My Youth and
Early Deaths

Also by Allen Stein:

Your Funeral Is Very Important to Us

Unsettled Subjects: New Poems on Classic American Literature

My Youth and Early Deaths

Allen Stein

MADVILLE
PUBLISHING

LAKE DALLAS, TEXAS

FIRST EDITION

This is a work of fiction and is not intended to resemble
anyone living or dead.

Requests for permission to reprint or reuse material
from this work should be sent to:

Permissions
Madville Publishing
PO Box 358
Lake Dallas, TX 75065

Cover design: Kim Davis
Author photo: Connie Stein

ISBN: 978-1-956440-97-3 paperback
978-1-956440-98-0 ebook

Library of Congress Control Number: 2024936311

Another for Connie

Unlike any other nation, here the people rule,
and their will is the supreme law.

—Governor William McKinley (1891)

The free man cannot be long an ignorant man.

—President William McKinley (1897)

I

This is the story of my education. It's not a formal story and it wasn't any formal education, either. It happened in just one summer, the summer of 1897, not so long back yet. The whole city was my school, more the ugly parts than the nice, and a lot of what I was getting taught wasn't so pretty, especially when the teachers were Monk Eastman and his lousy thug gang, and a lot of people died, mostly because of me, and some of them didn't come near deserving to. I'm not lying when I tell you that all of it still bothers me plenty. But, to tell you the truth, I figure that I learned some things I really needed to know.

It all started this one night with me laying there awake by the kitchen window. Everything's gone real still. Aunt Gabriella and Uncle Giulio's bed's not creaking loud anymore in the other room, and there's no noise down in the street or anywhere else. Everybody's asleep, I guess, but I'm not.

It was kind of cool for the start of June, so I didn't take my mattress off of the floor and put it out on the fire escape like I did when it was hot. But I did have the window up, and the breeze was right, so I could sometimes get a whiff of the river, and this night it seemed like it smelled fresh, the way it must have before everybody got here, before it even had a name, or at least any name that wasn't some Indian one. And the stars were looking clean and quiet and like if you could get close to them, you'd find they smelled good too, even though they might be pretty cold, being out there so far away from everything and even from each other. Mainly, though, I'm laying there trying not to think. I just want to enjoy the dark and the river smell and the peacefulness.

And then, almost like I was expecting it, I hear quick footsteps coming down the fire escape toward my window. I figure it's got to be either Davey Blumenthal or some guy up to no good. So just in case it's not Davey coming from the roof, I pull out the blade that I keep under my mattress every night and then slip back into the kitchen drawer in the morning. I get off of the mattress now and lean back against the wall, right next to the window, ready to stab any crooked son of a bitch who might sneak in over the sill.

A bony leg with the sock falling down over the top of the shoe edges in slow, and I know who it is right away, but I wait till the next leg is in, and the head and shoulders, and then I grab him from behind, put the blade to his throat, and say, "Make a move and you're a dead man." That's a line I read in a Billy the Kid book and I figured if Billy could use it, so could I, since Billy was just a little Mick shitass who went out west maybe ten years ago from only a few blocks over toward the Bowery from where I was right now, and where we don't have any Micks, just Jews and Italians.

Davey squeals, and I laugh. "That'll learn you not to be a housebreaker, you little *putz*."

Then Davey whispers, "Moish, you big *shmuck*! I almost pissed my pants, and then your crazy Dago aunt would see the puddle in the morning and pray to her bullshit saints to make you learn to use the toilet, and she'd tell everybody how big, tough Morris Levy, just a couple months short of sixteen, still pisses himself, and they'd tell her it's because her poor sister went and married a Kike, and so the kid ain't right in his head or *shlang* and never will be." And he gives me that crazy buck-tooth grin of his and then tells me, "But look, Moish, we got to hurry, no kiddin', or we'll miss out on all the fun. Monk's got something goin' on out on the bridge. I heard him tell one of his guys, 'It's gonna be da social event of 1897.'"

Now, of course, this isn't the first time Davey's come down the fire escape in the middle of the night to roust me out for some "fun." Usually it didn't amount to much more than sneaking around and maybe looking in through a crack in the wall at a whorehouse a couple blocks away or swiping some candy from some store where the lock is easy to jimmy. Once, we rolled some drunk laying on the street like a stiff, and we got some change off of him; and another time, over on Pell Street, we found some sappy Chink who'd been hitting the pipe and was spread out flat on his back in the gutter. We got a couple bucks that time and lived it up on candy and pop and even some beer and Sweet Caps and cigars for three days. Robbing from a Chink in that neighborhood, we were lucky we didn't get a meat cleaver up the ass. Davey also wanted to cut off his pigtail, but I said no, taking his dough was plenty enough. And anyway, I kind of felt sorry for the guy, figuring he probably had to iron a lot of shirts or cook up a lot of chop suey to make a few bucks, and maybe his joss pipe was about the only fun he had.

Tonight, because I wasn't sure what any fun having to do with Monk Eastman was going to be like, I took three rubber bands and tied the knife to my leg and then pulled my sock and pants on over it.

Monk is something scary to see, all right. He's about twenty-five, no more than five-foot-six, which is maybe half a foot shorter than me, but with a chest like a keg of beer and arms and shoulders like an ape and a neck thicker than his head, which isn't so small itself and looks even bigger because he's always wearing a derby about a whole size too small for it, and clothes that are too tight, so he's bulging everywhere. Monk's

3

been in more fights than he's been in bed with women, and he's been with lots of them. He's fought with bare fists, brass knuckles, clubs, guns, knives or razors, and his pale, splotchy face is so scarred up it looks like it's got trolley tracks on it going in all different directions. You'd figure no woman would ever get into a bed with him, but, like I said, lots do, some because they work in his dives and have to, but some, I guess, just because they want to. Maybe that's because he's boss of hundreds of hard guys and has lots of *gelt* and is in good with the politicians at Tammany Hall and with the cops, and some girls just get excited being around a guy like him. I can't figure it out.

I just know that when I saw him come down the street with his bowlegged strut, his coat so tight that it shows the gun it's covering on his hip, and with brass knuckles on his fists and a big club in his hand, I'd just cross over to the other side. And this was even though Davey, who sometimes ran small errands for him and his guys, said he was all right and that having a Yid gang tougher than the Mick and Dago gangs was something to be proud of, and this was also even though my no-good father, who left me and my mother, was actually part of the crowd working for him, which I didn't usually like to tell anybody.

So Davey and me, maybe ten minutes later, are at the ramp to the Brooklyn Bridge, but there are four Mick cops standing there, with their thick arms folded up on their chests. One of them pulls out a billystick as we come up, smacks his palm with it, and says, "Beat it, the bridge is closed for repairs tonight." And right then this little old guy with a load of clothes on his back tied together with some pieces of frayed rope comes up and says, "I hef got to get these clothes to Brooklyn tonight, please."

Still smacking his billystick on his palm, the cop says, "Look, Moe, I don't care where you 'hef got' to get your sack of rags. So beat it, if you know what's good for you."

"Mine name is not Moe, and you hef got no right to talk to

me this vay. This is America, and I am a citizen," the old guy said, but he was already stepping away.

"Go back where you came from, Moe. A Jew can't be no American."

The old guy calls back over his shoulder, "And you should go back to Ireland, and you and your Saint Petrick, you can vomit all your vhiskey and beer right onto the Statue of Liberty vhen you sail by, you Irish Cossack!"

"The Sheeny bastard," the cop snarls as he catches up to the old guy, and his first whack with the stick is right behind the guy's knees and drops him so that he's kneeling. The next, behind his waist, makes him sway backwards, and it sounds now like he's got something stuck way down in his throat that he can't get out, and the last, at the back of his head, makes him fall face-first onto the street. His load of clothes looks like a big lump of something that maybe fell from a star somewhere and crushed him under it. I think maybe I should go over and try to do something for him, but I don't know what. I mean, maybe I can take the load off of his back, but then what—am I going to call the cops or something?

"Don't do or say nothin', Moish," Davey whispers. So I stand there, feeling like an overgrown kid *shmendrick* who should still be in knee pants. I knew I had the kitchen knife tied to my leg, and I told myself I was ready to use it if the cop took his stick to me, but I didn't want any trouble and would just as soon go somewhere else for fun anyway.

The cop says to his buddies, "Old Moe'll be drinking his chicken soup through a straw for a while." Then he turns to Davey and me and says, "So what's wrong wit' youse lads' ears—ain't youse just heard me say the bridge is closed for repairs? Scram! Or youse'll get what Moe there got."

Well, Davey, he just pipes up, "We're invited to Izzie Goldstein's bridge party. Monk said that's the password and that we're his guests." And he stuck his chin up just like the snotty, smart-mouth little *momzer* he always was.

5

The cop looks at us and sneers, "Just get the hell out there, then, before I swat youse anyway."

Davey gives the cop a big wink, like they're pals in on the same joke, and says, "Youse is a officer and a gentleman, kind sir," and he does a big bow.

The cop raised his stick and gritted his teeth, but didn't do anything. I guessed being in with Monk gives a guy some privileges, but I always figured it's best not to overstep your bounds.

As we walked out on the bridge, I heard one of the cops say, "I hate havin' to kowtow to that Jew bastard Eastman," and another said, "Yeah, but he's one tough Hebe, an' he kicks in plenty each month for Boss Croker and Devery," and then for a couple minutes it was real quiet, just me and Davey's footsteps on the boardwalk, and a foghorn way off down river sounding like it was calling hard for someone but also knowing that it wasn't ever going to hear something back.

And except for the reflection of the lights of the bridge the river was dark, and you could almost tell yourself that there was no bottom to it, just a darkness that went on and on forever like the sky, but without any sun or stars to break up the monotony. I saw a small light from a tugboat heading away from the bridge and wondered if the crew ever looked down into the river at night and thought about all the blackness below them.

I looked back toward Manhattan and saw that except for the streetlamps it was mostly dark, just here and there some windows lit, where maybe there was a whorehouse or a tiger den with a game going on, or just a room where a guy and his wife were having it out. The bridge itself was all lit with big electric bulbs spaced out along the cables and going all the way up to the top of the towers. If you let your eyes run along the curve of the cables it was almost like we were on a lit-up road that would take us way up the towers and then out somewhere else. And the arches of the towers looked like they could be the way into a great big church, maybe like St. Patrick's uptown, except even bigger. I stared up at them. They looked as cold and quiet and blank as the stars way past them.

When Davey and me got to that first tower, we could hear some noise starting to come from over on the other side of it, and Davey says, "They're startin'. We better hurry, 'cause we don't want to miss a thing."

So we trotted through the arch and we see there's a ring of guys, maybe thirty or forty of them, and they're starting to sing something. At first, I can't make out that it's "The Sidewalks of New York." But when we get closer I hear, "East Side, West Side, all around the town, the tots play Ring Around Rosie and London Bridge is Falling Down," and they're singing it real loud now. So I say to myself, well, I guess it's a party, after all.

But it's really not. When Davey and me reach the circle, we see that Monk Eastman and Izzie Goldstein are in the center of it, and Izzie's not having any fun at all.

Izzie's fat and bald and usually pretty jolly. I didn't know him real well, but one time when I was having a couple keys made for Aunt Gabriella at his tiny little key and lock place over on Grand Street, he sees me pacing back and forth in front of his counter while he's working, and he says, "You look like you got ants in your pants, sonny," and I say, "Yeah, sometimes I'm restless," and he tells me "Well, come back here, Mr. Restless One, and I'll show you how we make a key." So I went behind the counter, and he took a blank piece of metal and cut in the grooves and notches. I remember looking at that shiny new key and thinking that maybe we're all of us like that blank key blade at first and then things happen that put grooves and notches in us until we can unlock stuff that we need to know, and maybe lots of it's pretty rough.

Another thing that morning at Izzie's was that I got to see Esther, his daughter. She came in from behind the curtain that separated the back of Izzie's shop from where he and his family

7

lived. Me and Esther knew each other from over at school, but we'd never been in the same class till ninth-grade American History this term. Seeing her that morning was like getting a present I wasn't expecting.

Esther was tall, maybe a little thin, with long, shiny black hair that she usually wore tied back with a ribbon. And she had these bright brown-green eyes that looked full of fun lots of the time, and smooth white skin and a straight nose with a cute little bump in it, and lips that were a teeny bit puffy, just enough to make them look like they'd be extra nice to kiss. I think a lot of the guys in class were sweet on her.

Yeah, Esther was pretty, all right, but lots of girls are pretty. There was just something special about her. She'd read more books than anybody in our class and talked better, and she took important stuff more serious, like, for instance, when we were learning all about slavery and she said it was wrong that the coloreds aren't getting a fair shake yet in America, and the Jews and the other new immigrants aren't, and that women aren't either, for that matter, and that she hoped she was going do her part to try to make things better.

Miss Friedman, our history teacher, liked all of the kids, and we liked her, but you could also tell that she had real big hopes for Esther. For one thing, both of them were socialists. I figured that maybe I might become a socialist myself because of all the stuff that my mother always said about how the rich get fat starving the poor people, but I never did anything about it, and both Miss Friedman and Esther did. Miss Friedman gave speeches and marched, and Esther, one time, got hauled down to the station by the cops because she was blocking a landlord from throwing a family out onto the street when they couldn't pay all the rent. And she didn't even know them. She was just walking by, saw some people trying to hold back the furniture movers and joined in. The cops had to pry her arms from around the leg of a beat-up old sofa bed. That's the kind of girl she was.

I never did stuff like that myself. I didn't like getting in trouble, and, besides, I figured it would worry Aunt Gabriella and Uncle Giulio, who were trying to take good care of me while my mother was so sick, and also it would probably make Davey and the other guys I knew laugh at me for being such a softie. I figured also that maybe I was just too much my father's son anyway to want to help other people much. I don't know. Instead, I just did stupid stuff sometimes with Davey, like I said. I remember that later on the afternoon when Miss Friedman had been teaching us about slavery, I saw Esther and her walking down the hall together, just like they were pals, and I wished I was walking with them, with one arm around each one.

Well, when Izzie saw me looking at Esther through the curtain that morning in his shop, he says, "Do you know, my daughter, the beautiful Queen Esther?"

I blush a little and say, "Yeah, we're in American History together."

And he calls to her and says, "Come on out, my beauty, and say hello to my customer, who is part of American History with you."

Well, she comes out and she's blushing too, and we say a couple things about class to each other, and then we both say we've got to go. Izzie laughs a little and he says, "Okay, youse kids. I can see you're a little shy, a couple of shysters." And he laughs again, and me and Esther do too. And then Esther and me gave each other a friendly little wave, and I left the shop with my keys and a goofy grin.

And now Izzie Goldstein was on his knees and Monk was standing over him, and everybody was singing "East Side, West Side" and whooping it up, but Izzie was crying. Every time, they'd sing "East Side," Monk would smack Izzie on the right side of the head with his open left hand, and when they sang "West Side," he'd smack him on the left side of his head with his open right hand, and when they sang "All around the town," he'd smack him with both hands at once, like he was

9

banging cymbals. The guys in the circle laughed like they were at the circus. Davey and I were with them now, part of the circle, and Davey, he was laughing and singing too, but I wasn't. Maybe it was because I knew Izzie and Esther, but maybe I wouldn't have even if I didn't know the poor *shlemiel*. If I did laugh and sing with the rest, I couldn't have looked my mother in the face next time I went out to see her at the TB hospital.

And meanwhile, believe it or don't, Monk and them, they had sandwiches and beer there on the bridge. There's these growlers filled to the tops with beer and there's big trays with sandwiches and pickles and potato salad, and these guys are singing with their mouths full and food in their hands, while Izzie is getting walloped again and again. A real party, all right.

I recognized some of the guys there, tough guys from around the neighborhood, Monk's guys, but I didn't know any of them personal. Except for Davey and me, who were both almost sixteen, most of them were in their twenties and even older. Droop-Eye Leibowitz was there, with his one eye that's got a lid that doesn't hardly go up and the other always wide open and bloodshot. You'd figure he couldn't see much, but the word was that when he was looking for you, he'd find you. And Big Tuchus Lifschutz, who guys said had once sat on some poor *shmuck* till he smothered the guy to death, was shaking his fat hips as he sang and laughed. And Tick-Tock Tannenbaum stood there, his long yellow face just like always without any expression, except that this time, his thin lips were curled up just a little bit. Even now in June he was wearing his black coat that went down almost to his ankles, the collar turned up, and, like always, the silver chain of his big watch was showing from his coat pocket. Guys said that when you heard a ticking sound coming closer and closer, and there were long, whistling breaths, but you couldn't hear footsteps under them, that was Tick-Tock and your time was just about up. I looked around to see if my father was there, but he wasn't. That didn't surprise me any, because this kind of thing wasn't really his style.

Then Monk raises his arms, yells, "Shush, youse loudmout' bummers, an' let's see what dis fat *shlumper* of a welcher has got to say for himself. 'Cause I mean dis is a party in your honor, Izzie, but it's also gonna be a fair trial for you, you *furshlugginer* fat little bald bastid, ain't it?"

Izzie sobs out now, "Yeah, it is, Monk, it is."

There's a dark stain at the crotch of Izzie's pants, and it's getting bigger. I'm hoping nobody else sees it, but Davey yells out, "Holy shit, he's pissed his pants, both the east side and the west side!"

Everybody just laughs like crazy at that, even Monk, and then he shushes everybody and says, "Okay, I'm gettin' Isadore Goldstein's testimony here, so let's have some order in dis here court. Isadore, you gonna tell the trut', so help you God? Grab your wet little dick and swear on it, you lousy pisspot bastid!"

Izzie grabs at his crotch and raises his right hand, but Monk says, "I told you, you tuchus-face shmeckle, grab your little putz and hold it—dat's what God and Monk Eastman want."

So Izzie, he's crying and shaking, and he unbuttons his pants, reaches in and takes out his dick, holds it in his left hand, raises his right, and, looking into Monk's ugly mug, swears to God that he's going to tell the truth.

Monk yells at him, "Okay, so tell me why you don't pay me my money!"

"Monk, I didn't know it was you that got hold of the debt, I swear. I thought I still owed it to Noogie Kaplan. He was the one who had the four kings in his hand!"

"So you didn't know not'in' about my buyin' Noogie's poker debts offa him? You didn't know not'in' about dat Louie and Hymie was collectin' for me when you told dem t'ree times—t'ree stinkin' times!—dat you didn't have the *mazuma* yet?"

"That's right," Izzie said, after waiting a second or two.

I remember thinking, "Oh, shit, Izzie, you're lying. Anybody could see that."

Monk calls Julie Rosenblatt out of the circle. "I got me a witness here, Izzie, who I don't t'ink is gonna back you up on dis point of testimony. What did he tell you, Julie?"

"He says to me, 'Monk Eastman can wait for his money, the ugly ape.' Excuse me for using such nasty language, Boss, but I'm testifying what he said, so help me God," and he raised his hand up toward the bridge towers.

Monk says real quiet. "Ugly ape." He nods a few times and then whispers, "Guilty."

Everybody's quiet now, knowing we're going to see something like we probably never saw before. I feel the rubber bands around my leg, the side of the knife tight against it.

Then suddenly Monk screams, "A ugly ape!" and has Izzie by the throat.

Izzie gasps, "I was just kiddin' Monk," but that's all he can get out.

Monk yells, "Miltie, gimme da paper and pen," and a skinny, pimple-faced guy puts a paper and pen in his hand, while Monk still holds Izzie by the throat with his other.

"Sign it!" Monk snarls to Izzie.

"What is it?" Izzie gasps.

"It says you're selling your shop to me for what you owe me."

"No, no. It's all I have. My wife and daughter—they'll be on the street."

"Nah," Monk says, showing his big teeth. "Maybe dey ain't gonna be on da street, maybe I'll find a place for 'em," and he laughs, and so do a lot of the other guys. And Izzie says no, he ain't gonna sign.

Monk says, "Sign it or you take a swan dive right now. You are guilty! You have got to pay! It's one way or da other—da ink or da drink. You go off, you ain't never gonna make a key again nowheres. Da river's gonna take you and lock you up for keeps."

So Izzie signs it, and Monk has Miltie put some kind of seal on it to make it all seem kosher. Izzie is laying on his stomach now and sobbing loud, Monk howls like a wild animal, grabs Izzie up, pushes him out over the rail and holds him by his ankles.

" 'Ugly ape' you called me!" he screams. "You done worse dan what your *farkakte* little shop can pay for, you *shvantz*. Guilty before God and Monk Eastman!"

"Drop him, Monk," yells one guy. "Yeah, let's see if shit really floats," yells another. And a few guys laugh, but most are quiet now. Davey, he's not saying a thing, which isn't like him. And I'm thinking I need to do something for Izzie, but I can't figure how, so I just stand there and feel like a helpless *putz* again.

"Swear right now," Monk yells down to Izzie, "dat you're gonna let me *shtup* your wife while you watch me do it, an' maybe I'll *shtup* your daughter too."

Izzie says nothing. Maybe he just can't get the words out. Meanwhile, some guys laugh, and one of them starts singing "ta-ra-ra-boom-de-ay," and some others join in, just like they were at some dive watching a line of girls picking up their skirts and doing a high-kick dance.

And right then I'm seeing Monk's muscles are straining and his jacket is stretching so tight across his big back and shoulders that parts of the seams are ripping. Izzie's not light. "Swear!" Monk says, "Swear, or I drop you right now."

From down over the railing, comes this high yell, "I swear it."

More guys are singing now, and it's getting louder, especially on the "boom" part.

Monk yells over the noise, "And, if I feel like it, your daughter, too, right? What's her name? Esther, ain't it? You got to watch her suck me off, right? Swear dat, too." Monk is panting now, and I'm thinking I want to kill him, have him panting up blood before he stops breathing altogether. I just stand there, though.

"Yes," comes the scream, "Yes, please, Monk. I swear. Please. Yes!"

But I see Monk's shoulders strain harder and then relax, and I hear the "yes" turn into a long shrieking "no" sailing up from Izzie before there's a splash in the dark down below.

The singing trails off. Then, for a few seconds, everything is dead quiet, and everybody walks to the rail to look down, but we don't see anything, just the river flowing to the bay, and some tugboat lights flickering way out there. Davey whispers to me, "*Oy, gevalt*, good-bye Izzie," and I say so no one can hear, "God, give him a break, he wasn't such a bad guy."

I looked down into the water and up into the sky and I didn't get an answer. There wasn't any key to unlock any kind of break for Izzie, now or later.

I don't know whether Monk dropped Izzie on purpose. I don't even know if Monk himself knew. Izzie might have just got too heavy for him. If that was what happened, though, there's no way that Monk was going admit it, so he says, "Dat'll learn him. You don't welch on Monk Eastman, and you don't get no loose, rude puss about Monk Eastman. I wanted youse all to see what comes of dat junk. But if youse are square wit' me, youse got a friend for keeps."

Then he says he doesn't want any party poopers there either, so he made us all sing along to another couple choruses of "East Side, West Side," while Monk, like a band leader, led us and watched our faces. I thought I saw him looking at me for a little longer than at the others.

Finally, Monk tells us, "Okay dat's it. I showed youse all a good time out here, and I want youse all to spread da woid dat Monk Eastman will show his boys a good time and dat da only ones what's got to worry are da ones what cross him. Ain't dat right, boys?" He looked at us, and we all joined in and told him that was right. Then he looks right at Davey and me and says, "See, even little *Shlemiel* and big *Shlimazel* over dere know it, don't youse, youse young nose-drips?" We nod that we do, and again I remember about the knife tied to my leg, and I think about stabbing Monk, diving into the river, and swimming away. But I know I'm not gonna do it, and I know that if you go in off the bridge you don't go swimming away anywhere. I'm feeling like a nothing, a piece of *dreck*. I'm the first in my family to be born in this country and I'm wondering what I need to do from now on to keep from feeling like maybe I'm already also the first to die in it.

II

I lean forward on my toes, my knees are bent just a little, my arms are stretched up high over my head, and I'm feeling a cool breeze playing at my *shlang*. I count one, two, three, and I dive in, eyes shut, and I feel the cold and the dark pouring over me. Some guys keep their eyes open once they go under, but I usually don't. There's no telling what you might see. For all I know, Izzie's here now, right below the pier I just dived off, his eyes wide open and staring.

It's the morning after Monk dropped Izzie into the river, and Davey and me didn't go to school. After we left the bridge last night, everything was quiet except for the clopping of a horse pulling an empty wagon. The hoofbeats made me think about cowboys out west somewhere, like where Billy the Kid went, somewhere maybe not much better but where there were no big bridges to drop guys off of, anyway. And just before we split up over at Ludlow, so Davey could go up to Broome, where he lived, where there wasn't anybody but Jews, he says, "Shit, some fun," like he wanted to mean it, and I says, "Meet me here about eight tomorrow, we ain't going to school, even if it is just two days before summer vacation." You see, I knew I wasn't going to be ready to look in Esther's face at school while she was worrying about why her father didn't come home. I'd need a little time yet, maybe time also to think of how I could keep Monk's mitts off of her if he really wanted to try something with her, and time to think of how maybe I could even get revenge on Monk Eastman for what he did to her father. I knew I needed to do something so I wouldn't feel so ashamed about the night before, wouldn't feel so much like a nobody and a nothing.

Now, to tell the truth, lots of times I didn't want to be in school, but mostly I went, because Aunt Gabriella cried and cried if she found out I played hooky, and told me that unless I made something of myself it was like I was driving a knife into my poor sick mother's heart, and that even if she didn't tell Mama, God would whisper it into Mama's ear, so she would know it anyway. I wanted to tell her that I wasn't so sure God's paying that much attention, but I didn't, because I didn't want to get her even more upset.

And Davey, he knew if he didn't show up at school most of the time, and his father found out, he'd get beat with a strap. His old man said it was because he didn't want him to be no bum, like his big brother who ran off. If he knew Davey did errands for Monk and his crowd, there probably wouldn't have been any strap strong enough to last through the beating he'd of given him.

I also went to school most of the time because Miss Friedman wanted me to be there, like she had some hopes for me. Maybe it was because she knew that I liked to read books sometimes, but I still can't figure why she expected anything much from me, because I really didn't, but I didn't like to hurt her feelings.

So, now, the very next morning after Izzie went in the river, Davey and me are at the pier over at the Fulton Fish Market, just a few blocks down from the bridge. And how did we end up here, with me diving into the greasy water where maybe I'll plop right down on fat Izzie Goldstein and get tangled up in his dead arms or something?

Well, me and Davey met, like we planned, and I said we

should go up to the Central Park and look at lots of grass and trees and try to forget what we saw last night. And Davey says, "Yeah, Moishele, we could eyeball all the peachy-lookin' nursemaids up there wheelin' the rich little brats along," and he gives me his cockeyed grin and sticks out his tongue like he's a slobbering mutt. But then he says, "Moish, it's so hot today, though, maybe let's just hoof it over to the ol' swimmin' hole and cool our dicks off instead of getting them hotter lookin' at nursemaid *knish*."

"Jesus," I says, "Didn't you see enough of the river last night?"

"The river's big," he says back, "and it keeps moving. It ain't the same river this morning. What happened last night is all washed away now, and it ain't gonna keep me outta the water today. I'm hot, and I ain't got the time or the money to go out to Coney."

I was going to argue back that the river can move along for a thousand years but it's still the same river and not what I want to jump into today, even if the sun bakes the street horseshit into cakes, but Skinny Lucchesi and Johnny Scelsi came along just then and Skinny says to Davey and me, "Hey Jewboy, hey half-Hebe, what are youse two punks doin' in an Italian neighborhood? Why don't youse go back east of the Bowery, where youse belong?"

Davey says, "We're goin' over to the Market for a swim. Youse come with us and wash the tomato sauce off your faces and the garlic stink from your asses."

Skinny and Johnny weren't such bad guys, really, but bad guys or not, they might have jumped Davey if I hadn't been there. Instead, Johnny just said, "Davey, you got a smart mouth. Just make sure it don't get too smart."

Anyway, they said they were going for a swim too, that school over with the nuns ended yesterday, and then they gave me some crap about why I didn't go to school with white men like them, instead of with a bunch of Yids at the public school.

They were kidding around and meaning it both. I didn't want to tell them what my mother thought about the church schools, so I just said, "because the mustaches on the nuns scare me," and all four of us laughed.

So that's how I was here now, going down deep and deeper into the river. And by now I've opened my eyes. Until you get way down deep in the river, you don't see just how dirty it is, with flaky pieces of garbage and greasy stuff that looks maybe like the fat globs in chicken soup. And the fish down there are nothing you'd want to put in a tank and look at. They're small and long and thin, mud-brown, some of them with yellow-white foamy stuff on their sides.

While I was down there, I looked straight up, and saw the masts of the boats and could even see some of the buildings along the river, and they gleamed in the sunshine. Everything up there looked so nice and clean, and I thought that maybe that was the way heaven looked to a lot of people from here in the world. And then I thought, well, the world, once you get up into it, out of the crummy water, is as crummy most of the time as the water is, so then maybe heaven, once you get up into it, is not so great either, if it's even there, which my mother always said it ain't.

My mother used to tell me that people like Aunt Gabriella who believed that everybody dead would meet again in heaven and be so happy forever were just dreaming, and they needed instead to try to make things better right here, because this was all we were ever going to have. I thought she was probably right, but I hoped she was wrong, because I wanted so bad for her to have something better when this was all over for her, and I was scared it was going to be over for her real soon, too, she was so sick. I figured I owed it to her to try to do something good, like she'd want me to, even if she wouldn't be around to see it, just like I also figured I owed Esther now.

When I came up, we all swum around some and then did what we called jousting, like in the books about knights charging each other on horses while the fair ladies watched and cheered and cried, and I wished poor Esther could be watching, because I was doing pretty good. We were in pairs, with one guy on top of the other's shoulders, shoving and laughing like crazy the whole time.

Then we went up onto the dock and we laid down on our backs and felt the sun warming us up. We didn't say much. Even Davey was quiet, like he knew that saying something could only take your mind off how good it felt. I closed my eyes, and it seemed almost like we weren't there on a smelly pier where men were hauling crates loaded with big dead fish with staring eyes and where just inside the open doors of the building behind us barrel after barrel got filled up with fish guts.

No, we didn't feel like we were part of any of that, and when some of the workers walked past and said that we were such godawful lazy little pissers that we were even giving playing hooky a bad name, we just smiled and laid there and felt good, and for a bit I didn't think about all the stuff that was on my mind.

After a while, Davey says to us, "I feel sorry for these poor dopes who have to haul fish around all day. And even for my lousy old man, at Bernstein's over on Cherry, cutting them up for the stores and restaurants."

"He prays a lot, doesn't he?" I asked.

"Yeah, when he ain't cutting fish or aggravated about something around the house, he's over at the *shul*, bobbing his head up and down, talkin' to God, but it sounds more like he's cursing than praying."

I say, "Maybe it's because of your little brother Manny getting killed under that wagon, like he did," and Davey says, "That ain't no excuse for him being like he is all the time."

"Maybe it ain't and maybe it is," I say.

Davey shrugged.

Johnny asks, "What do youse guys wanna do when you're through with school for good?"

I tell him that maybe I'd like to sail off somewhere, like on one of the big boats in the river, and see different places, like Arabia and China, and maybe have adventures where I help people who need help, stuff like that.

Davey says, "You're dreamin', big boy."

"Maybe I need to dream a little after what happened last night."

"Maybe what happened last night should wise you up a little."

Skinny pipes up then, "What happened last night, huh?"

"Nothin'," I say, but, of course, Davey can't leave it at that, and says, "Oh, just some stuff with Monk Eastman, nothin' nobody needs to worry about unless they get on Monk's bad side. Moishe and me, we're in wit' him, so we know all about it."

"I ain't in with him," I say.

"Yeah, you are, 'cause your old man is," Davey comes back.

"I ain't my old man," I tell him.

Then Skinny brags, "Yeah, well me and Johnny, we're in wit' Paul Kelly and his Five Points crowd, and an Italian gang is always better than a Yid gang, and Paulie, he's got control west of the Bowery, and he's gonna take over on the east side of the Bowery before too long, take everything Monk's got."

"Yeah," Davey says, "well if he's so tough, why'd he take a Mick name? He scared for people to know he's a Guinea?"

Johnny says, "His name is just from when he was a boxer, 'cause it's tough to get good matches if you ain't got a Mick name. Paulie's smart, he's from Sicily, but he speaks English like he was a college professor and he knows other languages, too, and he's real classy, but he ain't scared of nothin,' and especially he ain't scared of no Monk Eastman."

"Tell me another one," Davey says. Then after a few seconds, he announces, "Well, I'm gonna be a smart businessman, too. I'm gonna learn by watchin' Monk. I ain't gonna end up like my old man. I ain't gonna be bringin' the stink of the fish market home wit' me every day, and I ain't gonna be living in no two-room dump neither."

I'm laying there hoping he doesn't really mean it, but Skinny and Johnny don't see a thing wrong with it, except that they tell him he'd be better off if he decided to go in with Paul, that's if Paul would even want to take a runt Jew like him.

I close my eyes again and try to put all this stuff about gangs and what happened last night out of my head again for a while. But as I'm laying there now, it's back, along with something I remember from the Italian poetry that my mother liked to read to me when she was still okay. She read it in Italian and would tell me both in Italian and English everything it meant, and I didn't always understand, of course, but some of it sticks with me anyway. What comes to me while I'm on the dock is what Dante said was posted on the gate into hell, which in English is "Abandon all hope, everybody who's about to enter."

And it feels right now like maybe me and Davey and Johnny and Skinny and even all the guys working there at the smelly market and the smelly dock are already on the bad side of the gate.

I try to get my mind someplace else by thinking it might be real pretty tonight sleeping out on the fire escape and maybe catching a little breeze and seeing the stars, but now I can't help remembering right off about poor loony old Shmulewitz, the chicken-plucker, who walks the streets some nights yelling "Rivke, Rivke, fly back to the nest, my little sparrow," still crying for his wife, who ran off twenty years ago with some pants presser headed out to Ohio or Kansas somewhere, while people yell down at him to shut up, and that his sparrow's not coming back, that she's laying her eggs in somebody else's nest now.

And then, of course, I think again about Esther, and I can't figure out any way to protect her from Monk Eastman if I need to, but I promise myself that I will and that I'll always be good and kind to her, even though I'm still laying there guessing maybe we're all someplace where there's not much point in promising and hoping.

All this time Davey is still going on about how he's going

to join a gang and make himself the big dough. So finally I tell him, "Look, Davey, there's other ways to get what you want without being like any Monk or Paul."

"You want to tell him and the rest of us what those ways are, *boychik*?" I hear a man's voice say. He's come up behind us without us noticing. I'm surprised to hear him, but I know right away whose voice it is.

I start to put my hands over my *shlang*, but stop right away, because I don't want him to see that he makes me uncomfortable, but it's too late, because he sees my hands start to move, and he says, "It's okay, *boychik*, I got one too." I smile up at him for a second to show him that I'm not embarrassed by anything he can say. Then I get up and start getting dressed slow and easy so I look like everything is aces with me. And I say, "Hey, Papa, long time, no see."

He smiles and says, "Moishele, my son, look at you, *kaynahora*, you're growing like a cedar of Lebanon." And he reaches out, pats my face, and then his fingers tighten and he pinches my cheek till it hurts, but I keep my face looking like it doesn't. He says, "I'm glad I ran into you here. You can come with me and meet somebody."

I says, "Well, I'm kind of busy, Papa. Maybe I can go with you another time."

"Busy?" he says, "busy?" and he pinches my cheek again. "You don't look so busy, boychik. If you was in school, like the law says you should be today, then maybe you would be busy a little bit, *mein kind*. But I see you're just farting with these other bummers."

And he smiles at the other three in a way that's supposed to look friendly, reaches into his pocket, and gives each of them two bits. Then he says to me, "*Kumen avek mit mir*," gives my shoulder a nudge that's not so soft and tells me to finish getting dressed.

So I do. And meanwhile he's talking in a low voice to two guys he's got with him, who have just come out of the Market.

They're Monk's guys. One of them is Tick-Tock Tannenbaum, who I told you about already, and the other is another guy I saw on the bridge, a big redhead that everybody says is real scary, the Redkopf. These are the kind of guys my father always has with him on his job, which is like being an accountant for Monk, which he says is all he is.

But what my father also does is go around with a couple of Monk's boys and see people for Monk. Some of them owe Monk dough, and if they pay, I hear he's real polite and puts the numbers down nice and neat in a book that he carries and the money in a black leather briefcase. And if they don't pay, well, maybe he gives them another chance and maybe he doesn't. It depends on what they did before. But if he doesn't give them another chance, he never hollers at them or calls them bad names. He just tells them business is business, and he tells Monk's boys to go to work, and they beat up or cut up the guy, and the poor bastid knows that if he's not paying up in the next day or two, my father is coming back, and it's going to be more of the same, only worse.

And he goes around to restaurants and stores and signs people up to Monk's protection list, telling them real polite that it's like insurance, because if they don't pay Monk to protect them, something bad could happen to them or their business, and that the cops can't protect them the way Monk can. And sometimes, for shops that look like they're doing real good, my dad goes over and tells them Monk wants to be a partner and they don't have a choice in the matter. My dad gives them some dough and they sign some papers, and Monk is now their partner.

That's the kind of work my father does as an accountant, that and sitting in some hangout of Monk's and counting money up and working it out how to pay Monk's guys and the cops and the politicians and judges they've got lined up.

Well, I'm finishing getting dressed now, and my father says, "Those clothes are getting small on you. Where goes the money that I give to your crazy aunt for putting up with you? Does it go to the priests for their candles and their holy water and their fat nuns who say they're married to poor, suffering Jesus Christ, who probably doesn't know what to do with them all?" The Redkopf laughed out loud, and even Tick-Tock smiled a little at that. I says, "Mostly, she buys food. You don't give that much, you know."

My father was embarrassed now in front of Monk's guys, and in front of Davey and Johnny and Skinny. He gives me a cold look, like he's about to smack me one, which actually he never has, because he doesn't like to show when he's worked up. So he turns his lips into a smile real quick, and he says, "I give them plenty, *boychik*, your crazy aunt and that dopey Giulio, who's as dead in the head as the people whose names he carves on their tombstones."

"He's a big kid, Asher, a fast-grower, just like Monk noticed last night," the Redkopf said, "the kind you got to keep throwing money at for clothes."

My father didn't say anything, just stood there in his new tan pinstripe suit and gold vest and straw skimmer with a gold and blue band and shiny shoes. Meanwhile I put on my pants that had the patch on the knee and my shirt with the hole just getting started at the elbow, and my scuffed-up shoes that were down at the heels and my cap, with the button coming off the top and the bill ragged at the front. He lit a cigar and watched me through his gold-framed specs.

I looked like him, more than I ever wanted to. We were both about six-foot, with curly black hair and dark eyes, except his hair was gone at the front of his head, and his forehead was creased and his eyes looked tired all the time. My skin was maybe a little darker than his, from the Italian in me, I figure, and my nose was a little big, like his, but straighter, and both of us had cheekbones that showed. I had broader shoulders and more muscles than him. In fact, he was thin and without much of a chest, either, so I figured that if it ever came to a fair fight, I

25

could take him, but I also figured that if it ever came to a fight, he wouldn't fight fair to begin with.

So Monk had noticed me, and so now my father was taking me over somewhere to see him, was that it? Why? Was it so important that maybe my old man hadn't just bumped into me like he said, but had really been looking for me?

So I go off with my father and the Redkopf and Tick-Tock, and wave good-bye to Davey and Johnny and Skinny, and the three of them are looking at me like they're wishing they were going instead of me, and I'm thinking they're crazy if they are.

III

My father's not talking as we walk along, just puffing on his stogie, blowing streams of blue smoke, and looking like he's thinking deep about something every step of the way.

I say to him finally, "Where we going?"

He says, "You'll see when we get there."

I tell him that I have nothing to say to Monk Eastman, and he tells me, "Well, he's got something to say to you, and if you are a smart boy you shall listen to him good."

By this time we're getting to the City Hall Park, where he tells the Redkopf and Tick-Tock that he'll meet them over "at the place" and then has me sit down next to him on a bench. He asks me if I want an ice cream from the hokey-pokey man's cart there. I do, but I tell him I don't. "Okay," he says, "so you're either the only kid on the Lower East Side who don't want an ice cream or you decided that you don't want one from me. Okay, no is no, that is your right. The country is free even if ice cream ain't. But you should learn this: when somebody offers you something you like, with no strings attached, you take it—because this world, it don't offer you that too many times. You understand me?"

He turns to me now and looks right at me for a minute. His eyes looked more tired than usual, with more wrinkles around them than I ever saw on him before, but maybe I haven't sat so close to him in a long time.

His cigar was finished by now, but I could smell it on his breath, which was sour and fishy. He says, "I never had the time to tell you bedtime stories, but I will tell you a story now, a benchtime story," and he smiled a little. "And I tell you this not to entertain you or me, but so you will learn something. It's about when I was in Poland and only a little older than you. I believed, like your mother still does, that with socialism everybody shall work together and shall have equal food and an equal house and nobody shall be dressed in gold and nobody in rags. You like this idea?"

I told him that Mama had told me about this and I did like it.

"Yes, you got a good heart, and so does your mama. I know this. I see in your face how loyal you are to her and to your aunt and uncle. I understand this. I also see how angry you are at me for years. I understand this, too. Once I read books, and now I read faces. Usually the faces, they tell me more than the books did.

"My own face and my own heart, though, those I can no longer read so clear. Too much has happened. But back in Zychlin, in the old country, I thought I knew it was only goodness and kindness what was in me. I had read Marx, and Bakunin, and Saint-Simon, and Fourier. These are names that don't mean nothing to you, right? They might be tailors, for all you know."

I nodded.

He patted my knee. It was a soft touch, this time, and I felt my eyes start to get a little wet, so I looked away for a second, so he shouldn't see that he could make me almost cry just by being a little nice maybe.

He says then, "These writers said that all people, except for maybe Czars and nobles, and factory owners, have good hearts, only you must educate people to see how good their hearts are. This, when I was your age, I believed with no questions asked, and I worked so we should bring fast the better world. And I had a brother. This I have never told you. He was older than me and I named you for him. Like you, he had a good heart. He was tall and handsome, just like you, *boychik,* and his wife, she was a beauty, his Miriam. Well, my brother Moishe and his Miriam and I joined up with a man planning to start a socialist community not far from Zychlin."

While my father was telling me this, I thought about what that kind of place would look like. There'd be a square with tall trees and a little pond for kids to sail toy boats on. And around the square there'd be small houses with happy families that all had enough of what they needed, and the chimneys would let out soft fluffy puffs of white smoke into a light blue sky, not like the smelly, gray and black sooty stuff that came out of the factory stacks across in Brooklyn that gave you headaches and made you cough almost as bad as my mother. And I saw my father in a place like that. He was young then, and he didn't look so tired and wrinkled and cold around the eyes. And I saw my strong, handsome uncle, too, with his Miriam right there next to him, real pretty, tall and kind of thin, with long dark hair that maybe was tied back in a little white ribbon.

"So, *boychik,* we and others who thought like we did, we gave this man our money so that he should buy the land for the community, and the next day, he runs away with our money and with our Miriam, who he has made to fall in love with him. How could this be, we asked. He seemed so noble, so fine?

"Well, my brother, he goes crazy with love and shame and rage, and he follows them. And one terrible night, weeks later, he discovers that they are at an inn on the road to Lodz. What happened then is what brought me to this place. This is what I was told by one who was there. My brother rushes into the room where his Miriam is with the man we trusted. He pulls the man out of the bed where he was laying with

Miriam, and beats him, while screaming curses at Miriam. And this is the last thing he did in his life, because there were five drunken Cossacks there in the inn, and, drunk or sober, the Cossacks, they don't miss their opportunities where a Jew is concerned.

"So, the Cossacks were angry that my brother's noise should wake them up from their drunken sleep, and then because he was a Jew, they knew they deserved whatever fun they wanted. So that was the end of my brother and his enemy right there. Because the man with Miriam was naked, they cut off his penis and stuffed it in his mouth before they killed him. If my brother saw this before he himself died, maybe it gave him some satisfaction. Miriam they let live long enough to rape her again and again before they tore her insides open and threw her out to die in the snow. This is the story I heard.

"I loved my brother. That is why you got his name. Don't forget this." He touched the corner of one eye. Was he wiping away a tear or just rubbing an itch?

He pointed to the flags on the top of City Hall. "Things are better here than they were over there, but the world is still the world. Behind that beautiful city hall is the beautiful New York County Courthouse. Most of the money that the public spent on the courthouse went into the pockets of Boss Tweed and his friends at his political club called Tammany Hall that really runs this city. And he could do this for the same reason that the Cossacks could do what they did. He had the power.

"And where you live and swim, Monk Eastman has the power. The Mayor in that building over there, Mister Mayor William Strong, was elected because he crowed so strong that he would get rid of Tammany Hall and what he calls its 'corruption.' People think it is a bad thing, this 'corruption,' this 'graft,' where mayors and aldermen and commissioners and policemen take money so that they should not bother the gambling and the whorehouses and the protection collections.

But this is just business. This Mayor Strong, he is not so powerful as his name. He builds some parks, hires some more policemen, and makes the bigmouth Theodore Roosevelt his police commissioner. And the Mayor and Roosevelt, and this Reverend Parkhurst from uptown, they all make noise about 'reform.' A few dumb Irish cops who get too greedy go to jail, but nothing changes. Roosevelt gets bored and goes off to Washington to work in the Navy office, Monk pays Richard Croker, who was boss of Tammany when Strong came in and will be boss of Tammany when Strong goes out, Croker pays Big Bill Devery, the superintendent of the police, with some of the money Monk pays him, and Devery pays his men all the way down the line with some of the money Croker gives him. And nobody bothers Monk, not if they want to stay in good health. Nobody.

"Later this year there will be an election for the new mayor and Croker's man will win. Mark my words. And then there will be even less talk about 'corruption' and 'graft.'

"So, my big Moishe, if Monk, he wants you to do something, you just say 'yes' and you do it. He saw you last night on the bridge. He knows who you are, and he thinks you look smart and tough. I tell you, my son, be smart and tough for him if you know what is good for you."

He patted me on the shoulder, lit another cigar, and looked at me.

Then I say to my father, "What Monk did out on the bridge last night was wrong. Izzie didn't need to die like that. Monk's a stupid bum bastid."

My father's hand twitched, and I thought that I'd feel it hard across my face in another second, but instead he patted me on the head.

"I see you are still your mother's son," he said, and he took off his specs and rubbed the top of his nose like he had a headache pressing down on his eyes. Then he put his specs back on, took a deep breath and said, "Okay, we shall now go to visit

Mr. Monk Eastman, and I hope that for a change you will try to be your father's son."

Well, we ended up at a place Monk owned over on Forsythe. It's called The Palm, and it's a saloon and dance hall kind of place, with rooms upstairs where you could take girls that Monk always had there. The place stunk of beer and cigar smoke, and there were little ratty-looking fake palms that had tobacco-spit stains all over the pots they stood up in. I heard that at Silver Dollar Smith's place, where Monk had worked as a bouncer when he was about my age, the floor was made of real silver dollars, but here it was covered with sawdust that in lots of spots was clumped and damp, and there were oyster shells and peanut shells laying around in it.

Monk was sitting at a table and facing the door when we walked in. Tick-Tock and the Redkopf were with some other guys at a table in the back, and there were guys at other tables, and some at the bar. And strolling around or sitting with guys were girls, some of them drinking beer from big mugs just like the guys had.

Monk had a mug in his mitt and a girl in his lap. There was a plate with raw oysters heaped up in front of him. A small sharp knife for cutting them open was right next to the plate, and next to the knife was his club, which had a bunch of notches carved in it. Monk shoved the girl up to her feet when we came in and told her, "Go fix yourself up. T'row some more powder on your puss. You could use it." I could see that one of her eyes was black and swoled-up.

Then Monk wipes his mouth with the back of his hand, waves to my father and me to sit down with him and says, "So you brung him, Ash. I'll bet you didn't find him at school neit'er, did ya?"

"No, he was with his pals, jumping off of the Fish Market docks."

Monk says to me, "What, you seen Izzie take his swan dive last night, and you figgered it looked like a good idea on a hot morning to do what he done, huh? Only not from so high up, right?" And he laughed, said again, "Only not from so high up," laughed harder and looked around to see that the guys at the other tables were laughing too, and they were, some of them repeating the line and saying stuff like, "Hey, that's a good one, Monk."

Monk picked up an oyster from the pile in front of him, sliced it open, threw back his head, slid the slick, snotty-looking stuff down his throat and tossed the shell onto the pile on the floor next to his chair.

Then he turns back to me. He's grinning still, all greasy-looking around his mouth, and he says, "You ain't laughin', kid. You don't like a good joke?"

I know what I'm supposed to say, but instead I tell him, "Yeah, I like a good joke, I guess, but this one just doesn't seem so funny to me." My father puts his hand on my shoulder and gives it a quick pinch, while Monk just looks at me.

"Leave him be, Asher," Monk says. "You can't make him laugh if he don't t'ink it's funny. You, Moish, I seen you out dere on da bridge last night, with dat little pipik Davey Blument'al. I seen he got a laugh out of it, but you didn't look like you was enjoying yourself."

"What you were doing to Izzie didn't seem so funny to me, and I didn't think it was so funny either when he slipped out of your hands and into the river."

Monk gives me a hard look, but then the big grin is right back on his puss, and he says, "Slipped, nah, dat ain't right. Dat's why you didn't get it. If you'd seen dat I let him go, den you would of got da joke, kid."

I was scared, but I say, "Izzie Goldstein's wife and daughter loved him, I bet."

My father says right away, "This kid, he don't butter nobody up, Monk, says what's right on his mind. The kind of kid you can trust, even if you don't like him."

"Can it, Ash," Monk tells him, "I don't need you to tell me what kind of kid dis is or what I like and don't like. You're smart, Asher, but you ain't smart enough to do dat."

"Sorry, Monk," my father says.

Monk ignores him and says to me, "Okay, kid, feel what you like. I don't care. I could see last night what you was feelin'. I ain't blind, and don't ever forget dat."

I nodded.

"Now I t'ink you and me, we can do some business. You could do somet'in' for me, and I t'ink you are gonna wanna do it, 'cause I could do somet'in' for you."

"I've had my eye on you for a while now. People tell me you got promise. Remember, last year, you roughed up dose two Mick punks all by yourself who was callin' some graybeards comin' out of da *shvitz* over on Delancey old Hebe bastards or somet'in'."

"Those guys were nothin' but mouth, Monk. I ain't so tough."

"Well, you don't got a swole head, neit'er. Good for you. I don't like big talkers. But I liked da report on you, and maybe you don't know yet which side your bread is buttered on, but you look like a fast learner."

"Look, Monk, uh Mr. Eastman," I says, "thanks for saying nice things like that, but you already got Davey working for you. Maybe he could do whatever stuff you need done. He really likes doing stuff for you."

Monk stares at me. "And you don't t'ink you would, huh?"

I just shrug, and I hear my father sort of sighing and moaning real quiet.

Monk gives him a grin that's not all that friendly, and says, "Relax, Asher, da kid's got what it takes. I ain't gonna hurt him none," and then he grins back toward me, "not unless he *really* crosses me some time. And you ain't gonna do dat, are ya?"

I shake my head that I ain't.

"Good," he says. "Now, just so's you can be satisfied, *Mr.*

Moishie, I'll tell you dat da bucktoot'ed little sewer rat friend of yours, Blument'al, *who does what I tell him to do*, has got somet'in' else to do for me, and dat he ain't smart enough or good-lookin' enough to do what I'm gonna tell you *you* are gonna do for me. And he also ain't part-Dago, which you are and which might make you real useful."

And he nods and smiles. "So da point is dis, I can use a kid like you. And I'm gonna be generous wit' you, too. I know you got a mama dat you love who's at da sanatarian place over on Blackwell's Island 'cause she's a lunger, and 'cause da TB also messed up her head a little bit. You got my sympat'ies. And I know your old man, who's got his good points but also some dat ain't so much, don't want not'in' to do wit' her. So here's da way it is. You do some stuff for me. Don't worry, it's not beatin' up nobody, not'in' like dat, since I see dat you're a little dainty about dat stuff right now." And he smiles again, and I feel a chill go down my back. "So you go on my payroll now, just t'ink of it as a little summer job where you pick up a little dough so you can maybe buy your mama some t'ings, maybe even slip da doctors or nurses a little somet'in' so dey should give her some extra attention."

I nod back at him, and I ask, "What do you want me to do?"

He says, "I want you should get in good wit' Paul Kelly, and I'll tell you why. Dere are people right around here now who are bad for business. Dere sayin' stuff like 'Da Monk Eastmans of da world ain't good Americans 'cause of da stuff dey do. Hell, I was born right over in Brooklyn, and I got lots of people on my payroll and I pay good and regular and I give people what dey want. Dey want goils dat'll show 'em a good time, dey got 'em. Dey want booze on da cheap and lots of it, dey got it. Dey want da yam-yam pipe and a place to smoke it, dey got it. I'm a businessman, a good American businessman. You unnerstand?"

I nod that I do, and then he tells me that these "bigmout's" are talking about cleaning up the Lower East Side, and he says that he hears that a lot of these bigmouths are socialists, which means *"Dere* da ones what ain't American." And he yells that this is 1897, and business has got to keep growing right along with the country and has got to "fight off dese socialist bastids."

Then he tells me, "Look, you, Moishie, dat bitch Friedman who's your teacher, she's in wit' 'em up to her tits. She's runnin' some kind of summer school program wit' classes and sports, startin' in a couple days where dere gonna be warnin' kids about me, tryin' to toin da whole Lower East against me. Dere trainin' 'em to t'ink like socialists. You go to dat summer school, play up dat your old lady's a socialist, as red as da blood she's pukin' from her lungs, and get da Friedman bitch to trust you. Get her to take you to dis socialist meeting soon at some house uptown where I hear dat lyin' Dago bastid Kelly is gonna mouth off against me to some high-hat Protestant do-gooders. Friedman's summer program, which is in a couple schools down here, is gettin' most of its dough from him, 'cause he's tryin' to take over east of da Bowery and is pullin' da wool over dese high-hats' eyes by actin' like his shit don't stink. You meet da Dago and get him to t'ink dat 'cause you got a grudge against your old man, you're gonna spy on your old man and me for him, if he gives you some dough. Meanwhile, you spy on him and tell me what kind of stuff he's cookin' up. He ain't gonna tell you much, 'cause you're just a kid, but I know you ain't dumb, so find out what you can. And I also could maybe give you some stuff to tell him dat ain't true, but dat I could want him to t'ink is. So dat's da deal, Moishie. Dat's what you're gonna do for me."

I think to myself that this is something I need to do, not just because Monk is telling me I got to but because maybe if I'm in with Paul Kelly I can figure out a way to hurt Monk real bad for what he did to Izzie. And, right off, I can also maybe do something else I know I need to do, which is help Esther.

So I tell Monk, "Yeah, I'll do exactly what you want, but only if you give me something more than just the dough."

Monk waits a bit, like he can't believe that I'm giving him a condition, and my father's looking up at the ceiling.

Then Monk says, in a quiet voice. "Yeah, kid, whatta ya want?"

I tell him, "On the bridge, you were talking about doing stuff to Izzie's wife and daughter. I want you should lay off them."

Monk grins broad now. "Yeah, I heard you a couple minutes ago say you was sorry for the chiselin' bastid's wife and daughter, who wit'out knowin' it are squatters now in da keyshop dat I own free and clear, and I also figgered dat maybe you felt a little sorrier for da bastid's pretty little daughter dan you did for da mama."

The guys sitting at the other tables hear that and they laugh and wink at each other. Droop-Eye says, "She's gonna be a looker, all right. She already got some cute little boobies on her," and he reaches out and makes like he's squeezing. My face felt hot and I wanted to kill him, wanted to kill them all. Everybody's laughing harder now, except for Monk, who's watching me, and my father, who puts his hand on my shoulder. I shrug it off.

"Okay, okay," Monk says. "Youse guys, knock it off. Da kid looks like he could take youse all on and walk outta here in one piece."

"Okay, Moish," Monk says, "You win. You do dis job I want from you, and I don't make her become one of da goils on my payroll. It's hands off her and her mama. Okay?"

I say, "Okay, I'll do the job, and I'll do it good."

My father pats me on the shoulder, like I did the right thing, and Monk cuts open another oyster and swallows it in a gulp, tosses the shell onto the pile, and says, "Good. Young love's a touchin' t'ing, ain't it?" then laughs and winks at his pals, who laugh and wink back. And he hands me a few bucks.

And then as I pocket the dough, I can't keep myself from saying, "Look, why don't you just drop Miss Friedman and

her socialist pals and anybody who's 'bankrollin'' 'em off of the
Brooklyn Bridge?"

Next thing, I'm laying in the sawdust and oyster shells and
peanut shells and the spitted tobacco juice, with my chair laying alongside me and my jaw hurting.

But it wasn't Monk who hit me. It was my father, who walloped me with the back of his hand. I never saw it coming,
because whatever else he ever did in his stinking life he never
hit either my mother or me. He was sitting there, white in
the face, looking down at me. And I saw real quick that even
though he was mad at me for being stupid enough to say what
I said, he laid into me mainly because he figured if he didn't,
Monk was going to do me much worse.

Monk, meanwhile, his face is gone red, except for the
scars, which look kind of bluish, and he's staring at me on
the floor. It's so quiet in there, I can hear Tick-Tock's watch.
Everybody's waiting to see if Monk's going to let me get off
with just a smack from my old man. And he does. He says
real quiet, "It's a good t'ing for you dat I can use you, you
half-dago *shmuck*, but you better wise up fast. Your old man
was lookin' out for you just now. He might not be around next
time, and even if he is, it might not get ya off so easy. Now get
on your big feet, brush all dat shit off of you, and tell me you
apologize, an' maybe I won't break your head open before
you try to walk outta here."

So I get up, and with everybody watching me, and my
father rubbing the back of his hand, I brush myself off as good
as I can, and I tell Monk, "I'm sorry. I spoke outta turn. I'll try
and do a good job for you."

Monk nods. Then he picks up the club that he's got on the
table and steps toward me. I think he's going to belt me one
for good measure anyway and that I'll end up in the Eastman
Pavilion, which is what people call the emergency ward over
at the hospital because of all the guys that get sent there after
Monk works them over. But he walks past me, to the bar,

where there's this little old drunk slumped over, who's half singing and half mumbling some Mick song about his little old mother back in Dublin town, and Monk, he takes the guy's derby off his head, sets it down on the bar real gentle, and the guy, he doesn't even know Monk's there. And then Monk smacks him one right on top of the head, and the guy's face just drops straight to the bar, and a little trickle of blood runs down along his jaw from above his ear and starts to pool up at his chin.

Monk looks at him a couple seconds, turns back to the rest of us, and he's smiling now. He goes back to his table, picks up his oyster knife and cuts another notch into his club. "Dere," he says, "I got me an even fifty now dat dis club has done da job on. Forty-nine wasn't comfortable. I'd been stuck wit' it for too long. Maybe I'll pick up da pace now." Then he stares hard at me. I look back right at him for a little bit, and then I look away.

IV

So that was my morning the day after I saw Izzie go off the bridge. Right after lunch that same day, I was on my way to see my mother. I had the money in my pocket that Monk gave me, but even though I had the dough now to ride the trolley up to Twenty-Sixth, where the little steamer leaves Bellevue to ferry on over to Blackwell's, I was walking the couple miles anyway, because I was too worked up to sit, all nervous about everything that had happened since Davey had come down the fire escape. So, I'm on Allen, crossing Hester, working my way through the pushcarts and the freight wagons and all the people elbowing each other, and the heat's making the horse-shit and the sewers smell even stronger than usual, and there's all this jabbering and yelling, and then I see Esther. She's looking around like she doesn't know where she's going but needs to go there in a hurry anyway.

Her face was flushed, and she was staring up and down the street and into every store. She sees me, and she comes up and says, "Morris, have you seen my papa?"

I tell her no, and I say, "You look worried. Something wrong?"

"Papa went out after supper last night, and he never came back! Mama has gone to the police, and they said they can't even start searching for him until he's been gone for forty-eight hours, so we're looking on our own. And we went over to the

Infirmary Hospital, and Mt. Sinai, and she even went all the way up to Bellevue, while I went over to the school and told Miss Friedman why I didn't come in, and he's not at any of them. Nobody knows anything. He comes back late sometimes, but he never stayed out the whole night before. Mama went back to our place to see if he showed up finally, and I'm just walking around and looking. Maybe I'll go back home now and see."

I don't want her to walk away from me, so I lie and tell her, "I just was walking past there, and I saw your mother at the door, looking up and down the street. So I guess he ain't back yet. But let me ask you something. What's the point of looking, anyway? If your father's all right, like he probably is, he'll come home soon enough."

I didn't feel good lying to her, but I didn't know what else to do. I mean she really didn't need to be wearing herself out looking for someone she wasn't going to find. And meanwhile I could be with her some, anyway.

And then I say to her, "You look real tired, Esther, so why don't you at least go into a drugstore with me, and I'll get you a seltzer or a soda pop, and you could rest a bit, okay?"

She says yes, and I take her into Levine's, up on Delancey, and we sit down at the counter and she orders a strawberry pop and I order a root beer, and for a minute I just look into the mirror behind the counter at the two of us sitting there side by side, and it looks right. Still I can't forget that I'm paying for her strawberry pop with money I got from Monk Eastman, who dropped her father off of the Brooklyn Bridge.

I almost think I should tell her what happened, but I know I can't, because nothing good would come out of it. After all the terrible crying, she'd want to go to the cops, and they wouldn't do a thing, because of the money that Monk spreads around. And who would be a witness against Monk? Everybody who was there is on Monk's payroll, and, besides, they'd probably end up themselves in the river before they could testify, even if they wanted to. And Esther herself, if she went to the cops, well, something terrible would happen to her. And, besides, she'd hate me for not having tried to help her father, and she'd want me to testify about what happened, but fifty of Monk's guys would swear they were with him nowhere near the bridge and then I'd get killed and maybe Monk would hurt Aunt Gabriella and Uncle Giulio, too, just to top things off.

Meanwhile, she looks so pretty in her blue smock and white blouse that I want to think only about her and me right now. So I just stare at us in the mirror, and after a bit, I say, "I've only been in here a couple times. They make good sodas, don't they?"

She nods and says, "Yeah, this is very good. Thanks, Morris." And then she sighs.

"Aw, your dad's all right. It'll be okay," I say, trying to sound like I mean it, and I reach from my stool over to hers and put my hand on her shoulder and pat it a couple times. It's the first time I ever touched any girl besides dumb Skinny Minnie Hershkowitz that time with Davey up on the roof, and that wasn't so good really and I don't ever want to talk about it.

Esther smiled and said thanks, and I put my hands back on the counter.

Then she says, "I didn't see you there when I stopped off at the school today."

"Me and Davey Blumenthal, we went over to the Fish Market docks and went swimming. It was too hot, we figured, for school." And I shrugged and felt stupid.

But she smiled real nice and said that she wished girls could do stuff like that at least once in a while.

"Well, if you did, then me and Davey would have to get bathing suits."

And then we both blushed some and laughed a little.

"Davey's real funny at school," she said.

"Yeah, he makes good jokes," I say, and then "I'll be sure to be there tomorrow, 'cause it's the last day. I've got nothing against school, really. I was just feeling lazy. Anyway, I want to talk to Miss Friedman. I hear she's running some kind of summer program with sports and stuff."

"Yeah, I'm going to be in it. It's going to be fun and also educational about making the country better." Then she gets a little misty and says, "I'm just so worried about my father."

"You want an ice cream, even a big bowl?"

She says, "Where'd you get all the money?"

I look down at my hands. "Aah, I got it making some deliveries for people."

"Well, if you're working hard like that, then you don't need to be wasting your money on the likes of me."

"Anything I spend that makes you feel a little better ain't no waste, Esther."

She smiles and says, "I'm not so hungry right now. The soda pop's just fine. And you're a real nice guy, Morris."

Well, I hear that, and I don't want to look in that mirror anymore. So I say, "Why not let's take a ride uptown on the trolley? I got to go to Blackwell's so I can go see my mother at the hospital out there. You could keep me company till we get to the ferry. So take a trolley ride and rest, it's so hot out. And when we get there, I'll give you the fare and you can take the trolley back down here. And, besides, if your dad ain't home yet, which he probably is, you might spot him from the trolley."

So, in a couple minutes we're in a trolley car together heading uptown. And after a bit she turns toward me and she says, "How come your mother's out on Blackwell's, if you don't mind me asking?"

"No," I tell her, "you can ask. It's okay. I don't usually like to talk about it, but I don't mind telling you. My mom's in the charity TB hospital they've got out there."

I don't tell her, though, about laying awake at night when my mother and me still had our own place and me hearing her coughing, hacking like there wasn't going to be nothing left inside of her. She would try to smother it, so it wouldn't wake me up or scare me, but I was awake and scared. Sometimes I would ask her, "Mama, are you all right, should I run and get the doctor?" And she would say, "No, *mio bambino bello*. I no need *il dottore*, he can do nothing for this cold. It will just take time." And then I would lay there and pretend most of the time that I was sleeping. And when I saw spots of blood on her handkerchief, I didn't say anything. I pretended that I didn't see, because she didn't want me to see. And even when the doctor took her away to Bellevue while I was at school, and I got home and saw Aunt Gabriella there waiting for me and crying, I never said anything about TB, because no one wanted me to know and they felt better thinking maybe I didn't. They just told me she had a real bad cold and would probably be let out soon.

So for six months now, while I'm living with Aunt Gabriella and Uncle Giulio, and I hear them whispering in Italian that my mother, she's *molto male*, I don't let them know that I hear. Too much pain all around.

But, like I say, I don't tell Esther any of the details. I figure she's got enough bad stuff ahead of her. I do tell her, though, that somehow the TB, it's gotten into my mother's head, so that sometimes she doesn't act right, and they had to put her in a special building over on the island. I haven't told anybody else this, not even Davey. And my father, maybe he knows or maybe he doesn't.

She kisses me on the cheek, and it looks like she's going to cry. I shouldn't have told her, because now she's worried not only about her father, but also about my mother, which is just too much for her. So I kiss her on her head, and I see how nice her hair smells, like good soap that's not either too sweet, like the perfume Aunt Gabriella wears when she goes to church, or too sharp, like what the janitor uses to clean at school. The smell of her hair makes me think of walking in the Central Park, which I haven't done more than a couple times, or seeing a baseball game when the sun is making the grass shine and the flags are waving over at the Polo Grounds, which me and Davey snuck into once for a couple innings. And she smiles at me a little now, and I put my arm around her shoulder and she leans her head against mine, and I don't know if I ever felt better. Last night seems far away, and I don't want this ride to ever end.

But just when we're getting to Twenty-Sixth, we stop short, and I hear the trolley driver say, "Jesus Christ almighty." An old lady is sitting by the curb, near the corner, with her legs spread out in front of her, and she's hanging on tight to her shopping bag, which is all tipped over, and her eyes are staring wide. People are rushing over toward her, and I see there's blood on her black stockings, spreading down from somewhere up inside her, and a driver is getting down from his freight wagon and yelling something at the old lady and everybody else.

Well, Twenty-Sixth is where Esther and me are supposed to get off, so we step down, and Esther is pale and whispering "*Oy, gevalt,*" to herself, and we hear the driver, a big, dirty-looking guy with his eyes all bloodshot, screaming, "She didn't look where she was goin'."

The old lady's got a cross around her neck, and in her bag that's laying there she's got a big *ciabatta*, and there's tomatoes that's rolled out of the bag and are sitting now against the curb. I go over and pick the tomatoes up and put them into her bag. I don't know why, because they're not gonna be any good by the time she gets out of the hospital, if she ever gets out. But the way she was holding onto that bag, like it was a lifeline to keep her from going under, it seemed like something I ought to do. Esther helped me get them back into her bag and was stroking her head and smiling gentle and whispering to her that she was going to be okay.

Meanwhile, a doctor comes up and kneels by the lady and starts working on her and a guy yells at the wagon driver, "You was goin' too fast. You didn't give her no chance to get back up on the curb, like she was tryin' to." And another guy yells, "Yeah, it was your goddamn fault!"

Well, then the driver's two horses are scared by all the commotion, and one of them whinnies, and then the other one does. And the driver, he says, "The old biddy wasn't lookin', and if I was goin' a little too fast, it was 'cause of these two bastids here." And he grabs a big thick black strap that he's got up at his seat on the wagon and he starts beating the horses on their heads.

"Stop it," Esther screams, "You're going to kill them, you brute!" and she rushes up to try to get the strap out of his hands, but the guy just says, "Shut up, you," shoves her away and keeps hitting them. I grab the strap from him before he knows what's happening, and I start beating him with it on his head and then on his back and shoulders and hands when he tries to cover himself up.

Nobody stops me. A couple guys even yell stuff like "Give it to him good." Then the guy falls down onto the street and lays on his side moaning and bloody and still trying to cover himself up, and I hit him some more, wishing I had a club to smash his head with. And now Esther's yelling, "Stop, Morris. Please. That's enough!" Then I hear cop whistles blowing from maybe a block away. I throw the strap down on the bastid, and I say to Esther, "Let's get out of here."

So we head west, toward Second Avenue, and nobody comes after us. I look back when we're about a block away, and I see one of the horses move backwards when someone's trying to grab hold of its reins, and I see it step on the head of the guy that I left laying there in the street. I don't tell Esther that, and I don't let it bother me any either.

We walk fast and don't say anything for a few blocks. Then, about when we're getting to Lexington, she starts crying, so I put my arm around her, and I tell her, "Don't worry, Esther, it's gonna be all right."

She says, "Oh, that poor old lady. And those horses, they

were so frightened. Oh, Morris, why is everything just so awful?" And then she says, "But you were brave, Morris."

I shrug and tell her, "You were brave first, yelling at the guy and trying to stop him from beating the horses, and I didn't do anything so special," but I do feel a little bit like a cowboy hero in the books, especially when I remember that they always grin and shrug and say, "Aw shucks, it was nothin', ma'am," after they've done something that the pretty girl thinks is real special.

Esther says, "I never knew you could get so mad, though. It was scary. I thought you might kill him."

"I don't usually get mad," I said, "and I won't do it anymore if you don't like it. I don't want to do anything that you don't like." But after beating that wagon driver bum like I did, I knew now that there wasn't anything I wouldn't do to Monk when the time came that I'd have to. And I kissed her on top of her head again and got that great smell again that was in her hair.

Then I look up, and I say, "Hey, ain't that so pretty there with the sun shining right on it like that?" You see, we were at Madison Square by now, and I saw the gold statue up on top of the Madison Square Garden building, the one of the girl standing tip-toe on one foot and she's pulling back on a bow and ready to fire an arrow.

Esther said that, yeah, it's real pretty and that it's Diana, and I ask her, "Diana, who?" And she smiles and says, "It's Diana, the goddess of the moon, silly."

And I tell her that I didn't remember any goddess of the moon from the Bible, though I admit to her that there's a lot in the Bible I don't know, because my mother always told me religion was just a bunch of stories rich people want poor people to believe, and the couple times Aunt Gabriella took me to church I got bored and didn't listen much. And Esther laughs now, and she tells me Diana isn't from the Bible but was a Roman goddess. I asked whether that made Diana a Catholic, and she laughed some more and kissed me on the cheek. I was glad I could make her laugh a little, even though I didn't know I'd said anything so funny.

So, anyway, we looked up at the statue, all shiny in the sunlight, and I've still got my arm around her, and I tell myself I bet that Esther looks something like that without her clothes on, and with her dark hair done up like Diana's in a bun and showing off her long neck, pretty like a swan's, and with her nice little pointy pears standing up real cute.

And then I do something that surprises the both of us. I look back up at the statue and I raise my arm, like I'm saluting it, and I recite out loud without missing a word, I don't think,

> *I benedico il loco e 'l tempo et l' ora*
> *Che si altomiraron gli occhi mei*
> *Et dico: 'Anima, assai ringratiar dei*
> *Che forte a tanto degnatta allora.'*

Then I blush and look down.

Esther says, "Wow, Morris, was that Italian? I didn't know you could speak it."

I told her, "I really can't, I just understand it a little. That's from this poet named Petrarca, a long time ago, and he's saying he blesses the day and the hour when he first looked at something so noble as this girl named Laura that he loves, and he says his soul should be real grateful that it has the honor of loving her. My mother taught it to me. She thinks Petrarca isn't talking so much to this Laura lady as he is to a spirit of justice and kindness for people."

"So that's what you were reciting it to, then, when you were saluting Diana?" she asks with this sweet little smile.

"No I was really reciting it for a girl who's even prettier than Diana." I want to whisper to her that if she had an arrow like Diana's, she's already fired it at my heart and hit it square, but I figured that was maybe too mushy.

Well, for a few seconds neither of us says anything, and then Esther sighs and says, "Morris, thanks for spending so much time with me, but I really need to get back to my mother now."

So I took her over to the downtown trolley, gave her the fare, and she says just before she gets on, "Thanks, Morris. I want us to do more stuff together, even though Mama says I'm not really supposed to go anywhere with a boy. I think that kind of rule is silly nowadays. I trust you and know we could have good times going places together. Papa understands that kind of thing." Then she gets choked up and gets on the trolley, while I give her a little pat on the back.

I watched the trolley move on down the avenue till I couldn't see it, and then I headed over to the dock at Twenty-Sixth to take the little steamer boat out to my mother on Blackwell's Island.

V

The *Minnahanock* is a boat just for the sick people and their relatives. My pal Billy Higgins who works on it told me that the name of the boat is what the Indians use to call Blackwell's Island, and that what it meant in Indian was something like "A Great Place to Live." I like that. It lets me daydream for the few minutes while we're going across that I'm on the river back in early days, and that the island doesn't have any hospitals or workhouse or prison or insane asylum on it like it does now. No, it's just got trees and maybe some tepees, and I'm canoeing across to rescue somebody who's been kidnaped by the Indians, maybe someone like Esther, and she'll love me and stay with me forever. And while I'm thinking about all that right now I'm trying not to look down the river toward the bridge.

Going over today are four people laying on stretchers on the deck, all of them pale and with eyes that look too big. They're sweaty, even though there's a nice little breeze out there on the river. And they're all coughing, especially a young guy who's saying over and over that he'll be coming back in a box. It gave me the creeps.

Well, Billy Higgins sees me, and says "Moe, old man, you doing okay?"

I don't mind if he calls me Moe. He doesn't mean anything

by it, the way some guys do when they call Jews that, or "Abie" or "Ike." For him it's just short and friendly for Morris. I tell him I'm not doing so great.

"I see you got some pretty roses there for your mama. That'll make her feel better."

I smile and nod. I don't tell him that I paid for them with dough that Monk Eastman gave me.

Billy always smiles quick and easy, makes you like him right off, but things haven't been so easy for him. He's twenty-six or twenty-seven and would be handsome except that his face has red splotches and pockmarks all over it from when he got the smallpox back in '85, when he was a little younger than what I am now. The sanitary board people hauled him out to the island back then and stuck him in quarantine over at the smallpox hospital that's now a nursing school right next to the hospital where they have my mother. He said that the people who could pay something got to be on the top floors in wards with windows and real nurses and with doctors coming by a couple times a day because they figured you were worth saving. But people like him, he said, who didn't have anything, went downstairs to the charity ward, where it was crowded and dark, and where they didn't get too many visits from the doctors, and where most of the so-called nurses were just women they brought over from the workhouse that they still have on Blackwell's, which is mostly for pickpockets and streetwalkers, you know, small-timers that don't get away with it. These ones they brought in as nurses back when Billy got the pox had already had it, so they couldn't get it again, and Billy told me that lots of times they'd just laugh at the sick people, especially the sick young women, and shove their pocked-up faces right next to them and tell them stuff like "Dearie, I'm your mirror now. Take a good long look, 'cause this is what you is gonna be seein' the rest of your life, sweetie." He said they all weren't like that, but lots were, and some did even worse stuff he didn't want to talk about.

And while he was there, when he was about at his sickest, that was when he and everyone else was boated over to the new smallpox hospital up on North Brother Island, a little place right next to the Bronx. It was a cold, windy, gray day when they took them, and the water was rough, and the steamer was crowded and having a tough time against the wind and the waves and the currents up near Hellgate. Sick people were crying and yelling, and the charity patients didn't get to go inside, but were just left laying out on the deck.

Well, there was this lady laying near Billy, and she was wrapped tight in a wool blanket, and wrapped up tight with her was her little boy, maybe a year or two old, and he had the pox, too, and she's rocking him a little, but he's moaning, with his eyes stuck shut with crust and pus. And she's moaning, too, and pale and sweating, and Billy, well, he's just a kid then, but, sick and scared as he is, he's telling her that at the new hospital everything was going to be better. And then the boat rolled hard to one side, and all the stretchers went sliding down toward the rails, and everybody was screaming. But screaming the loudest was the lady that was near Billy, because her baby went sliding out of her arms. Billy was sliding too, but he scrambled over and reached out for the kid but couldn't grab him. He told me, "Moe, I felt the toes on his tiny foot, just at the tips of my fingers, but he slipped under the railing and down into the drink, never made a sound." He said the kid's mother died just a day or two later over at the new hospital. Once she saw what had happened, Billy said, she never made another sound herself, not even a moan. "Moe," he said, "sometimes when it's gray and windy and chilly out here, I swear to God in heaven, my fingertips start getting the feel of those tiny, soft toes just brushing against them, and it's all I can do not to start crying and crying, grown man here like I am, working the boat."

I had tried to keep that kid out of my mind ever since I heard the story. I didn't even tell Davey about it. And even on the bridge, with all the stuff going on with Monk and Izzie, I made myself not think about it, but now, being back on the river with Billy, I could see the kid sliding in just like it must have happened. I wondered whether anything was left of him after all those years and if it could get mixed up with what was left of Izzie.

And I wondered if socialism could have kept stuff like what Billy told me from happening. One rotten socialist guy back in Poland didn't make socialism itself so bad, maybe, which my old man would have known if he hadn't gone so rotten himself. And Izzie having gone into the river like that little baby made me see that Monk was just like all the selfish rich guys uptown and all the mine owners, and factory owners and all the rest that liked President McKinley so much. They were all on top and they wanted to keep it that way, and if the people on the bottom got sick and bled and coughed their lives away or even ended up falling into the river, so what?

Billy told me more, too. When he finally got well, and he went home to where him and his folks lived over around Hell's Kitchen, nobody was there anymore. His father, who drank, had beat his mother with a leg off of a table and by the time the cops got there she was dead. And Billy's little brother and sister had been put in some Catholic orphanage, and his old man had hung himself in his jail cell. And nobody had come to tell Billy.

Since then Billy's been on his own. His brother ran off from the orphanage a couple years later and joined the Army, and Billy hasn't heard from him since, and when his sister got out of the orphanage, she took a job typing, but she got in trouble with some married guy, had a baby, ran off, and Billy hasn't heard from her either.

And now he works most every day on the *Minnahanock*, the same boat that took him out to Blackwell's back when he had the pox. Maybe he couldn't get any other job, or maybe he just feels like this is where he became who he is and he can't really be himself anywhere else. I tell myself out there on the boat with him that I don't want to end up trapped in bad memories, like Billy is in his way and my old man is in his own way.

Well, we reach Blackwell's, and I head over to Metropolitan Hospital, which used to be the insane asylum, but now is just for people without dough who got TB. A small part of the place is for people whose TB poisons their heads, and that's where they've got my mother.

The building's a big place, gray stone, with two long wings, sort of an L shape, with each wing four stories high. Where the wings meet there's a tower that goes up about seven stories. It's round, with a dome at the top, and windows all the way up, even in the dome. Both wings have porches on every floor, with roofs on them for shade, so the sick people can sit out and get fresh air, which is part of what you need if you have TB and are trying to get well.

There's ivy growing on the walls, and the place doesn't look so bad when the sun's shining, but when it's cloudy or rainy, then it looks dark and scary, maybe like an evil baron's castle, or maybe, even worse, it just looks more like what it is, a place for very sick people that most of them won't leave except in a box, including my poor mama.

I go through the main entrance, into a round lobby that I once heard some nurse call the rothunder, and then I go up this twisty, winding staircase to the fourth floor. When you get up there and look down, it's like you're seeing a coiling snake of stairs, and if you look up to the top, which is the dome of the tower, it's like seeing the head of the snake reaching up above you.

Then, I go down the hall to the big room where they keep my mother with a bunch of other sick ladies. Some new nurse who's got wall-eye so bad that it looks like she can only see what's on the sides of her, like a fish sees, tells me my mother is out on the sun porch. She looked about Billy's age, and, except for her eyes, wasn't so bad-looking, and she smiles at me, shakes my hand, tells me her name is Mary-Margaret Shannahan, and as she walks me to the porch she tells me, "I've only been here for six days now, and already your mother has told me more than a few times how proud she is of her 'big, fine boy with his big, fine heart.' She thinks the world of her Massimo, she does, and she's going to love those roses you were so sweet to bring her. I'll bet you had to save your pennies and nickels to buy them, too."

I said, "Yeah, well, she deserves nice things, but I ain't so special, really."

"Well, even though she's not herself now, you know, I'm thinking she's a good judge of character, Massimo," she says, turning to face me full now, which makes me wonder whether she's seeing me at all.

"Morris is my official name, like on my birth certificate and school papers," I tell her, "but some people also call me Moishe or Moishie."

"And which do you like best?" Mary-Margaret asks me.

I tell her it doesn't make much difference, but that for out here "Massimo" is fine.

We're at the entrance to the sun porch now, and Mary-Margaret says, "I'll let you go and surprise her by yourself, Massimo. It'll do her so much good to see you." I felt rotten now for not coming maybe every day, even if it takes so long to get there and makes me sad for days after I do.

I stand there in the doorway and look at my mother. She's sitting in a beach chair, with her legs stretched out in front of her, and she's wrapped up in blankets and has a white night-cap on her head. She's staring across the river at the city. And she's sweating and shivering at the same time.

She doesn't see me or hear my footsteps on the wood planks as I walk over to her.

"Mama," I say real soft, "Mama, how you doing?"

"Ah, Massimo, my Massimo," she says, turning to me, "you come all the way over here to see me, my good boy. I sit here and think lots about you, you know."

I bend down and kiss her on her forehead. It feels damp and both hot and cold at once. "How are you feeling, Mama?" I ask her. I see that in her dark eyes she looks like maybe she's thinking clear right now, not so mixed up in the head like she is other times.

"Ah, not so good, not so good. My head, it don't stop hurting. And my throat, it's sore and dry, and I cough, but what can I do? Complaining don't help. So. Maybe I get better soon. Now let's talk about what is important. Are you a good boy? You listen to your aunt and uncle?"

I nod yeah and show her the flowers.

She leans her head to them and smells hard. "Ah, beautiful. *Bellisima*. So sweet. Both them and you. Where do you get the money for this?"

I don't answer. I just take one of the flowers from the bunch and put it behind her ear. She smiles and says, "I bet I look just like when I was a girl back home, barefoot in the grass."

I say, "You do, Mama. Just like a pretty *ragazza contadina*."

She laughs and asks, "And you go to the school and you learn, like I always tell you?"

I say yeah and don't exactly look her in the face, but she doesn't seem to notice.

"Good," she tells me, "but make sure your aunt, she don't send you to the church school. You go to the city school. She means good, but the church school ain't what I want for you. If she tell you to go to church sometimes, you do that for her, so she don't feel bad, but I tell her you could do that only sometimes. And, listen to me good, you don't pay too much attention to what goes on in the church, okay? When I come to this country, I say to myself no more church for me, and you know why?"

I knew why. She told me lots of times, but if she wanted to tell me again now, out here, I wasn't going to stop her.

"The church, it blinds the people, Massimo, and it steals from them their minds and it steals from them their souls. And it tells them they got it good waiting for them in heaven, but that's just so they don't know how bad they got it here. The rich, *gli uomini ricchi*, they want it that way. Back home the church and the *Camorra*, this is how they have it—you know the *Camorra*, how do you say, the mob of crooks and killers, *capisce*?"

"*Io capisco*, Mama."

"Si, *la Chiesa, la Camorra, y gli uomini ricchi*—you got nothing with them around. So I come here to think for myself and to live my own life, and this is what I want for you, Massimo."

She turns toward the city again. The sun was over by Jersey now, and the city looked like it was glowing. "Look at all this, Massimo," she says, "New York, America, where I was to make my new life, *mi vita nuova*. It didn't go so good for me, but in that city is where you got to make your life. Make it good, Massimo. Be strong, 'cause you got to be, but be good, too. Your poor papa, *il povero*, he wanted to be good, but he no strong enough. Don't go his way, Massimo, *caro* Massimo."

And she sings soft now,

> *A l'aura il vigile*
> *Grido mandate:*
> *S'innova il secolo*
> *Piena e l'etate*

She used to sing this lots of times. It means something like there's a call in the wind that better days are coming for all the people. I feel a breeze now, and being with her like this can almost make me believe I hear that call on it, even though I know if I'm hearing anything it's just a tugboat way off somewhere.

And her eyes get wet, and she pulls her arms from under the cover and grabs my shoulders, squeezing them hard. People tell me my shoulders are big, but right now they feel small and weak. I'm surprised at how strong her large hands still are. Mama is a big woman, almost as big as my father, tall and broad. She sits up higher, pulls me to her hard now and kisses my forehead, holding her lips against it for a long time. I feel the fever that's burning in her, and I smell the sweat from her body and something that's like mold in her breath. It's not comfortable, but I don't want her to let go.

But then she slowly lays back down again, and she's wheezing, trying to hold back the coughs. Strands of her hair, black with streaks of iron gray, have come down from under her cap, and they're sticking to her forehead. I kiss it. It's wetter and hotter than it was before.

"I'll be good, Mama," I said. "I won't forget what you taught me." Then I took a deep breath, and I say, "Mama, why did you ever marry Papa?"

She smiles and says, still wheezing some, "Massimo, your papa, like I just said, he wasn't always like now. I met him almost twenty years ago at a meeting, *La Lega Socialista*. Me and some girlfriends, we was there, and your papa, he was there with some guys, and we ended up after the meeting, sitting at a big table and having coffee with them, and even though, your papa and me, we didn't speak the English so good, and he didn't know the Italian, and I didn't know the Yiddish, we could talk a little and we could look in each other's eyes. His eyes were so dark and serious, but so *dolce*, and he had a sweet smile, and he was so serious to make the world right, even though life had hurt him bad. You know about this?"

"Yeah," I say, "actually, he told me this morning, after I kind of bumped into him and we talked on a park bench."

"Your papa, he's gone *la via sinestra*, the wrong road, but he's your papa. You shouldn't be strangers." She took a few wheezy breaths. "Your papa, he work hard when he come over here. He take classes, he learn English better, and how to work with numbers for businessmen, and he make a little living keeping the books for a guy who got a business making clothes, and life is not easy, but we're together and we love each other, and we was sure we was part of the new way that was coming, with *pace y amore per tutti personi*, you see."

She stopped for a minute to catch her breath, and I thought that maybe me and Esther could be happy like that, being together and trying to make the world better, especially after I took care of Monk.

"But then when you was just a *bambino*, things go bad," my mother says. Your papa's boss, he's no good. The people who cut and sew for him got to work too long for too little, and sometimes the boss, he makes the girls there, the pretty ones, do other stuff for him and his customers that's an *infamia* that maybe you can guess. Well, your papa, he talks union with the workers, 'cause even after what happen to him and his brother in Poland, he still has the cause in his heart. He no tell you this?"

No, and he didn't tell me what Mama then told me happened, that he got beat up bad by some guys his boss hired, got beat up right in front of the workers eating their lunch and none of them lifted a finger to help him. They were all too scared, too scared or too selfish, maybe. The boss comes in later, says that he doesn't know anything about these guys, and tells my father, that any hours he misses at the doctor because of this he's going to lose pay for and that, oh, yeah, because times are hard, he's going to have to cut his pay back some, anyway. Mama told me he wouldn't fire him, because my father did good work for him. And he knew that my father couldn't quit anyway, with the times being hard.

Well, Mama said, that was when he got himself into Monk's crowd. He knew about the gang and what it did, and he got somebody to meet him up with Monk, who was really only a kid then but who was already making himself a name, and he tells Monk that he's good with numbers and that over the next couple months he's going to play with the numbers for the boss's business and swipe money out of it, till his boss doesn't have a business anymore. And he tells Monk, he's going to give half of the dough to Monk's crowd at first on condition that the gang protects him, so that when the boss finds out about it and wants to call the cops, guys from the gang would come by and tell the boss that wouldn't be such a good idea. And if Monk's boys protect my father good, he tells Monk, he'll give them another quarter of the dough, so they'll end up with three-quarters, and he himself keeps just one.

So, that's what happens. My father does what he says he's going to do, and the gang does what he wants them to, and everything works out swell, except that my father, by making the business go broke, puts a bunch of workers out of work and also decides that he likes being with the gang and they decide he's a smart guy they can use. And when Monk becomes the big boss on the Lower East Side pretty quick after that, my father's his accountant.

Mama looks away from me now and across at the city again, where the sun is starting to drop closer to the tops of the tall buildings, and she says, "I could not accept this that your father done, putting people out on the street and joining a *Camorra*. And he cannot accept that I don't accept, so he leaves us, when you are still little. And I go out and do the sewing in the sweat- shop, and I go to the meetings still, but not with your papa, and I march with the *Lega*. This is the whole story, not a happy one."

"And do you hate Papa?" I ask her.

"No," she said, shaking her head slow, "I feel sorry for him." Then she smiled at me and said, "And he did give me a fine big boy, my Massimo."

Then she reaches down below her blanket, and her hand comes out holding a little key. "Here," she tells me. "You take this. Your papa, he give it to me, when he come to visit me, just before they take me away to here. He was worried about something, and he tell me I'm the only one he can trust even though we don't never see each other no more.

"What's the key for, Mama?"

She's got a strange look in her eyes now, like I seen before. It means that she's not thinking so clear right then, and she says, "Don't tell the Pope you got it, you promise me this?"

I tell her I promise.

She pats me on the head, tells me I'm a good boy, and that she can trust me. Then she tells me that "This key is to a treasure, my big, brave boy, and you got to find it. It's in a tin box where your papa put some things, *cosi molte, molte importante*, that could get Monkey Eastaman into big trouble if he turn on your papa. And he tell me that that's not all that he got hid there, that's there's lots more, a big prize for whoever finds it if your papa is gone. But, me, I cannot be able to get it if sometime I need to, Massimo. So this key, it's for you, my boy. Use it if the time should come."

I ask her where's the box and she tells me, "I don't know no more. Your papa, he say to me to put it where that Monkey Eastaman, he never find it, a place he never go. But I can remember no more where I put it. It's a secret." And then she reaches down into her pocket, pulls out a piece of black ribbon, slips it through the hole in the top of the key, reaches up, opens my shirt and says, "You don't got no cross or no Jewish star at your throat, good, good. You don't need that stuff. But you need this, just in case. You got to keep it with you! You got to!"

And then she pulls her hands back to her mouth and starts coughing like she's never ever going to stop and then I see there's blood on her hands where she's coughing into them.

I get real scared and I'm saying, "Mama, Mama" and holding her shoulders and I'm screaming for Mary-Margaret, but just before she comes running in, my mother catches her breath for a few seconds, says what sounds like "sand Jew today oh" a couple times, throws her arms around my neck and ties the ribbon to it. Then she lays down against her chairback, with her whole body heaving like a machine that's about to break. My chest feels like it's got a warm wet spot, and I look down at it and see that the key has blood on it. I wipe it and I wonder if this was a key that Izzie Goldstein made. I slip it under my shirt and close my shirt up to the throat.

Well, Mary-Margaret is there now, and she gets my mother into a wheelchair and takes her back to her bed. I don't go with her, but stand there on the porch, looking across the river toward the city. I'm trying not to cry, and I keep whispering to myself "sand Jew today oh."

After a while, I walk down the hall to the room where my mother and other sick ladies are laying on their beds, kind of taking turns coughing. Mary-Margaret is sitting there next to her, and my mother is breathing easier now, her eyes open, the rose still behind her ear, and a little smile on her face.

I tiptoe in, kiss her on the forehead again, put all the flowers, except for one, in a little water pitcher Mary-Margaret brought in, and then Mary-Margaret follows me out into the hall.

I thank her for helping Mama.

She chokes up, then smiles a little and says, "I'm sorry, Massimo. I don't mean to get like this, but sometimes all this is hard, you know? Your mom is strong and brave and good. And she's suffered so much. And now, well . . ." And Mary-Margaret gets choked up again and I do too, and she pats me on the head.

Then I think maybe I can do something nice for her, so I tell her, "Look, you got some time right now?"

"Time for what?" she asks me.

"Time to walk me to the boat, because I could use some company. I'm feeling way down in the dumps, because of Mama. It's gonna leave soon, so you don't have to stay with me any."

"I'll stay with you, Massimo, lad, right up till you step onto the boat, don't you worry. This is the end of my shift, my time to have my supper and then take a nice walk before going to the dormitory for the night."

That's just what I want to hear, because the boat isn't really going to be leaving for about a half-hour, and I want her to have some time there, so she can meet somebody. Then I say, "Here, I kept this one for you. Thanks for being so nice to Mama," and I give her the rose that I didn't put in the vase with the rest, and she smiles and holds it in front of her with both hands.

So we walk over to the dock together, and as we go by the little church they have there on the island, she asks me if I go to church and pray for my mom. I tell her, yeah, that I do sometimes. I don't say, though, that I only go when my aunt makes me, which ain't often. But I also don't tell her that sometimes at night I lay on my mattress on the kitchen floor and I pray and pray, and clench my eyes so hard that the tears come out, but that it doesn't feel like God is listening even a little bit, either at the church or when I'm on the kitchen floor begging him to help her.

Mary-Margaret tells me this is the Church of the Good Shepherd, and that it's an Episcopalian church, which is a kind of Protestant church. She had to spell 'Episcopalian' out for me, because I never heard of that, and, besides, I didn't know any Protestants, so far as I could tell. She says that she's Catholic, but that she goes in there sometimes, anyway, "for the comfort of being in a house of God." Then she asks me, "Do you think it might do you some good right now, Massimo, to stop in and say a little prayer for your mother in her time of trouble?" And she gives me a kind, encouraging sort of smile.

I didn't want to tell her that I guessed my mama had never had a time that wasn't trouble and that this was just more of the same, only worse. So I just smiled back and said that I needed to get to the boat, but that maybe another time I would for sure. And, still smiling, not even a little less, she said, "Well, then, lad, let's make tracks to the dock."

So we got there, and I was real happy to see that Billy

had stepped off of the boat and was standing on the dock by himself, smoking his pipe. Sometimes he chewed tobacco and spit all over the place, and I was glad this wasn't one of those times, because I wanted Mary-Margaret to see him at his best. And he smiled at me and Mary-Margaret when we got closer, and Mary-Margaret, she's kind of shy and she's got the rose up right in front of her mouth with her face down, but I saw that she smiled back, and apart from the eyes not really looking where they're supposed to, she's got a real nice smile, straight white teeth, you know, and cheerful. Billy, his teeth are kind of crooked, but when he grins, it doesn't matter anymore than her eyes do, because you can see what's more important than either straight teeth or straight-ahead eyes.

Well, right off the bat, it seemed like each one of them could see the other just the way I saw them. At first, Mary-Margaret said that she'd go off and leave me to have time with my friend, but I said, nah, that since he happened to be there, she might as well meet him. She hemmed and hawed a bit, but finally she came right onto the dock with me, which I could see she really wanted, and I introduced her to Billy, and we started talking a little, and, then after a minute or two, I acted like something down at the other end of the dock really got my attention, so I left the two of them alone.

When it was time to push off, Billy asked her if she'd come down to the dock again sometime soon, and maybe ride across to the other side with him, and she told him that she'd like that. And I knew I had done a good thing in meeting the two of them up. And when we pushed off, she stood on the dock, waving at the both of us and holding my rose up against her cheek, and we waved back, with the three of us all smiling.

Then I looked toward the city as we got closer to it, and it was like I could almost see Monk's grinning mug and Esther's sweet, pretty, sad face both of them there ahead of me, both waiting for me. And when I stepped onto the dock at 26th, I felt a kind of chill at my neck, and I reached into my shirt, whispered to myself a couple times "sand Jew today oh," and looked back across the water to Blackwell's, which was all in a dark shadow by now. I whispered, "sand Jew today oh," again a couple times, almost like it was a prayer, though I figured it was nothing but nonsense words out of my mother's poor TB brain, and the key felt both hot and cold at my chest. And as I started walking downtown, I could've sworn that there was somebody watching me while I went.

VI

A couple days later, I started in the summer program, and began trying to get in real good with Miss Friedman so she'd take me to the meeting at the rich guy's house uptown where Paul Kelly was going to speak, and the day after that I stopped by Izzie's key-shop to see Esther, who hadn't showed up at all for the program because her mother wanted her to stay close. She and her mother still hadn't heard anything.

Well, I got her mother to agree to let Esther take a walk with me. We started uptown, neither of us saying much, until right before we got up near the Madison Square Garden again, we saw this big, fancy restaurant, Delmonico's, and stopped to look at it, because we'd never seen anything like it.

The window's about half a block long, with boxes of all kinds of bright flowers on it, and the people inside get to look not only at those window boxes but also at the flowers and trees in Madison Square Park. I say to Esther, "The view's a lot better here than what you get when you're eating at Epstein's over on Delancey, ain't it? I mean you ain't looking out a window plastered with signs and seeing pickle barrels by the door and pushcarts in the street."

Esther smiles and says, "But I bet you can't get a good hot pastrami sandwich in this place."

Well, then we look inside. There's big crystal chandeliers

and the ceiling's painted with tree-tops, birds, and a blue sky with puffy clouds.

And in the center of the room is a white stone fountain surrounded by flowers. It's got statues of four big fishes spouting water, and riding on top of each one is a cupid without wings but with a bow and arrow slung over his shoulder. And in the middle is a statue of a naked lady standing in a big oyster shell. And just like when I saw the Diana over at the Madison Square Garden, I can't help wondering if Esther would look like her when she's not wearing clothes. And then I see Esther looking over at me, and I start to blush, so I say real quick, "Hey, look at the thick carpet and the pretty dark wood furniture, and the little trees in big pots over there."

The ladies inside are wearing big hats with gorgeous flowers in them, and their dresses look like something a queen or maybe Lillian Russell or some other famous actress would wear, and the gentlemen have suits that they didn't get at Schwartz's Gents Shop, but at a swank place where some other gentleman helps you and everything fits good and you end up looking classy instead of like a guy who throws people off of the Brooklyn Bridge or who works for a guy that does stuff like that.

Of course, my clothes are scuffed and patched, and I have my sleeves rolled up above my elbows, so no one sees that they don't reach down to my wrists anymore, and if some hatless hobo found my cap laying in the street, he might just leave it there. And Esther, well, her stockings have little tears in them, her smock has got some stains that her mother probably couldn't get out, and her white blouse isn't as white as the ones the ladies inside are wearing.

Well, while we're looking in, a man at one of the tables picks up a black cane that's got a gold knob and points at us with it and says something to the others at his table, and they all laugh and watch us like they're looking into a cage at the zoo.

I'm hoping Esther's not noticing this, but of course she is, and she says, "Come on, Morris, let's go. We're not here to be the floor show for those swells."

She's right. But I'm not going to leave with them thinking they laughed us away. No, they need to be reminded that windows go both ways. So I make a big show of nudging Esther's shoulder with my elbow, and when she turns to me, I smile and point straight at the bigshots sitting there. And then I laugh hard and tell Esther to do the same. Well, she sees what I'm doing, and she manages a smile, good enough to send the message anyway. I can see the guys inside don't like it one little bit. And then the guy with the cane calls the waiter over and points to Esther and me. I wave my hand at him, like him and his pals at that table aren't worth my time, give them a big horse laugh, and walk off back downtown with Esther, thinking that if I had a thick club I wouldn't mind carving a notch in it for each of their heads that I'd crack.

Well, we turn and start back downtown, and we go a couple blocks, and don't say much, and I look over at Esther and see she's crying. "Morris," she says, "Papa must be dead, but I can't tell Mama I think that, because she couldn't take it and needs to hope."

I nod and don't say anything, and she stares me in the face, takes my hand, and says, "Morris, you also think my father is dead, don't you?"

I make myself look straight in her eyes, and I say, "Yeah, I guess I think he must be or he'd be back by now. He was a good guy, he wouldn't go on the lam from his wife and daughter, who he loved so much."

She held my hand real tight now. "You just said he *was* a good guy. You *know* something, don't you?"

I shook my head back and forth real slow and answered her like it was the most sincere thing I or anybody else in the world ever said about anything, "If I did, I'd tell you, so at least you wouldn't be wondering anymore. It's just that if he ran up bills with gamblers, well, those are guys who play real rough, people say. And your father would get word to you if he could. So I don't think it's good."

She says, "Thanks for telling me what you honestly think, Morris."

We're getting downtown now, and I look over toward the river, and I can see the towers of the bridge, and just then she kisses me, right on the lips, and I feel like the worst skunk in the city, and the happiest, too.

A lady comes along pushing a baby carriage that's got twin boys in it. They both look pretty cute, but it's kind of funny, too, because one of them has a real pretty smile, soft and gentle, and the other is looking around like he's almost ready to punch somebody in the nose. Esther says, "Oh, they're so sweet, aren't they, Morris? I can't wait to have children of my own. I don't see why I can't be a teacher, like I want to, and have kids too, right? And she looks at me and smiles like maybe she's thinking I'm the guy she's going to be married to and having kids with. I hope that's what she's thinking, anyway. And I smile back and say, "Sure, why not? You're the kind who can be a great mom and a great teacher, too."

She kissed me on the lips again, and I feel even happier. But something makes me turn around, and I see someone, someone kind of small, duck into a doorway in the shadows, and I got the feeling again that maybe I'm being watched close, and that feeling didn't go away until after I left Esther at the shop, got back to my street and went into the building where I was staying with Aunt Gabriella and Uncle Giulio.

When I got in, nobody was around, so I took what was left of Monk's dough and snuck it into the little jar in the drawer where Aunt Gabriella kept money for food and rent and clothes and stuff. I figured if she noticed there was some more there than she remembered, then maybe she'd just think she hadn't counted so good the last time she looked in it.

In the summer program, Miss Friedman and the other ladies there were teaching us that the guys who owned steel mills and railroads and rundown apartment buildings were not being good American citizens when you really stopped to think about it, and that right near us Monk Eastman was no better than they were, and that when the people realized it and banded together and got rid of all the big capitalist guys and big gangsters, who were really about the same, then America would be what it really ought to be, and I was acting like I believed all of that, which mostly I did.

And some of being there was fun, too. Up on the caged-in roof playground, we played indoor baseball and dodgeball and capture the flag. I'm not bragging, really, because being bigger and stronger than the other kids, I had a real advantage, so I slammed some home runs and smacked guys pretty good in dodge, and got away with the flag more than anybody, except for Davey, who was quicker than me most of the time.

I liked having Davey there in the program with me, but I wasn't so sure why he was there, since he'd never said a thing about wanting to make things better. So the day after Esther and me had walked up to Delmonico's, while him and me are sitting on the roof, leaning back against the fence, and sweating hard from running around up there in the baking sun, I say to him, "Davey, you just here going to this program because you like to do what I do? Or do you have another reason?"

He smiles kind of nervous, says that, no, there's no other reason. But I keep looking at him, because even though he can lie pretty good to other people, he can't with me, and I say, "Monk wants you to keep an eye on me, right, to make sure that I'm playing up to Miss Friedman like a good little socialist, right?"

"Yeah," he says, looking away, because he's so ashamed.

"And tell me something else. You been watching me on the streets, following me around some, right?"

He nods and says, "Yeah, Monk wanted to make sure that you weren't gonna go and tell anyone what happened to Izzie, especially Esther. He figured that if you told her, I could see it from the way she was acting."

"So he doesn't really trust me all that much, huh? Well, you just tell him that I ain't told Esther or anyone else, and that I ain't going to, because I ain't. I'm going to do just like he wants me to because I don't want any trouble. You got that. It's the truth, you little bum, you little *shvantz*. I ought to bust you right in the jaw for spying on me and on Esther."

Then down below I see East Houston Street all crowded like usual with people shoving past each other, going back and forth from one place they didn't really want to be to another they don't want to go to, and all the pushcarts and the wagons and stores are selling either stuff they want and can't have or stuff they can afford but that's not so special. And the people who own the stores don't seem to be doing much better than Izzie did, with him and his family just living behind a curtain right there back of the counter. And then I look above the stores at the apartments. Some of them have little flower boxes and pots on the windowsills, like the people who live inside just feel like they've got to see something pretty growing once in a while. And in others, you've got old people sitting with their elbows on the sills and just staring out, and they probably haven't ever been anywhere else since they came here and they sure ain't going anywhere else anytime soon. And I figure I'm not going to be too hard on Davey.

Meanwhile he's saying, "Moish, mainly, I'm just trying to help you. I don't want you to get in no trouble with Monk. I wouldn't do you dirt. You're my pal." He has tears in his eyes while he's telling me this.

"And if I wasn't showing up every day and getting in good with Miss Friedman, or if you thought maybe I'd told Esther what happened to her old man, what would you do then?"

With the tears still in his eyes, Davey tells me, "I don't know, Moishie. I don't know, but I swear on my mother and God that I'd never do you dirt, I'd never rat you out."

I pull my arm back like, okay, now I'm going to slug him, and he kind of shrivels up, but I reach down instead, of course, and rub his head. "Okay, you little *vantz*, it's all right by me. You're doing what you gotta do, just like I am, and I know you wouldn't do anything to hurt me."

He looks up and grins, his buckteeth big and yellow in his skinny runt's face, and I can't help it, I grin right back at him and rub his head again. Then he says, "Hey, what's that black ribbon you got hanging around your neck? I never noticed it before."

I say, "It's a black ribbon."

"Yeah, but what you got it on for?"

"Because I want to."

Well, before I can swipe his hand away, he pulls the ribbon out of the top of my shirt as I'm leaning over him. So then he's got to know why I've got a key on a black ribbon around my neck. So I tell him my mom gave it to me last time I was over to Blackwell's, because she told me it was a lucky charm and she wanted me to have it.

"What's it open? It don't look like it opens any door. Looks like it could open some kind of small box, right?"

"How should I know? Like I told you, my mother gave it to me, and she ain't doing so good, lately, is she?" While I'm thinking the key's probably not so important, I'm also remembering 'sand Jew today oh' that I can't get out of my mind sometimes. I'm not going to tell Davey anything about that, though.

He says, "I'm sorry about your mother, Moish, no kidding." And then he asks, "Hey, what's this stain on the ribbon?"

"That's my mom's blood. She had a coughing fit while she was giving it to me."

"Then it don't seem to me like it's any lucky charm."

"Yeah, well, probably it ain't."

Then Miss Friedman comes along and asks me and Davey to go down to the basement and help her bring up cold drinks for everybody. So the three of us lug up a case of Moxies, and she carries her share, maybe more than her share, because Davey, being both small and lazy, doesn't do all that much, really. But she didn't seem to mind, smiling and talking the whole time we're going up the five flights of stairs.

Miss Friedman wasn't so hard for me to be friendly with, always cheerful and encouraging, and wanting to help people. And she wasn't so bad to look at either. She wore glasses and had thick eyebrows above them, but her face was kind of pretty, and she was maybe a little chubby but it was in a good, *zaftig* way, and I was always sneaking looks at her big melons and at her slim ankles that were showing sometimes when she walked or sat. I think she caught me staring sometimes, and it always made me go red and look somewhere else real quick, which must have made her know for sure I was looking. I figured her for no more than twenty-seven or twenty-eight, and it worried me that Monk Eastman hated her.

So then we're back up on the roof, and everyone's having soda pops. Davey's off on the other side of the yard, bragging about something to a couple girls and I'm just sitting there by myself, drinking my Moxie, and I'm looking at the guy on the label. He's handsome, with a white coat and a tie knotted up real tight over a light-yellow shirt and a clean, crisp-looking white collar. And his black hair is combed up neat and shiny, and he's got a serious look on his puss and he's pointing his finger right at whoever is looking at him. I guess he's supposed to be just a drugstore counter guy who's only asking you what you want to have, but he looks like he could be a doctor telling you, and not for the first time either, what you've got to do for your own good and asking why you're not doing it.

Well, then Miss Friedman comes over and sits down next to me, right on the floor, her legs straight out, like mine, her back up against the fence, like mine. Her ankles in their blue stockings are showing.

She asks in her soft, husky voice, "Morris, are you liking the summer program so far?"

73

I say, "Yeah, I am, Miss Friedman."

"Why are you here, Morris? I know you're smart, smarter than you like to show, but still you strike me as a guy who wouldn't want to come to school in the summer."

I tell her that my mother's a socialist and that I want to learn more about socialism so that I can do some good in the world. And, of course, more or less, this isn't a lie.

She knows my mom's sick and asks how she's doing.

I shrug and tell her not so good, that she's still out in the hospital on Blackwell's Island.

She asks, "Is she getting good care out there?"

I shrug again and tell her I don't know, because I really don't, but that she's got a nurse now named Mary-Margaret Shannahan who's real nice.

"Oh, so she's got a Jewish nurse," Miss Friedman says.

I say, "No, I think she's Irish," and then I see that Miss Friedman is laughing, and I blush and laugh along with her.

Then she tells me, "Look, Morris, your mom might be getting pretty good care, but it's not as good as the care she and the others out there would be getting if they had some money. Right?"

I nodded, and she starts telling me how socialism would make everything fairer and better.

I nodded again. Then she asks me, "Morris, do you think that this America we have under President McKinley is an America that you're happy to grow up in?"

I could tell her there's a lot that makes me unhappy right now and that I don't really know how much President McKinley has to do with it, but I just shrug and say, "I guess it ain't."

"You're right, Morris, it really isn't. And the Democrats are no better than the Republicans. We need a government that is truly of and for the people, and it's got to start in every neighborhood of every city and in every town in every part of the country."

I'm nodding and looking every other second at her legs, because she's pulled up her knees and leaned forward to put her arms over them, and I can see further up now. I feel kind of like I'm doing her dirt, but I can't help it, and I can also see where her blouse is sweaty and sticking to her left boob and showing its outline real clear. If her left elbow would move just a little, I think I could maybe see the nipple.

Then she says, "Well, one reason for having this summer program is to get the children in this neighborhood to start thinking about a better society, and one way to start moving toward getting one is to work to get rid of the criminal element that runs the whole Lower East Side."

"You mean get rid of people like Monk Eastman?" I ask her.

"Yes, people like Monk Eastman."

"What can us kids do about him? He's got maybe hundreds of guys in his mob, and he's mean and tough, and he kills people, I hear, and gets away with it because he pays off the cops and the politicians."

"Yes, Morris, that's all true," she says, and she moves her elbow a little and I can see her blouse is sticking real tight to her melons and I can see the tip of the left one standing up. "But, Morris, people like you and your friends and schoolmates, can report what you see to honest policemen and honest politicians and honest newspapermen and encourage your families to do the same, and then people like Monk Eastman will lose his power and the government will start to change. This can happen everywhere in this country. It can start with children, with boys like you."

I know my father would smile at her like she was a kid herself and tell her she was dreaming a dream that didn't have any future to it.

She tells me now, "I've seen how all the other kids look up to you. And it's not just because you're the big, very handsome boy you are. People see that you're also smart, even though you don't like to admit you are, even to yourself. And they see you're sensitive. You read people well and you care about people, and the other kids notice that. You're special, Morris. You can be a leader." And she puts her hand on my shoulder.

I feel myself get big and tight in my pants, and I'm blushing and getting sweaty all over. I look away and I ask her if there are people in her group who are strong enough so that they don't have to be afraid of Monk and his friends.

"Yes, there are," she says, "people uptown, wealthy and well-respected people who pay for summer programs like this because they want reform and good government, and who have friends in politics and in the newspapers and magazines."

"Do any of them know what guys like Monk Eastman can do when they're mad?

"Yes, we actually do have people who know. Have you ever heard of Paul Kelly?"

"Yeah, I heard of him," I says. "He's a Dago gangster who changed his name."

She smiles and kind of strokes my shoulder, which makes me get bigger down in my pants, and I kind of shift just a bit, so that my thigh just brushes hers. And if she notices it, she doesn't do anything about it. She just says, "He's an *Italian* man, who used to have a gang that did some criminal things but who has now reformed and wants to help people."

"So Paul Kelly's gone socialist."

"I don't know," she says. "Not all the people in the reform movement are socialists, but once we've reformed the city, then we can start educating more and more people about social-ism." And she smiled and had a look in her eye like my moth-er's. "This will all be better someday," and she waved her arm out toward the whole city, and when she did, her thigh pressed against mine, and I didn't pull mine away.

Well, anyway, she tells me that Paul is going to be speaking in a couple days to these uptown reformers about how to stop mugs like Monk Eastman from doing what he does, and I ask her if I could go to hear him, and she grins like I've just given her a real great present and tells me she was just getting ready to ask me.

So it's working out so far just like Monk wanted, but what's more important is it's working out so far just like I want. And meanwhile my thigh is still against hers. Then she pats my shoulder one more time, gets up, and says she's got to get back downstairs to get ready for class and that I should "play for a while with the rest of the kids."

I sit there for another minute, and I stare at the label of the Moxie bottle and see the guy on it still staring hard right at me.

Then, right after school this same afternoon that I'm sitting up on the roof next to Miss Friedman, I go over to see Esther. There's a guy behind the counter, right where Izzie used to stand, and I just stare for a second, and he says in this thick Yiddish accent, "Do you need a key, sonny, or hef you just come in here to see the sights, maybe?"

He's a tall, skinny guy, maybe thirty, and he's got black hair that he's losing, a long skinny face, big hooked beak, and thin pale lips. I give him a hard sneer, and the look that comes over his puss shows that he's scared of his shadow.

Esther comes in from behind the curtain now and says, "Morris, this is Mendel Katz, who is working for us till Papa gets back." And she tells him I'm a friend of hers.

Mendel moves his lips like they're a couple skinny worms and nods toward me. I figure his being there has something to do with Monk, and I'm right, because me and Esther take a walk and she tells me that two days before, Monk comes into the shop with this Mendel guy, who's a cousin of his or something, with a wife and kid who both died back in Russia, and he's been in the country a couple years now and hasn't had any luck with jobs. But he knows how to make keys and fix locks, and Monk tells Esther's mother that Mendel's going to work there till Izzie shows up.

Esther says that Monk looked rough but talked nice to her mother. "He said that he hated to give her more to worry about, but that Papa owed him money that he'd borrowed, for gambling, I suppose, and then he showed us a paper that Papa had signed in May giving Monk our shop if he didn't give Monk his money by the end of the month. He said he'd given him more time, and then when he heard Papa was gone, he still waited because he knew how worried we must be, but he said he just couldn't wait any longer now. He didn't really want our shop, and he'd figured out a way to help us and poor Mendel both." Well, the way, he told them, was to have Mendel work there, share with Monk the money he earns, and meanwhile Monk would let Esther and her mother go on living there for free and even give them dough sometimes to help out with groceries and stuff.

"He's got a big heart on him," I say. Of course, I could tell her that her old man actually signed that paper in June and I could tell her exactly where and how, but, then again, of course I can't.

"Well, he does own the shop now, Morris. We saw the paper, with a legal seal and everything on it. He doesn't owe me and Mama anything, and he's been patient. We would have to be out on the street tomorrow if he wants it that way, but he's not being mean. I know his reputation, but he *is* being nice to us. He even said that he thinks Papa ran off because he was afraid that he would get rough with him about the money." And then she puts on a tough guy face and tries to sound like Monk, "What he said was 'I gotta admit I got a little rough with some chiselers and welchers, but I know your old man ain't that kind of no-good bummer, so if your papa writes you, you should tell him that Monk ain't mad and that me and him can work out a deal. And you could tell him I'm worried about him 'cause I know he ain't no bad egg.'"

I say, "You do it pretty good, almost perfect."

Esther laughs. "Should I put in the 'dats' and 'dems'? He sounds funny, all right."

"'Funny' is only a little part of how he sounds, Esther. 'Scary' is the biggest part."

And then, like she's trying to convince herself not to worry, she says, "Well, he could have been a lot worse to Mama and me."

And I figure maybe he will be sooner or later, if I don't stop him.

Then I took Esther to the drugstore and got her a lemonade. And while I'm sitting at the counter with her, I think of Miss Friedman and how good her leg felt against mine, so I brush my knee up against Esther's real light and keep it there, but she moves her leg away pretty quick. I just keep talking like nothing's happened. Esther's a good girl, and I'm proud of her for that, and it just makes me love her more, even though I'm still thinking about Miss Friedman and how it felt sitting next to her like that on the roof, with our thighs touching.

I suppose while me and Esther were sitting there at the drugstore counter the cops were already getting to the key-shop, but we didn't know it, of course, and we still didn't know it while we were having a good laugh out on the street on the way back. You see, we were watching Rabinowitz, the butcher, push Mrs. Nachman out of his store while she's holding a plucked chicken upside down by its legs. "Liar!" she's yelling, "Crook! *Gonif*! I caught you mineself! I knew it vas not as big as your scale said, and you told me I vas crazy. Crazy, hah! I veighed the bird on mine husband's brother's scale at the fish market, and it is six onzes light, *six*! Crook! And now I come into your store and ask like a lady for mine money back and now you are throwing me out! You *grobe bondit*! You *momzer*!" And Rabinowitz, who is fat and red-faced and sweating, and who puts his thumb on the scale if you don't watch, and whose meat isn't always so fresh, is screaming that she's a lunatic which the American government never should have let get on the ferry from Ellis Island and that a chicken weighs different on a fish scale. And then Mrs. Nachman, who really is kind of bughouse anyway, is hitting Rabinowitz over the head with the chicken, and Esther and me are laughing now like we're bughouse ourselves. "Crooks and crazy people all over, ain't there?" I say to Esther.

Then, when we turn the corner and we're just down the block from Izzie's shop, I see a couple cops standing at the door and a police wagon at the curb.

Esther and me go running up, and one of the cops steps in front of us with his arms at his chest, and he says, "And who would youse two be?"

Esther can hardly talk, she's so nervous, so I tell him, "She lives here, and I'm her cousin. What's going on?" I see that there's two more cops inside, and Mrs. Goldstein is holding her head and crying, and that weasel Mendel has his arm around her shoulder like he cares.

The cop says, "Well, we got some bad news for youse, so maybe you'd best go in there and see what it is." He said it just like he was saying that the garbage men weren't going to be coming to pick up the trash tomorrow.

Well, what's happened is that a body washed up on some rocks down near the Battery, and in one of the pockets the cops found a money clip with nothing in it, but with "I.G." written into the metal, and Izzie's name was on the list of missing people the cops had, and now they wanted Esther's mother to come and see if the guy that washed up was Izzie.

Well, Esther's mother remembers when Izzie cut the initials into the money clip with some tool he had in the shop. And now when Esther walks in, her mother runs over, throws her arms around her, screams "Papa's dead," and starts howling. And Esther's hugging her and crying, and Mendel tries to put his arms around them both, and I shove him away, and he gives me a look, but I make a fist at him, which Esther and her mother don't see, and he backs off.

So, a little later me and Esther and her mother are getting out of the cops' wagon, down where they've got the body. Because the regular morgue is so filled up with all the people dead from the bad heat this summer, we're at what they call the annex morgue, which is just a big wooden warehouse right near the stables for the police horses and the big barn for the police wagons. And I see three freight wagons pulling out of the yard, and painted on the side of all of them it says, "Moylan's Ice Keeps it Cold," and when we go in, we see the dead people, three rows of them, maybe fifteen or twenty to the row, and each one of them is laying on their back, packed in ice, in what looks like a long dresser drawer. Also, there are big blocks of ice a couple feet in front of six electric fans sitting on crates, so the air they're blowing around could get a chill to it, and it did, because I was shivering a little almost from when I walked into the place.

I'd never seen electric fans before except in ads in the newspapers, and I wanted to feel what the breeze was like right up close to one and maybe even tear up a piece of paper and see how far it would fly away, but I couldn't do that, because of why I was there.

It was dim and shadowy, but there was enough light for people to see what they had to. And even with the ice and the fans and the shadows making it cooler than it was outside, it was still June and hot, so there was this smell. It's a smell you try to forget, but it comes back to you sometimes, no matter where you are or what you're doing.

Well, sure enough, of course, one of the bodies laying there in those dresser drawers is Izzie, or what used to be Izzie. I couldn't help looking some. Izzie had gone black-purple and green and all swoled up. His eyes were open, and it was like you could still make out the expression the face must have had when it was still Izzie's and he yelled "No!" just before he hit the water.

Then Esther's mother started to sink down to her knees, and Esther grabbed her, and I grabbed them both and got them over to one of the benches that was over against a wall. While we sat there, some guy in a uniform comes over. He's holding a big accountant's book, like maybe my father uses, and he says, "So you can make an official identification of the deceased, then, Mrs. Goldstein?"

Well, Mrs. Goldstein can make the official identification, but just not right at that minute, because the main thing is to keep Mrs. Goldstein from passing out or maybe even ending up dead right now and put on ice in one of those drawers. So the guy walks away for a while and she's all hunched over and moaning and sobbing "Why, Izzie, why?" She's rocking back and forth so hard that the bench we're sitting on is shaking. Esther has got her arms around her, and she's crying plenty, too, but she's saying over and over, "Mama, Mama, it's going to be all right," She's being so brave, and her being not even sixteen yet, and I'm proud of her for it, and I'm also thinking that I don't want to just hurt Monk, I want to fix it so his body, if they ever find it after I'm done with him, is there laying on ice, until they put the stinking bum in the ground.

Finally, Mrs. Goldstein signs the book, and she's asking the guy, while she's still crying, "Tell me, who did this to him? Who?"

I turn and watch another ice wagon pulling into the yard.

And he says, "Ma'am, I wouldn't know anything about that. I just help take care of things once they get here."

"But how did he get here?" she's yelling. "*How?*"

When we're finally ready to get out of there, the cops don't offer to take us back to the neighborhood. As far as they're concerned, they did their duty bringing us there, and after that we're on our own. It was a slow walk back, with nobody saying much of anything and Esther and her mother crying off and on the whole way, and Esther's mother asking, "What are we gonna do now?" and "What's gonna happen to us?"

The first thing they do, it turns out, is stop at Feinberg's Fine Funeral Parlor back on Delancey to hire Feinberg to go and get Izzie's body, fix it up some, and set up the funeral. I left them when they went in. Esther whispered in my ear that her mother had already told her that it was going to be family only, which was just fine with me. I didn't need to say good-bye to Izzie a third time.

After I left them at Feinberg's, I saw some guy leaning on a lamppost across the street and watching me. I didn't recognize him, but something told me he was one of Monk's guys. He nodded toward me and motioned for me to come over to him. When I did, he slips some dough in my hand, tells me, "Monk says to keep up the good work and don't do nothin' stupid, 'cause the river's got room for more." Then he walks off whistling "East Side, West Side."

I pocket the dough and head home, figuring that I'll put some in Aunt Gabriella's jar. I'm more ready than ever to meet Paul Kelly at the socialist meeting uptown.

VII

Two days later, in fact, the night of the day that Esther and her folks put Izzie in the ground, Miss Friedman took me to the reformers' meeting, and I told Davey to let Monk know that I would be there. Her and me went uptown together on the trolley.

When I was leaving right after supper, Aunt Gabriella asked me where I was going. I told her that Miss Friedman from the summer school program was taking me to a meeting. Aunt Gabriella says, "You going to the kind of meetings where your mama, she met up with that bum, your father? Why you want to do that, Massimo? They no gonna change nothing for better. You no wanna go to the church, okay, so I say you don't got to go to the church so much, but why you want to go with these people and their *socialismo?*"

She shook her head and squeezed the towel she was holding. Her hands were big, like my mother's, and red from all the work she did, and the veins stood out in her arms. The shadows under her eyes were dark, and her eyes, which were soft and brown, looked worried lots of the time now, about me and my mother mostly, I figure. And they always looked sad, probably on account of how the only child she and Uncle Giulio ever had died right after it was born.

Uncle Giulio, who never said much usually, took his pipe

out of his mouth, blew some smoke toward the ceiling and said, "Be careful, my boy. You no want these people who tell you they gonna change *il mondo* to get you inna big fix with people who no want the change and can do the rough stuff to stop it. I no want to be carving 'Massimo Levy' on no headstone." And he came over and gave me a kiss on the top of my head.

So, like I said, after that I'm on the uptown trolley, sitting next to Miss Friedman who's told me that I'm going to be "impressed and inspired" tonight, and that she especially wants me to meet some Protestant minister guy who's become a good friend of hers. And I nod and smile, but I'm a lot more eager to meet Paul Kelly and get in with him and use that to get Monk. But then I start thinking about how Gabriella and Giulio are so worried about me, and I get this crazy, scary feeling that the trolley is taking me straight ahead on its iron rails to what the rest of my life is going to be, and there's no getting off, and what's ahead is dangerous.

I tried to get my mind off that by looking at the signs in the trolley. One that's in every car I've ever been in says "Don't Expectorate." I looked that word up in the dictionary at school, and found out the sign was just a fancy way of saying not to spit, which seems dumb to me, because the kind of guys who would spit on the floor of a trolley aren't the kind of guys who are going to know what "expectorate" means in the first place, and they'll spit anyway, if they feel like it.

Another sign was telling guys that they could learn to be a lawyer by studying at home. It showed a handsome, classy-looking guy, with shiny shoes, a nice striped suit with a vest and tie, and a mustache that was trimmed neat. He's sitting in an easy chair and reaching out with both hands to this little baby angel who's on the chair's footstool and is holding up a book for him to take that has "LAW" written on it in big letters. Thing is, it looks to me like the guy in the chair is already doing good enough as it is so that he doesn't need to be studying at home. I figure if they want to make it so most guys can think this

Sprague Correspondence School of Law of Detroit, Michigan really put this advertisement up for them, they maybe ought to show some guy at a small kitchen table, next to a wall with a crack in it, and he's got his suspenders over his undershirt and a mug of beer in front of him and his elbows on the table, and he doesn't look too pleased with anything. And maybe his wife looks mad and his kids are dirty and crying. Then learning the law at home, if he could get some peace and quiet to do it, might seem like it was worth a try for him and for guys in the trolley who look at the sign. And I think maybe I'd like to be a lawyer and get guys like Monk and his bums, including maybe my father, all thrown into the clink.

Then another sign gets me looking at it pretty hard. It's for Quaker White Oats. It's got a poem on the bottom of it that says:

> Ceres, fair goddess of the harvest fields,
> Now to the world her choicest treasure yields.

Above the poem, there's a box that says "Quaker White Oats" in big letters, and on it is a picture of a Quaker walking through a field of oat grass, and smiling, like he's showing off what a good crop he's got. This picture doesn't do much for me. But they've also got one of a lady who's part leaning and part sitting on the box, and that's different.

I guess she's supposed to be Ceres, the fair goddess, but it isn't what she's supposed to be that matters, but what she is. She's real pretty, that's what. And she's wearing a kind of sheet dress that's got a strap over her right shoulder, but the strap didn't keep it on her all the way, and it's slipped down to just below the points on her tits, and you could see them pretty good. Also, while she's got the left part of her ass on top of the box, the sheet droops in between her legs, showing you that her thighs have a real good shape, full without being fat. She looks better than any of the whores me and Davey ever got a peek at. She probably isn't as pretty as the goddess Diana over on top of the Madison Square Garden, but she looks more like a woman who could be around somewhere, even like she could be sitting next to you on a trolley sometime.

Meanwhile, the trolley goes around a bend, and that makes me lean toward Miss Friedman, and when it does I slide my leg up against hers again, just like it was up on the roof of the school, and she doesn't pull her leg away. So we sit like that the rest of the trip, while she's telling me about how none of the people who are going to be at the meeting are at all stuffy, especially this Protestant preacher guy she already told me about.

Well, the meeting's at a big brownstone house way up Fifth Avenue. If it's not as swank as Delmonico's, it's still more swank than any place I've ever been inside of. It's somebody's home, with lots of rooms, high ceilings and dark furniture all polished up but not so much that it looks too shiny. And there are paintings of lakes and trees and hills. And I don't see any wall that's got a cross hanging with Jesus nailed to it, like we have at Aunt Gabriella and Uncle Giulio's.

The guy who lives there is a thin, pale old man with a white bushy mustache that droops down around the corners of his lips and with white hair combed straight back almost down to the shoulders of his black coat. His name is Mr. Norton, and Miss Friedman whispered that he was from Massachusetts and fought in the Civil War in some big battles and once even got to shake Abe Lincoln's hand when President Lincoln visited the Army, somewhere in Virginia. So when I got to shake Mr. Norton's hand, which was dry and bony, I was holding something from history, I guess, touching something that touched Lincoln.

I wanted to ask Mr. Norton lots of stuff, but I didn't know what, and while I was thinking of what it could be, he had already let go of my hand and was shaking somebody else's. But he said to me, with a little smile before he let go, "Glad to have you enlisted in the cause, sonny." Oh, and he had this long narrow scar that went from near his eyebrow right down to near the bottom of his jaw. I figured it might be from a Rebel sword or bayonet.

In one of the rooms we were all moving around in, three of the walls were filled up with books. There were some preachers there, who were eating cookies and drinking coffee, and a bunch of men and ladies who looked like not one of them had ever seen Monk Eastman, or anyone like him, in their lives. None of them had rough hands like Uncle Giulio's or Aunt Gabriella's, none of them looked like they'd ever worn something that had holes in it. That didn't mean that they weren't probably good and smart people, but I figured maybe it meant something.

There were also some other kids there who looked about my age, probably from summer programs in other neighborhoods downtown. Most of them, both the boys and the girls, were wearing glasses and looked like they were smarter than me and most of the kids I knew. I figured Miss Friedman really must think I'm somebody that I'm not so sure I am or ever will be.

So I walked around for a while with a plate of cookies and some different kinds of stuff on little pieces of bread. I didn't know what a lot of it was, but it tasted okay, most of it. I even ate the stuff that didn't taste so good to me, because I didn't want Mr. Norton to think I didn't like the cooking, just in case he was watching. Some of the men and ladies came over and talked to me, and they all did seem pretty nice, though I didn't know what to say when they asked about "conditions among the youth" on the Lower East Side and stuff like that. One lady told me she thought it was "wonderful" how me and my "brethren" were beginning to leave our "troubled past behind" and become "good Americans." I thanked her, but I wasn't sure what she meant.

Then Miss Friedman brought over this husky guy who's over six-foot tall with curly blond hair and a big smile. And he takes my hand and gives it a strong pump and shows me all his teeth. I don't know that I ever saw anybody before with teeth that white and big. His name is the Reverend Mr. Nathaniel Fanshawe. He's the Protestant preacher that Miss Friedman was telling me I'd like, while she was sitting with me on the trolley with her leg touching mine.

This reverend says that Miss Friedman has been telling him all kinds of good things about me. "Indeed, she speaks so highly of you, Morris, that were I a different sort of fellow, I might almost become jealous, as I assumed I myself was the person Rachel thought most highly of in our movement." And Miss Friedman blushes, and he shows his teeth again, and pats me on the shoulder like he's my uncle or something and knows I can take a joke the right way.

I nod and smile to show that I figured he was kidding, and he goes on that I should "start spreading the word to the fellows in the community downtown that the Concerned Citizens League is going to get up some baseball teams, and that we'll supply the equipment and uniforms, and we'll take you fellows around the city to play other teams that we're funding in other communities. It will be a time of good, clean athletic competition and mutual education."

He puts his hand back on my shoulder. I want to shrug it off, but I know that's not what either Miss Friedman or Monk want me to do, so I don't. He says, "Now, Morris, what I mean by 'mutual education' is that you can tell those of us in the League about concerns and difficulties in your community, and we can share suggestions on improving conditions there."

"And," I say, "one of those suggestions is for us to be socialists, so everybody could have stuff fair and equal, right?" I say this with a smile of my own, to show him and Miss Friedman that I'm right with them on all this.

"Why, yes," he says, "because many of us modern men of

the cloth, ministers, that is, Morris, genuinely believe that the truest way to follow the genuine teachings of Jesus is through following the teachings of socialism."

And I just answer, "Yeah, socialism's the real stuff. My mother is a socialist, and my father, he used to be."

"Used to be, huh," this Reverend Fanshawe says. "Did you lose your father?"

"Well, he kind of lost me, but that's another story."

The Reverend pats my shoulder and says, "Well, chin up, old chap. You are a stout-hearted fellow who is going to play an important role in your community and our movement."

I smiled and said, "Yeah, I hope I can, sir" and reached out and patted his shoulder.

He smiled over at Miss Friedman, who smiled at him bright and happy and then at me, and everything seemed honky-dory between the three of us, about as good as either of them or Monk could have wanted.

Just then, Mr. Norton tells everyone that we should go with him to another room because he's got something for us to hear that's "truly inspirational." Well, what he's got for us to hear is a tube he's going to put on a phonograph for us. Now, I'd never heard a phonograph before. So I was kind of excited. I thought we were going to hear maybe the John Philip Sousa band, playing something like "Stars and Stripes Forever," which our school band plays, and not real good, but that I liked anyway.

But instead, it's going to be, Mr. Norton tells everyone, Eugene V. Debs, who's one of the big socialists, and who Mr. Norton tells us went to jail just for leading a strike of poor railroad workers. Then, after a lot of scratchy noises from the machine, you could hear this Mr. Debs saying that the working people in America can't get a fair deal and that's going to have to change. As I hear this I'm remembering what me and Esther saw at Delmonico's, and I'm seeing my mother laying there in the charity hospital and Aunt Gabriella and Uncle Giulio eating pasta at their rickety kitchen table, with Uncle

Giulio's hands hurting him so bad from all his carving on the gravestones that he can't hold his fork all that good. And then Mr. Debs says as long as people in America don't have a fair shake and people go to jail for saying that's not right, then he's not ever going to be free himself, even if he's out of jail. And I'm thinking this is a good and brave man, maybe the kind I'd really like to be.

And, also, I'm thinking that my father would say something like, "Yes, this Debs maybe is sincere and brave, but look at the clothes on the uptown men and women here tonight, *boychik*, look at the suits, the shoes, the dresses. They didn't get them at Shapiro's or Horowitz's, did they? Look at the faces, my Moishele. Are they faces like the people have who shove the pushcarts through Delancey Street or who argue about whether the carrots should cost a penny less or a penny more? These people here, they don't know us, and they got nothing to do for us. These are dreamers, my son, dreamers who want to feel how good they are and how much we and God shall love them."

I look around the room now and see that Miss Friedman and Mr. Fanshawe are whispering together by themselves in the back, and Miss Friedman looks upset. I'm worried that maybe Fanshawe told her that he doesn't trust me and that he's going to tell Paul Kelly not to.

And then Mr. Norton gets up when the phonograph show is over and talks a little bit about how great Debs is, and then a door opens in the back of the room, and a small, slim guy walks in, soft and quiet. He looks familiar. People are nodding and smiling at him, and he's nodding and smiling back, but he doesn't show all his teeth, like this Reverend Fanshawe does, or like Monk does, for that matter. He's wearing a dark suit that fits him perfect, and his slicked-down hair is parted razor sharp, not one strand where he doesn't want it. He's got dark eyes and olive skin, like my Uncle Giulio, and a long nose that looks like it's been broke at least a couple times, and when I see that nose and some scars over the eyes—prize-fighter's scars they look like, something clicks for me, and I think, "Okay, yeah, I saw him once or twice in the papers— this is *Paul Kelly*."

Mr. Norton sees Paul and calls out, "Friends, our new comrade Paul Kelly is here. I've asked him to say a few words this evening, and he couldn't have come at a more auspicious moment than right after our hearing, through the marvel of Mr. Edison's invention, the voice of Eugene V. Debs. Mr. Kelly has embraced the cause and is a shining example of its power to transform and triumph."

Paul walked toward him, moving light on the toes and balls of his feet, almost like he was still moving in a prize-fight ring. And Mr. Norton shakes Paul Kelly's hand with the same hand that had once shook President Abe Lincoln's.

Then Paul starts to talk. He sounds much more like Mr. Norton or the Reverend than he does like Monk, and he's no more than a couple years older than Monk, either. I'm kind of surprised, and then I remember what I heard from Johnny and Skinny about Paul being so smart and knowing all sorts of languages.

Paul says something like, "Well, I have to echo what Mr. Norton said about this being an auspicious occasion, and maybe go him one better, because here I am, little Paolo Vaccarelli, as I was christened by my late and lamented dear mother and father, speaking to people like you, some of the very best people of this great but troubled city. It's truly an honor.

"Now, I suppose that some of you know that I own restaurants and dance halls. And though that means I therefore sell liquor, which I know must trouble the teetotalers among you—whom I truly respect, by the way—it doesn't mean that I in any way encourage or tolerate heavy drinking, nor does it mean that I am not appalled at the gambling parlors, brothels, and opium dens and such that infest large parts of this city. And some of you might also know that when I got out of prize-fighting a few years back, I ran with a rough crowd.

But before long I got out of all that, mainly because I thought about how my late mother would have regarded it, both she, in fact, and the priest at St. Dominic's who tried to keep me and other poor little Italian kids on the straight and narrow. I owed them both something, and I told myself I owed God even more."

He was smooth, and if it wasn't for Monk telling me that Paul was angling to move in on Monk's own turf, old Paolo Vaccarelli might have had me believing all that stuff. And Johnny and Skinny hadn't said anything about Paul going legit. So I wasn't buying what Paul was selling. And while he was telling everyone at Mr. Norton's how he wanted to work with them to get rid of "dark elements," like Monk Eastman, who he called "a major example of what is polluting our city and infecting our youth," I was watching the people who were watching him.

They liked what they were hearing. I figured they wanted to believe in a guy like Paul, because they wanted to believe that they could live uptown and still do good for people downtown that they really didn't want much to do with, any more than the people eating at Delmonico's wanted to have Esther and me come in and join them for dessert.

Well, Paul's telling them he wants a city that's honest, and if educating people about the criminals and corrupt politicians will someday lead to socialism, well, then, he doesn't have any beef with that, because even socialists are going to want to have nice places where they can get a good meal that's not too expensive and maybe dance a little and have an innocent drink or two. And he says, that's why he's giving dough to help run summer programs to educate kids and to set up baseball teams, which he knows is right up the Reverend Mr. Nat Fanshawe's alley, on account of how good a baseball player the reverend was back at Harvard, and the reverend shows his teeth and makes like he's swinging a bat. And Paul says, "I know your truly lovely wife, whom I met with your beautiful kids at your parsonage last week, is your biggest fan, and, frankly, I don't know if I ever saw a happier couple."

The reverend grinned like it was Jesus himself who told him how special him and his wife were, and Miss Friedman, standing next to him, was smiling some, too, but didn't look like she really meant it. And I'm still worried that maybe he was telling her that he could see something wrong with me.

Paul finished up, telling them he would teach the boys on the teams he's going to pay for to stand up against "the criminal elements, like the Monk Eastmans, who terrorize the Lower East Side and its environs." And he tells everyone that they need to talk to their newspaper friends and people they know who are in the government but aren't with the bosses at Tammany Hall about how there's got to be a public spirit campaign "against Monk Eastman and everything he stands for," and that Paul himself is going to get information and give it to them.

After Paul finishes up and everybody's clapped, Miss Friedman comes over and gets me in a group of people to meet him personal.

The men and ladies there can't get enough of Paul. It's like they get a big thrill hanging around a tough guy like him, something they can tell their friends about, like if they went up and petted a circus lion and were now more exciting themselves. It doesn't make sense to me, because they've got Mr. Norton right there, who got his scars fighting in the Civil War, not like Paul got his, fighting two-bit guys in a ring in front of a bunch of screaming mugs. I don't know, you'd figure they were too smart to be so dumb.

Then me and the other kids who were there got to talk to Paul. He spread the olive oil around thick. He said how proud he was "to be associated with such fine young citizens" and that if we saw any "suspicious activity," particularly by Monk and his crowd, to be sure to take what we knew to some "incorruptible" reporters, cops, and politicians whose names he gave us printed up on a list.

While Paul was telling us kids this stuff, it seemed his eye was mostly on me, like he was sizing me up, kind of like Monk was that night out on the bridge. I thought that if the reverend maybe thought there was something a little fishy about me, then Paul would for sure. Well, after Paul finishes his spiel, he comes over, puts his hand on my shoulder and says low, "Here, Massimo, let me speak to you in private for a little bit, if you're not too much in a hurry to head back to where Monk Eastman makes everybody's lives so miserable."

So he has me sit down with him on a couch, and he says, "A couple of your pals have told me that they think highly of you and that I ought to get to know you, Massimo."

"Yeah, who was that, Mr. Kelly?"

"'Paul,' call me 'Paul,'" he says, "though with your Italian blood, you might feel more comfortable calling me 'Paolo.'"

I nod but don't say anything.

"The friends of yours who told me are two good kids who are also friends of mine, Johnny Scelsi and Skinny Lucchesi."

"I know them. They're okay, but they ain't really pals of mine."

He smiles and says, "Well, maybe you ought to become friends with them, then. They think you've got smarts and spunk, Massimo, and that if you were to join my organization, it would be a nice friendly arrangement for us all."

I smile and say, "Well, we're already in the same organization, the Concerned Citizens."

He laughs just a little bit. "Of course, what was I thinking? You're already on the side of the angels, *dalla parte deglie angeli*, fighting against crime and corruption, of course." And he chuckles another second and then he says, "Ah, but Massimo, I was born in *Sicilia* twenty-eight years ago, not in Manhattan yesterday. When that Miss Friedman of yours and that Reverend Big Teeth came to my restaurant to set up my little speech tonight, and she talked you up as a special kid who was going to be here listening, I didn't think *per un minuto, un secondo*, that you were coming because you think as they think. I know who your father is, of course, and I hear from Johnny and Skinny what they hear from that little friend of yours, this Davey Bloomingflower, or whatever—"

"Blumenthal," I say.

"This friend of yours who likes to talk too much tells them that he is not just a nobody punk but someone who is in with you and that your father has you doing significant work for Monk. So I hear this, and I can only think that Miss Friedman, a nice young lady who trusts in good intentions, is being fooled by you and your father and Monk Eastman. Now, to what purpose is she being fooled, I ask myself. And the answer is not hard to see, Massimo. You're to find out what we are doing against Monk and learn who our friends are among the police and politicians and newspaper people. Am I right about this, Massimo?"

It's scary what I'm doing, trying to trick both Monk Eastman and Paul Kelly, putting myself in a spot where I'm going to be lying to both of them, right to their face, but Paul is saying the kind of things that I hoped he would say, giving me my opening. So, scared as I am, I take it. I tell him, "Yeah, I'm working for Monk."

"Good," Paul says, "like I thought, you have a good enough head on your shoulders not to lie if you know you can't get away with it. Now, you can tell Monk whatever you want. It doesn't matter. So he knows for sure that I'm bankrolling the summer school program in some neighborhoods downtown and some ball teams, too, and that I've got a big in with the Concerned Citizens League, and that my whole point in getting into all these things is to tell people that Monk is a plague, *una piaga*, on their lives. So what? Monk's crude, but he's cunning, He's probably figured all that out for himself already. You're just one way to confirm it for him. And if you want to give him the names I just gave out to you and the bunch of little four-eyed *mamelukes* that Miss Friedman and these other concerned citizens think are going to lead the revolution, be my guest. The people I named are on my payroll, and Monk can't buy them off, because they know that he's on his way out and that before long I'll be controlling both what's east and west of the Bowery downtown, and friends of mine will have the neighborhoods that stretch uptown from there. And if he kills those on my list off, it'll cause a stink so big that even he can't handle it, and I can replace them quickly enough anyway."

"So, as I say, kid, you can tell Monk the whole story. It's okay with me, no joke. I know you don't want to get in Dutch with him." Paul smiled his tight little smile, and I could see his dark eyes were still sizing me up.

I take a deep breath before I tell Paul what I'm going to tell him next, because I know that if things don't work out in the long run with what I'm trying to do, it could end up that the rest of my life that I felt the trolley was taking me towards on its iron rails could be a real short one. And meanwhile I look over and see Miss Friedman and Reverend Fanshawe are both quiet now. He's sitting with his legs apart, his elbows on his knees, and his hands hanging locked together in front of them. He's looking down. And Miss Friedman, her face is red, and she's sitting up straight, her hands in her lap, and she's looking off away from the reverend.

I look back at Paul, sort of gulp and then tell him, "Monk and my old man actually wanted me to do more than just see if you're mixed up with this Concerned Citizens League and socialist stuff. They wanted me to get in with you and your gang and spy around and tell them anything I could find out."

Paul looks me right in the eyes. His own are flat and cold now. "Why would they think I would take you in, because I'd think you're a good little socialist? They're not that dumb, neither of them, to think I'm that dumb."

"I was supposed to tell you that I hate Monk and my old man and that I want to do them dirt and that for some dough from you I would spy on them and report to you. But the plan was that I wouldn't tell you anything important and that meanwhile I'd find out any stuff I could about you and your guys and your plans and pass it on to them."

His eyes don't change, and he asks, "And why are you telling me this?"

I had thought for days about what I was going to say, and now I said it. "The thing is I really do want to work for you. I do hate Monk. My mother, who's a socialist herself and is dying out on Blackwell's now, always said that it was because of Monk that my father left her and me. I don't know if that's Monk's fault so much as my old man's, really, but I do know one thing that's for sure Monk's fault and I hate him for it." And I wait for him to ask me what it is.

"And what's that?"

"There's this girl I like—a lot. Her name is Esther. She's real pretty and real good. And Monk killed her old man a few weeks ago. He dropped him off of the Brooklyn Bridge. I was there. I saw it happening, and I couldn't do anything about it. Izzie Goldstein was his name. He had a little key-shop, and he owed Monk some gambling money and he said some dumb stuff. But he was an okay guy and none of that was enough to kill him for. And Monk talked about some ugly stuff he might do with a pretty kid like Esther, too. Finally, Izzie's body washed up, but Esther doesn't know how he died, and right now it could get her in trouble if she knew, so I haven't told her. I probably can't ever. But, maybe, if I'm working with you, I can do some things to hurt Monk plenty, one way or another. And one other thing that I thought about a lot before deciding that I wanted to come over to you is that Monk ain't going to last and you are. You're smoother. The rough stuff that bastid's pulling is going to catch up with him, and I want to help it do that and meanwhile maybe get in on some big things and some dough with you."

He smiles now and nods. "And your mother, the socialist, how is she going to feel about this, if she finds out?"

I don't smile back. I just make sure I look as sad as I always feel when I talk about my mother. "She's dying, and her head ain't right anymore. She's not going to know anything about it." Then I do get really a little choked up, which, of course, doesn't hurt me any with Paul right then, and I get myself back together after a couple seconds and I say, "Till a long time off yet, rich people are going to eat at Delmonico's and poor people are only going to be looking in the windows. I don't want to spend years looking in windows."

"Okay, so you tell me you're double-crossing Monk, and maybe you are. How do I know you won't double-cross me?"

"You don't. I figure you don't really know that about anybody you have working for you. But the fact is I hate Monk. I've got reasons to. I've got no reason to hate you, and I don't. And like I say, you're on the way up. He ain't." I'm surprised at how calm I am, now that I'm talking to him like this, how easy it all comes to me.

He nods again. "And how do you feel about your old man, deep down?"

I tell Paul the truth, or what I think is the truth. "I don't like him for ditching my mother and me. Sometimes I hate him. But I don't know. He went through some bad stuff, and maybe he's just doing what he thinks he has to do to get by. He's smart, I know that."

He gives me a long, slow look and then says, "You're not so dumb yourself, kid. Maybe you can be of some use to me. We'll see. Meanwhile, you go ahead and be sure to tell Monk you're in with me and give him that list of names. And do this, too—see if you can get your father to come over and work for me. I don't have any Jews in my crowd, except for a half-one," and he smiles and nods at me, "but I'll make an exception for your old man. I can use a guy with his brains and with all that he's got on Monk."

Right off, I say, "Monk would kill him," and I'm surprised that I actually feel worried about it, but Paul says, "I want you to tell him two things. First, tell him, as you yourself were shrewd enough to say before and as your father probably already realizes, that Monk Eastman is too rough, too wild, too crude to last. He's making the people he's paying off look bad. It's not just these dreamers here tonight who are talking about getting rid of the cheap politicians and cops who are letting Monk act like the ape he is. It's people who've got some political know-how and muscle, and the boys down at Tammany aren't going to put up with him much longer. They can get their payoff from somebody who's polished and discreet, a better business-man who can pay them more, because he can also branch off into legitimate enterprises.

"President McKinley's going to win again in 1900. Put out of your head anything you heard here tonight from these nice people—Debs or anyone like him is not going to win. And even William Jennings Bryan, who isn't nearly radical enough for these dreamers, is still too radical to win. And business is going to be bigger and better than ever for those who know how to adjust and grow with the times. Nothing will stop it. *Capisce?*

"And the second thing you need to tell your father is that he's already in danger from Monk. Tell him about what happened to Sid Schachtman. You ever heard of him?"

I tell him no, and Paul says, "Sid had your father's job with Monk before your father did, and, just like your father, he knew everything about Monk. And Monk doesn't trust smart guys next to him for too long. They have too much on him. So one night, the story is, Monk tells Sid, who always liked the ladies, that he's got a pretty little thing he's found that he thinks is going to be just about the best girl in his stable. She's a virgin, and he's going to let Sid cop her cherry and break her in. Monk usually likes to do that himself, but he says he's letting Sid have the opening night with her, because Sid's been doing such good work for him. This is a real honor for Sid, and he's a proud man. But just a couple of hours later he's a dead one.

You see, as Sid is doing it with this little thing, who, of course, is no virgin, and probably never was, if you know what I mean, Monk is hiding behind a curtain watching. By the way, I hear that he enjoys playing with himself while he watches people doing it. Like I say, he's an ape. So, as Sid's getting his rocks off, Monk jumps out from behind the curtain, and cuts Sid's throat with a straight razor. Now whether the girl knew this was gonna happen or not, I don't know. But she's under this guy who's spurting blood, and she screams, and Monk cuts her throat, too, because he didn't want her blabbing to anyone.

"And you know what Monk said afterwards? He said, 'Dey came and dey went.' That's what happened to Sid Schachtman, the man your father replaced, Massimo. If your father doesn't know that, he needs to. Monk liked to brag about what he did to Sid, to let his mugs know who was boss. But Sid, like your old man, was no mug, and if you're not a mug and you know the kind of stuff about Monk that Sid knew and Asher Levy knows, well, you've got to worry, and so do those who care anything about you."

And Paul tells me I could help my father and destroy Monk by getting my old man to give Paul big stuff that he knew about Monk that Paul could use to get the newspapers to pressure everybody to send Monk to jail and break up his gang.

"So, Massimo, pretend like you're spying on me for them, but meanwhile you're spying on them for me, and you tell me anything you can find out about what Monk's up to, but what's even more important is that you talk to your father about what I just told you. Massimo, I can use him as I move ahead, and I'll make it worth his while. You tell him that. Get back to me in about a week or so. You can find me at Vaccarelli's, my little restaurant over at Mulberry and Grand. I'll be waiting to hear from you."

Paul gets up now, and I do, too.

And he says, "And if I don't hear from you in a while, I'll get in touch, Massimo."

I nodded, and he flicked out a left jab toward my nose. I ducked my head down quick to my left, dropped my left shoulder, and pulled back my left hand, ready to punch him in the ribs, but he opened his fist, put his hand around my neck, and laughed. "Say, you *are* a tough guy, all right," he says, and he lets go of my neck. "Most kids would have pulled their heads straight back and looked scared. You looked startled, but not frightened, and were ready to belt me one. You're okay, kid. 'Kid Massimo,' that'd be your ring name, or 'Monahan,' maybe, if you wanted to try and pass for a Mick, which you don't look like any more than I do." Then he smiled and told me, "But don't forget, if I'd really wanted to hit you, you couldn't have ducked fast enough. Remember that."

I told him I'd remember for sure.

Some lady came up and took Paul by the wrist over to a couch to sit down with him.

Then Miss Friedman came over and told me it was time to go. Her face was red, and Reverend Fanshawe, I saw, was still sitting where he'd been next to her before, and he was looking at the ceiling now, his hands in his lap. He could have been praying, but I don't think so.

So we leave right then and head for the downtown trolley. And Miss Friedman's not saying a word for the whole first two blocks, not asking me a thing about what I thought about the meeting and everybody there. And that wasn't like her, so I know she must be really upset, and probably about this Reverend Fanshawe guy. I want to find out if it has anything to do with me, so I say, "That Reverend Fanshawe, he seems like a real nice friendly guy, all right."

And she laughs, but in a hard way like I never heard her laugh before, and says, "Yes, he's just so terribly friendly," and next thing I know she's got her hands up to her face, and she's crying right there in the street.

I asked, "Did he make a nasty crack that it was stupid for you to think I belonged there?"

Well, when I say that, she cries and laughs at the same time, and it's like she can't even catch her breath. I start patting her back, like I used to do when my mother would have one of her bad coughing spells, and Miss Friedman gets her breath after a minute, though she's still crying, and I say, "Maybe we ought to walk for a few minutes, because probably you don't want to get on the trolley with people around when you're so upset, right?"

She nods, and we walk for a while, and then she says, "Poor Morris, you just don't trust yourself enough."

So I start to ask, "Well, why are you—?" and she cuts me off. "Why am I crying? You mean you can't guess after my sitting there with the oh-so-charming Mr. Fanshawe, who has such a lovely wife and such lovely children, why I walked out of that house in tears?"

I guessed I knew what she meant, but just in case I was wrong I didn't want to her to get mad about the kind of stuff I was thinking, so I only said, "Yeah, I figure I can."

She nodded back and didn't speak for about a block, and then she says, "He made me think he loved me, and that some- how we could eventually find a way for things to work out. Oh, I was so stupid, so trusting, such a *fool*." And she started to cry hard again.

I felt myself starting to get stiff and big down below and was kind of ashamed about it but couldn't make it stop.

I put my arm around her shoulders as we walk along. The streets are dark where we're walking, except for the streetlamps, and it's kind of misty. I say soft to her, "Look, it's a long trip back downtown, but maybe we should just walk it, anyway. The air might help, and if you get tired, we can catch the trol- ley and take it the rest of the way."

She says okay to that, so we walk along, with my arm around her, and after a bit, she sighs and leans up against me with her head on my shoulder.

We got all the way downtown that way, and by the time

we got there Miss Friedman had told me that this Reverend Fanshawe got to know her and liked her, or made her think he did, and she was lonely and he was handsome and real friendly, and she fell for him, and they got into bed together, and then over at Mr. Norton's, he told her that his wife was getting suspicious about him, so he couldn't see Miss Friedman anymore. "He was the first man I'd ever been with," she says to me, "and he made me feel things that I didn't want to stop feeling. Oh, I shouldn't be telling you this, Morris. It's wrong. But I need somebody to talk to tonight, and I know you're caring and sympathetic, but forgive me if this is upsetting you."

I held my arm around her tighter and told her it was okay, I wasn't upset. And I wasn't. I felt sorry for her, and I also was all excited holding her and hearing this stuff from her.

So, now we're at the building where Miss Friedman lives, on Barrow Street, over in Greenwich Village, and she thanks me for walking her all the way home and listening to her so patient. My arm is stiff from holding it around her the whole way, and when I take it off her shoulders, I accidentally knock off her hat, this little straw thing she was wearing. So I pick it up, but it's got the hatpin sticking out of it and I jab my finger on it, let out a little yell, and hold the finger up as I give her the hat, and there in the light of the streetlamp I can see it's starting to bleed.

And Miss Friedman says, "Oh, poor Morris, that must really sting." I tell her it's okay, and then, without thinking, I act like a little kid and put the finger in my mouth. And she says, "Come upstairs, and I'll wash that off and bandage it for you, Morris."

So we go up to her place, and as she opens the door she tells me, "the girl that I share the apartment with is away visiting her mother," and I start to get hard down below again, and I'm thinking that she would probably feel as good to touch all over as that Ceres the fair goddess of the harvest fields would, even if Miss Friedman was a little more *zaftig* than Ceres was.

And after I felt her breath soft on my fingertip while she bent her head down and took care of it, and then raised her face up again, I couldn't keep myself from putting my arm around her neck and pulling her face to mine real gentle and kissing her on the lips. For a couple seconds, she kissed back, and then she backed off, blushing and with tears in her eyes, and said, "No, this is all wrong, Morris. Because I'm feeling lonely and hurt, and you're such a sweet, big and handsome boy, I've taken advantage of you. More than I wanted to admit to myself, I was probably inviting what just happened, inviting it all the way home tonight." And she moaned, "Oh, I'm a selfish, filthy pig!"

I didn't like her talking like that about herself. So I kissed her again, real quick and light this time and told her she was just swell and that I was the one who needed to apologize, which was the real truth, I figured. And I also told her not to worry, that I would never tell anybody about anything that happened that night.

She smiled, wiped her eyes, told me she knew I'd never tell and that I'd better go.

So I left. It was way past midnight by then, and I guessed I'd better hustle, because Aunt Gabriella might be up, worrying about me, and if she was, she'd have Uncle Giulio up, too, and the guy needed his sleep.

All the way home I wondered what Miss Friedman would be like in bed, and if it could be as good with her as it could with Esther, maybe, someday. And all the way, I felt that I still was moving straight down the rails towards my future, whatever it was going to be.

VIII

To get in quiet at home that night, I used the fire escape, and climbed through the kitchen window, like I always do after sneaking out with Davey. Just as I was laying down on my mattress, Aunt Gabriella calls out, "Massimo, is that you?" I says, "Yeah, I just raised the window up to get in some more air." She didn't say anything back, so I couldn't tell whether she knew I was trying to put something past her, and at breakfast she didn't say much either, except for giving me a long once-over and telling me I looked tired. I shrugged and told her the meeting ran late and I didn't believe most of what I heard there. She said, "But you going back to that summer school, anyway, where they tell you that stuff you don't believe, right?" I told her that, yeah, I was going back because that's what Mama would want. She shook her head and sighed. Uncle Giulio had already left for work, so I didn't have to lie to him, which was good, because it was bad enough doing that to Aunt Gabriella.

Well, at school Miss Friedman just smiled and said, "Good morning, Morris," like nothing had happened. I could see, though, that behind her glasses her eyes looked like she hadn't slept a lot and maybe had done a lot more crying.

I said, "Good morning, Miss Friedman," and hoped nobody could see I was blushing. And then Miss Friedman began the lesson just like always, except that she talked a lot this morning about Eugene V. Debs, and she said she'd heard him give a speech on a phonograph the night before and it got her so inspired that she could hardly sleep. And she told everybody I'd gone to the meeting too and asked if I could tell them what I thought about Debs.

So I stood up in front of them then and told them that, yeah, this Mr. Debs had some really good things to say, and that President McKinley was making the United States of America more and more a country just for the rich and that by joining together, all the hardworking, poor people could make America more like what our parents wanted when they came over the ocean to get here. And Miss Friedman, who was standing now behind the class, looked over their heads and gave me a smile.

And then she started talking about Monk, telling the class all the stuff that Paul Kelly wanted her to say, and telling them about Paul's ball teams and that I had said I was going to play on one of them and they should spread the word about the teams, and a lot of the kids looked excited about that, but Davey whispered to me, "Monk ain't gonna like none of this."

I whispered back, "Don't worry yourself. She ain't real important to him, and Monk already figures this is the kind of stuff she's saying, but I'll let him know anyway."

Later, when we're up on the roof getting our exercise, Miss Friedman still isn't acting like anything's different than it was before, but then when me and Davey are starting to haul drinks up with her, she calls me back, saying she needs me to help her lock something up, and she tells Davey he can just head on up with his load.

So, next thing, we're down there in the storage room alone together, and she's saying again she's ashamed about what happened last night with me. And then she's crying again, so I put down the case of Moxie, and put my arm around her, just like the night before, and I kissed her forehead, and I said,

"There, there," like I read the hero always did when he was comforting some beautiful heroine.

And then suddenly we're kissing again, and right away I hear a soft step on the stairs, and I see that Davey has come back down and his eyes are as wide as two gold double-eagle coins. I give him a look that tells him to get out of there as quick and quiet as he knows how or when I catch him he'll go flying off of the roof. So Davey tiptoes back up the stairs, and she doesn't know he was there, but in a minute she stops what we're doing, and she says, "Look, Morris, this doesn't change anything I've said. We cannot do this anymore. I mean it."

On the roof two minutes later, Davey sits down next to me, and he says, "You and big-boob Rachel, huh, Moishele? You touch her *knish*? You get any *knish* from her before, like maybe last night?"

I look at him cold. "You better not tell anybody what you saw, or I'll fix you good."

He's grinning. "You know I can keep a secret. But ya gotta tell me, did ya touch her *knish* just now, and have you ever got your salami in her? She ain't bad-lookin', you know."

I say, "Look, I never touched her before, and what happened today was that she was upset about something with her family, and she started to cry, so I gave her a little hug, and then I got excited being so close to her, and I kissed her, which I shouldn't have. She didn't do anything wrong. It was me, and I just hope she's not mad enough to run and tell my aunt or even the cops."

"Yeah, sure," he says, looking over at Miss Friedman now with a sneaky smile on his face, and I say, "Davey, I'm telling you, the whole thing was just a quick mistake that doesn't mean a thing, so shut up about it, or you're gonna lose some teeth in the next minute."

"All right, all right," he says, "but just one more thing. It ain't about this exactly, so don't get mad, 'cause I want to keep my teeth, okay? I'm kind of attached to them." And he grins again, real big this time, shows me the whole bunch of them. He's bucktoothed, like I said before, and the rest of them are kind of all jumbled up with each other and not too clean either. And I don't want to, but I smile back at him.

"Okay, what's the one more thing, Davele?"

He's not smiling now. "What about Esther?"

"What about her?"

"You still sweet on her, Moish?"

"Yeah," I tell him, and it's the truth, too. It's all *meshugge* with me right then, I guess, because I'm thinking about maybe *shtupping* Miss Friedman sometime, but I also want to marry Esther someday. And meanwhile I'm doing her dirt. "Yeah, Davey," I say, "I'm still sweet on her. What's it to you?"

He says now, without looking me in the face, "Nothing. I don't know. I was just curious." Then for a minute he just sits there looking at his skinny, dirty hands, and then he says, "Well, if you like her so much, then you don't need to be kissing Miss Friedman, do you? Is it 'cause Esther ain't as *zaftig* or won't put out for you?"

And I realize right then from the way he said Esther's name that he's hoping I'm so sweet on Miss Friedman that I'm not so sweet on Esther anymore, because he likes Esther himself.

"No," I say, "Esther doesn't put out. She's a good girl. And Miss Friedman doesn't put out either."

He says, "Yeah, that's what I figured about Esther," and he looks relieved. "I feel sorry for her 'cause of what happened to her old man."

"So do I—plenty," I tell him. "And I'm going to marry her someday," and then I get up to go and run around some with the other kids. Davey just sits there for a long time, staring again at his scrawny hands, and then he goes downstairs by himself. When we go back down to the classroom, I don't see him anywhere.

I don't talk to Miss Friedman anymore that day, but when school's over, I hang around outside the building, waiting for her, thinking maybe I can walk her home before I head over to The Palm to report about my talk with Paul.

Before she comes out, though, the Redkopf shows up and tells me I need to go with him to see Monk.

I ask, "Anything wrong?"

"Nah, not a thing."

"All right, tell Monk that I'll be there in a little bit."

He looks surprised and says, "Look kid, let me tell you something. You never keep Monk waiting, okay?"

I nod, and then he chuckles and says, "I'll give you a break, kid, 'cause your old man's okay, and you probably ain't so bad yourself. Partly he wants to see you so quick because he just wants to give you a little of the old razzoo about something that come up. Monk, he likes to joke around, you know, so just roll with the punches, so to speak, and even if you get mad, don't show it. A word to the wise, right?" And he winks at me and gives me a hard clap on the back.

So we go back to The Palm. Everything looks the same, except Monk's got a different girl with him, and she's not much older than Esther, real pretty, bright blue eyes and a tiny turn-up nose, but with lots of makeup on her. She looks tough and smart, too, and proud to be Monk's girl. He sees me, yells out, "Hey, it's our big *Moishe Pipik*. Look you, Moishe, at how good my little goil Sadie here treats me. Dese dames, dey get a guy eatin' outta dere paws." She's got an oyster in her mitt and she holds it up to his mouth while he slurps the meat out of the shell.

Of course, my father's there, like I expected, and off sitting by himself.

Monk says, "So, big shot, what you got to report to me about dat high-hat phony bum, Paul Kelly and everyt'ing else?"

So I give him the list of names that Paul gave us kids and then tell him about the meeting and that Paul thinks I'm in with him now and that he even wants me to bring my father over with me. What I was figuring was, if I tell Monk all that, he's going to trust me just as much as Paul seems to. The only thing I don't tell Monk is that because of Davey's loud mouth Paul already knew for sure I was working for Monk. I'm mad at Davey, but still I don't want to get him in big trouble. I just tell Monk that when Miss Friedman told Paul my name he must have put two and two together and figured out who my father was. Monk says, "Maybe so, but Paul ain't got his ear up to God's mout', and he don't know everyt'ing, so maybe somebody could of told him or told somebody who told him. People need to watch their yaps." And he yells out, "Does youse hear dat, everybody?" And they all say they sure do, including my father.

Next he says, "So Paul wants you should make your papa da Dago's pet rat, huh?"

And he looks over at my father like maybe it's my old man's fault that Paul would come up with something like that. My father doesn't look too relaxed about this, and I feel a little sorry for him, but I had to tell Monk because it helps me look out for myself and Esther. Meanwhile, though, I'm wondering if my father knows about this Sid Schachtman guy and what happened to him.

And then I throw my old man a bone, because my mother, I figure, would still want that after everything, so I say, "And, of course, I told Paul I'd try, but that my old man's loyal to Monk straight down the line, which, of course, I know is the truth of it, Monk."

Monk nods and looks over at my old man and says with a smile on his ugly puss, "Your kid's stickin' up for ya, Ash. I figger he's a good judge of character. He better be, for bot' your sakes," and he laughs like he's just kidding, which, of course, he's not. Then he says, "Now what's going' over at da school? What's dis bitch Friedman and de other bigmout's over dere sayin' about good old Monk?" And he grins at me and sticks his tongue in the ear of Sadie, who's on his lap now and giggling, and then he says, "Any of dem whispering little sweet not'in's about me in your ear, Moishele?"

I don't like him calling Miss Friedman a bitch, but I just say, "Well, today, Miss Friedman for the first time said that one big way us kids could work for a better society is to not get mixed up with you or your guys."

"Is dat all she said about me?" he asks then, looking at me real close, and still with an ugly smile on his puss. I don't want to tell him that Miss Friedman said we should rat Monk out if we know about anything he's doing, but I figure Davey might tell him if he hasn't already, so I tell him right up, "No, she said that if we got any dirt on you, we should tell it to what she calls honest cops and reporters and stuff."

"Proba'ly none of what dey could say is gonna amount to a t'ing, but I don't like it none, anyways. It's insultin'. She's got a mout' on her, dat *shlooche*, dat's almost as big as her *knish*."

Some of the guys there laugh, and Tick-Tock says, "I can shut her up, boss," just as relaxed as if he was saying, "I can get up and get a mug of beer, boss."

Monk says, "Now ain't da time. It could cause a stink. Let's wait and see." He looks back at me and grins again. "I saw you didn't like it none when I called dat slut a slut. Ain't dat what she is, Moish?"

I look down and blush and hate myself for it. "I don't know. She doesn't like what you... what *we* do, but other than that she ain't so bad."

Right away everybody's laughing, and even my father's got a smirk. Then Monk says, "So, *gantzeh knocker*, I hear you got your ashes hauled by dat *shlooche*."

Right away, I tell him and everybody there, "Davey Blumenthal doesn't know his ass from his elbow about anything. What he saw was me giving her a hug, because she was crying about something that happened in her family. He's a lying little weasel!" My voice went up high, and everybody's laughing, even Sadie on Monk's lap, and she whispers something in Monk's ear, and he grins like the gorilla he is and says, "Sadie here says you look like a big baby wit' jam and cake crumbs all over his puss who keeps yellin' dat he didn't get into no sweets."

I don't say anything.

Monk says, "Okay, you can let up on dat little puke Davey. He didn't tell us a t'ing except dat he saw you and Friedman grabbin' at each ot'er over at da school like youse was two drowning people. And, besides, he's just doin' what I tell him to do. So don't you do not'in' to him." And he waits for me to tell him I won't touch Davey.

"I ain't gonna do nothing."

Okay. So how do I know you was puttin' your knockwurst up that bitch's cooch last night? I know dis 'cause a couple of my boys just happened to see da two of youse go strollin' arm in arm, cool as you please, up to her buildin' and on upstairs for a quick one. You gonna tell me different?"

"No."

"Like I'm sure your old man told you, 'cause he got your best interests at heart, you don't keep not'in' from me. Ain't dat right, Asher?"

My father said, "That's exactly what I have said to him, Monk."

"So tell me, kid," Monk says, "Was she a good ride, dat *zaftig* one? Did she yell dat your *shlang* was the biggest and best she ever took inside of herself? Dey always tell you dat, you know."

They wouldn't believe me about what really happened, so there was no point in saying a thing. And again everybody, even little Sadie, was laughing, like they knew from way back all this stuff that I didn't.

"Aah," Monk says, grinning, "you can *shtup* her till she's too sore to *shtup*, for all I give a piece of horse-cake. Just don't let her fool ya. And now I'll tell ya somet'in' else," and he wasn't smiling anymore, "don't let dose big fat *knaidlach* she got stuck on her chest make you forget dat you're woikin' for me and dat she ain't right about not'in' and I am."

I tell him that I won't.

He grins again now. "Good, and don't you worry none, den, 'cause it ain't me nor no one else gonna tell your little sweetie over at da key-shop, what's goin' on wit' you and da juicy lady what's givin' you an education this summer. And, oh yeah, my cousin Mendel who's woikin' dere now, he's kind of sweet on your sweetie, too, but I told him he can't do not'in' unless I tell him he can, and I ain't gonna tell him dat, as long as you don't forget what's what wit' me."

I tell him I'm not going to forget. Then Monk says for me to come over and sit down with him. So I do, and he asks me if I'd like to take Sadie upstairs and "have some fun." He says, "If you ain't too scared of dis little *machshaifeh* snappin' your putz off like it's made of matzoh, she can show you a better time dan dat cow Friedman. Dis one, she got a *punim* on her like an angel, but in bed she's an angel of deat'. She'll make you forget bot' Friedman and da one wit' da ripe lips at da key-shop." Sadie winks and licks her lips, and meanwhile she's still sitting on Monk's lap.

I tell Monk, thanks, but not today.

He laughs and says Friedman must have me all sore in the *shlang*. I can't tell whether he's pleased that I turned down Sadie or angry, because he's still smiling at me.

Well, then he gives me some dough, more than ever before, and he tells me, "Take about a week or so, like you're woikin' on your old man to get him to go over to da Dago's side," and he laughs and looks over at my father and says, "which we all know he ain't gonna do, right? and den go see da Dago and tell him dat Monk is talkin' about openin' a big saloon and dance hall, maybe two or t'ree even, over in Five Points, just west o' da Bowery. Him t'inkin' dat I'm gettin' my mitts into his territory, will give da greazeball somet'in' to worry about. But tell da greazeball dis, too, tell him dat you was sneakin' around and heard me sayin' to your old man dat when Paul hears about da dance halls, he's gonna offer to ease up on gettin' everyone riled up against me, and if he offers, I could hold back awhile on da dance halls as long as he's bein' a good little Dago. And tell him, too, dat your old man might get interested if da dough's right. Ain't dat so, Asher?" he says, grinning at my father.

My father looks unhappy and shrugs. "So, he can say it's so, if it fools Paul Kelly, but that don't make it so, and it never would."

Monk nods and says, "Yeah, Ash, right as rain."

I think again of poor Sid Schachtman.

When I leave, my father walks me to the corner, and he says, "Be careful, Morris, both for yourself and for me."

IX

Before I went home, I went over to the key-shop and saw Esther and set up a trip for us to the Central Park for the next day, which was Saturday. When she asked her mother if she could go with me, Mrs. Goldstein looked like she said yes only because she didn't want to have to fight with Esther about it.

When I came in, Aunt Gabriella was crying. She'd gone to see my mother, and my mother couldn't recognize her. "She was so smart," Gabriella was saying while she walked back and forth in the kitchen "so smart, she read all the papers, had ideas about everything. I cannot always agree with her, but smart, *una buona testa*, and now, she don't even know her own sister, her big sister who loves her. And she coughs and coughs till she throws everything up, and the pain, it don't never stop. Maybe I no pray hard enough. She thought I was from the Sanitary Board, and she was scared I was gonna take her away from her little Massimo, who was only three years old." And Gabriella sat down at the table, put her head down on her arms, and sobbed and sobbed.

Giulio had just come in from work, and he got down on his knees beside her, put his arm around her, and kissed her head. He hadn't had a chance to wash up yet, and some of the stone-carving dust on his hands and arms got on her shoulder and some of it fell down onto the table. I started to cry, too, and I got down on my knees on the other side of her, put my arm around her, right alongside Uncle Giulio's, and told her I'd pray more for my mother, and harder.

That night, while I was laying awake on my mattress, I kept looking at the stars and praying for my mother to get better, or, at least so she shouldn't suffer so much and that things should be easier for my aunt and uncle, though, like my mother, I didn't really figure that anybody could pray hard enough to make God listen, even if there was a God out there to listen. And then I got to thinking about Miss Friedman's body, and even started to touch myself some, while I was still praying, so I pulled my hand away and tried to get her out of my head. I made myself think about Esther and how good she is and what a nice time we were going to have walking in the Central Park, away from everything that was so mixed up. And then I prayed some more.

And in the morning I went into a *shul* to pray. I'd been in churches a few times but in a *shul* only once, and, of course, my mother wasn't Jewish, but it was Saturday, and I figured that maybe if I was there in the *shul* with a service going on, then maybe God would pay more attention than if I was in a church on a Saturday without many people around.

The one time I was in a *shul* before was when I was a little kid and my father took me on a Saturday morning. He said, "I stopped bowing down to this nonsense a long time ago, so don't you let them fool you, *boychik*. All that their prayers mean is that they're scared of a God who ain't really there but who they think is telling them again and again, 'Do what I say or you're in big trouble.' And the *goyim* are just the same in a church. But I want you should see that this is where you have come from. You are a Jew, at least from me, and, for good or bad, I want you should remember this." He was still a socialist then, and he said a good socialist can't believe in God. Now he's in Monk Eastman's gang and doesn't believe in anything.

So, just for the second time in my life, I'm in a *shul*. I went into one that looked big enough so that nobody would notice me too much, because I didn't know how to pray in Jewish. Way up over the altar there was a big round window, and the sun came through and poured all over the rabbi when he was leading the prayers, and it made me think that just maybe it could be a sign that God was looking in to watch what everybody was doing in there.

So I started to pray. In the back, behind everybody else, I prayed for God to help everybody who needed help, which was pretty much everybody I knew, especially my mother. And I even asked God to maybe try to help my father some, because if things hadn't been so tough for him, he could have maybe ended up a little better than he had. And then I asked God to forgive me for any bad things I already did and to let me know what to do about Miss Friedman and Esther and to help me hurt Monk Eastman, and, finally, I asked him to help Mr. Eugene V. Debs and people like him make things better in the country.

I was down on my knees, with my eyes closed and my hands pressed tight together right up under my chin and my face turned up toward the round window above the altar. And when I opened my eyes and saw that the sky was still blue and there was still sunlight shining onto where the rabbi was praying, I thought maybe it wasn't so stupid to hope at least a little that there was a God and he had a heart.

I see that an old guy is staring at me, and as I'm getting up, he comes over and says, "A Jew does not pray like this, down on his knees."

"I'm sorry," I say, "I didn't know it wasn't right."

"Are you a Jew?" he asks me.

"Yeah, half, anyway."

"Vhich of your parents is Jewish?"

"My father."

"Then you are officially not a Jew. If it vas your mother, then you vould be. You vas not Bar Mitzvahed, vas you?"

"No, my father doesn't like religion."

"Ah, this is a shame" He looks tired, his suit has got some patches, his tie is stained, and his shirt and collar aren't so clean either. I feel sorry for him, but he's looking like he's feeling sorry for me. And he says, "I see you vant so much for God to listen to your prayers. Am I right?"

"Yeah," I tell him.

And he says, "Vhy don't you vait for avhile after the service and I can take you up to the rabbi, and maybe he shall help you so you can pray here as a Jew, if your father, he don't mind?"

I say, "Thanks, maybe some other time, but right now I have somewhere I gotta be."

He smiles sadly and says, "Okay, a good *shabbos* to you anyvay, young man. And come back some time. Don't be a stranger."

I say, "Good *shabbos*" back and leave, hoping that my hoping just before wasn't stupid.

A couple hours later, Esther and me are in the Central Park. Even after I slipped some more money into the jar in Aunt Gabriella's drawer, I've still got plenty left from what Monk gave me, and I'm trying to show Esther a good time, and she's kind of enjoying herself, but something's bothering her, something added on top of her father being dead. I asked her a couple times if everything was okay, and she said yeah, but I could see she didn't really mean it.

We went over to this place, the Belvedere Castle, that's built right up on top of the highest rock in the whole park. It's where scientists look at the stars through their telescopes. Me and Esther stood there on the part of the castle that I said to her was the battlements, which I knew from a book about knights, and we leaned on the wall and looked out over the park, that was stretching below us there so pretty. And I say to her, "If you were a young maiden trapped in this castle, I'd find a way to climb up here and rescue you, just like a knight in shining armor."

And she laughed and says, "I don't think you could do any climbing wearing armor, whether it was shiny or not. And all the clanking and clanging would wake up the wicked wizard or the evil prince or the dragon spitting fire, and then what, Sir Moishalot?"

I laugh, too. "Well, I'd strip down to my armor underwear, which ain't nearly as heavy." And we both laugh.

And then I say, "Well, the main thing is, really, that I'm gonna protect you from Monk Eastman and Mendel and everybody else that's no good."

She says, "I don't want to talk about them right now, Morris."

"Okay, I won't. Boy, it's pretty here, though, ain't it?"

"Yeah, it's lovely. Thanks for bringing me here. I want to come back here with you, lots of times." I give her a little kiss on the lips, and we stand there together quiet for a minute, looking out over everything.

After that we walked some more, holding hands, and went over to the toy sailboat pond, and I rented a boat for each of us. Esther named hers "The Moishele," you know, the little Moish. And I told her that mine's "The Fair Esther."

Well, the sailboat pond is maybe two feet deep and closed in by a cement curb, and me and Esther are walking around the curb with the poles they gave us for steering our boats, and the water's shiny in the sun and the boats are bobbing up over the ripples and down again, and everything's just perfect. And I'm thinking how I'd like to be on a real sailboat with Esther, just the two of us, on a day exactly like this one, as long as the waves weren't too big, kind of like a Coney Island ride that isn't too wild.

Except this would be prettier than any Coney Island ride, and me and Esther would have everything to ourselves, just like some people I saw when I was on the Staten Island Ferry once with Davey. We were leaning on the railing and looking out toward the Statue of Liberty, when this beautiful sailboat comes cruising along. It's called "The Happy Rover." A handsome man and pretty lady were on it, dressed in shiny white clothes, except for the man's blue jacket and blue tie and a bright red neckerchief on the girl and a red and white polka-dot handkerchief tying up her blond hair, and when they saw us watching they smiled and waved, and I waved back. Davey did, too, waved wild enough so he was sure they were looking right at him, and then he turned around, stuck his can out at them, and wiggled it back and forth.

I yanked him back and asked why the hell he did that, and he's all worked up and says, "They think they're so special, don't they? Smilin' at us while they're showin' us what they got and we don't, you know? Like a pretty boat and someone good-lookin' to be with just by yourself. And they ain't got no ugly dirty stink-smelling old man to go home to and no old lady who just yells and complains all the time. No, they just go sailing right on over the fish that my old man has to cut up."

And I say, "C'mon, Davey, you've got somebody real good-looking to be with. You've got me, ain't you?" And he laughs and punches my shoulder, and I laugh and punch him back soft.

But I still think sometimes about that couple on the boat that day when everything looked so perfect. Meanwhile, though, I'm here with Esther and the day's plenty nice and she's doing better than before, and we're having fun. And then our boats smash into each other, and they go over on their sides and just lay there bobbing, one of them halfway sinking. A couple seconds later, Esther's looking miserable, and in a few more she's trying not to cry.

So right away, I'm thinking, "So the boats bumped each other, so what?" And then I say to myself, "It's Izzie, you *shnook*! She's thinking about him drowning."

Well, I take her pole out of her hand, and with one pole in each hand I start working hard to get the boats up and going again, but I can't do it, and she's just watching and sniffling, so I finally just take my shoes and socks off, roll up the bottoms of my pants, step over the curb and wade on over to the boats and set both of them up straight and wade back to her. She's laughing now and looking at me like maybe I really am some kind of a hero, and I says, "'The Fair Esther' and the 'Moishele' have got a lot of places to go together yet. You watch, I'm going to take us cruising all over."

She smiles, says, "I'd like that, Morris," and then looks like she thinks it's never going to happen. I tell her, "Just you wait and see, kid" and kiss her.

Then I ask her if she'd like to go home, and she says, no, that she's "not at all ready to go back there," and would rather walk some more. And that's what we do. She holds my hand as we go, not talking much.

We get to this long straight path shaded by big trees, called The Poets' Walk, with statues all along it of famous writers, and Esther says we should sit down on a bench there. And while we're sitting, she asks me if I like any poems besides the Italian one I recited for her when we looked at the statue of Diana. I tell her that, yeah, I guess so, that I liked "Oh Captain, My Captain," and "The Midnight Ride of Paul Revere," and some others too. And she asks me if I remember who wrote the Paul Revere poem, and I laugh and say, "Oh, so you're testin' me, huh? Okay, smarty Miss Goldstein, it's Henry Wadsworth Longfellow." She smiles like she's proud of me, like maybe I showed her I really am more what she hopes I am than I sometimes look.

And then she asks me if I know a poem by Longfellow called "A Psalm of Life." I tell her I don't, and she asks if she can recite her favorite stanza, so I tell her, yeah, sure, I'd like to hear it, which I really would. So she looks up at the trees and she says these lines that I looked up since then and can remember now, too. They go:

Lives of great men all remind us,
We can make our lives sublime
And, departing, leave behind us,
Footprints on the sands of time.

I like that, and I say that I guess "sublime" means really good.

She says, "Yes, it means everything that's right and true and beautiful and inspiring." And then she smiles in a dreamy way and says, "I want my life to be sublime. I don't know how, just yet, maybe by being a great teacher, like Miss Friedman."

"Yeah, that might be good," I tell her, looking at the trees, so I don't have to look her right in the face, which I can't do now after she said Miss Friedman's name.

The last place we went to in the park that day was this clump of woods and rocks called The Ramble. When you're walking in there, it's like you're not in the city anymore. I wished that I could have come up here with Davey and other guys when I was a little kid and played Hide and Seek or Cowboys and Indians. Of course, we played it downtown, but it was too crowded. Only the alleys, especially if they had some barrels or crates in them, were okay, but usually they didn't smell so good. The trouble is, wherever you are down there, you just have too hard a time pretending.

But this Saturday, walking through this place with Esther while the sun was getting a little lower and there was more and more shade and shadows, I didn't want to pretend. What I wanted was just to enjoy every second being where I was and with exactly who I was with.

We walk along in The Ramble, holding hands and quiet, and Esther seems happier, and I tell her, "It's sublime here," and give her hand a squeeze, and she laughs a little and says, "It is," and squeezes back. And then she whispers and points over into the shade under a big wide tree and says, "They must think it's extra sublime." And there's a guy and a girl laying there, hugging tight and kissing hard. Esther and I turn to each other and smile and then look away.

We walk along some more, and I see a tree with a nice big branch that's not too far up and I say, "Hey, let's go sit in that tree," and she says "Sure," so I help her up the trunk, and I'm trying to be a gentleman, but I can't help touching her some around her hips, and then we're sitting up there together and our legs are dangling down, and I got my arm around her and there's a breeze that's cool and sweet moving the leaves around so that her face is sometimes in the sun and sometimes in the shade and sometimes both at once and always just so pretty, and everything is as good as anything ever was.

And Esther starts humming a tune and then she's singing it in a voice that's so nice, but the song is "The Sidewalks of New York," which I don't ever want to hear again, especially from her, so I say real quick, "You know the words to 'On the Banks of the Wabash Far Away'?" And she does, so we start singing that, swinging our legs in time together, and my arm's around her and she puts her arm around me, and while we're singing together about stuff like the "breath of new-mown hay," I lean over and give her a kiss, and her breath smells as fresh as new-mown hay must, and when we sing about candlelight gleaming through the sycamore trees in the moonlight I picture Esther waiting for me in a little cottage in the country, and we're married, and I'm coming home from work, maybe even from farming, and she has the candles lit up and supper waiting, and maybe there's a little kid or two there, and we're the mom and dad.

We're looking at each other while we're singing, and we're smiling. And I think about the first time I ever saw Esther that I can remember. She had her sick little sister with her, and they were out in front of her father's shop, listening to an old hurdy-gurdy man crank the handle on his organ wagon. And she took her sister's two little hands in hers and the two of them started skipping around together to the music. The little kid was having such a good time. It was like she could have been in a big palace ballroom instead of that dirty, noisy street. She wasn't strong, though, and a year or so later I heard that she died, maybe of diphtheria. I still remember the look on both of their faces when they were dancing. I liked Esther from then on, I suppose.

And now Esther and me are singing "When You Were Sweet Sixteen," and after a bit she stops smiling. It happens when we get to the chorus part that goes

I love you as I never loved before
Since first I met you on the village green.
Come to me or my dream of love is o'er.
I love you as I loved you
When you were sweet, when you were sweet sixteen.

I'm looking at her like I do love her as I never loved before, and she sees me doing that and she looks so sad again.

"What's the matter?" I ask her.

"Nothing. We just better go, Morris, that's all."

"Did I do something wrong?"

"No, nothing."

"Then what's the matter? Tell me, Esther."

We're walking now, and she says, "It's… well, when we were just singing that song, I thought about how everything seems so innocent and right in it, and how nice it could be if, you know, the two of us could be together… when we're old, and we could look back at us now and remember how good everything was for us, and, well… it's not." And she starts to cry.

"I know. It's rough about your father."

"It's not just Papa being dead, it's something else, too."

She's sniffling, and I put my arm around her and say, "Esther, you've got to tell me what's what here."

"Okay, Morris, just don't get angry, because there's nothing you can do about it."

"Just tell me."

"Mendel's been putting his hands on me."

Both my own hands clench up into fists.

"When Mama isn't there or just isn't looking, he touches me, touches me in places where nobody ever touched me. It's not like he's rough or anything. It's like he's lonely and can't help himself. I feel sorry for him a little, but I hate it. I just hate it." And she's got her face in her hands and she's crying while she's telling me this.

"At first I pushed his hands away, and once I slapped him, but then he told me that if I don't let him touch me some, he's going to tell Monk that Mama and I are saying bad things about Monk and that we're not grateful for how good he is to us, and then Monk will put us out on the street. So the last couple of days, I just tried to stay away from him, but when I can't, I just have to stand there like a lamppost till he's done. I don't know what to do."

And I get tears in my own eyes, I'm so sad and so angry, and I hug her tight and say, "Oh, Esther, I've just got to do something to help you," and I kiss her, and she's still crying some, but she's smiling, too, and she kisses me back and hugs me tighter and says, "Being with you more and more helps so much, Morris."

I let go of her after a bit, and we stand there smiling at each other, sad and happy.

Then suddenly a rock goes whizzing by my ear and lands a few feet away. I look around and see somebody ducking back into the bushes, maybe a hundred feet from Esther and me, and running away. It's a small skinny guy.

Esther doesn't notice the rock, so I don't say anything to her. And it's shadowy in there, like I said, so I can't be sure about it, but the guy I see running off sure looks like it could be Davey.

X

That night, as I laid on my mattress and couldn't sleep, I thought about Monk. I knew that if it hadn't of been for him, Mendel wouldn't be in the shop putting his hands all over Esther, and I knew that Monk might get me good if I did something bad to Mendel, but still I wanted to hurt Mendel right away and take my chances with Monk. I was so mad, and I was so tired, and I wasn't thinking so straight, and I also couldn't keep from thinking about Esther's body and Miss Friedman's, too. I knew that the next morning I was going to church with Aunt Gabriella and Uncle Giulio, and I hoped that maybe something there could help me think clear and figure out what to do, but, really, I wasn't expecting anything much.

Like I said, I promised Gabriella I'd pray for my mother, and because I did it at a Jewish place the day before, I figured I needed to do it in a Catholic place next day, and I knew it would make her happy if I went with her. We went to the one over on Mott, the one called "The Church of the Transfiguration." I asked Uncle Giulio what that name meant. He said, "It means you go here and you get better." I thought, okay, that sounds all right.

And I guess, even though I hadn't slept a lot, I looked like I'd got a transfiguration. I was wearing my blue suit, and I had a clean white shirt on and a blue tie that was Uncle Giulio's, and Aunt Gabriella patted my hair, and looked at me and said I look like the son of a *padrone* or like I was *un grand giovane principe*, a grand young prince. And she showed me off to everybody, and I could see she was almost as proud of me as if I was her own son instead of her sister's, so I was glad I came with her, even though I was sure if she knew me better she wouldn't be so proud of me.

And the priest and his helpers were all in their beautiful gowns, and the organ was playing music that sounded like it was coming from the sky, and everything in the church was making me look up. And when I did, I could see the stain glass window pictures, and they were lit up by the sun, so Jesus was glowing when he was holding out his hands and blessing little children, and even the blue-gray dead guy coming out of the cave after Jesus made him alive again looked healthier. And the faces on the statues of the different saints all looked gentle and like they wanted to help. So I prayed and prayed, even if I couldn't go up and get the wine and cracker. And I figured the praying was what really mattered, if you really meant it.

After it was over, Aunt Gabriella took me over to meet the priest, Father Basilio, a short chubby guy about fifty with fat little hands that he kept rubbing together when he talked, and a broad beak, and teeth that looked small and sharp.

He says, "Your aunt has told me how sick your dear mother is. I want you to know that I have been lighting candles and praying for her, Massimo. I hope it comforts you to know that."

I say, "Yeah, thanks."

Then he says, "I hope you'll come here more often to pray with your wonderful aunt and uncle who care so much for you, Massimo."

I tell him, "Yeah, I might do that, Father."

He smiles, and he rubs his hands some more and says, "You know, Massimo, that even though your sinful father is a Jew, you always have a place here, and, Massimo, you owe it to your eternal soul to come home to our Holy Father and our Mother Church, the one true faith. Remember, the devil is clever above all things, and I know you don't want to spend eternity in hell with those who killed our Savior. Please don't turn your back on us, Massimo."

I says, "No, I won't turn my back on you."

After lunch, I went out to Blackwell's to see my mother. She wasn't any better, and there wasn't much that she did or said that I want to talk about. Maybe it was because I was still wearing the suit I wore to church, but she mostly thought that I was my father, and she was telling me that we needed to fight together for *giustizia per sempre, il paradiso in terra*, justice for all, heaven on earth. Would Father Basilio say that she was headed to hell for thinking like that, and that she's going to be there with Miss Friedman and Esther?

Then, just as I'm leaving, she knows me for a second. She says, "Massimo, you still got the key I give you, the key to the box I tell you about?"

I say, "Yeah, Mama, I do."

"You show me, Massimo, show me."

So I unbutton the top of my shirt, and pull out the key on the ribbon around my neck.

"*Bene, bene, Massimo.*"

Then I ask, "What's 'sand Jew today oh' mean, Mama?"

And she says something that sounds like, "*buon santo*," which means "good saint," and I figure she thinks I'm a saint for something I did, like maybe for keeping the key she gave me, but that doesn't help me any, and then she's mumbling and coughing herself off to sleep. So I kiss her on the forehead and leave.

Both Billy and Mary-Margaret were off on that Sunday, so I didn't get to see them, which would have helped me feel maybe a little less rotten after seeing my mother. And when I got off the boat from Blackwell's, back in Manhattan, I headed right towards Miss Friedman's place, even after being in the park with Esther the day before. I guess my mind still wasn't clear about a lot of things.

It was getting dark when I got there, and I saw a lamp on in her apartment when I looked up, so I ran up the stairs two at a time and knocked on the door, probably harder than I needed to.

A real skinny lady maybe a couple years older than Miss Friedman opens it. She's got thick glasses, a little nose, no chin, and a scared look, and she's got her finger in a book that she's holding. I can see right off that she's another teacher. I'm panting from running up the three flights, and all I can get out is "Miss Friedman?"

She asks me, "What's happened? Is something wrong?"

"No," I say, catching my breath, "Nothing's wrong,"

"Rachel's all right, then? She hasn't had some accident?"

"Yeah, no, I mean no accident. I'm sorry. I didn't mean to scare you, Miss. I was just looking for Miss Friedman. You know where she is?"

She looks at me like she doesn't know whether she ought to tell me.

Real quick I tell her, "My name is Morris Levy. Miss Friedman is my teacher in the summer school program, and she took me to the meeting over at Mr. Norton's a couple nights ago. I need to talk to her about the ball teams that Mr. Kelly's setting up."

She relaxes some now, "Oh," she says, "I was so sorry to have to miss the meeting, but I was away. And she holds up the book that she's got her finger in. "This is Bellamy's *Looking Backward*, have you read it?"

I say no, not yet, and she goes on, "It's such an inspiring book about the world that people like you and Rachel and Reverend Fanshawe and Paul Kelly and even I in my small way are working for. Oh, when Julian West wakes up in the year 2000, after sleeping for more than a century, and sees the wonderful new America that socialism has created, it's just like a new Eden!" And her eyes get watery, because she can see what's coming, just as sure as my father and his brother Moishe saw it coming back in Poland.

"Yeah, sounds great."

She smiles now, and says, "I'm Florence Cohen, and I wish that I could be teaching with Rachel this summer, but my mother is ill, so I'm running over to see her in Brooklyn all the time." I see just how pretty she isn't, and I feel sorry for her, and it's wrong, maybe, but when I look at her it just makes me want even more to get close to Miss Friedman's body.

"Rachel thinks so highly of you, Morris," she says.

I thank her and ask again if she knows where Miss Friedman is.

She sighs. "The last couple of days, something has been troubling her. I suppose that's why I jumped to the conclusion that something was wrong when you knocked on the door. She's over at her school now, playing the piano. It helps her when she's in one of her troubled moods."

"Well, I'll go and see if I can catch her over there. Maybe I can cheer her up."

"Yes, she'd like that, Morris, and I hope we meet each other again."

I tell her, "Yeah, that would be swell," and then I go hustling over toward the school.

Well, when I get over there, I see there's a light on in the music room on the second floor, and I find an unlocked door outside and go tip-toeing up the stairs to where she's playing, and come up right behind her and whisper, "You oughtta be playing in Carnegie Hall, lady."

She turns around, all surprised, and I say, "I like good music, so I came by to hear some."

She smiles a little, but also looks like seeing me there isn't a surprise she's really enjoying all that much, and she says, "Well, usually I just play for myself, especially when I need to think things through, but, sure, Morris, I'll be happy to play a piece for you." And she starts, and I'm leaning on the piano, right near her, and listening close. She turns to me and says, "It's Chopin." Well, this Chopin music could make you feel like you and Ceres, the fair goddess of the harvest, were walking through a field with your arms around each other, and the sun was going down and a breeze seemed to whisper sweet stuff, and the grass looked like the softest, greenest carpet there ever was.

So, I leaned over, put my arms around her tight, and tried to kiss her, but she pulled her face away, stopped playing, and said, "No, Morris. Really, no more. We can't do this. It's wrong. I do mean that."

"Why is it wrong?"

"Because you're just a boy, and I'm your teacher."

"Yeah, well, that Fanshawe guy is married, and a preacher, too, and look at what you did with him!"

She went all white, stared at me hard, slapped me, and said, "Morris, leave the building right now, and if you want to return, you will come back only as my student, nothing more. Now go!" And she dropped her arms onto the piano keys, making a loud crash, put her face on her folded arms and started crying, with her back heaving way up and down.

I wanted to go over and put my arm around her and tell her that I knew what I said was dumb, but I was afraid she'd just get madder. So, finally, I just say, "I'm sorry, Miss Friedman, I didn't mean it. Don't take it too hard. There ain't a thing wrong with you or a thing special about me, except maybe that I'm just a no-good *putz* and always will be." And I left.

When I got home, I pulled my mattress onto the kitchen floor, laid down on it, and stared out at the stars, so far away and so cold, and I remembered the name of that book that Miss Cohen didn't want to take her finger out of, *Looking Backward*, and I was scared that maybe there wasn't ever going to be much worth looking back on in my whole life.

XI

The next day was July Fourth, so there was no summer school, and I didn't have to make up my mind yet about whether I was going back after what happened with Miss Friedman.

I did make my mind up, though, that I was going go over to the key-shop first thing, take Mendel aside, and tell him that if he thought his being related to Monk scared me any, it didn't, and that if he ever put his hands on Esther again, I'd slug him plenty.

As I'm heading over there, I see the lampposts with their red, white, and blue bunting for the holiday, and I figure that maybe I'll ask Esther if she wants to go see the fireworks show that the city's having over at the bridge once it gets dark. Since she doesn't know what happened out on it, I guess it's not so bad for her to be there.

When I get to the shop, I see that Esther is sitting outside.

I smile and say, "Hey, Esther, you look so pretty sitting out here, you know? I saw you, and I just started walking faster."

"Oh?" she says, "so nice of you to say." Her voice seems cold and she's not smiling back any, and I'm sure Mendel did something to her again, but before I try to find anything out about that, I want to cheer her up, so I tell her, "You know I was thinking, it might be fun if you would go with me tonight over to the bridge for the fireworks show."

She doesn't say a word, so I go on and tell her, "Of course, instead of the fireworks, I'd be looking mostly at you because you'd be more beautiful to see than any fireworks they could set off." I figured girls like sappy talk like that, and, besides, it was true, anyway.

She says, "Come around with me into the alley, where we can talk in private."

So I follow her, and as soon as we're there, she asks me, "Do you think I look as pretty as Miss Friedman? Huh, Morris? Do I?"

I can't look her in the face, and I can't think what to say. I just want to walk away and then maybe come back tomorrow. But that wouldn't change anything, and I know it. And finally I say, "Yeah, I think you're prettier than Miss Friedman, why?" I'm trying to sound like I'm not nervous.

"Oh? I'm so glad you do. I guess that explains why you and Miss Friedman were grabbing each other all over and kissing at the school the other day."

I take her hands, and she's trying to pull them away from me, and I say, "What are you talking about? Who's been telling you lies?" And I know that I sound exactly like a guy who's lying already.

She says, "What's it matter who told me? Are you going to say you weren't doing it?"

"No, I won't lie. We kissed, and we shouldn't have, but it ain't like you think it was."

She laughs cold and angry.

"No, it ain't, really, Esther. She was upset. I think her mother, no, her father got real sick all of a sudden, and she was crying, so I gave her a friendly hug, and then, well, I just kissed her, and she sort of kissed me back, 'cause she was so sad and worried, you see. It was a mistake, and we both apologized to each other. That's all it was."

She was looking at me like she wanted to believe me, because even though what I was telling her was pretty bad, it wasn't as bad as what she thought it was at first.

And then I tried to help her to believe me by telling her more, and said, "We never did anything over in her apartment, either, when I took her home and her roommate wasn't there," and maybe it was the way I said it, or maybe that I said it at all, that made her know that even if we didn't, it was something I'd wanted to do.

So, she yanks her hands away from me, says, "She's your *teacher*! You're disgusting, both of you," and as she's saying it her spit is spraying all over me. "And *she's* probably a whore, a *shlooche*."

"No, she ain't. She really ain't."

She says, "I don't ever want to see you again. I could vomit now from thinking about our afternoon together up in the park. You're even worse than Mendel, that poor lonely greenhorn *shmo*." And she slaps me across the face and goes running out of the alley.

So I'm standing there by myself now, with nothing around me except for the garbage cans and their stink, and the crowd out on the street is going back and forth past the alley, and it's like I'm not only not part of that crowd, but like I'm not part of any bunch of people anywhere. My face is hot and stinging from where Esther slapped it, which is just where Miss Friedman slapped it over at the school the night before.

And then I'm chasing after Esther. I catch up to her just as she's going into the shop. She hears me behind her and she tries to close the door on me, but I push it open and go in while she's yelling "Get out, get out." And I see Mendel in there looking at me and smiling his snaky smile. And then he's saying, "You hear Esther, get out. She don't vant you around."

His being Monk's cousin only makes me madder. I hate him more right now than I did that wagon driver that I beat with his whip. I grab Mendel with both hands at his throat, and he looks as frightened as if I was Billy the Kid and I had beaten him to the draw. I smile at him now, take his shirt up near his throat and pull it apart hard, so that the buttons go ripping off and he's standing there staring with his mouth wide open and his dirty gray undershirt showing.

I says, "Mendele, honey, you like to touch people when they don't wanna be touched none. This is how that feels." And I haul off and punch him in the stomach, harder than I ever hit someone before.

He goes "Oh," and he bends over holding his stomach, and he starts to crumple to the floor, but before he does, I reach behind his neck with both hands and bring his ugly puss down hard onto my right knee, which I bring up to smack it. Then I figure, okay, he can fall down now if he wants, so I let go, and he does. Blood's pouring out of his nose, which maybe is broke, because I heard a crunch when I brought it to my knee, and his mouth is bleeding too.

Esther and her mother both, they're standing there and screaming. And her mother's starting to yell now, "Police, help! Police, murder, help!"

I say, "Don't worry, he ain't dead, though he ought to be, and you don't want to call the police on me, because Monk Eastman won't like that."

And Esther yells, "What does that mean?"

"Nothing. Only that Monk needs me a lot more than he needs this *shmuck* who's laying here."

Her mother's bending over Mendel and putting a handkerchief to his face, and the handkerchief's got blood all over it already, and Esther just looks at me with eyes that are dead, and she says, real quiet, "Get out, Morris. Just please, please, get out, and don't ever come back."

I don't say anything, and as I'm going out, Mendel chokes out, "You vill pay for this. As God is my vitness, you shall pay."

And I tell him, "He ain't witnessing this, you bastid. He ain't witnessing a thing."

For the next fifteen minutes I'm walking around, up one street and down another. And I'm wishing that Esther and Miss Friedman aren't hating me.

And then I see Davey. He's with Louie Zaslofsky and Hymie Birnbaum, who aren't bad guys. In fact, if I was to help start a ball team for Paul Kelly, they'd be two guys I'd want to have on it. Davey's got a pickle in his hand this time instead of the rock he had the last time he saw me. And as he's nibbling away on his pickle, he's laughing about how he got it. He swiped it, just before, at Rubenstein's grocery by saying to Rubenstein, "Hey, ain't that your wife going down the street with Handsome Harry Rosen?" Rubenstein, who's got a good-looking wife and worries about her, turns, Davey pulls the biggest pickle from the barrel and shoves it in his pocket, and says, when Rubenstein turns back, "Nah, it was somebody else. I think I gotta get my eyes checked."

Louie and Hymie tell him he's a real character, and I say, "Yeah, you're always good for a laugh, Davey."

He sees I'm not really finding him so funny, and he says, "What's the matter, Moish, you got money invested in Rubenstein's pickle barrel?" Louie and Hymie laugh, but I don't.

I say, "Why don't you go with me back to Rubenstein's right now, so I can stick your head into that barrel and you could tell me if I've got any money down at the bottom of it, huh?"

Davey takes a step back from me, and Louie and Hymie both take a couple steps away from him. Louie says, "C'mon, Moish, if Davey done something to you, he don't mean nothing by it. He's just a clown, don't get mad at him." And Hymie's nodding and saying, "Yeah, don't take him too serious. You know, it's just Davey."

I tell them, "You don't know what he did, so butt out, because I've got nothing against either of you right now. Let's just keep it like that. In fact, why don't you both just get lost? And Davey, you just stay here. Don't you go running anywhere, or I will catch you and drown you in the lousy pickle barrel that you like so much."

So Hymie and Louie walk away, but before they do, Louie says, "Moish, don't do anything that you're gonna be sorry for later."

I laugh out loud and say, "Too bad you couldn't have told me that yesterday." Then I turn back to Davey, who's still keeping a smile on his puss but looks like he's ready to crap his pants.

"Davey, how could you pull that stuff with me?"

"What stuff? What do you mean, Moish?" The smile ain't going anywhere, but he's got tears in his eyes.

"Spying on me and Esther, Saturday in the park. Were you following us all afternoon? And then throwing a rock at me? Davey, I thought you were my pal."

He puts his head down, and the smile is gone, but he doesn't say anything. At least he's not trying to lie.

"And then you go and tell Esther about what you saw me and Miss Friedman doing at school? You told me you'd never do me dirt." I'm more sad now than I am angry, and I'm still plenty angry. I can feel tears getting into my own eyes. "Why, Davey?"

"Why? Why?" he yells now, and people passing are looking at us, and I yank him around the corner and into the doorway of a store that's closed for the holiday. It's got a couple of little American flags crossed over each other and pasted up on the inside of the door so you can see them through the glass.

I push Davey up against the door, and I say, "Yeah, why?"

He screams, "Because you tell me you wanna marry Esther, and meanwhile you and Miss Friedman are hugging and kissing, and 'cause you take Esther to the park and you walk with her and sail boats with her and sit on a castle wall with her and in a tree with her, and I ain't got nobody and all I can do is watch you with her, you bastid, and wish it was me instead of you, except I wouldn't never be crooked with her, the way you was." And he reaches out and smacks my face with the back of his hand, and he's crying now.

"Well, get somebody, then, you little rat," I say, grabbing his shoulders as I'm thinking that's three people now who used to like me who have smacked me in the puss since I got off the boat from Blackwell's yesterday after praying to God all weekend.

"I love Esther. You don't deserve her. *You're* the goddamn rat, Moish. I hate you now, you son of a bitch." He's crying hard and trying to get his arm loose so he can hit me again.

"So you went and told Esther about what you saw with me and Miss Friedman, 'cause you love her and you hate me."

He nods and answers, "Yeah," his whole face clenched up and angry, "Yeah."

"Well, you ain't ever going to have her. She's mad at me, sure, but she also told me just now that she hates snitches, especially a snitch that would rat on a friend and, besides, she thinks you look like a skinny, little rat-face monkey and she could never figure out why I kept you around for a pal and that she never trusted you and knows that nobody else other than me ever did. So, you fixed yourself, Davey. I ain't your friend anymore and you ain't ever gonna have Esther, either—you can just put that out of your head. It'll be a miracle if you ever get any girl, except maybe crazy Minnie Hershkowitz or somebody just like her." I shake him hard, and I'm nearly crying myself now. "Davey, I mean it, I ain't your friend anymore."

He spits in my face and screams, "Your mother's dying 'cause God is cursing you for a louse. If you was better, she wouldn't be like she is."

I give him a shove, and his head goes back into the door, and I hear a loud noise and see that there's a long crack in the glass now. The little flags that were pasted on it are on the floor, and Davey's crying and rubbing the back of his head.

I say, "Here, let me take a look," and reach for his head. He pulls it away and says, "Don't touch me, you big dumb bastid."

I grab his head anyway and turn it, so I can see. "No, you ain't cut. Your *keppele* is still in one piece, Davey, but if you do like you did me anymore, it's not going to be. And if you ever come down my fire escape again, I'll throw you off of it." Then I kiss the back of his head where he hit it and I walk away from him.

That night I'm sitting on some rocks right down low at the river, not far from the Fish Market dock, and I'm watching the fireworks shooting up off of the bridge, lots of explosions of red, white, and blue. The rockets look at first like they could keep going forever past the moon and the stars, but they end up just dropping into the river, with a few sparks left for just a second to show they'd ever been here.

Somewhere a band is playing, and people are cheering. Maybe somebody's giving a big speech. I wonder if Esther's in the crowd and if she's cheering, or if Miss Friedman is there. Probably she's not. And what about Davey? Izzie, I know, is not there.

After a while I head home. Lots of people are walking around with red, white, and blue ribbons pinned to their clothes and having ice creams and soda pops, laughing and talking. Little kids are waving sparklers. I just want to get out of the crowd and go upstairs, and maybe sit by the lamp on the kitchen table and read about someplace else and sometime different.

But when I get to the building I see a big, heavy guy there, leaning next to the doorway, and he's got his straw skimmer pulled down low over his eyes, a cigar in his mouth, and his arms folded at his chest like he's waiting for someone. I haven't seen him before, but I figure I know who he's waiting for and who sent him. I think for a second that maybe I ought to just keep walking past, like I don't live there, but where would I go? So, I take a big breath and walk up the couple steps to the door.

He moves over in front of me, just like I expected, and he says, "You're Asher's kid, ain't ya?" He's taller and broader than me.

I tell him I am, and he says, "You gotta come wit' me now. Monk's got something he wants to say to you."

I tell him okay, but that I want to tell my aunt and uncle where I'm going. He says he was up there already, looking for me and that he told them that he would wait for me because my father needed to see me. "I told them there ain't nothin' wrong wit' Asher, but he's just got to talk to you about some stuff. I'm lookin' out for them, you see, kiddo. I don't want them losin' no sleep over you tonight. And if you wanna look out for them, too, you'll just come wit' me wit'out makin' a peep."

I'm not gonna make a fuss, and I go with him. We just walk along block after block, neither of us saying anything, until I say, "I figure Monk's gotta be mad about something to send somebody for me, right?"

"It ain't for me to tell you dat," he says, "but he ain't happy."

Monk's saloon is crowded. There's a band playing, and people are dancing, and waiters are running around hoisting trays with big schooners of beer over their heads, and there are flags and bunting all over the place and cigar smoke drifting everywhere.

Some of the guys from the band stand up and start singing:

> Please, oh please, oh, do not let me fall,
> You're all mine and I love you best of all,
> And you must be my man, or I'll have no man at all,
> There'll be a hot time in the old town tonight.

And everybody in there joins in on the last line, yelling more than singing. And, like usual, the floor is full of oyster shells, and the dancers are stomping them into smaller and smaller pieces with every step they take, grinding them into the sawdust that's wet from the spilled drinks.

And everyone's got grins plastered to their pusses, except for my father, who's sitting at the same table as Monk and looking in the dumps, and except for Monk himself when he looks over to the swinging doors and sees me walk in. He's got his club with the notches on it right there on the table, like always.

The guy walks me over to Monk's table and motions for me to sit down in a chair right across from Monk. Monk tells Sadie, who's leaning all over him, to scram. She does, but not before giving me a dirty little grin and shaking her head back and forth at me like she's letting me know I was a bad boy and I'm in big trouble now. My father stares off like he's just watching the cigar smoke drift.

Monk says, "Your father ain't no dumb man, Moish, but he didn't do no good job teachin' you not to cross Monk Eastman. You was dere on da bridge watchin' what happened to dat stinkin' piece of *dreck* Izzie Goldstein. And you heard what I says happens to guys what cross me, didn't you?" And he grabs his club and smashes it down on the table, right in front of my face. Stuff goes flying and the table's cracked now.

"Yeah, I did hear, Monk."

"You t'ink because you're a kid, I won't fix ya good?"

"No, Monk, I know that won't get me off the hook."

He nods. "Okay. So where does ya get da noive to beat up dat *shmendrick* cousin of mine, who I got in dat shop to do *you* a favor by not puttin' little Miss Esther and her old lady on da street like I ought to?"

And before I can answer, he screams "Where?" and smashes the table again. The band's still playing, but most of the dancers have stopped clomping around and are looking over at us.

"He was puttin' his hands on Esther, and she didn't like it."

"So she didn't like it. So what? She t'ink her tits and ass are gold? She better watch out, givin' herself airs, like she's da Vanderbilt dame, or I got plans for her. Look, so she don't like Mendel so hot, but she don't like you neit'er, I hear, 'cause of you stickin' your sausage in dat Friedman bitch's roll. Who d'hell you t'ink *you* are? Mendel's my cousin, my *blood*! You're just Asher's blood, here. And dat don't matter as much as you t'ink, tough guy.

"Now your old man, he promises you're gonna be good from now on, and I told him and I'm tellin' you now, dat if you ain't, I'm gonna take it out not just on you but on him too. Ain't dat right, Asher?" And my father stops looking at the smoke, turns to him, and says, "That is right, Monk."

And then Monk looks back at me, "And you're *gonna* be good from now on, ain't you?"

I tell him, yeah, I will.

Then he says, "Okay, but still you got to pay for what you done to Mendel. You hurt him bad, and 'cause of your old man and 'cause I can still use you, I'm gonna go easy on you, but still you got to get some pain, ot'erwise you are gonna t'ink I gone soft, which I ain't gone. Here, I wanna show you somet'in'." And he calls out, "Heshie, bring over some guy who's dancin' out on da floor. I don't care who."

And the big guy who took me over to Monk's place just now grabs some bald guy about forty who came in looking for a good time on the Fourth. The guy's got a smile on his kisser, but he's not happy now or confident-looking. "Hi ya, Monk," he says.

"Hi, yourself," Monk says. "I don't know you, do I?"

The guy says he doesn't think Monk does.

Monk says, "You havin' a good time here at my dance hall tonight?"

The guy smiles nervous and says he is.

Monk says, "Swell. Here, see some fireworks, on me." And he grabs his club and smacks the guy right over the head. The guy goes down without a sound. "Dat ain't wort' no notch," he says, "unless it was gonna take me to anot'er nice, round number." Then, with everybody still watching him, he takes a small glass that he's been drinking some hard booze out of, and he holds it up and says, "I hope none of youse t'ink dat because times has been good to us, dat Monk's gone soft or not'in'." Then he bites it and then bites it again and again, till it's all in his mouth and he chews it up slow while he's looking at me and everyone in the place is watching him, and then he swallows it. Then he spits a little blood out on the table.

"No, I ain't gone soft, Moish. I cut my lip once as a little kid on a glass what broke in my mouth when I was tryin' too hard to lick some sweet stuff sticking to da inside of it and I started to cry, which made my old man pop me one across da face for being a crybaby, and he says to me, 'Okay you started eatin' dat glass, now finish it, and wit'out no more tears, neit'er.' So I did, and now once in a while, to remind me and everybody else dat I ain't never gonna be soft no more, I take me anot'er as a snack. It builds up da backbone, Moish."

Then Monk waves over towards the corner of the bar, and a guy who's been sitting there in the shadows gets up and walks over slow and sits down next to me. It's Tick-Tock, and even in July he's wearing his long black coat with his collar turned up. He doesn't speak. He doesn't have to. I can hear his wheezy breathing and his clock ticking away.

Then Monk says, "Okay, Moishie, now it's your toin to hoit and to show you ain't soft. Are you a righty or a lefty?"

"I'm a righty."

"Dat's da mitt you hit me cousin in da gut wit'?"

"Yeah."

"Put your left mitt out on da table, den, wit' da palm down. See, I'm goin' more dan a little easy on you."

I put my left hand out.

He says, "Do you need Tick-Tock or your old man to hold it down for you?"

"No." I hope I don't have to say anything more, because I'm trying not to puke.

Monk looks me hard in the eyes, then lifts his club up over his head. I keep my hand where it is and I turn away now and look over at my father, who's turned his face away too and is staring over at the bar, where everybody is looking at our table. The band stopped a while back and everything is quiet.

The smash hurts, but I've got my jaw tight, and I don't do anything but let out a soft 'oh.'

Monk says, "When I saw you was gonna stay put and be game and take your punishment like a man, I pulled me punch some, so I don't t'ink it's broke. I didn't hear no crunches."

I said, "Thanks," and I halfway meant it, because it hurt

so bad I figured I ought to be at least a little grateful that it wasn't worse.

"Okay, den, maybe you learned your lesson, and den maybe you din't. We'll see as da days, like da clouds, roll by." He smiles, and I can see blood still spotting his lips. And he yells for a bucket of ice for me. When it comes, and I stick my hand in it, I don't know whether it's making it feel better or worse, but I keep it in.

"I think he did learn," my father says. "He has been acting dumb, but dumb he isn't."

"Like I says, Asher, we'll see," Monk tells him.

The music is going again, and people are dancing. The guy Monk knocked over the head was drug out, and only the two trails that his heels made in the sawdust showed that he was ever there. My hand was aching hard, keeping time with the drum in the band.

Monk says, "Okay, let's talk business now, Moish. It's time for you to go to da Dago and tell him what I told you to tell him about me startin' up dance halls over in Five Points, and remember, you make it seem like you is woikin' for him now and dat you t'ink you can bring your old man over, too. And den tell me what dat Guinea is t'inkin. And just so's you can do your woik proper, I'm gonna fix it so you don't have to worry none about dat *shmuck*-face cousin of mine. I'm gonna tell him if he don't keep his paws off dat Esther, he's gonna get woise from me dan what he got from you. Dat ain't no daisy to be picked by da likes of him.

"Meanwhile you still got dat Friedman cow to milk, anyways. And you do right by me, and I'll keep little Esther and her old lady off da streets and even put in a good woid for you, an' maybe if you play your cards right you can get your little piece of *knish* back."

I said yeah. I couldn't do anything else for the time being.

XII

When I got home after Monk had smashed my hand, it was late, but Aunt Gabriella and Uncle Giulio were still awake. They were out on the fire escape watching the fireworks and worrying about me. Right off, Aunt Gabriella notices my swole hand. I say, "Oh, yeah, I got it jammed some trying to help some guy fix a busted wheel on a wagon. It ain't so bad. See, he gave me four bits for my trouble." And I reached into my pocket and give her four bits that I had left from what Monk gave me a while back. She takes the money without looking at it, but she looks close at my hand and says, "You not been fighting?"

I tell her I haven't, and she probably doesn't believe me, but she doesn't say anything, and I feel worse than if she did. And Uncle Giulio looks at my hand, but he doesn't say anything either other than that I should soak it in Epsom salts, which I see him doing with his own hands a lot when he comes home from work.

So, a few minutes later I'm sitting there with my hand in a bucket of warm Epsom salts water and listening to the popping and banging still going on outside, and there's a loud knock on the door. Right away I think maybe Monk's decided that he let me off too easy.

I kind of jump, with my swole hand coming right up out of

the bucket, and Gabriella crosses herself, says "*Dio ci protegga!*" and whispers, "Massimo, don't you open that door!" Uncle Giulio, he's picked up a big hammer that he uses for his work and he's right beside her now, looking scared but ready to try to protect us all if God doesn't.

I don't want to get my aunt and uncle hurt or the place tore up, so I figure if it's Monk or anybody he sent I better just go with him, like there's not a thing wrong. So I open the door, ready for anything, I guess, and standing there is someone I'm never really ready for, and that's my father.

He sees Giulio behind me with the hammer, and he gives him a cold little smile and says, "Giulio, my son, he maybe needs a knock on the head, but he don't need it from such a big hammer as you got there."

Gabriella says, "Shut the door in his face, Massimo. You not let him in my house."

Then, while my father is standing there, because I don't shut the door, Gabriella's letting him have it. My old man might have been better off getting hit with Giulio's hammer than he is with what Aunt Gabriella is throwing his way. She's yelling at him that he's a no-good husband, a no-good father, a crook, a louse, *un uomo senza onore*, a man without honor. He just stood there, even shrugged his shoulders a little, like he was saying, okay, that's how it happens sometimes. I felt a little bad for him, even though I didn't want to.

Uncle Giulio has his hand on Aunt Gabriella's shoulder, trying to calm her down so she doesn't make herself sick and also because he's not the kind that likes to see some other guy take too much heat. He said once, "Massimo, carving on all the headstones like I do, it tells me how little time any of us got and that it's *stupido, molto stupido*, to waste what we do got by being angry or mean. Remember what I tell you." Well, remembering it and living it aren't the same for me, not yet anyway.

Then my father says soft, "Thank you, my sister-in-law, I have heard what you tell me, but I have come to talk to my son about something very important," and Gabriella starts right in again, but this time she says something that I never heard before and that makes my father look more upset than I've ever seen him look. First she yells, "Look at his hand! This I know must come from his being wherever you was tonight. He will end up *morto* under the ground and all because of you, *suo padre*." And she goes on, "You say 'my son', but you no act like he's *tuo figlio*. That *bambino* you got with that Jew whore you live with like she's your wife and who you got now in your fancy apartment what you never took Massimo to, you lots better to *that* son than to Massimo, no? Why, because he's all Jew, like you? You think I no hear this about you? Massimo wants to love you, but you no let him."

Giulio is saying, "Gabriella, *basta*, *basta*, enough" and looking at me like he wishes I'd gone deaf about a minute before, but I'm not all that worked up about it, really. So what if I've got a half-brother somewhere that my father cares more about than he cares about me? I stopped looking for anything much from my old man a long while back.

My father, though, has gone pale. He says, "Like always, it's a pleasure for me to have a conversation with you Gabriella. But now I need to talk to Morris private. I will take him out onto your fire escape unless you got an objection."

So then my father and me are sitting out on the fire escape. I don't say anything about what I heard about his living with a woman who's not my mother and having a son with her. He doesn't mention it, either. Instead, he says, "Morris, you think maybe that because Monk went easy on you tonight, this is the end of it with him. It ain't. Monk can use you now, but don't think you are the only way he learns what Paul Kelly is up to. Your information is just a little stream that flows into the river. Monk has more than fifteen hundred men who work for him. I know this. Remember, I do his payroll. And Monk pays good, better than Paul. His men, they are loyal to him, and they are scared of him, and they do what he tells them, no questions asked.

"So listen to me good. He needs you a little, but not so much that he won't hurt you right away if you make him angry again, hurt you so bad that what happened tonight will seem to you a picnic. But this you can control for now if you keep your nose clean. Later, though, when Monk does not need you no more, then is when you must really watch out, maybe even go away to another place. I can help you with this maybe. Monk don't like you, and if Monk don't like you, then you are in big trouble."

"How do you know he doesn't like me? He let me off pretty easy tonight."

"What you did to Mendel, you never should have. You were smarter than that, I thought." Then he shook his head, "Maybe you are too much like my brother that I named you for. Monk didn't like you already, now he hates you."

"Why didn't he like me before?" I ask him, but I'm guessing that I know already.

"Why?" my father says, "Okay let me give you the reasons, my boy. Monk saw the look on your face that night on the bridge, and he has not forgotten it. The next day, he says to me, 'That big strong son of yours, Asher, he looked like he wanted to toss me off of the bridge. I'll have to keep my eye on him,' and then he laughs, but, you know, some laughs ain't like others."

There were loud pops in the sky just down the street and then flashes that made my father's face go red, then white, then blue, before it faded back into the shadows.

"You must get better at hiding what you feel, Morris, if you are planning to get yourself someplace in this world or even to live in it. Monk also saw the looks what crossed your face when he made fun of you and that Miss Friedman and when he even says the name of this Esther that you are so crazy for. Do you really think inside that brain of yours that Monk don't hate you now for what you done to his precious Mendel?"

"Aah, he doesn't care a thing about Mendel, I bet."

"Do you have a *Yiddishe kopf* on you at all or is it all thick *Italianer?*"

I answer, "Well, it ain't as *Yiddishe*, I guess, as the *kopf* on that half-brother I've got that I didn't even know about until ten minutes ago."

"Like I was telling you a minute ago, *boychik*, you got to learn how to hide your feelings a little bit better. Listen to me. Of course, Monk cares nothing for this Mendel. With him it is the principle of the thing. You touched his relative, so, as far as he is concerned you have done dirt to him personal. And when you held your hand on the table by yourself and you didn't pull it from the stick, he saw that you are not so afraid of him as he wants. And for you to be both angry at him and not scared, this he cannot tolerate. What will you grow up to be, he must be asking himself. I saw the look he gives to Tick-Tock after he hit you, and the look that Tick-Tock gives him back. You are stubborn, you could cause problems later on, so they don't want you around them for long, my boy. Also, you and me, we both know that I have told you nothing about Monk's business, but he don't know that, so he is worried that you know what you shouldn't. This, too, he cannot tolerate."

"Did he say any of this stuff to you?"

He laughed like I'd just said maybe one of the dumbest things he'd ever heard. "What would he have to gain by telling me he wants to hurt my son after my son ain't no use to him no more? I know this because I have been with Monk now long enough to know how he thinks. I *use* my *Yiddishe kopf*, Morris."

"Yeah, I know you do. Can you use it to help me if I need you to?"

He smiled now, reached over and patted me on the knee. "*Boychik*, I don't know that I can even help myself. If I could make him to think you are trustworthy, I would do this, of course. But he has made up his mind about you, and with him that is that. Have you heard about this Sid Schachtman, who did my job before Monk decided it was my turn to do it?"

I told him I'd heard it from Paul Kelly.

My father says, "Kelly, another one not to trust, Morris, remember this. This Sid Schachtman, there is not a day that goes by that I don't think of what happened to him. I worry for when Monk shall decide, like with Sid, that I know so much already that he don't want me around no more, so I try to show him all the time how I am a man that he can trust. But the problem is that Monk, like me, is not a man who trusts.

"And by the way, *boychik*, you didn't do me no favors when you says to Monk that Paul Kelly wants I shall join up with him. It is almost now that the better I do my work for Monk, the more dangerous it is for me, because he sees what a plum I should be for Paul to pick and suck down to the pit."

More fireworks went off, and my father shakes his head and says, "Hurray for the Independence Day in the Land of the Free."

I ask him, "And you've got no ways at all to protect yourself?"

"I got maybe one way," he says, "and it is the last news I came here to bring to you tonight. He is afraid that I got something hidden somewheres that could get him in big trouble. You see, when Monk was just getting started in Silver Dollar Smith's gang that had some pull for a while, there was a young judge who was giving Smith a hard time. He was new and honest and he would not play ball with the Tammany Hall crowd like every other judge was playing. He was Goldman, a Jew, the first Jew to be a judge in the whole city, and the Jews were all proud of him. He was handsome, strong, and he was not scared, no matter what threats. He was trying to send Smith's men to jail or to the Death Row, even when the prosecutors were scared to push it so much. This Judge Goldman, he even had a special gold ring made for himself that he wore every day. It had engraved on it the lady of justice with her scales and blindfold, and it had in Hebrew the word for 'justice,' and there was a picture of it in the newspaper.

"He was, of course, murdered, and when his body was

found, both the ring and the finger that wore it were missing. This the newspapers reported in big headlines. Everybody figured that Smith had put somebody up to it, but they couldn't prove nothing. The Jews, they were furious, and if anybody should know for sure who murdered Judge Goldman, it maybe would be the end for the killer, even today. So much outrage. It maybe would put him on the Death Row, no matter how much he bribed and what big people he knew."

And I say, "It was Monk, right?"

He nods. "He's got a little safe that he keeps always locked, and one day, while I was in the rat's nest that is his office, I saw the door was not closed tight, and he was not around, so I peeked inside, looking for anything, I did not know what, that could protect me so I should not be a Sid Schachtman. And what I tell you now is true, I swear on my dead brother, though it is something I could not believe even when my own eyes saw it. In a little case was Goldman's ring, still on the bone that was his finger. I took it and left the safe door like it was. Whether Monk knows it's gone I don't know. He has never said nothing about it. But sometimes he gives me looks."

"Well, if he thinks you've got that over him, you could be safe, 'cause he might be afraid you gave it to someone who'll rat him out if something was to happen to you."

"Maybe, maybe not. Nobody is safe from Monk if he gets mad enough, even if he knows I have it, which I'm too scared to tell him I do. So. But I keep it, just in case it should maybe be useful, if not for me, then for you."

"So where is it?"

"That I don't know no more, *boychik*. I put it in a tin box with something else that is very important. And I give it to your mother to hide it careful, where no one but her shall find it. This was after your mother and me we were not together no more, but still I trusted her that she should keep it. And then, when I heard she got sick, I asked her where she had put it, but her brain had gone wrong and that was that."

"She never told you 'sand Jew today oh'?"

"No, what does this mean?"

Some drunk was yelling curses in the street now, and Shmulewitz the chicken plucker was down there, at it again, calling for his Rivke, and the yells coming from the two of them while some last fireworks were going off, made about as much sense as 'sand Jew today oh' did.

I tell him "I don't know. It's what Mama said to me out at the hospital on Blackwell's when she gave me a key to a tin box she said you gave her that was real important. I asked her where the box was, and that's all she said."

My father laughed cold, "Once more, life is playing little tricks on me. If you ever find the box, and I am gone, decide what is the right thing to do. Just use your head and don't be in no hurry to trust nobody more than yourself."

Aunt Gabriella sticks her head out the window now and tells me it's time to come in. She's heard the last thing my father said, and she points her finger at him, and it's trembling, and she tells me, "If you're smart you no trust *this* one, anyways, not one word that he say to you."

My father gets up and says, "You have a mouth on you, Gabriella, but you are a good woman. You don't like me, okay, you don't have much reason you should like me. I thank you for taking care of this boy. Now be so kind and go back inside, so I shall say one more word to him private and get out of your house, like you want."

She says, "Don't come here no more" and goes back into the bedroom.

My father puts his hand on my shoulder and says, "I did not want you to be involved in what my life has become, but when Monk told me I should bring you in to work for him, I had no choice. I tried to tell you in the City Hall park that you should not let your feelings get in the way, but you are what you are, and this he has seen. I know I have not been a good father to you, but you are my son not less than this other one you have heard about tonight. He is a baby, though. You are not. Take care of yourself, *boychik*." And he gave my shoulder a couple pats now before he stepped through the window and into the kitchen and out the door.

I stayed on the fire escape and watched him leave the building, his hands in his pockets and his head down. I heard one last firecracker from far off and then I went back inside, and laid there, knowing it would be another long night.

XIII

The next morning, first thing, I went across the Bowery over to Vaccarelli's, the restaurant Paul told me to come by when I was ready to talk to him again.

On my way over, I ran into Johnny and Skinny on Grand. I hadn't seen them since the day we were swimming, and they say that they saw Davey over at the fireworks the night before and that Davey was telling everybody that I was a no-good bum and that he saw me and Miss Friedman feeling each other up together over at the school and that he heard from some of Monk's guys that I'd even done the big thing with her in bed.

They were grinning at me like they thought I was some kind of hero. Davey told them Miss Friedman's put together so rich and sweet you just want to dive right into the *gelato*, and Skinny is making slurping noises and kissing his fingertips and saying, "*Maddone!* you are a lucky half-Yid son of a bitch," and Johnny's asking, "Is it true that these Yid women, they ain't got no stoppin' in them till the guy's just wore out?"

I tell them, "You know, Davey ain't got the truth in him, that little pisser, and he doesn't care whose name gets dirty. That Miss Friedman never did a thing with me. She's got a man that she sees. She doesn't need a kid like me."

Skinny grins and says, "Yeah, sure." And he and Johnny look at each other and snicker.

155

I tell them, "I'm gonna kill that skinny bucktooth rat liar!"

Johnny says, "Davey told us your girl Esther, she knows all about it, and she don't like it and don't like you no more, and that she's gonna be his girl soon."

"That ain't ever gonna be." I want to tell them that I don't care what Esther does anyway, but I can't make myself say that. What I do tell them is that I'm working for Paul now, except nobody knows it except me and Paul. Skinny says that's great, but he's a little bit jealous, I can see, and he says he and Johnny do stuff for Paul, too, like carry messages or get stuff from the grocery sometimes. And I say that's fine, but that Paul has me doing important stuff that has to do with Monk, and they look at me like this is even bigger than anything I was doing with Miss Friedman. I figure they're gonna tell Davey the next time they run into the rat and that he'll tell the first one of Monk's guys he sees, and that's good, because Monk is going to think that I'm doing just what he wants me to do.

After the two of them go off, still talking about how lucky I am, I go into Vaccarelli's, which isn't a dive like The Palm. There's nice tablecloths on small round tables and good silverware and pretty plates laid out and shiny wood floors, and walls with no stains or cracks on them, and some nice paintings of places that look like they're in Italy— mostly small mountain towns with the sun shining down on a church and tan buildings that have roofs with curved orange tiles on them, and there's one of a volcano that's smoking near some big town by a bay.

The place isn't open for business yet, but there are guys sitting around inside who I figure are some of Paul's gang. Right off you can see that they're dressed better than Monk's mugs are. They're wearing suits that are pressed neat and fit pretty good, not tight, like Monk's guys usually wear because Monk wears his own tight to show off his muscles. And none of the suits have big screaming check patterns on them, like Monk and some of his guys, even my father, wear sometimes.

And Paul's office is the best I ever saw. I mean I haven't seen many, just the principal's a couple times and a couple doctors' offices, but they weren't like this. Polished furniture with soft and pretty chairs, a big desk that Paul is sitting behind, and healthy-looking plants in beautiful vases all around, and a bookcase on one wall that went up to the ceiling and was filled with books all the way up, books, I could see, that were in different languages. Also on one wall he had a big painting that was the same as the volcano one that I saw out in the restaurant, just bigger. The volcano is sending flames and rocks into the sky. It's nighttime, and people from the town near it are running away down a road along the water, and some are falling in.

Paul sees me looking at it. "Vesuvius," he says.

"Yeah, *Formidibile monte, sterminator Vesevo*."

He looks kind of surprised, then smiles and says "Ah, so you know Leopardi, then. I told you I figured you for an impressive kid. 'Stupendous mountain, destructor Vesuvius.'"

"My mother use to recite that sometimes."

"Your mother must be a woman of refined taste, Massimo."

I nod. I know my mother would say right off that he could recite all the beautiful poetry he wants and still be a guy who hurts people.

Then he says, "A boy like you from such a background, you don't belong with the Monk Eastmans of this world, and neither does your father. He's not that sort of Jew, Massimo."

I nod again. Meanwhile I'm thinking of those words from Dante that I thought about when I was at the Fish Market docks, the ones that are over the gateway to hell, that tell you to give up on any hopes you have, and I'm feeling again like I'm either at the gate or have maybe gone through it already. Paul smiles now, waves for me to sit down on this soft couch, and he comes around from the desk and sits on a chair near the couch and turns it so he's facing me. He asks, "Massimo, would you like me to send out to the kitchen for something?"

I tell him that I wouldn't mind.

In two minutes, I'm gobbling up the best cannolis I ever had and gulping a tall glass of sweet ice coffee, which is a drink I never had before, and Paul lets me take my time before he gets down to business. He even asks me if I'd like some more. I would, but I tell him no, because I don't want to seem like a pig.

He also asks me if he can get me something for my hand, which he can see is swole up, but I tell him no, and, of course, he asks what happened, and I tell him everything. He shakes his head, sighs, and mutters "that *animale*." Unless I didn't know better, I could almost forget how many guys they say Paul's either got killed or killed by himself.

And then I tell him, like Monk wanted me to, that Monk is planning to move into Five Points by opening dance halls. What I don't tell him is the second part of what Monk wanted me to say, that I secretly heard that Monk's not really going to do it, but just wants Paul to think he is so he can force Paul to make a deal with him. You see, the plan I firmed up for myself after the talk with my father out on the fire escape is that I'm going to try to get Paul so riled up against Monk that he's going to lose his temper and do something real soon to bring Monk down, maybe even kill him.

Well, Paul hears this stuff about the dance halls and his jaw goes tight, and he says in a quiet voice, "So the gorilla said that, huh? Well, tell him that you heard me talking with some of my associates and that we're planning to have our guys fan out all over the Lower East Side and chat with the rabbis about what a menace Monk Eastman and his bums are to the community just in case the rabbis have had their noses too buried in the Talmud to know what's going on. We'll show them this, too, that Monk started circulating two or three days ago." And Paul gives me a printed-up advertisement that says stuff like "Ear chawed off: $15, Leg or arm broke: $19, Shot in leg: $25, Stab: $25, Doing the big job: $100 and up."

Paul says, "Most of the rabbis must know the sort of stuff Monk pulls, but seeing this kind of thing being circulated and getting the handsome contributions that my men will offer if they speak out against Monk might make them feel that enough is enough. Tell him you overheard me saying all this, and maybe he'll wise up and act like something other than *che brutta bestia* that he is. If he does wise up, fine. We'll let him hang on for a while, even as we're keeping the pressure on him. And if he doesn't wise up and tries something raw, well, we'll return the favor, and meanwhile everyone will know that he caused the trouble in the first place."

Just then, a guy comes in and says, "Sorry, boss, the butcher and the vegetable guy are both here. They don't like the new deal you told them you were setting up. I think you need to talk to them personal."

Paul's jaw goes tight again, and his nostrils open a little wider, and I'm thinking, okay, I'm maybe going to see Vesuvius shoot out rocks and fire right now, and I stand up and say, "I'll just go outside into the restaurant to wait, or out on the street, if you want, till you're ready."

But he smiles, and says, "No, Massimo, you just make yourself comfortable here. It won't take me long to tell these two *insetti*, these *pezzi di merda*, what's what." And he walks out like a man who's not going to do any bargaining. I know the two guys waiting for him won't see the guy that Mr. Norton saw.

A couple minutes later, Paul is back, looking like a man who didn't like the time he just had to waste swatting bugs or rubbing horsecrap from his shoes. But then he smiles and says, "But you haven't told me anything about your father. How is he doing, Massimo?"

"He's okay."

"He couldn't have liked seeing what that *animale* did to his son."

"I don't guess he did, but he couldn't do anything about it, so..." and I shrugged, like what else was there to say.

"You've spoken to him about coming over to work for me? You told him I could use a man with his skills?"

I said that I did, and that I asked my father if he knew what happened to Sid Schachtman and that my father told me that he did and worried about it a lot and was thinking hard now on whether to come over with Paul.

Paul smiles again, and I can't tell whether it's because he believes me or because he figures that either me or my old man told Monk all about him trying to steal my old man away and now it's aggravating Monk. He says, "Well, tell your father to keep thinking about it. I can work out a nice deal with him, and I can protect him from Monk and offer him the respect and trust that he deserves and that Monk's never going to accord him."

I smile back at him and say okay, and I get up and shake his hand and tell him I really think my father might want to come over. I figure the longer he thinks he needs me to work on my father, the longer he's going to want to keep me around.

He gives me some dough. I thank him for letting me work for him, and he gives me his smile and walks me out, telling me to take care of my hand.

An hour later, I'm at Monk's saloon, but Monk's not there. Kid Twist Zweibach is at the bar, and he's got two rats in a cage. He's poking them with a stick, trying to get them to fight, while a couple guys are putting money down on the bar, betting on which rat will win if Kid Twist can ever get them to go after each other.

I tell them that I've got something important to tell Monk. One of the guys laughs and says, "Yeah, what is it, kid, that your hand hoits?" And they all laugh. I laugh with them, because there ain't any use in letting them think they're making me mad.

Well, Monk's over at his apartment, which they tell me is

on the third floor on the corner of Broome and Chrystie. And Big Jack Zelig giggles and says, "Hey, kid, a woid to da wise, don't get into no scrapes wit' da Chinks over dere, 'cause if you does, dem guys'll take dat swole hand of yours and cut it up into da chop suey." I laugh along with the others, but I'm wondering what he's talking about.

Then I see that Monk's place is above a Chinese laundry, and there's two Chinks sitting right beside the building door. They're wearing Chinese clothes, and they have pigtails, and when I come up to the place, they get up real quick and block the doorway. Their arms are folded across their chests and their hands tucked into their big loose sleeves, and it's not hard to guess their hands aren't empty in there. One says to me, not very friendly, "Why you come here?"

I tell him I work for Monk, and I'm thinking I'm glad that these guys don't know what Davey and me did way back when we found that Chinese guy laying in the street. I'd heard what Mock Duck and his new Hip Sing Tong and the old On Leong Tong were doing to each other feuding over in Chinatown. Lately, every couple days, the cops would find pigtailed heads laying in the gutters and alleys.

Anyway, after one of the guys goes up and checks with Monk, I'm climbing up the stairs and feeling how hot it is in this place, because of the laundry below. I wonder if Tick-Tock would wear his coat even in this. Up on the third floor, Monk is sitting at a table, without a shirt on. I tell him, "I saw the guy you wanted me to see," and I don't say anything else, because there are other people there. Sitting next to him is Sadie, with her blouse open down to her waist, so you can see how little she's got on underneath it. Walking around, without anything on except for some understuff and lots of makeup, are three girls, who, just like Sadie, are none of them much older than Esther. They're cooking stuff and serving it to Monk and Sadie, who have their elbows on the table, each of them with a knife in one hand and a fork in the other.

Monk grins and calls out, "Goils, dis here is Moish, who's doin' some important woik for me. Sadie's already friends wit' him. I hadda straighten him out a little last night, but he's okay in my book. Moish, dese goils all woik for me, too, in my best sportin' house. Dese are good goils, good oiners, and good cooks, too."

I say I'm pleased to meet them, and Sadie shows me her teeth and licks her lips a little and says, "He's a cutie, this one, but kind of shy," but the others don't do more than nod. So Monk says, "Goils, mind youse manners," and then the other three smile big and say they're pleased to meet me. But they don't really look that happy about it or about anything else. One of them's got a big bruise on her left cheek, and another's got a lip that looks fuller than it's supposed to. They're all sweating as they're working over the stove.

I smile back and I say, "Monk, I didn't know you had Chinese guys working for you."

"Aah, it never hoits to have friends in Chinatown. You rent some Chinks from a guy like Mock Duck, he can let you in on some stuff he's doin' over in da town. It's just good business."

He grins at me. "How's da paw? Still looks kinda swole up. But you had to learn your lesson. Anyways, I'm glad I didn't hit it no woise. No hard feelin's, right?"

"Nah," I say, smiling, "Tell you the truth, I figure I probably deserved worse. The hand hurts, but I'll be okay."

He grins again. "Sit down an' eat somet'in' while you tell me what you got to tell me."

I'm not hungry, but I'm not going to say no to Monk right then, so I tell him, "Yeah, I could stand to have something. It smells good." And then I'm sitting there with Monk and Sadie and filling my face with *kreplach* soup and *flanken* and potatoes and chopped liver and stuffed derma and kasha. I haven't eaten that kind of stuff since I was a young kid and my father took me and my mother a couple times over to Gluckstern's or Pollack's. My mother never much liked this kind of stuff, too heavy for her, she said, "*troppo pesante*," but she waved for us to keep on going, which I did pretty good for a kid. I always had a big appetite.

Well, the food's not bad, so I'm chewing away, sitting across from Monk and Sadie, and the sweat's pouring off of us. There's a window there, but it's so covered up with steam that you can't see out of it. Sadie is putting stuff right into Monk's mouth and he's making like he's going to bite her hand off and she's giggling, and the whores are cooking and carrying stuff over to the table and they're sweating, too, and Monk tells them they're not being friendly enough to their guest, so every minute or two one or another of them comes over and runs her hand slow and soft across my neck or breathes into my ear that I look so big and strong, or rubs her belly and boobs up against my shoulder, sighing while she's doing it. I knew they didn't mean it, but I couldn't help getting worked up some, even though I didn't want to, really.

So I sat there, eating and sweating and blushing, and Sadie is watching me and nudging Monk and saying how cute I am and that she figures something else is getting swoled up now along with my hand, and Monk, he's laughing. Sadie's kind of small, but with a big chest and these wide blue eyes that look real innocent and curly hair that falls down around her face, especially when she's sweating like now, and that makes her eyes look even wider and more innocent, and she's got plump lips that you think could give you sweet kisses, but then you figure that she's not really someone you want to get mixed up with. I feel kind of sorry for her, though, for being Monk's girl and a whore, which is what she is, even though she's just a kid.

She says, "Oh, Moishele, you look so sad. What's the matter, you don't like a little attention?" She flicks out her tongue and runs it over her lips back and forth a couple times and says in a voice that she makes sound like a little girl's and kind of husky at the same time. "Aw, Moishele, anytime you do feel sad you can come see me, and I'll make you feel lots better," and she giggles and winks at me, and Monk laughs and says, "Ain't no skin off of my *tuchus*, Moish, if you want to *shtup* dis one. Just watch dat she don't leave you wit' not'in' more dan a wet piece of spaghetti for dat Red bitch Friedman." This is the second time he's told me I could have Sadie in bed. Would she and me end up like Sid Schachtman and the girl that was under him?

I tell him, "Maybe another time," and he says, "Just say da woid" and then, "Okay, goils, fun's over, get lost. Dat means you, too, Sadie. Me and Moish got woik to do."

The girls leave, and me and Monk are sitting alone at the table. "So, you seen da greazeball already today, huh?" he asks.

"Yeah, I just left him about an hour ago."

"Good, I see you're really on da ball. Maybe you learnt somet'in' last night."

I say that I think I did. And then I tell him everything that Paul wanted him to hear about what he was going to tell the rabbis.

Monk asks me, "You told him you hoid me say secret-like dat I wasn't really gonna put my dance halls on his toif?"

"Yeah, I told him that, but it didn't seem to make any difference. He says to a couple of his guys that he's gettin' you nervous and that he's gonna twist the screws tighter yet, till you give up a chunk of your turf this side of the Bowery to him or just get driven out altogether and go back to being nothin' more than 'a cheap headcracker and stick-up man,' a 'brutal beast' is what he called you in Italian. I'm sorry I've got to tell you this kind of stuff, but I figure you want to know what's what with Paul."

Monk grins big. He's mad, sure, but there's something about his being in a big fight that he likes. I also make up that I heard Paul tell his guys to go around to all the priests and tell them to get everybody at their churches to fight against Monk, because the Jews want to run everything downtown and you couldn't trust the Christ-killers ever, anyway.

Still grinning, Monk says, "So da Guinea Dago bastid said dat, huh? What, he don't t'ink I got enough nails to hammer him onto a cross wit'? I t'ought I could save some dough for da two of us by makin' a little deal wit' him and headin' off a fight dat ain't gonna do us no good wit' da guys from Tammany. But maybe I'm startin' not to care so much what da guys from Tammany t'ink, at least where Paul Kelly is consoined."

I want to get on out of there. It's not getting any cooler, and I ate too much, and I'm starting to get a little nauseous. So I say, "Well, anyway, that's all I got to report to you," and I make like I'm starting to get up.

Monk says, "Sit down, Moish, don't be in no hurry."

I sit, and he says, "You didn't tell me what Paul had to say today about your old man."

"No, I forgot, because he didn't say much. He just asked if I spoke to my father about coming over to work for him, and I told him I did, but that my old man said he wouldn't ever do Monk dirt like that, which is the truth, of course. And Paul says, 'Keep working on him and tell him I'll pay him real good and protect him from Monk, who won't be much of a threat too much longer anyways.' So I told him I would. But you and me both know, Monk, that Paul's just dreaming as far as my old man goes."

"Yeah, sure he is, kid. And one t'ing he ain't got clear in his greazeball brain is dat dere ain't nobody you can protect from Monk Eastman, not nobody." And he grins at me, and I think of what my father told me on the fire escape, and I'm getting even more nauseous.

Monk comes round the table, stands over me, and puts his hand on my neck. "You done good, Moishele," he says, and he gives it a squeeze hard enough to make it hurt a little. "You can go now. Next time you see Paul, you tell him you're still woikin' on your old man, and if you want to have one of da goils now before you go, and dat still includes Sadie, you got her, 'cause I got a room right here where you can get your ashes hauled so good dat you'll forget dat you ever want to do it again with Friedman or dat little Esther what you took care of Mendel over."

His hand's still pressing on my neck. "Esther ain't ever done it with me or anyone."

He laughs. "Oh, yeah, I forgot. Dat's right, she ain't never done it yet. Well, anyways, go and have some fun wit' one of my goils dat's here today."

I tell him thanks, but I've got to go see my mother, who's not doing so good.

XIV

The day after I talked with both Paul and Monk, I went back to the school program. I needed to let Miss Friedman see that I was so sorry about what I told her and that maybe we could at least be friends even if she never let me get near her again. But the couple times that our eyes met up, hers were cold, and I looked somewhere else real quick. If she noticed that my hand was swole, she didn't say anything about it. She didn't call on me in class, and I didn't speak up any, either.

Like I expected, Davey hadn't come back to the program after the Fourth. I saw him out on the street once since then. He was on the other side from me, and I knew he saw me, but he acted like he didn't, which was fine with me, because I had nothing good to say to him anymore.

On the second day I'm back, I'm sitting up there on the school roof and kids are playing, and I'm watching, and I decide that even if she gets mad, I just need to tell Miss Friedman again right away how sorry I am. So I'm waiting for her to come back upstairs with some little kids who were helping her with the Moxie bottles, and then suddenly a little kid is running out from the stairs onto the roof and he's screaming and crying, and about fifteen guys are after him. I see that they're all a couple years older than me, rough-looking guys, a few of them I'd seen around, but I didn't know any of them, except that I recognized that the leader, a husky guy who got a lot of his right ear cut off in reform school, was Hymie 'One Ear' Kaplan, who worked for Monk.

One of the guys grabs the kid that's screaming and slaps him back and forth across the face, then shoves him down and kicks him hard in the can three times while the kid is laying there curled up and crying. And the guy's yelling, "That's what you get for running, you little punk!" Meanwhile, the teachers, three ladies, have gotten all the kids, even the older ones, who are thirteen, fourteen, and fifteen, huddled together behind them, and a lot of them are crying and screaming for help, as these bums head for them all.

And what am I doing? Well, right off I'm trying to help the kid that's taking the beating, but three guys grab me, pin me up against the screen and keep me there. I'm scared about what happened with Miss Friedman downstairs because the three teachers who were trying to shield the kids are getting it bad. The guys are calling them "Red bitches" and "Red whores" and slapping them around, and putting their hands all over their bodies, until all three of them are collapsed onto the floor and sobbing. And then they're getting hit with clubs on their asses and even jabbed with them between their legs. And the kids, even the little ones, are getting slapped, and the bigger girls are getting about what the teachers are, and the bigger boys are getting punched and kicked and clubbed, and getting extra if they try to fight back, which almost all of them aren't trying.

And these guys are yelling at the kids the whole time that they're punks who ain't American for going to "this Red school," and if they catch any of them here again, they won't get treated as easy as this time. And just to prove it, a couple of them cut holes in the screen fence that keeps you from falling off of the roof, and they grab three of the boys and stick them halfway off the roof through the holes and make like they might let go. And just like with Izzie, I can't help. The kids are crying and begging and promising everything now as their heads are hanging there lower than their bodies, and these three guys are still pinning me, and all I can do is watch. One kid's glasses go falling off of his face and down to the street.

Well, after a couple minutes, they pull the kids back in, and the kids lay there like they're never going to get up again. One pukes, and when he finishes he still just lays there, his face right next to the vomit.

After about ten minutes, when it looks like these bums are finally going to leave, and I say to myself, okay, now it's my turn and I'm really going to get it, one of the bums points over to me and yells, "What about the big guy, ain't he gonna hafta take his medicine like the rest of the Red punks?" And One Ear says, "Nah, dat's Moish Levy. Monk says to leave him be. He ain't really wit' da rest of 'em."

So, of course, just when he says this, and the guys holding me let me go, Miss Friedman comes out onto the roof and hears him. Her nose is bloody, and her blouse is ripped off of her shoulder, so you can see her underwear all the way down to her waist. Her cheek is bruised bad, and one of the lenses in her glasses is cracked, and her hair's all messed up. She should have stayed downstairs and hid after what they did to her, but she came up, I guess, because she was so worried about everyone.

She gives me a look across the roof like I'm the scariest one that's there, and I want to yell to her that I'm not. But One Ear and his guys are heading towards the stairs right where she's standing. They shove her around some as they go by, calling her "Filthy Red *Shlooche*," and One Ear, he doesn't just go past her, he stops in front of her, pulls her tight to him with his left arm and reaches down with his right and brings his hand up under her skirt and feels her real rough up at her knish. She tries to scream but it comes out like choking. I start rushing over to shove him away from her, but before I get close, a guy pulls a pistol and points it right at my chest.

Maybe Billy the Kid could have done something to be a hero, but I couldn't figure what it was, so I just stood there with this guy's gun aimed at me and watched till One Ear stops grabbing and feeling Miss Friedman, tells her to tell Paul Kelly that he's a "Grease-dripping Dago son of a whore bitch who's through downtown and who'd better watch out before he ends up a dead man," and finally he tells her to "stop *shtupping* kids, like everybody on the whole East Side knows you're doin', or next time we'll *shtup* you like you ain't never been done, you filthy Red cooch."

Then him and the rest of them are gone, and I go over to Miss Friedman, who's curled up and making little wheezing sounds. She looks at me cold through her broken glasses and she whispers, "You're one of them, you . . ." She doesn't finish, either because she doesn't have the strength or just can't think of any word bad enough to call me. I say, "No, Miss Friedman, I didn't tell anybody about us, I swear, and I ain't one of them. I *ain't*. My father, he works for Monk, which I was ashamed to ever tell you, but I ain't one of them, I swear."

She doesn't answer, and I look at her and at everyone else laying there, and I know that not only is Monk to blame for it all but probably I am, too. I hadn't figured that this was what could happen because of what I told him Paul said, but I should have. And I hated myself maybe worse than ever yet.

Three hours later I got Miss Friedman back to her place. First I took her to the hospital. I yelled over to the other teachers, who weren't hurt as bad as her, that that's what I was going to do and that I'd send help for them and the kids, and then I got her up on her feet and walked her downstairs and out of the building. She told me to leave her alone, but I told her I wouldn't and that I was going to help her whether she wanted me to or not, and she didn't answer.

When we got to the street, I saw a cop right away and told

him he better get some help upstairs to the roof gym because there were a lot of people hurt up there. Well, it turns out he's in on what had happened, because he says, "Nobody dead or crippled, is there?" I say no, and he says "Okay, we'll see how all those whining Godless little socialists are doin,' don't you worry yourselves none," and he went strolling off down the street. He never asked me how they got hurt, who did it, nothing like that, but I guess that didn't surprise me any, not in Monk's territory. As the cop walked off, I saw a freight wagon, and I paid the guy to take me and Miss Friedman over to Mt. Sinai. The whole way there, she's leaning away from me.

Well, they cleaned her up at the hospital, saw that nothing was broke, then pinned up her ripped clothes and asked her about what happened, but she didn't tell them anything except that some guys attacked her and she didn't know who they were or why they did it. She said all that in a low, flat voice. The only time she sounded anything like herself was when she said she was worried about the children and the other teachers. Well, while we were there, one of the other teachers came in to check on Miss Friedman, and she said the cops finally came with some ambulance people and they gave everybody the once over and said they were okay except for cuts and bruises. And when nobody could say who did it, the cops just chuckled and said it must have been just some drunken hooligans having fun and they'd keep their eyes open.

Then me and her got Miss Friedman back to her place. Florence Cohen nearly faints when we come in, but then she calms down and gets Miss Friedman into bed. When the other teacher goes home and Florence goes out to a store to get some bandages and stuff to help take care of Miss Friedman, I'm alone there with her. Maybe it's only because she's too weak to say anything at all, but she doesn't tell me to leave.

I sit down on the edge of her bed, and I tell her, "Miss Friedman, Rachel, look, I've got to apologize about what I said up in the music room. It was mean and stupid, and I can't really figure out why I said it, except that I just wanted so much to kiss you and my feelings got hurt, or something, when you said it was wrong. I guess lots of times I'm just no good, you know."

She says, so weak I can hardly hear her, "You need to give yourself a chance." And then it's like she's too exhausted to say anything else.

I lean over and kiss her on the forehead, and I say, "You better get some rest." And she nods and seems like she's going to drop off to sleep, but then a shiver goes through her, and she says, "Those boys, those terrible boys, what they did to me, and the things they said." And she shivers some more and starts to cry, and she's saying, "And the program, it's over, it's all over."

She's right, of course. Who'd want to go back there after all that happened? "I figure Monk got scared you were going to hurt his business," I said.

"I tried so hard, and people like Paul Kelly had so much faith in what we were doing."

I don't say anything.

And then she remembers what I wished she didn't. "They didn't hurt you. Was it just because of your father, Morris?"

"Yeah, but I feel like it ain't right I didn't get roughed up too."

"No, Morris, I'm glad you weren't hurt."

I says, "I ain't like my father."

She falls asleep, and I sit in a chair watching over her until Florence gets back.

XV

The next day I find out that what happened over at our school happened at both the other schools on the Lower East Side where they had the same program going, and two of the kids and one of the teachers ended up in the hospital with some busted bones. And Monk's guys weren't just busy at the schools. Paul had these two S.A.C.s over in Five Points, you know, what they call 'Social and Athletic Clubs.' One was the 'Sons of Italy S.A.C.' and the other was 'Kelly's Italian-American S.A.C.' They were clubhouses where guys like eighteen and nineteen and up into their twenties who played on Paul's sports teams could hang around and do some drinking and card playing and hold dances and take girls to some rooms upstairs. Paul got lots of guys started in his gang by getting them first to his S.A.C.s. Well, at the same time that Monk had gangs busting up the programs at the schools, he sent two other gangs of guys over to these clubhouses, and they wrecked up the places total and everybody in them. The furniture was smashed, the windows knocked out, and the sports equipment stolen or broke and in the gutter. Some of Paul's guys got hurt pretty bad.

I tell myself that sooner or later Monk would have attacked the schools this summer, and maybe he also would have sent his guys over to Paul's S.A.C.s sometime too, even if I hadn't told him what I did over at his place above the Chink laundry, but

I wasn't sure, of course, and I figured there'd be a lot of people who'd be out to get me good if they knew what I'd pulled, and maybe I'd deserve everything they'd give me.

And then, when Paul heard what Monk did, he sent five guys to rough up Monk bad and teach him that Paul was no one to cross. I wished he'd sent them over to kill him. I guess he figured that having some guys just shoot Monk dead would have left all of Monk's guys ready to kill Paul and with no leader for Paul to deal with. But getting Monk roughed up is not that easy, it turns out, because Monk is, well, Monk is Monk. The story that one of Monk's streetwalking whores told the other whores and then that got around the neighborhood was that late at night the day after everything at the schools and clubhouses, she sees Monk is coming down Chrystie from spending the evening at The Palm, and then she sees these five guys come up sudden and grab Monk and drag him into an alley. She runs down the street and around the corner, and she gets the two Chink guards, and runs back with them to the alley. But when they get there, they find Monk's done just fine on his own. Two of the guys are already running off way down the street, and in the alley a guy is on his back with a knife sticking in his chest, and laying next to him is a guy with the front of his face squashed up and the back of his head dented in and bloody from Monk's smashing it into the brick wall a few times, and Monk's got a headlock on the fifth guy, and he's pounding the guy's face with brass knuckles, which Monk has got on each paw.

Monk has a knife gash in his side, but he doesn't even care. He tells the Chinks to let the two guys lay where they are in the alley, "'cause da rats around here probably ain't never had no garlic nor no olive oil neit'er and dey might like a greasy Dago treat for a change." And he says to take the guy he's got in the headlock back to the laundry. Meanwhile, he gets a handkerchief off of the streetwalker, stuffs it into the cut in his side and walks home with his arm around her. He's happy as a lark, she says, and he's yelling he's "da king of da whole sout' end of Manhattan," and that "I get what I want when I want it."

The next morning, people find the two bodies in the alley, and, just like Monk wanted, the rats did chew some on their faces and hands. The story is that Monk says when he hears about it, "I'm just scared dat' da guy wit' da knife in him was dead before dey got to him. For da record, I don't know what guy killed dem' Dagoes, but I know for sure he's gotta be one tough customer. It'd take ten Dagoes, maybe, to kill a bird like dat." And then him and the guys with him laugh and slap each other on the back.

And the morning after that, the guy that Monk had the two Chinks take back to the laundry was found laying in the gutter a couple blocks from Monk's apartment. People said that his face looked scalded all red, like maybe he'd been dunked in a vat of lye cleaning fluid, his head was crushed in, almost like a horse's hoof had stomped on it a couple times, and his body looked like it had been run over by a wagon back and forth and back and forth.

Nothing happened for the next few days, and everybody was guessing what Monk or Paul was going to do next. Meanwhile I went over to Miss Friedman's each day, and I sat with her some when Florence was away. Miss Friedman was sad and quiet. Mostly she'd lay in bed holding some book that she wasn't reading, and looking out the window, where you couldn't see much except for a little bit of sky and the building across the street. She had some pretty flowers in a window box, but I don't think she was even noticing them.

I was calling her "Rachel" now as much as I was calling her "Miss Friedman," and she seemed to like that. It was quiet being with her, and that was fine. Maybe we both needed a little peace.

Monk wasn't ready to rest, though. Three days after he took care of the guys in the alley, someone throws a brick through the big front window of Vaccarelli's, and when one of Paul's guys runs out to see what's going on, he gets shot high up on his side. He goes down but yells "You bastids, I'll take you with me," pulls out a gun, raises himself on one arm and shoots back at three of Monk's guys who are firing at him from across the street. Two more guys come running out of Vaccarelli's shooting, but they're hit right off, too. According to the newspapers, the whole thing lasted maybe a minute. The first guy that got hit, after taking three more bullets, rises up to his knees, calls out "Sweet Mother Mary, just let me get off one more shot," but falls flat on his face dead, laying there in his nice suit that's covered with holes and blood. The other two of Paul's guys are laying there not hit so bad that they're not gonna make it, but some kid coming down the street got hit accidental and is crumpled up crying for his mother, till he bleeds to death a couple minutes later. Monk's guys, of course, are gone in a hurry, and nobody can describe them to the cops.

The kid, it turns out, was Johnny, who the last time I saw him was grinning because he heard that I was doing stuff with Miss Friedman. He wasn't a bad guy, really, and now he's not ever gonna get to do that kind of stuff with anyone. When I heard, I felt maybe it was like my own hand fired the shot that got him, because of what I'd started. And I knew for sure that since the night I heard Izzie hit the water the world wasn't any better for having me still walking around it, and maybe was even worse.

That same night that Johnny got killed, two of Monk's guys got shot leaving one of his saloons and some old lady just coming down the street when the gunfire started, got hit in her leg. Nobody died, but everybody knew more would, and then Tammany told Monk and Paul to hold off, because this stuff was getting the newspapers all riled up, which could be bad for business. So the bosses at Tammany called Monk and Paul in for a meeting, and they said the two of them had to decide how they were going to get along better so that everybody could make money like always.

Well, at the meeting, Monk is yelling, Paul is talking calm mostly, but they're both saying the same stuff, that they want to destroy each other. My father was there and he told me all this. So Croker, the big Tammany boss, mashes out his cigar right on the table they're all sitting at, slams his fist down, and says, "Okay, you two fools just want to have a go at each other, so we're going to oblige you. One week from tonight the two of you fight it out in the ring, man to man. We'll set everything up. Winner takes control both west and east of the Bowery and the other guy gets out of the city for keeps. And if he doesn't on his own, we'll see that he does. You guys both have big gangs, do you? Ours is forty times bigger. It's called the New York City Police Department. And don't anybody do anything stupid during this next week. I want both sides of the Bowery quiet, understand?"

Monk and Paul both said okay.

"Any objections to you two duking it out?" he asks.

Monk said, "I'll moider da greazy bum." Paul answered, "We'll see about that, you ape." It took five guys to keep Monk from going for Paul right there.

The fight was set for a place way up in the Bronx, and not the papers or anybody not in Monk's or Paul's crowds was supposed to know. Tammany wanted no publicity and no riots.

My father also told me that Monk said that he wanted me to be there and had put my name on the list of who was allowed. I asked him why, and he said all Monk would tell him was, "He's done good woik. I want to give him a treat." And my father warns me, "He is not about to give you a treat, Morris. Still, if he wants you there, there you should be. Just be careful and don't make him more against you than he is already."

Over the next week, I saw my mother and left all choked up. I also checked in on Miss Friedman a couple times, and I guess she was doing better, but it was still like something had changed for keeps. She didn't even keep the shade up in her room anymore. Florence told me that since the day she got roughed up, Miss Friedman hadn't been out of the house for even ten seconds.

And every day, I went by the key-shop, but only from across the street, to see if I could just get a look at Esther, even from far away, but I didn't see her, not once, just Mendel or her mother.

And then I was at the fight, which was set to start at ten at night in a huge trolley-car barn way up at the end of the line in the Bronx, on Jerome Avenue, right across from the Woodlawn Cemetery. Except for the moonlight, it would have been dark there because there was only a couple little one-family houses and a lunch place that got all of its business from the trolley workers and was closed at night. But the Tammany guys had emptied all the trolleys out and lit up the whole inside of the barn with torches, because the gaslights inside wouldn't have been bright enough, and they also had torches all around the outside of the building. And right across from the barn, the cemetery stretched out forever, just more headstones and crosses, and angels with big wings, and little white houses for the dead than you could ever count or want to. So with all the torches and the noise at the car barn, it was just death on one side of the avenue and like hell on the other.

There were cops all over, all holding their guns in their hands. Tammany had sent them out to make sure that there wouldn't be any riots between Monk's guys and Paul's.

I go inside, and I see guys crowding up to a bar set up out of planks and barrels that goes along almost half one of the walls of the place, and behind it they've got about a dozen bartenders, big kegs of beer and enough booze, it looks like, for both everybody in the car barn and everyone laying in

Woodlawn across the road. And at one end of the bar, there are five guys wearing green eyeshades, taking bets on the fight from guys standing in long lines. The cops don't mind. In fact, they're happy, because they know they're all going to get their cut of the take. As the money is piling up in stacks, they're standing there and guarding it. Of course, you have to ask yourself who's guarding those sticky-fingered Micks while they're guarding the dough?

The fight ring is in the center of the place, and rows of chairs are set up on all four sides of it. I figure they've got room for maybe two thousand people.

Well, the seats start filling up, and Monk's guys, of course, are all sitting together and so are Paul's. I go and sit where it looks like the edges of the two groups will end up near each other. By a quarter to ten every seat is taken except for a few next to the ring on opposite sides. I figure those are reserved for some of Monk and Paul's top guys.

About five to ten, just about everyone in the joint is stamping their feet and clapping their hands. They want action. It's like a big drum pounding away, one-two-three, and in a minute more they're all chanting in time with the stamping. On one side they're yelling "Monk-East-Man!" And on the other it's "Paul-Kell-y!" Each side's trying to out-yell the other. And the cops are in lines three deep against the three walls where the bar isn't, and they're in the aisles, and a line of them is standing around the outside of the ring, and all still have their guns in their hands.

So the yelling and stamping get louder and louder, and it's five after ten, and there's still no Paul or Monk, and the torches almost seem like they're flickering in time with the stamping and yelling. And then on Paul's side there's a cheer, and they're getting up on their feet and yelling at the top of their lungs.

It's Paul coming in, wearing a robe with red, white, and green stripes, like the flag of Italy. He's got a trainer with him and three guys wearing nice suits, and each of them with a girl who's dressed like the queen of the dance halls. Walking beside Paul, though, is a tall lady in a beautiful black and gold dress, and she's got a long pretty neck, and her chestnut hair is piled up perfect on her head, and she doesn't look like she belongs in any dance hall. Instead, she's like one of the Gibson Girls that look so classy in the magazine ads, a real lady. I hear someone near me say that it's Dora Madden, who runs Paul's classiest whorehouse.

And even though Paul's in his robe, he's carrying himself like he's the best-dressed guy in the place. His hair is combed perfect, his head is high, and he's got a little smile on his face as he raises his hand a couple times toward everyone cheering him. It's like he's walking into a high-tone restaurant and saying hello to high-tone people like Mr. Norton and his crowd.

He takes Dora to her seat, right up front, and kisses her hand as she sits down with his top guys and their girls. Then him and his trainer climb into the ring. And for a minute or two he stands there waiting, and the people on his side start stamping their feet and yelling "Where is Monk? Where is Monk?" And some guy yells, "The yellow Kike ain't gonna show!" And guys on Monk's side look like they're ready to go for them, but the cops raise their guns to their shoulders, the barrels up but ready to point straight ahead in a second, and the guys sit down.

Then after another minute, guys in the back on Monk's side of the place start yelling, and then others are, and they're standing up and clapping, and they're chanting "Kill him, Monk!"

And in a few seconds, I see Monk and the group he's got with him. Up front is my father and Tick-Tock, neither one with a girl. Then there's Big Jack Zelig, and he's got his arm around a girl who's grinning and waving at people, and it's Sadie, and then there's some guy working as Monk's trainer. And then I see Monk. He's got a beat-up old robe on that looks like he might have pulled it from the bathroom of his place above the laundry. He's wearing his derby mashed down on top of his head like always, and he's got a big crazy-looking grin, and then I see he's got a girl walking next to him, and he puts his arm around her. She's tall, kind of thin, with dark black hair, and she's all painted up and wearing the kind of dress that Sadie likes to wear, lots of bright colors and cut to show off whatever her body's got, and she's smiling. I know who it is right off, of course. And I'm thinking maybe if I hadn't done what I did with Miss Friedman, then Esther wouldn't be here like this with Monk, and I almost start crying from thinking about how much has gone wrong because of me. Monk spots me watching and waves at me like we're pals from way back, and then he leans over to Esther, says something, and points my way. She sees me, turns to Monk and kisses him on the cheek. And I see my father looking over at me, and now we both know what Monk's big treat for me tonight is.

My father and Tick-Tock and Big Jack and Sadie sit in the first row, and Esther sits down next to Sadie, but not before Monk pulls her to him, gives her a big kiss on the mouth and she puts her arms around him and kisses back.

I'm praying for the first time in a while, and what I'm praying for is that Paul kills Monk so that Monk will end up right across Jerome Avenue in the cemetery. And then I can go over to Woodlawn anytime I want and spit and piss on Monk's grave. And I'm thinking that if God and Paul don't kill him for me, then I will finally do it for myself and pretty soon.

Now I see that a guy with a big horn is announcing in the ring that there isn't going to be any kicking, gouging, or biting, and no hitting below the belt, and that they'll fight till somebody is dead or knocked out, or gives up. The last doesn't seem likely to anybody that's there.

They don't shake hands, and then there's a bell and they come at each other. Monk, though, still has his derby on, which he doesn't know, and when the ref reaches over and swats it off of his head, it goes rolling over to where Esther is, and she reaches into the ring, picks it up, and puts it in her lap. Right off, Monk charges at Paul, firing wild lefts and rights, and Paul, who didn't lose too often when he was boxing for a living, sidesteps and tags Monk with two left jabs and a right uppercut. Monk is right away bleeding out of his nose, and I'm hoping that a guy could bleed to death through the nose. And all the first round Monk keeps rushing and Paul keeps side-stepping and smacking him. Near the end of the round, Monk waves at Paul to come towards him and yells, "Fight like a man, you lousy Dago!" Paul stands there and waits as Monk rushes him again, and then he pops the ape some more. A couple times I look over to see how Esther's taking all this, but she's looking straight ahead, so I can't see an expression.

When Monk is in his corner after the first round, he doesn't sit down, he just stands and yells across the ring that Paul's "yellow, like all Guineas." Guys from Monk's crowd are standing too, screaming the same sort of stuff and cursing and waving their arms. Guys on Paul's side are yelling stuff back, but Paul's just sitting on his stool and swallowing some water and resting. Meanwhile, the cops have their guns up at their shoulders.

The second round goes like the first, except that Paul is starting to hit more at Monk's body. Monk's got a bandage still on his left side from where Paul's guy got him with the knife, in the alley, so now Paul keeps moving to Monk's left, getting in shots where the bandage is, and by the end of the round, the bandage is red through. Monk just keeps rushing in, throwing punches like a crazy man, and getting hit two, three shots every time. I don't know whether he's hit Paul even once, except on the arms.

It's just like what I read Gentleman Jim Corbett did to John L. Sullivan when they fought for the championship. He was faster and smarter than Sullivan, and there wasn't anything that Sullivan could do to stay champ. And that's the way it went for Monk for the next seven or eight rounds. If it had been anyone else than Monk taking that beating, I would have felt a little sorry for him. He was cut up over his eyes, his nose and mouth were bloody, and his trainer had ripped the bandage off of his side and just stuck tape over that knife cut that Paul had opened up again, and every two rounds the tape got so loose from getting wet with all the blood that the trainer had to pull it off and stick on another piece.

And the whole time, Sadie was jumping out of her seat and screaming up into the ring, but not Esther. She just sat there facing forward and hanging tight to Monk's derby. I wanted to see what she would do if Monk died right there.

Well, Monk, he didn't have any quit in him, of course. He just kept coming forward and taking punches that made his face look like a sponge that had sopped up too much blood and now was oozing it out. Monk's guys were still yelling for him, but they weren't yelling so loud now.

After the ninth round, one of them was just so aggravated that he goes tearing towards Paul's corner, yelling something like, "You Ginzo bastard, I'll kill you myself." He doesn't get near Paul, though, because one cop grabs him and another comes over and clubs him one-two right on the head with the butt of his pistol. The guy goes down, out ice-cold, and two more cops come over and carry him out. Meanwhile all the rest have their fingers on their triggers now, just waiting for someone else to try something.

After ten rounds, I was wondering how long Monk would last. He hadn't gone down yet, though you had to figure most human beings would have long before. Of course, Monk wasn't a normal human being. He was both less and more. He still didn't sit between rounds.

Paul meanwhile still didn't have a mark on his face, and his hair was still parted neat, and it almost didn't look like he'd even been in a fight except that his arms were bruised up from blocking so many of Monk's wild shots and he had Monk's blood splattered on him.

When they rang the bell to start the eleventh round, and

Paul saw Monk start rushing across at him again, I thought I saw a look cross his face like he was wondering was he ever going to finish this animal off. And then it was like he made up his mind that he would try to end it right now. Maybe he was tired of hurting his hands and arms, or just getting tired, or maybe because he hated Monk so much he wanted to kill him once and for all.

So this time, when Monk rushes, Paul sidesteps and tags him, like before, but now he stays right there and keeps hammering Monk, punch after punch, body and head. Monk's blood is getting splattered everywhere. His legs are getting like rubber, and Paul's crowd, they're up and yelling at the top of their lungs. And I'm up yelling, too, yelling "Kill him! Kill the ape! Kill him now!" When I realize what I'm yelling, I figure I better sit down and shut up before anybody sees me.

Paul throws a left hook to Monk's jaw and a right to his chin, and Monk drops down to his knees, tries to get up and falls over on his right side.

Everybody's standing now. Paul's guys are whooping and cheering and Monk's are yelling for him to get up. Paul's kind of crouched, like a panther, right over Monk, ready to sock him as soon as Monk gets back up on his feet, and meanwhile the referee's counting.

It looks like there's a better chance of Monk dying than there is of his getting up before the count gets to ten. I see Esther's head is down, like she can't look anymore. She's hanging on tight, still, to the derby. Sadie's screaming at Monk to get up, and my father's sitting there like he's staring straight at a wall. Tick-Tock, wearing his black coat like always, says something into my father's ear. My father nods and then turns and gives me a look and then stares straight ahead again.

Well, when the ref yells "six," Monk rolls over to his hands and knees, and at eight he's leaning on one knee and pushing himself off of the floor with the other, and that's when Paul finally makes a mistake. He steps toward Monk to hit him right as soon as that second knee is up, but Monk, just when he gets it an inch off of the floor at nine, bullrushes Paul, drives his shoulder into Paul's chest, and Paul staggers back on his heels and falls back onto the ropes, Monk is on him in a second, pounding away. Paul's trying to cover up. He knows what he's supposed to do, but he can't do it, because Monk is hitting him all over, like he's got maybe six arms instead of just two. Paul tries to lock up Monk's arms and hang on in a clinch till the round ends, but Monk's arms are too thick and going all over too fast.

Now Monk's guys are the ones yelling "Kill him," and Paul's crowd is standing there, not saying much. Monk hits Paul with a short, clubbing right hand behind Paul's left ear as Paul is trying to hang onto him, and Paul slumps forward, with his head resting on Monk's shoulder. Then Monk steps back, pushes Paul off of him, and hits him square in the puss with a right, and Paul, whose hair's not so neat now, falls straight onto his back.

Paul looks like he could be dead, except that his left foot is shaking back and forth faster than a dog's tail wags when it's all excited, so I figure he's not dead but maybe dying. And Monk is walking all over the ring, screaming something that's not words, and his arms are up, and he's grinning and he's leaving a trail of blood wherever he's walking, and his guys are jumping up and down and cheering, and calling his name.

And then Paul somehow gets himself up. And maybe if Monk hadn't been so busy celebrating he might have knocked him right back down for keeps, but by the time Monk hears the yells and rushes over, Paul, even though he ain't steady on his feet, is able to keep getting away from most of Monk's rushes and wild punches, and makes it to the bell.

Paul somehow got off of his stool for the twelfth, and Monk was right on him again. Paul, because of the beating he took, can't get away from Monk now, but Monk, who's slowing down too, is still getting tagged by Paul, even if Paul can't hit as hard anymore. So, all through the twelfth and thirteenth, both of them are getting hurt bad.

By the fourteenth, even this crowd seemed to be getting upset from what they were seeing. So it was mostly quiet now, except for the smack of the punches and the panting and groaning of the two guys trying to kill each other in the ring.

After Monk and Paul both went down in the eleventh, neither guy had gone down again. And they were grabbing and leaning all over each other more and more, both of them covered with their own blood and the other guy's and both exhausted. If it had been a regular boxing match with a regular crowd there, people would have been yelling it was time to stop it already.

Finally, in the fifteenth, Paul steps out of a clinch, gets his feet set as steady as he can and rips a right into the cut on Monk's side. Monk lets out a groan you could hear through the whole place, and Paul hits it again, and follows with a left to Monk's jaw. As Monk starts to go down, his left hand drapes over Paul's shoulder, and he has just enough still in him to let out a snarl that sounds like "Die, Dago!" and to drive a right into Paul's belly. You could hear the air go sucking out of Paul, and he and Monk go down together and lay there side by side. Everybody's on their feet, watching and quiet.

The ref starts counting. If one of them gets up, and the other doesn't, that guy wins, and he's got the other guy's business. Neither one makes it up all the way, and by the time the ref reaches ten, both of them are laying there again.

The ref stands over the two of them, waves his arms, and yells that the fight is over and that it's a draw. Then Boss Croker climbs into the ring and yells, "Okay, each guy keeps his business and keeps his nose out of the other side of the Bowery, and the first guy that acts like he ain't happy with that will find out fast what the City of New York and its grand police force can do. I won't ask the two of you to shake hands. I just say you better live and let live if you know what's good for you. So everybody, good night to you all, and get the hell out and go back downtown, with no trouble, or else."

And the cops start moving everyone out, and up in the ring the trainers get each guy onto his stool. And some of each one's top guys come into the ring, too, and even Dora over in Paul's corner and Esther in Monk's. Esther is looking at Monk like she's worried about him, because she's Monk's girl now, which makes me want to go running into the ring and look her straight in the face and tell her how her old man ended up in that morgue. But if I ever do that it can't be yet. So I just stand there and watch.

I start to go out with the crowd, and I'm thinking this is the worst I ever felt in my whole life. Then I see my old man looking over towards me. He nods like I should meet him right now.

I follow my father over to a corner in the shadows, and he says, "You didn't listen to me like I told you out on the fire escape."

"What do you mean?" I ask him.

"You couldn't keep from showing what you are feeling. Tick-Tock, he saw you yelling that Paul should kill Monk. He told me this, and he will tell Monk, who don't need any more reasons already why he should hate you. I said you were just trying to show Paul's people that you are really working for Paul. He nods, but I know what he's thinking. I'll put in good words for you, Morris, but I am not full of hope about this."

He goes back to the ring, and I leave. The cops have set up one way out for Monk's crowd and one for Paul's. I go with Monk's crowd, and, outside, the cops are marching us to one trolley line and Paul's group to another. They've got maybe twenty cars set up on each track and they're telling everybody that the cops will ride with them and that both lines are heading straight downtown with no stops, one ending up on the west side of the Bowery and the other on the East, and no one will be getting off till they get to the end of the line, and once they do, nobody will walk across the Bowery tonight either. There's some yells back and forth from the two crowds as they go trudging along, but it really doesn't look like either side wants a battle tonight. I figure they'll both be spoiling for a brawl soon enough, but for tonight they all saw enough and they're tired.

I wasn't in a hurry to get back downtown or anyplace else either. Aunt Gabriella and Uncle Giulio wouldn't be sitting up worrying where I was, because I'd told them I'd be spending the night over at my father's place. It got Aunt Gabriella aggravated when I told her, but I figured that was better than telling her where I was really going. And now that I'd been there, it didn't seem like there was anywhere I wanted to be or anyone I felt like seeing.

I pretended like I had to tie my shoe, and I stepped out of the crowd. I got down on one knee in a place under some trees and then I ducked away. Nobody noticed. A couple minutes later I was across Jerome Avenue, and I climbed up over a wall and was in the Woodlawn Cemetery. I was in a city of the dead. I walked down a narrow avenue in there, and I could read the headstones in the moonlight. Maybe Uncle Giulio had carved some of them.

I was tired, and I laid down on a stone bench, but it was too hard, so I figured what the hell, and I laid down right on the ground between a couple graves. I figured the people buried there wouldn't mind and that maybe I was where I belonged. The ground was soft, and the smells of the grass and the dirt were strong, and I told myself that it wouldn't be all that long anyway before me and everybody I knew and everybody in the car barn tonight would be under the grass. And right now that didn't make me sad at all.

A breeze starts up, and the branches start moving around and making a whispery sound, and maybe once I'd have gotten scared, thinking maybe about ghosts, but not now. I just laid there and told myself that there wasn't a thing about ghosts any scarier than what I'd just seen right across Jerome Avenue inside of the car barn.

I slept some, finally, and when the first birds woke me, I got up, all damp and smelling from the earth, climbed back over the wall and headed downtown. I walked the whole way, real slow, and tried not to think of anything. When I got back home, it was almost eleven. Mrs. Canzoneri, who lives on the first floor and sits at her window and watches people going in and out of the building but usually doesn't say much, sees me coming and says, "Massimo, you doing all right?"

I say, "Yeah, I guess so, Mrs. Canzoneri."

And she gives me this sad look and says, "*Povero ragazzo*," and I do feel like I'm a poor kid today, but I wonder how she knows it.

Then I go upstairs.

The door to Aunt Gabriella's place sticks and doesn't shut full unless you close it hard, which Aunt Gabriella and Uncle Giulio remember to do all the time, and I don't sometimes. But this morning I notice it's not closed all the way, and right away I feel like something ain't right.

And as soon as I'm inside, I know that it's not. Aunt Gabriella's sitting at the kitchen table, her head is down on her arms, and she's crying. Uncle Giulio's got his hand on her shoulder. And standing there talking to them in a soft voice is Father Basilio. So I'm guessing what happened. And my hands and my feet start tingling and I feel weak all over, and my lower lip and chin are quivering, and they're all looking at me like there's nobody in the world to feel more sorry for than me.

Father Basilio takes my hand. "Massimo," he asks, "how old are you?"

I can hardly get it out, but I say, "almost sixteen."

"Then you're old enough for me tell you man to man that

your mother died last night. A messenger brought the news over from the hospital early this morning."

I shake my head back and forth, and I say, "Then all the praying I did for her to get well didn't do any good, huh?"

He looks a little upset and says, his voice like sticky-sweet cherry cough syrup, "I know how hard this is for you, my son. But remember that God's wisdom is infinite, and not for us always to understand and never for us to question. Perhaps He saw how much your mother was suffering and He released her from her it."

"Yeah," I say, crying now, "then why did he have her get sick in the first place if he was sad because she was suffering so much?"

"My son," he tells me, and his voice doesn't sound as soothing now as it did before, "God had a plan for your mother, a good one, as He does for us all."

I think about all she went through, and I think about Esther, and Miss Friedman, and poor Johnny, and Izzie, and about my father's brother Moishe back in Poland, and I think about Billy with his pock marks and Mary-Margaret with her crazy eyes, and the sick lady and her baby that drowned off of the smallpox boat going to North Brother Island, and I think about everything I saw in the car barn the night before, and even about what a lot of the people below the ground that I slept with up at Woodlawn Cemetery must have gone through before they were finally done with everything, and I can't take this stuff that he's telling me. So I say "Listen, my mother wasn't in any plans of His and neither am I."

He backs off and looks at me like I slapped him across the mouth, and he's about to tell me, maybe, that, yeah, God does have a plan for me and it's to send me straight to hell sooner or later, but Aunt Gabriella gets up now and screams, "It's not his fault, Father. He don't know what he says. It's all because of his mother marrying a Jew, that Jew with the *malocchio*."

And she starts sobbing and sobbing, and Giulio takes her

in his arms, and I go over and I kiss her head, and she kisses my hand. And I just want the priest to leave us alone, which finally he does.

Two days later, we had the funeral. Aunt Gabriella wanted to have it at Father Basilio's church and then have my mother buried in some Catholic cemetery in the city, but I got her to agree that Mama should be buried out on Blackwell's. She liked it there as much as she could like anything at the end. Mary-Margaret was kind to her and made sure everybody else treated her good, and she enjoyed sitting on the sun porch and watching the river flow past the city. And the cemetery out there gives you a good view of everything she liked to see. Also, it didn't cost anything to get buried there, because it was all paid for by the city, which it wouldn't have been at the Catholic place, and I didn't want Gabriella and Giulio to have to pay to put my mother where she never wanted to be anyway.

Aunt Gabriella did have a priest come out to the island with us, but it was a Father Ranzini, a little old guy who didn't have much to say the whole trip, which was fine with me.

There was a small chapel there in the hospital, nothing but bare walls and some benches, and a couple windows. The walls had some cracks and needed a paint job, but I didn't care. The less it looked like a church or *shul* the better. Father Ranzini said some prayers over the plain wood coffin where they had put my mother, and since I got my way about her being buried out on Blackwell's, I wasn't going to fight Gabriella about that. I figured my mother would understand.

There wasn't much of a crowd there, just me and my aunt and uncle and the priest, some sick ladies from my mother's floor, who looked like they'd be joining her in the ground before too long, and there was Mary-Margaret and a couple other nurses, and Billy, who Mary-Margaret told what had happened. My father, who Giulio had told about it, wasn't there.

When Father Ranzini asked if anybody wanted to say something about my mother, I couldn't, because I wouldn't have gotten the words out even if I could have thought of something to say that wouldn't get people all aggravated. And Aunt Gabriella was too broke up also, and Uncle Giulio wasn't the kind to make any speech. So there was this quiet that didn't seem right, and then Mary-Margaret speaks up, and she says, "I'd like to say something, if Mrs. Levy's family wouldn't mind."

I managed to get out that I would like that, and Aunt Gabriella and Uncle Giulio nodded that they would, too.

So Mary-Margaret said something like "Now, I only got to know Alda Levy late in her life, when she was so terribly ill, but I consider myself fortunate to have known her even for a short time. I remember that the day I met her, she noticed a religious medal that I wear, and she asked me what it was. I told her it was an image of Saint Jude, also known as Thaddeus, and Alda recognized the name, 'Ah,' she said, 'San Giuda Taddeo, he is the saint for the lost causes. If I believed, then he should be my saint, because I myself am a lost cause,' and she chuckled at that. One pretty afternoon, in fact, I took her to the little Church of the Good Shepherd that we have here, and I showed her the statue in there for St. Jude, and she said he had a noble and mild face. So did she. Though her health failed her, she was anything but a lost cause. She was a strong and loving woman, with the courage of her conviction that people ought to help people. I'll miss her, and I know that she's going to a place where there won't be any suffering like what she went through so bravely here." And then she said, "Thanks for letting me say a few words on her behalf. I loved her."

I went over and hugged her and cried on her shoulder, and I saw the St. Jude medal hanging from her neck and thought "San Giuda Taddeo, Sand Jew today oh," and as I cried, I also knew now what it was my mother had been trying to tell me.

Then we were outside at the grave. I dropped in the first shovelful of dirt on her coffin. When I heard it hit the lid, I remembered the splash I heard from way down in the river when Izzie fell in. I wanted to believe that Mary-Margaret was right and that my mother was in a better place and that maybe Izzie was too. Mary-Margaret was good, and maybe good people have a better shot at knowing these things, but I wasn't so sure about any of it.

I watched while Gabriella and Giulio, and then Mary-Margaret and Billy all tossed some dirt on the coffin, and then Billy says, "Moe, old man, how about if I finish off filling this in, so you can know it was done by a friend instead of by these guys from the hospital, who don't know you and probably could use a rest after the digging they did already today?" And I told him that would be fine, and we hugged each other, and I thought it would be so much nicer if God was like Billy and Mary-Margaret, instead of being like He was, or not being at all.

Then just as we were all leaving, except for Billy, I saw a guy standing by himself on a little hill a ways off. He was in the shade from a tree, but I could see it was my father, and he was putting what looked like a handkerchief into his pocket. He saw me watching, nodded towards me, and walked away. By the time we got to the dock for the steamer, he was gone. He'd probably paid somebody to bring him over in a private boat.

As I was on the steamer that afternoon heading back to the city, where Monk and Esther and all the rest of them were, I finally figured out how I could bring down Monk and what I was going to do about Esther and about a whole lot of things, and I knew I'd travelled a lot farther along the track towards where I was going.

XVI

The next day, I went back out to my mother's grave as soon as I could. The dirt there still looked so fresh, and that was the only thing, except for her name on a little metal tag stuck into the ground, that made her grave any different from all the others with their own little metal tags. There weren't any headstones like in the Woodlawn Cemetery, because the city wouldn't pay for them. I told her I missed her and that I was always going to think about her and all the stuff she believed in.

When I left the little cemetery, I saw Mary-Margaret, who was taking a walk. She asks, "Are you doing okay, Massimo? Billy and I are worried. The last few times we saw you, we could tell something was troubling you, something besides your mother's condition."

I say, "Yeah, some things have been going on, but I'm going to be able to take care of them now, I think."

She looks like she's not so sure. "You know you can always call on either Billy or me for help."

"I know. Thanks. And in case I need some, I'll let you guys know for sure. One thing, though, I want to go into the Church of the Good Shepherd, where you took my mother. I'd like to see the statue of St. Jude."

She tells me it's set back in a little kind of nook in the shadows, and it has its hands out, like it's saying, "Come over here, I can help you, even if you think nobody can."

So I go, and I notice that there's a little space between the bottom of the statue and the wall that it's up against. I can't see into that space because the whole nook is in the shadows, and the space is so narrow, but I can get my hand in, and I'm expecting I'll find something besides cobwebs or a mouse nest, and I do. I feel the edge of something metal, and I get my fingertips around it and pull it out slow, and it's a tin box with a lock on it.

I make sure nobody's around, and I take the key my mother gave me and stick it into the lock, and it fits. The stuff that's inside is a certain special ring, and what it's ringing around gives me a shiver, and there's also a thick yellow packet that says on it that it's for me and that I shouldn't open it unless my father is dead. I lock the box up, put it back where it was, and put the key back around my neck and inside my shirt.

Early that night, I went over to the key-shop to talk to Esther. We hadn't spoken a word since the day I beat up Mendel. No one was in the shop when I got there, except for Mendel, who was closing up, and when he saw me, he picked up a hammer and backed away from me. I raised my hands open in front of me and said, "Mendel, I ain't here to fight you anymore. I was mad at you 'cause of you touching Esther like you did, but I hurt you worse than you needed, and I know that. I'm sorry."

He was still holding the hammer up and looking at me like I was some kind of wild animal that was going to spring at him and rip him apart.

So I say, "Look, Mendel, we buried my mother yesterday out at the TB hospital, I was there again today, and, believe me, I ain't going to leave her grave and go and get in a fight right away, okay?"

He lowered the hammer now, nodded, and said, "May your mother be in heaven."

"If there is one, that's where she is." Then I say, "Now, you don't owe me a thing, I know that, but could you please tell me where Esther is? It's real important."

He shrugged, looked sad, and says, "Vhere should she be? Vit' Monk, of course. So, Big Shot, you beat me up so bad because I touched the girl, like I know I should not have, but I vas lonely and she vas so pretty and I couldn't make myself not to do it, but now she is vit' Monk, who touches her plenty, so vhat are you going to do about *this*, Mister Big Shot?"

"Why is she with him?"

Mendel sighs, "Vhy is she vit' him? Vhy do you t'ink? Because she is pretty and because he vants her to be vit' him, and my cousin, he gets vhat he vants. You know vhat I t'ink? I t'ink if you had not made so big a fuss over her, he vould not hef decided that maybe he vill hef her for himself. But vit' him, who can know?"

"He forced her to be with him, didn't he?"

"Force?" he says, "there vas no force. There vas money. My cousin, he tells Esther that if she is nice vit' him, then her mother shall own this shop, free and clear, and that he shall pay more than half of my salary. So now her mother owns the shop. But this I should tell you also. I don't t'ink the money by itself vould have been enough. Also, Monk uses his charm, the charm of a strong young animal vhat got no doubts and no fears and grabs vhat it vants. And vhen Monk smiles at a girl and shows she is vhat he vants, she is flattered, because she sees how everybody is scared of him, and that vhen she is vit' him, he can grab for her vhatever she shall vant."

"But he's an ugly ape, and Esther is too smart not to know it," I says.

"Yes, but he has never smiled at you like he does at these girls who he thinks they are special, and he has decided for now that Esther is the most special of the special. She vas scared of him first, but he kept smiling and acting even bashful, like he is only a boy who likes his mischief but is good at his heart, and soon she vas not so scared of him no more, especially vhen he was treating her mother so good, vit' candy and flowers, just like he brings for Esther, and taking them both to restaurants.

"This vas going on for about a veek, and then the night came vhen he took Esther out by himself, and he had brought her a dress for this, a dress like she had never had before, and the kind that a girl like her she should not put on her body. But she vas flattered, and vhen I saw her look in the mirror and smile, I vanted to tell her vhat my cousin is, but vhat could I do?

"Her mother smiled vhen Esther and Monk vent out the door together, because it had been settled that morning who shall own the shop and how I shall be paid. And vhen I came in to open up the next morning, Mrs. Goldstein said I should be quiet, because Esther vas sleeping. She had not come in until it vas four o'clock, and about this Mrs. Goldstein vas not so unhappy like many mothers vould be."

"She's not even sixteen yet."

Mendel nodded. "But Monk, he is only twenty-six, and he took up vit' this Sadie, that now is second vit' him to Esther, vhen Sadie vasn't fifteen yet. He likes young best. And he likes Esther better than he has liked anyvun in years. He has told me this."

"So where do you think she is with Monk tonight?"

"He's just taking her to dinner tonight, because he has some business to take care of after. She said they vas going to Ostrofsky's Hungarian, over on Delancey."

So ten minutes later, I'm standing across the street from Ostrofsky's, and looking at Monk and Esther, who are sitting at a table next to the window. Monk always likes to be seen, and Esther doesn't seem to mind. She's smiling and even giggling. It seems like ten years ago that I was outside of Delmonico's with her and trying to keep her from knowing that her old man was dead, and now she's sitting and eating and laughing with the guy who murdered him.

Ostrofsky's Hungarian isn't Delmonico's, of course, but it's no dump either, and the food isn't cheap, and I'm still outside looking in, but Esther's in there looking out now, and wearing a dress that's not as bad as what she wore into the car barn, but still the kind she shouldn't be wearing. She sees me, and then a guy pushing clothes on a cart passes in the street, and then a wagon passes from the other side, and when I can see in again, now Monk is looking at me, too. And even from across the street I can see he's got a big grin on his puss, even though his mug's all cut up and swole still from Paul's fists, and it's like he's showing off to me with that grin how he's got everything his way, and I don't. I want to thumb my nose at him, but I don't want to show I'm upset, so I just smile back and wave a little, like I just happened to be passing by and spotted the two of them, and it doesn't mean anything to me, the two of them together. And I walk off, telling myself that Monk's not gonna be laughing at me for much longer.

From way off, on the corner of Norfolk, I wait for Monk and Esther to leave the restaurant, and then I follow them, waiting to see if Esther's going to be back in the shop alone soon. Her and Monk are holding hands. She's carrying her head high, like she ain't ashamed of a thing, like she's the queen in the Bible that she's got the name of. Some of the men they pass tip their hats to Monk, and he doesn't take his derby off to them, but nods like a king getting cheered by the crowd. Guys at fruit stands offer Monk stuff, and he has them give it to some guys of his who are walking behind them. By the time they've gone two blocks, the guys are carrying armloads.

So I'm walking along, watching all this and hoping that Mendel was right, that they aren't headed to The Palm, with the rooms upstairs for guys and their girls, or to Monk's place above the laundry. And while I'm following them, something out of the corner of my eye tells me maybe I'm being followed myself from across the street. So I stop and look in a store window. It's Halperin's shop for Jewish religious stuff. There are prayer caps and prayer scarves and prayer books, but what I'm looking at is the reflection off of the glass, and what I see is myself and, watching me from across the street and pretending he's not, Davey. It makes me mad, but not so mad that I don't realize that it could be good for what I've got to do tonight if Davey follows me all the way to the key-shop, if that's where Monk is taking Esther now.

Well, that is where he's taking her, just like Mendel said. When they get there, Mendel's gone, and Monk pulls out a key from his own pocket and unlocks the door. He has his guys bring the groceries inside, and then take off, and then him and Esther are alone, just inside the door. They're standing in shadows, but it's not so dark that I can't see what they're doing. Monk's pressing Esther tight to him. Her hands are resting on his shoulders, not shoving him away. Their mouths are mashing together. Then Monk's hands go down her back till they're on her *tuchus*, and he's rubbing it, and he's grinding his front up against hers.

And then Monk lets go of her, and he's giving her a sweet little kiss on the cheek and heading down the street. I see Esther lock the door, smooth out her dress, and look in a mirror.

I wait till Monk's out of sight, and I cross the street. Davey's watching me from behind a wagon stopped at the curb. I don't know if he could see the stuff that I just saw with Esther and Monk. Maybe it would serve him right if he did. Maybe it serves me right, too.

I come up to the door of the shop and rap on it. Esther looks out, sees that it's me and waves at me to go away. I point that I want to come in. Again she says no. I put my hands together like I'm begging her, but it doesn't make any difference. She gets up and she's going to turn off the light, and go into the rooms in the back, but I yell so she can hear me, and I pick up a broken piece of the curb and make like I'll throw it through the glass door if she doesn't let me in, and so she comes over, looking at me like I'm the most disgusting guy in the world, and she opens the door just a crack and tells me that she's got nothing to say to me.

I tell her, "You gotta let me in, Esther, it's real important. There's stuff that you've got to know, right now. I know I acted bad, but that doesn't mean that you shouldn't hear what I've got to say. I promise I won't stay and bother you."

She says nothing, but she opens the door wide enough for me to come in, and she sits down and looks at me with her chin high in the air, so that even though I'm the one standing it's like she's looking down at me. "So what do you have to tell me?" she asks in a cold voice.

"Well, first, and this ain't the real important stuff I came to tell you, but it's important to me, 'cause it's something I owe you. I owe you an apology for kissing Miss Friedman and thinking about her the wrong way. I never should have done it. I liked her, but I loved you, so it was dumb and wrong. I was a *shmuck*."

Her chin is still up there, and her eyes are cold.

I shrug and say, "I'm so sorry it worked out so wrong, 'cause all the time I was thinking, *dreaming*, I guess, that you and me would get married to each other someday."

She drops her head a little when she hears that, and maybe even looks a little sad. When she looks at me again, her chin's not so high, and her eyes aren't as cold.

I say, "I lay awake at nights a lot now and think about that afternoon when you taught me about the statue of Diana on top of the Madison Square Garden, and I also think about when we looked into Delmonico's and saw those people with their fancy clothes."

She looked down at her dress now.

"And I think about the day we spent up at the park, and I feel lousy about what I did to Mendel here in the shop. He didn't deserve to get beat up like that, and I had no right to do it anyway, 'cause of what I did with Miss Friedman, but I beat him up because I was angry and embarrassed about that, and I loved you so much, and I just let go. So, like I say, I want to apologize for all that."

She gives me a little nod and then she says, "Okay" real soft.

And I can't help saying to her, "If I hadn't been such a *shmuck*, maybe you'd be with me now, instead of with a guy like Monk Eastman."

And, yeah, she gets a little angry when I say this, but it's more like she's trying to tell me that she hasn't really been doing anything wrong. She raises her chin up a little again and she says, "I think lots of people, including you, make Edward out to be a lot worse than he is. In case you didn't know, that's his real name, and he likes me to call him that instead of his ugly nickname."

I say, "You know what *Edward's* guys did to the kids and teachers in the summer programs at the schools around here, and especially to Miss Friedman?"

Right off she comes back, "Yeah, and she deserved whatever she got, the *schlooche*." And then she looks a little embarrassed, like deep down she really doesn't mean it. "Edward said that he just wanted to get them to stop saying bad things about him, and he sent his younger guys over there so the teachers and kids wouldn't be too scared, but the guys just went too far."

"Don't let him sell you any bill of goods about that or about anything else, Esther."

"Edward has helped Mama and me a lot."

"And he's bought you lots of clothes, I see."

She blushes and says, "Yes, he's been very nice to me, and he's also been a gentleman."

"That ain't typical of him."

"Well, like you and Miss Friedman, we've kissed a little… that sort of thing, but we've never done… well, you know, what you wanted to do with her. Edward promised me that there wouldn't be any of that until… *unless* I was, you know, ready to do it."

She's blushing redder than before and she can't look at me when she's saying this. I really want to believe her, and I guess I do.

And now I start to tell her the truth about Monk and what

I'm going to try to do to make things better for her and every-
body, but I want to kind of ease her into hearing it if I can,
"You can't believe his promises, Esther. He doesn't keep them.
The guy's a murderer."

"That's not true," she says. "I asked him about that. He
admitted that he killed a few men but only when they were
trying to kill him."

"You believe that?"

She's still not looking at me. "Yes, I do. He's crude. I know
that. You're pretty crude yourself, you know. But he wasn't
treated well when he was a kid. His father used to get drunk
and beat him. And his mother, who tried to stop his father
from beating him, died when he was just a kid, and he hung
around on the streets over in Brooklyn, where he grew up, so
he wouldn't have to be at home with his father. And out on the
streets, he got mixed up with rough guys, which made him act
rougher than he really is."

I just say again, "Esther, he's a murderer. I know it. You've
seen that guy Asher with him some, right?"

She nods. "Yeah, I saw him once or twice."

"I ain't ever told you this, 'cause I was ashamed to tell
you it, but Asher's my old man. I know from him what Monk
Eastman is."

She looks down at her dress and smooths it. I look over at
the counter and see the little machine where her father once
showed me how he made keys.

"Esther, look I've got to tell you now the important thing
that I came here to tell you, and I swear to you, I wouldn't lie
about something like this. I don't need my father to tell me that
Monk has murdered guys. I saw Monk murder someone."

"Oh?" she says, like she's trying to show both to me and
herself that she's not going to believe what I've got to tell her.

"Yeah, a while back, I saw him hold a guy off the Brooklyn
Bridge by his legs and drop him into the river. I wish I could
have done something to stop it, but I couldn't, because there

were too many of Monk's guys there, and probably I was too scared to, anyway."

She looks frightened. "Well, maybe the man deserved it. Maybe he was a killer himself." Her hands are all over the skirt of her dress now. I'm so sorry for her, but she has to know.

"No, he didn't deserve anything like that. He was a good guy, mainly, a real good guy." I take a deep breath and I'm about to tell her, and I see Davey behind a wagon, looking in at us.

"Wait a minute," I say, "there's somebody here who'll tell you that I ain't lying about any of this." And I go and open the door, and I yell out, "Davey, I know you're out there watching. Get in here. I ain't going to hurt you. Esther needs to talk to you."

I say to Esther, "Davey's been your friend, right?"

She says, in a choked voice, "Well, he's been coming by and talking with me sometimes, and asking if my mom or I need him for any errands."

"Yeah, he loves you. He told me that over at school. That's why he told you about me and Miss Friedman, even though him and me were friends. He ain't going to lie to you about this when I put it to him. He ain't going to lie to you about Monk either, even though he works some for Monk, in case you don't know it, and even though, like everybody else, he's scared of him."

Davey comes in, giving me a dirty look. He still wants Esther for himself, even if it's after Monk is finished with her and maybe has made her one of his whores. I'm guessing Davey figures that by then she'll be glad to have even a sneaky little punk like him show up and say, "Marry me, no matter what, I don't care."

"Davey," I say, "tell Esther what we saw out on the bridge that night."

"What night?"

"Davey, just tell her. She needs to know."

He looks nervous, so I grab his arm and twist it behind him, and I say, "Tell Esther who Monk dropped off of the bridge."

"Ow," he says, "you're gonna break it, you dumb *bulvan*. If I tell, Monk will kill me when he finds out."

"Yeah," I say, twisting some more, "and *I'll* kill you right now if you don't. But if you do tell, then we could maybe help each other. So who did Monk drop off the bridge that night, Davey?"

"You bastid, Moish. He dropped Izzie into the river."

"That's what I came to tell you, Esther," I say to her, "it was Monk that killed your father. I figured you needed to know. I'm sorry."

Esther looks at me for a second, like I was the one who did it, and she starts sobbing and then she's ripping at her dress, like she wants to tear it off of herself.

I try to put my arms around her, but she pushes me away, and says, "You always knew, and you never told me! You *are* a bastard!"

"Esther, I *couldn't* tell you. Monk made me work for him, spying on what Paul Kelly was doing against him, and he said that if I worked good for him, he'd make sure nothing bad would happen to you or your mother, that the two of you wouldn't end up out on the streets, and that he wouldn't force you to become one of his whores, or... make you his girlfriend if he felt like it. That's how he made me do it, 'cause he knew how I felt about you. So what was I going to do? He pays off the cops, and he could also get fifty guys who would swear he wasn't even near the bridge that night, so what good would telling you do?"

The tears are pouring down, and the make-up she's got on that she never used to wear is all smeary. I want to go over and wipe her face, but I don't try. I just tell her, "But when I saw up at the fight that Monk had broke his promise to me and had you there with him, then I figured I had to tell you. I also wanted to tell you because I've got something on Monk now that I can use to maybe get him sent to jail or even to the death-house, which is where he ought to end up. It was something in a tin box that my mother was hiding. She died out at Blackwell's a couple days ago and I discovered it and then hid it away someplace on my own."

While she's still crying, Esther says, "Oh, I'm so sorry about your mother, Morris." She looks like she wants to maybe touch me to show that she's sorry, but she holds back. Still I realize this is the first time she said my name so far tonight.

Davey says, "I'm sorry, too, Moish." And I see that I got so worked up trying to tell everything to Esther that I forgot Davey was there and that he might go spilling everything to Monk. But I see that Davey does really look a little sad for me, and I'm thinking maybe he's not rat all through and through. After all, me and him had been pals since the first grade.

I say, "Thanks, Esther. Thanks, Davey. But at least she ain't suffering anymore, and that's something, anyway." And because I figure I've got to trust Davey some now, I tell both him and Esther, "I'm going to take what she was holding onto and use it to get some important people, honest cops and honest political guys and honest newspapermen, to see that now's the time to take Monk down. And it could help plenty if the two of you were in with me. Davey, I know you've been working for Monk, just like me, but neither of us owes the guy anything, and you just can't trust him. If you was to swear along with me to people that we were there and saw what happened to Izzie, it could help a lot, along with what I'm going to show them from the tin box my mother was hiding. And then if Esther and her mother could tell people about how Monk came by the shop with this paper that we swear we saw him make Izzie sign, then they'll really know we're not making this stuff up."

Esther tells me, "I'll do whatever you think can hurt Monk," and then, in this cold, low voice, that doesn't sound like anything I ever heard from her, even when she was her most mad at me, she says, "I want him dead."

Davey and me both look at her for a second. I say, "I ain't gonna argue with that, Esther," and then I turn to Davey, "Whatta ya say, Davele?"

Davey looks nervous, but he takes a deep breath and he says, "I'll help, but I'm doin' it just for Esther and not for you, even though I'm still sorry about your mother."

I tell him, "Okay, fair enough."

Esther says, "I gotta tell my mother tonight when she gets back from Aunt Hilda's. She's going to drop dead or run through the streets yelling about it to everybody and then drop dead."

"You've got to keep her calm," I say. "I don't want Monk finding out nothing about this until after I've done it."

She says, "Let me get out of this thing that I'm wearing and wash up, and let's go to the newspapers tonight and tell the whole city the story."

I see that Davey looks so nervous now he could almost cry. I say, "Davey, don't look so worried, the ape won't know anything until it's too late for him."

"I'll do whatever Esther wants."

I tell them that I don't have the tin box with me, that I'm hiding it somewhere safe, and she's got to be patient, and Davey and me will meet her at the shop the next afternoon, and go talk to some people, and that she shouldn't tell her mother a thing until afterwards.

She says, "Okay, I'll try not to let her know, though it's gonna be tough not to, if she starts telling me again about how good Edward, I mean Monk, really is. Oh, I was so *stupid*!"

"Is he coming by tomorrow?"

"I don't know. He said maybe he'd be by tomorrow night and take me out somewhere."

I tell her that I'll try to think of something to make sure that she doesn't have to see Monk's face again, unless it's in a courtroom. And then I ask, "Are you still real mad at me?"

She doesn't look right at me, and her head's down some. And she says, "Not so much."

"Thanks, that makes me feel a little better, anyways," and I see that it also makes Davey look like he feels a little worse, and he says to Esther, "I'm real sorry too about how things have went, and if I should of did anything different, I apologize."

Esther looks over at him, like you'd look over at a runty little kid that you feel sorry for more than you like him, and she gets up and takes his shoulders and kisses him on the forehead. She's taller than him. Davey looks like he could cry.

So we set up a time to meet back at the shop and Davey and me walk out together. We go along for about a block and a half, without saying anything. I buy myself some chocolate drops and a Moxie. I ask Davey if he wants something. He says he ain't hungry. We walk along some more, and I say, "Here, have a chocolate drop. Eat, you need the weight or the girls ain't gonna like you." He takes it, gives me a look, and says, "There's only one girl I want to like me."

We walk along quiet for another block, until we're at the corner where we have to split up.

I say, "See you back at the shop tomorrow."

He says, "Yeah," and walks off.

I'm starting to wonder right then whether he really could be rat all the way through, and I know my old man would say I got careless back at the shop. But I tell myself, well, I took my chances with Davey tonight and I'm just going to have to live or die now with how it turns out. I look at my Moxie bottle and see the guy on the label looking at me just like he did before. I feel like I can look him right back in the eye now, because I'm doing what I know I've got to do.

XVII

Early next morning, I showed up at my father's apartment, where he never expected to see me, because he never gave me the address. I'd gotten it a couple days before by asking a kid I knew who delivered from the cleaners. My old man was living a few blocks north of Houston, where it wasn't so crowded as where I lived.

When he let me in, he saw right off that I noticed he had real nice furniture and more than just a couple rooms, and this made him look a little uncomfortable, like he figured I was thinking maybe he hadn't done so right by me. But I wasn't thinking that, not much anyway. I was just thinking that he gave me and my mother what he figured we were worth to him. After all, he was an accountant, and he'd learned how to work out the numbers.

I wasn't there to try to make him feel bad. If he wanted to, that was up to him. I was there to tell him I found the box and warn him about what I was going to do with what I found in it. I figured I owed him that much, anyway.

Well, it turned out that Monk knew already that I had it, and I was in big trouble. You see, this meeting that Monk went to after he took Esther home from Ostrofsky's Hungarian, was a big one, with Monk and Paul both there and all their top guys, including my father. What happened was that Monk and

Paul decided that they didn't like being told what to do by Croker, the Tammany guy. So they agreed to secretly pay off a guy named Van Wyck that Croker was backing for mayor in the fall, and then when Van Wyck got in, he'd double-cross Croker, throw him out as Tammany boss, and put in some guy who wouldn't order Monk and Paul around so much and who they could bribe cheaper. Paul was going to use the people he knew from the reformers to help Van Wyck and put Croker on the skids. And then Monk and Paul would either work together on business downtown or start trying to wipe each other's business out, whatever they felt like. That was the plan, and they were happy with it.

And my old man said the meeting was ending with everybody in a good mood, and then a couple bad things happened. The first was that as Monk and Paul were chatting away before heading out, they got to talking about the stuff that I told each guy the other one had been planning to do to him and his business, and they doped out real quick that I had been lying to the both of them. My father said that Monk looked crazy-mad, like he wanted to strangle me, and that Paul just looked cold, "like he was your hangman," my father said.

Monk then turned to my old man, and asked, "Asher, you got somet'in' to spill about dis?" My old man said he told Monk that he had never suggested for him to bring me into the gang, which he said Monk didn't like hearing one little bit. And then Monk snarls at him, "You gonna object, Asher, if I give da lying *momzer* what he deserves?"

My father tells me, "I shrugged and answered Monk the only answer I could, which was 'What he deserves, he should get, son or no son. I warned him, like a father should, not to fool around, and he didn't listen. This is how it is.' And Monk, he gives me a wolf's smile, and he says, 'Sooner or later everyone gets what he deserves, Asher,' and a chill goes through me."

I say to my father, "I'm sorry. What I did didn't do you any favors."

He shrugs, smiles a little, and says, "Life has never done me no big favors, *boychik*. The Cossacks are everywhere." He's wearing the same suit that he had on the morning that he came by the Fish Market dock. It still looks fresh and new, but his face is lots more tired-looking.

My father then tells me the second bad thing that happened right after the meeting. They're all walking out onto the street, and Davey comes rushing up and says, "Mr. Eastman, I got to talk to you. There's big trouble."

Monk says, "Okay, kid, you interrupt me when I'm talkin' wit' my pal Paul Kelly, like two gentlemen, dis better be good."

And Davey, who doesn't have the good sense to think about it, says right out in front of Paul and everybody, according to my old man, "Moishe Levy says he found something real important in a tin box that his dead mother was hidin', something that he's gonna take to honest cops and important people, he says, and bring you down."

Monk, who doesn't even try to pretend like this doesn't bother him, looks over at Paul, who's acting like he didn't hear anything he wasn't supposed to, and then grabs Davey by the neck and yanks him over where Paul and his guys can't hear, and he says, "Do you know what da bastid lying traitor found, you stupid little piece of horseshit you?"

Davey says he doesn't know what, just that it was big stuff. Monk looks over at my father, like he's figured it all out, and says, "Jeeze, I wonder why your dead wife would of had it, Asher, unless your kid's just making up anot'er story, huh?" Then he says, "Nah, dere's somet'in' to it, I t'ink. What could be in dat box? You wouldn't know not'in' about it, would you, Asher?"

My father said Monk was saying his name like it was a curse word. Well, my old man says he shrugged and told Monk, "This boy, he's crazy from his mother, crazy from the start. I don't know nothing about what he talks about. He tells stories, like you just heard from Paul. There's nothing there but sickness in his head." He says that Monk doesn't look for a minute like he believes this, but all he says is, "Yeah, but he's *your* kid, too, Asher."

My father says he shrugged again, and Monk stared at him a long minute and turned back to Davey, who he's still holding by the back of his neck, and he says, "He didn't tell you dis by yourself, runt. He don't like you dat much no more. Who else was dere?"

Davey didn't want to answer, my father says. The little rat didn't want Esther hurt, just me. I figure Davey saw that Esther was maybe starting to like me a little again, and he got so jealous that he ratted on me so that Monk would put me out of the picture. He was just too mad and dumb to know that he was putting Esther in danger with me, the lousy punk. I was surprised that he hadn't growed a tail by then.

So, my father tells me, "Davey says nothing, but it don't matter, because Monk says to your little friend, 'So he told Esther wit' you standin' dere, ain't dat it?' And he squeezes the back of this Davey's neck so hard that the boy is howling with the pain. And Monk says, 'And he told Esther about what happened on da Brooklyn Bridge dat night, right?' Davey says, 'Right, right.' And then Monk asks, 'And now she's gonna work wit' him to do me dirt, right?' And again Davey, he screams with the pain and he says, 'Right, right.' Then Monk says, 'Asher, I knew your kid wouldn't like me bein' wit' his darlin', but I didn't know his mot'er was hidin' no tin box dat he was gonna find, right, Asher?'"

My father answered him, "Who knew, and who is to say there is such a box as this, or what could be in it?"

"Yeah, Asher," Monk says to him, "who's to say?"

Monk kicks Davey in the balls, and while Davey's laying there, holding himself and crying, Monk says, "T'anks for bringing me da news, and dat's for bringin' dat big mule of Asher's along in da first place to da bridge dat night."

Then he tells my father, "You go home, Asher, to dat new woman and new kid of yours and spend a little time wit' dem, which you probably don't spend enough. I'll let you know real soon what me and da boys decide we're gonna do about da big kid, but you ain't gonna be part of the decidin'."

My father says to me now, "Don't you make no mistake about this, Moishe. He wants that you should be killed before you can go to talk to someone. Whether his men are to do this themselves when they find you or bring you to Monk for him to do it himself like he would enjoy so much, this I cannot say."

"Why didn't they come for me last night?"

"To grab a boy from out of his Italian aunt and uncle's apartment and kill him, Monk, he knows this would seem to the Italians too raw to take from a Jew. Even Paul would think this is what the Italians call an *infamia*. It could cause a fuss which right now Monk don't need. To snatch you where no one should see it, or want to talk about it if they do, this is more to their liking. Also, Monk probably does not believe you would have this tin box with you. He thinks that if he has you followed, then you will lead him to it. And then he will have the judge's ring and have you dead and no more worries.

"I promise you, you did not come here sight unseen, Moishe. They are watching you every step that you are taking now. And they will be making sure that you shall not contact anyone who can hurt Monk and that I shall not do this, neither. Because I too am being watched. Go to the window, Moishe, don't open up the blinds. Just look through the slats. Is there a thin man across the street, leaning against a lamppost? He is in a gray suit and a straw hat with a red band, and he looks like he is reading a newspaper."

"Yeah, he's there, all right."

"He has been there since I woke up and looked out of the window this morning. He is watching my doorway, and when I leave, he shall fold up his paper and follow, and he shall not be following alone, neither. Monk, he knows that I am afraid for my life now, and he wants to make sure that I don't go to talk to nobody about him."

"Do you think they're watching Esther, too? Would Monk do that?"

"Why wouldn't he? He is considering to himself what he shall do with her. Monk might make it so she shall end up like her father, in the river, or it might be his pleasure to force upon her opium and make her a drug slave who works in his whorehouses till she ain't so pretty no more and then gets sold to the Chinks for their dives. This has happened with some of Monk's girls. So she is in danger every bit as much as you are."

"Big joke on me. I came here to warn you about what I was going to do, so you could maybe protect yourself."

He smiles and says, "Thank you for thinking about me, though whether I deserve that you should might be another story. Ah, Moishe, I think there is nothing that we can do that could help me now. I am frightened, but I must also be resigned. Still, I am glad you came today, because I have for you these pages, which I was trying to figure out how I should get to you. They could maybe help you. It is my testimony about some of the crimes that Monk has committed and the people he has paid off. I have worked on this through the night. There is a lawyer in this building who put a legal seal on it that means that I swore that everything I have here is the truth.

"And I have this, too," he says, showing me another paper. "This is a list of the politicians and police officers that Paul is paying off and how much each gets. I'm sure they would be very upset if they thought Paul got so careless that their names should come out public. And the reformers he's fooling wouldn't be fooled by him no more. I got my ways of investigating, and I was going to give this to Monk to convince him I was somebody he should still keep around. But now, no matter what, he don't want me around anymore. You keep this with everything else I am giving you. You could use it maybe to protect yourself from this Paul Kelly."

213

"Why don't you use it yourself?" I ask him.

"Because Mr. Paul Kelly cannot protect me from Monk, even if he wanted to. That is why I never even gave a second to the thought that I should leave Monk to work for him."

Then he puts all the papers in an envelope, and tells me, "You take this now." And I open my shirt, stick the envelope inside, and button up.

He says, "When somebody comes to do what Monk wants him to, I shall tell him that there is testimony that will go to people if I am killed. It will not help, because Monk has made up his mind to end me. I am to be an example, for failing him or betraying him or just for knowing too much, or whatever his wild mind tells him I should be made an example for. And he will be willing to take his chances getting rid of me instead of to change his mind, which he does not like to do, especially in front of his guys."

"And you, my older son, you must try to get to people who can protect you, and maybe help you make Monk pay for what he has done, for what I have helped him do, since you want so much that he should have to pay." He shook his head, smiled real sad, and said, "But, remember, his kind don't pay so often in this world, like I told you before."

He didn't say anything for a minute, and then he rubbed his nose up between his eyes, and said, "Moishe, my Hannah, she ain't nothing but a baby herself. She came off the boat just three years ago with her father and her big brother. The father is sick with his heart and drops dead a couple weeks after they are here. The big brother, he runs off somewheres like Chicago or Detroit with some bum friends he made, and Hannah, she knows nobody here except a married cousin who takes her in. I know this cousin, and through him I meet her, and right away I am drawn to her. There is something about her that reminds me of Miriam from the old country. So I am with her now. But she is only nineteen. She still knows no one, and she hardly speaks English. I don't want her to end up no seamstress in a sweatshop or even selling her body, so maybe if you come out of this all right and I am not here anymore, you could look out for her and the boy a little bit."

I say that I'll try to look out for them, and for a second I feel like maybe that would be doing my mother dirt, but I realize, no, that helping them is just what she would want me to do. And my father reaches out and pats my back, like I'm a good son, which I'm not any more than he was a good father. And I feel bad for us both. I say to myself that if I ever have a kid of my own, I won't go off and leave him, and maybe then he'll turn out better than I am.

Then I hear a little kid's voice from a room inside, and my father turns around and calls out, "Hannah, I want you should come in here now and that you should bring Danny with you. There is someone here I want you both should meet." Then he whispers to me, "When you knocked on the door, I sent her inside with the boy, in case they had come from Monk to take me. I didn't want any of them should see her and right away get ideas. I told her that she should stay inside because I had to talk some business, and that if I had to leave I would be home for supper. She thinks I am a legitimate accountant, so don't make her think different."

The door opens then, and first there comes in this cute little kid, who's not two yet. He's got a grin on his puss, and he runs over to my old man with his arms reaching out, and the old man scoops him up and tosses him in the air a couple times, and the kid's laughing like crazy, and then my old man hugs him, tickles him in the ribs, and the kid's loving it and throws his arms around my old man's neck and hangs on like he doesn't ever want to let go. My father's smiling when he looks at me, but his eyes are a little wet. He doesn't want to let go of this kid.

I'm wondering right then if I ever went running to the old man like that and if he scooped me up, the both of us grinning, and my mother watching with her hands together up at her chin and smiling like there's not a thing wrong in the whole world. This was how my father's Hannah was standing and looking at the two of them. Then, when my old man put Danny down, and the little guy hugged his father's legs, she looked over at me, and my father tells her in Yiddish who I am. I can't speak Yiddish, except for some words here and there, but I can understand some of what I hear. He tells her the truth, that I'm Moishe, his son by his dead *Italyener* wife.

She looks at me a little nervous, like she thinks I'm going to hate her and maybe even her kid, too, but I don't, not either one of them. They didn't do anything wrong. Of course, she was with another woman's husband, but she's not the first, especially not on the Lower East Side, where a lot of husbands come over by themselves from Europe, and they tell their wives that when they make enough dough they'll send for them, and after a while the wives don't ever hear from them anymore. My father probably told her that him and my mother were finished with each other, which was true. And he's not a bad-looking guy and he dresses pretty good, and he had some dough, so Hannah, with her mother and father dead and her brother having run off somewhere, figured what could be wrong here? Maybe she didn't follow the rules, but I was learning that lots of people don't.

So I smile at Hannah and go over and shake her hand and say hello. And she smiles back and says hello, too, and still looks a little scared of me. Her teeth are a bit crooked, but they're small and white, and her skin is kind of dark, like she almost could be part Italian herself, which she's not, and she's got greenish eyes and a cute, chubby face with dimples, and her hair which is a light brown, is piled up under a pretty, blue, green, and yellow flowery kerchief she's got tied around it, and there's a strand here and there hanging loose, dangling near her ears, which are small, and look good with the little pearl earrings she's wearing. I can see why my father liked her right off. She's tall, like Esther, but not as slim, maybe because she's had a kid, but she's not as big in the hips and boobs as Miss Friedman is, either. And she's real shy.

I say, "Danny has a *sheyn punim*," you know, a pretty face. She just grins and bobs her head, I go over to the kid, who's a little scared of me at first, but I pick him up kiss him on the cheek, and I say, "You don't know me yet, buster, but you and me are kind of brothers, and I'm gonna get to know you better if I can, like your old man wants." And the kid doesn't seem scared of me anymore.

So I put him down, kiss him on the head again and tell my father that I'd better get going. He walks me out to the staircase, and he tells me again to be careful and to warn Esther, which is what I was headed to do right away, and he reminds me that I have to figure that I'm being followed all the time now. Then we say good-bye without looking in each other's faces. My eyes are damp, and I don't want him to see, and maybe it's the same for him, I don't know.

When I get outside, the streets are so crowded, I can't tell whether I'm being followed or not. I figure if I start zigzagging from one street to another long enough I could maybe make out if anyone's tailing me, but for now I want to act like I don't suspect anything and go straight on over to Esther in the shop, like nothing's wrong, give her the word about what's going on, and tell her that I'll come back for her as soon as it gets dark and find a safe place for her—I'm thinking it's going to be out on Blackwell's, maybe with Mary-Margaret. And wherever I go the rest of the day, I'm going to be out in the open, like I don't suspect a thing, so it'll be easier for me to give them the slip tonight when I go sneaking out, like they're not gonna be expecting.

I go into the shop, and Mendel's there working, and he nods to me like we aren't friends, but also like we're not such bad enemies anymore. Esther's mother is out shopping, and Esther's in the back, at the kitchen table, and I'm glad that she's wearing the same blouse and smock that she was when we spent our first afternoon together. She's got a book in front of her, laying open on the table. She must have heard me come in, but she doesn't even look up.

I say, "Esther, what you reading?"

She looks up now, and I see she's crying. The book's about King Arthur and the Knights of the Round Table, and Guinevere, who's Arthur's queen that he loves so much but who runs off with Lancelot. I read about that and liked all the jousting and sword fights. If that's what's making her cry, I don't know why. I figure it's lots more than that, of course.

Anyway, I say, "Look, Esther, I had to come by early. I've got bad news. That rat Davey, he told Monk that I told you about your father, and now Monk is maybe after us both."

She says, with the tears rolling down her face, "Do you think Monk would hurt me? He told me he loved me."

"Yeah, Esther, he would, I think, and that's what my father says. Monk doesn't love anybody but himself, and if he thinks you want to hurt him—"

She interrupts, "I *do*. I told you last night I want him dead, and I still do."

"The thing is, Esther, you've got to get away. I don't think they're gonna come till it's dark, but if they do, scream like crazy, just don't go off quiet with them. I'm going to come back tonight and sneak you to somewhere safe for a couple days. They're probably watching the street now, so I'm gonna have to be careful when I come back. And don't try to go to the cops, because the ones around here ain't gonna help you, and if you try to leave the neighborhood, I figure that Monk's boys will grab you right off."

"I want him dead," she says again.

"Okay, we'll work on that, don't worry. You ain't told your mother yet about what happened to your father, right?"

She hasn't, so I say, "Well, right now, when your mother gets back from shopping, you tell her, and tell her that I've got plenty of information to get Monk in jail or executed and that meanwhile I'm going to take you someplace safe and that she should go hide at some relative's place. She should just walk out, like she was going shopping or something. No one will follow her, probably, if you ain't with her."

She says, "Okay, and I'll get some clothes together to take for when you come back tonight."

We're talking low the whole time, and I peek through the curtain to make sure Mendel isn't hearing any of this, but he's with a couple customers. "You ain't said anything about this to him?" I ask her.

She says no, that she doesn't trust him, and I tell her that she shouldn't, but that he's not as bad as I thought and that he would never want her to get hurt.

When I tell her I'm going till it's getting dark, I want to kiss her, at least on the cheek or the forehead, but I'm not sure she's ready yet, so I just smile and give her a little wave.

After I leave Esther's place, I want to see how Miss Friedman's doing. I haven't been there for a few days now, but I know that if I'm being tailed, she doesn't need me coming up to her place and getting her and Florence involved. So I decide instead to go home and rest up, because it might not be so easy getting Esther over to the last boat for Blackwell's.

I still don't try to lose anybody who could be tailing me. Instead, I walk home like there's not a thing on my mind. I even stop to get chocolate drops and a Moxie and stroll along slow and easy, looking in some store windows, stopping at Wasserman's newsstand and reading in a baseball magazine about whether Kid Gleason with the Giants or Wee Willie Keeler with the Orioles is better. And when Wasserman says to either buy the magazine or put it down, I buy it and walk along reading, just like I would if I didn't think Monk's guys were watching me.

When I get home, Mrs. Canzoneri is at her window, and I say, "Hi, Mrs. Canzoneri, nice day, ain't it?" like I always would, and she says, "Yes, Massimo, un bel giorno, ma un po' troppo caldo," pretty, but just a little too hot, which it's been all summer mostly. And she says, like I heard her say before, "Look at the big, puffy clouds. They look like they could have the angels sitting on them." I know that if I turned quick now, I could spot somebody tailing me, but I just stroll on in, while I hear Mrs. Canzoneri whisper to herself 'povero ragazzo.'"

Aunt Gabriella's going out to do some stuff at church when I come in, so I go into the bedroom and lay on her and Uncle Giulio's bed, reading and resting up. I'm starting to think maybe I should go and get Esther right away, but I figure it'll be a lot easier to sneak her away from the shop later, and that, besides, Monk wouldn't try any rough stuff till most of the shops are closed and the streets aren't so crowded.

I get drowsy and daydream that I'm out where the cowboys are and that I shoot Monk in a gunfight and leave him laying in the street to get run over in a cattle stampede, and Esther and Miss Friedman, and, maybe Hannah and Danny and even my old man are watching from the doorway to the saloon and see what a big hero I am.

Then I sleep for a while, wake up and have supper with Gabriella and Giulio, and try to act like everything's usual, but I look over to the window and wonder if I'm ever going to be back to see that fire escape again or lay on my mattress on the kitchen floor and look out at the sky.

Aunt Gabriella looks at me and says, "Massimo, stai bene? You look like you gonna cry."

I say I'm okay, that I'm just missing my mother, which isn't a lie, because I am missing her all the time, but which I shouldn't have said, because, of course, it made Gabriella cry.

I get up and kiss her on the head, and I put my arm around Uncle Giulio and I kiss him on the head, too, and I say, "You're both real good to me, and I love you both," which I ain't ever really said to them before, though I figure they always knew I liked them pretty good.

Uncle Giulio kind of gets choked up, and him and her sit there and can't say anything.

I wish I could tell them that I'm going to go out now and get started doing something that could make them real proud of me, and make Mama so proud too, if she could just know about it, but I can't tell them that, of course. It would just worry them sick. So I tell them I'm going out to see some friends and I won't be late, but that they should go to sleep and not wait up. Meanwhile I'm hoping I can have Esther out at Blackwell's and settled in by ten and maybe get back here not too late after midnight. And if everything works out tonight, then tomorrow I'll get Esther and the tin box, sneak back into town, and start telling people who maybe could do something about it everything we know about Monk.

I leave Aunt Gabriella and Uncle Giulio after supper. And when I close the door behind me, making sure it doesn't stick, I don't go downstairs. Instead, I walk real quiet up the two flights between our place and the roof, and when I get up there I see it's empty, just like I hoped, and so are the roofs that connect to ours. There's just clothes lines and little two-foot-high walls between the different buildings. All I've got to do is step over a few of those and I can go around the street corner.

So I go across the roofs, to a building around the corner and then downstairs into the street as easy as could be, and anyone watching for me is still back at my building, waiting for me to come out of it. I'm thinking maybe this is a good sign for my whole plan. But when I get to the key shop by going up to a roof down the street from it and walking across the roofs to Esther's building and come downstairs to the shop's back door, I see it's part open and Esther's mother is laying on the kitchen floor.

At first I think she's dead, but then she moans, and I kneel down and see that she's got no marks on her. There's this smell, though, that's real sweet and kind of familiar. It's coming strong from her face, but it's all around, too, and I sniff it a couple more times, and I start to get dizzy, and I remember this smell now from when I had a rotten tooth pulled out at Dr. Schwartz's Painless Dentistry Parlors. It's the stuff Dr. Schwartz used to make me dreamy so I wouldn't feel the pain. He said you use a lot of this on someone, it could knock him out cold, and use some more and it could kill him. It was called Chlorafoam, or something like that. And now I see there's a handkerchief laying near Mrs. Goldstein, and I pick it up, and it's just drenched with the stuff. So somebody must have held it over her face till she dropped.

Of course, I'm calling for Esther, but she's not there, and then I see there's another damp handkerchief laying in the kitchen. Her book is still open on the table, just where it was when I saw Esther there in the afternoon, but her chair is knocked over and laying on its side.

Mrs. Goldstein starts moaning louder now, and I say, "Mrs. Goldstein, it's Morris. What happened? Where's Esther?" and she cries and spits up some vomit. I turn her over, so that she doesn't choke on it, and I grab a blanket from a couch and wipe her mouth with the end of it, and I ask again, louder this time, "What happened?"

She just moans some more, and I want to shake her, to get some words out of her, but I just ask her again, but this time softer, to maybe calm her down some, and it seems to get her head a little clearer. She says, "They came in."

"Who? Who came in?"

She says, "Rough men. They scare Mendel and tell him to go get out, and he goes."

She spits up some more vomit. I wipe her mouth with the corner of the blanket again, and she says, "My good blanket, from my mama."

"Sorry. Then what happened."

"They grab Esther and me. We try to scream, but they put wet handkerchiefs over our mouths. Sweet smell. Sick. And I faint on the floor."

"Do you know where they took Esther?"

She howls, but she's not strong enough to make it loud, "They got my Esther?"

"Yeah, I think so. But don't worry, I'm gonna find her and get her back to you."

"Oy vey is mir. Gevalt! Esther, Esther!" She's calling now like she thinks Esther's gonna hear her and come running. Then she's choking on her vomit.

I pat her back and she says, "Oy, my head hurts so bad, so bad."

"Mrs. Goldstein, did you hear them say anything about where they were gonna take her, anything at all?"

"Oh my head! I can't think nothing clear. Esther! Izzie! They was talking something about palm trees."

Okay, I figure now that they took her to The Palm, and I'm going to go there right off, but Esther's mother's moaning louder about her head, and then she's twitching around on the floor and her mouth is drooping open, with drool oozing out of it, so I have to do something quick for her. I look around and grab a pillow and put it under her head, and then I run out on the street and yell, "Somebody go get a doctor 'cause Mrs. Goldstein's sick and needs help quick!"

I come back in and see that she's not twitching anymore, except for her left arm and her left eye, and she's almost purple in the face. I tell her everything's gonna be okay, that I'll bring Esther back and make sure nothing bad happens to her anymore. I can't tell whether Mrs. Goldstein's seeing or hearing me or anything else right now, but I can't hang around, because I've got to save Esther if I can. I run into the kitchen and open some drawers till I see what I want, a knife that's not too big, but big enough and sharp enough. I wrap it in a napkin and slip it down into my sock, under my pants, the first time I'm carrying a blade since Izzie got killed.

When I go back to Mrs. Goldstein, I see a couple ladies have come in, and one is yelling to her that a doctor is on his way, but Mrs. Goldstein's acting like she doesn't know they're there. I say to the ladies, "In case you wanna know, Monk Eastman's guys did this, and they got Esther and took her somewhere. I'm gonna find her. You could tell the cops if you want, but they probably won't do anything. If things don't work out so good for me, you've got to tell people that it's time they do something about Monk."

XVIII

I'm mad enough when I leave the shop to go charging straight
into The Palm, stab anybody I need to, especially Monk, and
rescue Esther, just like Billy the Kid would go straight into
some saloon out in Tombstone, but by the time I've gone a
block, I realize that busting in there that way won't get me
anywhere but dead, just like Billy the Kid, and that I've got to
get in with nobody noticing.

When I get to Chrystie Street, I stop on the corner and I
see Kid Twist Zwerbach and Dopey Dorfman standing at the
door to The Palm, so I can't sneak in through the front, and
there's no other door and there's no windows on the first floor,
except for right in front, where they're standing, and the fire
escape is right above them.

I figure Esther, if she's there, is probably in one of the
whores' rooms upstairs. Now, The Palm is five stories, and it's
attached on one side to a corner store that's only one story,
and on the other side, there's a narrow alley not much wider
than a couple garbage cans between it and another five-story
building. And there's an even wider alley behind it.

So a couple minutes later I'm five stories up, on the roof
across the alley from The Palm, and my stomach's sick because
of what I know I've got to do. The six feet, or so, I've got
to jump looks a lot wider up here than six feet looks on the

sidewalk. And if I don't make it, then Gabriella and Giulio and Billy and Mary-Margaret won't even know that I died trying to do some good for a change. There's a low wall around both roofs to keep people from falling off, and that means that as I'm running across the roof to jump, I have to slow a little to step on the wall of the building I'm on and push off it just right and hope I've got enough steam left to clear the wall on the other side.

As I'm thinking about this, I'm dumb enough to look down. It's pretty dark out now, but lights from windows and from a streetlamp across Chrystie let me see it's a long way. And my stomach shoots some burning stuff up into my mouth, and I gag a little and spit out as much as I can, then feel dizzy, and lay down up there, smelling roof tar, telling myself Davey and I jumped over puddles maybe twelve feet wide and more all the time, so there's nothing to be scared of, but that doesn't help a whole lot.

I'm wondering if I'll have time to think of anything on the way down except how crazy I was to try to jump across. And I wonder if Izzie even realized he was yelling "No" and if I would yell anything. He fell from higher, so he took longer, and I don't know whether that makes it worse or gives you some time to try to get ready for what's waiting. I do know that even if I have time on the way down, I won't pray. My mother would be proud, maybe, that I didn't die begging some God she didn't believe in. And I tell myself, too, that since I felt like I haven't been really all that alive after watching Izzie go off of the bridge, then maybe I ought to feel lucky that I went on a couple months more and got to do some things I liked, anyway.

So I get up, take a deep breath and try to shake off the dizziness, and think again of the guy on the soda pop bottle. Then I just back up to the wall on the other side of the roof, take another deep breath, and run fast as I can toward where I've got to jump, and I'm seeing Esther and trying not to see

Izzie, and suddenly I say a word out loud, just one, without my knowing I was going to say it, and the word is "Moxie." Not what I figure Billy the Kid would say during a gunfight or some knight would yell out when he storms the castle, but that's what I say as I put my foot on the wall and raise up my arms and take off into the dark. At least it's not "No!"

I stumble as I come down on the other side, and I fall flat on my face on the roof of The Palm. My hands are scraped, and my knees are scuffed, and I feel like I could pass out, but I know that I'll be okay quick. And just a couple minutes later, I'm holding my knife, opening the roof door, and tiptoeing down to the top floor. There's one dim light burning, and the walls along the staircase have ugly drawings scrawled up on them of girls with their legs spread wide and of guys with their shlangs big and hard.

When I get down to the top floor, I see that at the end of the hall there's a bathroom with the door open and four doors along the hallway, two on each side, and they're all shut. So I put my ear up to the first door, don't hear anything, open it soft and slow just a crack and peek in to see if Esther's there, and there's just an empty bed and a washstand, and over the bed there's a picture of a big naked lady, with melons on her like Miss Friedman's and she's laying on her back on a couch, and she's got one hand behind her head, and she's smiling like she's glad you're coming toward her. The second room I peek in is also empty, with the same kind of picture over the bed. At the third door, I hear some girl yell "Gevalt, you're a reg'lar bull," and a guy answers, "You better believe it, Toots."

At the fourth door, I don't hear anything, so I open it careful, and just as I see these four feet laying there in the bed and a huge red tochis going up and down, the door squeaks, and the ass stops and rolls over and the guy it belongs to turns toward me and yells out "What the fuck is it?" It's Big Tochis, and I pull back and say, "Sorry, wrong room," shut the door, and trot quick down to the next floor. I figure he couldn't see who it was, and he wasn't going to leave what he was doing to find out.

Down on the fourth floor, the doors have keyholes that I can look through. Again, two of the rooms didn't have anyone in them. In another, a girl was sitting on a guy and letting out whoops, and the guy was whooping it up too and yelling that she was queen of the rodeo. Then I heard footsteps coming up, so I scrammed on into the bathroom at the end of the hall, and when someone knocked, I growled out "Busy" and made noises like I was working hard to take a dump, which I figured would make whoever it was go off to a toilet on another floor, which he did after he cursed through the door and said if I was as sick as I sounded I needed to be in the hospital.

When I peeked in the keyhole of the last door on that floor, what I saw was a guy and a girl doing stuff with a whip and ropes, and it was real ugly, so as soon as I saw that the girl wasn't Esther, I said to myself, almost out loud, "I gotta get Esther outta here quick!"

Well, just as I'm going down to the third floor, a couple turns the corner and starts coming up. The staircase is dim, so I hold the knife against the side of my leg that's closer to the wall and hope that they won't see that I have it. The guy is someone I don't know, a gray-haired, part-bald, red-faced guy in a cream-color suit, with a cigar in his puss and a belly that's pulled his cream-and-white-check vest so tight, it looks like the buttons are about to pop right off of it. And stretched stiff across the vest, he's got a gold watch chain that looks like it can barely hold together, and the shiny little knick-knacks on it look like they're ready to go flying with the buttons. One of them is a little gold four-leaf clover. He sees me a couple steps above him up and says, "Ah, a lad's never too young to get his ashes hauled now, is he?"

I smile and say, "You bet."

The girl with him giggles. She's wearing his straw skimmer tilted back on her head, and she looks like I saw her somewhere, but I can't remember where, and then she says, "Hey, cutie, why ain't we seen you back for another spread over at Monk's flat?" and I see she was one of the whores that was cooking for Monk in his place over the laundry.

"Who was you with, honey?" she asks me.

"Huh?"

"Whose room was you in?"

"I forget her name, but she showed me a real good time."

So I'm standing there, two steps above them, and I want to go by, but the staircase is narrow, and this is no small guy. I take one step down, hoping they'll make some room, but she puts her hand on my shoulder and asks, "Maybe she just really didn't make so much of an impression after all." And she's stroking my shoulder now, trying to drum up business, I suppose.

I play along with her, so she'll let me go by, and ask, "What's your name, then, sweetie?"

She tilts his skimmer over one eye, licks her lips, and says, "I'm Hortense," and then she whispers, "and you can guess, can't you, what they call me for short, even though it ain't real nice?" And she makes it sound like I should think it is real nice, actually.

Her hand's still on my shoulder, so I figure that since she's in the mood to talk to me, maybe I can see if she knows something, and I say, "Yeah, Miss Hortense, I'll look you up next time, if you don't think I'm too much of a kid for you and maybe ought to go instead with that young girl that Monk got brought in here tonight."

And she laughs and says, "Her! I seen her come in. Someone said Monk was goin' with her till she did him some dirt, but I don't believe he'd waste his time on a skinny, weepy thing like her who thinks she's too la-di-da to be with the likes of us. Monk's got her in a room next floor down, with Sadie trying to talk some sense into her. You're better off with someone like me," and she leans over and kisses me hard on the mouth.

Well, the guy with her wasn't so drunk or jolly that he liked this. "Hey," he says, "What's the big idea here? She's with me, you mangy gutter mongrel!"

I get mad, but I'm not going to do anything about it, because I don't need a loud brawl now to make everybody come running. I just want to find Esther.

So I say, "Sorry" and try to push by him.

Well, he gives me a shove and knocks me backwards, right on my can, two steps up from him. When I fall back, my arm that I'm holding against my side goes flying out, and Hortense says, "Oh my God, he's pulled a knife!"

He hears her and he says, "Why, you..." and he reaches for my throat. And I don't know whether I decide to do it or not, but next thing I know, I shoot my arm forward and the knife is sticking deep somewhere high up in his fat belly. He's got this surprised look on his face, like if you had of given him a million years, he couldn't have guessed what just happened to him was what was going to happen when he started up those stairs.

He falls on his knees one step down from where I'm sitting, and he opens his mouth like he's trying to say something but is too scared or too hurt to get anything out except for little hiccups and belches. And he's looking into my face now like he's begging me to do something for him, like maybe pull the knife out or yell for help. And the only words I can get out are "I'm sorry. I'm so sorry. I didn't mean to, really," which I'm gasping and whispering both.

And Hortense, she's got her hands up to her face, and her eyes have gone big, and she doesn't look so much like a tough hooker now but like a scared girl who probably isn't even twenty yet. And her and me and the guy himself are all staring down at what's happening to him in front. There's a red stain that's spreading all over his vest and chain. It's got the gold four-leaf clover covered with blood, and the blood is running along the chain toward the watch that's slipped out of his pocket and is just hanging there.

The guy then reaches his hands, all trembly, toward the knife handle, which is pushed right up to his body, so I see I must have reached out with the knife harder than I thought. And he puts his fingers on the handle and starts trying to pull the thing out, which I don't know is gonna do him any good if he can do it, but he groans after pulling it back maybe a half-inch and lets go, because he's either too weak now or it hurts too bad when he pulls at it.

He's still looking at me like he's begging me to do something, and Hortense is all pale and dazed, almost like she got as big a dose of chlorafoam as Mrs. Goldstein. So, I grit my teeth and close my eyes a little and grab the knife handle and give it a big yank, and it comes out, but when it does, the blood splurts up out of the guy like I uncapped a little fire hose inside of him. It shoots onto my white shirt and even up into my face and over onto Hortense's skirt. The guy tries to get up, but can't get more than a couple inches, then reaches out his arms and falls forward, his arms shaking and his hands grabbing at my ankles. I see his watch laying there, all covered in blood now. And then his hands aren't moving anymore, and nothing else is either. I step up back from him, so his hands, which are on my shoes, just lay on the stairs.

Well, seeing the blood go shooting out from the guy wakes Hortense out of her daze, and she looks at me now like I'm Jack the Ripper and like she's going to be my next victim. And she's getting ready to scream almost loud enough to wake up the guy that's laying there with his blood starting to drip from one step down to the next. So I put my hand up to her mouth and hold the bloody knife up to her throat, and I whisper, "Hortense, I didn't mean to do that to him, and I ain't gonna do nothing to you, not unless you yell, and then there's no one can get here fast enough to keep me from cutting your throat and leaving you laying there beside that fat bastid."

I didn't mean any of that, of course. No matter what, I wasn't going to hurt Hortense for being a scared girl, but I had to make her think I would. And I say, "Now, if you keep your trap shut, I'm just gonna get out of here, but if you scream or go to get somebody before I'm out of this building, I'll come back and finish you now or do it someday after I'm out of here, and you'll always be wondering when I'm coming. So you gonna be quiet, like a good girl?" And all the time, I still have my hand over her mouth and my blade at her throat.

She nods that, yeah, she's not going to yell, so I take my hand away from her mouth and keep the knife where it is another second, just to let her know I'm making sure that she's not gonna double-cross me right away. Her head's tilted way back, and the guy's skimmer has fallen off of her and tumbled down to the bottom stair. I wipe my knife on her skirt and go running downstairs.

On the third floor, the first door I peek through I see Esther laying on a bed and see Sadie sitting on it, talking to her. I open the door, walk in and shut it quick behind me. They both see me standing there, a knife in my hand and lots of blood on my clothes, and Sadie looks like she wants to yell but figures she better not because she doesn't know what I'll do, and Esther jumps up like she's either gonna come toward me or move away fast.

I whisper that I've come to rescue Esther. Sadie says fast and low, "You can't get her out of here. And Monk won't make it no easier on her when he catches her. I was just tellin' her that it ain't such a bad life, to wise up, like Monk wants her to, 'cause if she don't, she'll end up in the river. So get outta here and leave her alone, you'll both be better off."

I says, "Yeah, well maybe I'll end up making Monk wish he was in the river. Let's go, Esther."

Esther throws her arms around my neck, and says, "How is Mama? You've got to tell me."

I kiss her on the forehead and all I tell her is that when I saw her mother she was waking up from the chlorofoam and told me that Monk's guys had taken Esther to The Palm.

Well, just then, I hear a scream from upstairs. Hortense has figured out that she needs to be more scared of Monk if she doesn't do something to catch me than she needs to be scared of me. And right after she screams, I hear guys yelling and footsteps all over the place.

I look over to see if Sadie's about to yell to let them know where I am, and she says, "If yous two catch hell from Monk, it ain't gonna be on account of me. I got that much of a conscience anyways." Esther meanwhile says, "Morris, give me the knife and go. I'll hide it in my dress and stab Monk tonight."

I tell her, "Maybe some other time" and ask Sadie, "Where's the fire escape?" I'm thinking that if everybody's running up to the fourth floor, maybe the guys out front came in to see, too, and we can get down to the street. Going up to the roof and trying to jump with Esther over to the other building isn't something even to consider.

Sadie says, "It's right across the hall."

So I grab Esther and run into the room across the way without anybody seeing us. Well, there's a whore laying there in bed with nothing on, and there's a guy standing up just finishing getting his pants on to go see what all the commotion is. It's the Redkopf, the guy that told me that time not to take it serious if Monk gave me the raspberry about Miss Friedman. He looks up and says, "You, you son of a bitch! Monk wants you and now!" I want to back away, but I've got nowhere to go. And he grabs a blackjack and steps toward me and Esther. I bring my right arm around like I'm throwing a roundhouse and slash him solid on the left side of his throat with my knife.

The Redkopf looks as surprised as the guy on the stairs did. He drops the blackjack, and both hands shoot up to his throat, and he holds them there, but the blood is coming quick between his fingers. He gurgles, and his eyes look already like he's real far away.

Me and Esther head for the window and the fire escape, and in another second the whore is screaming.

I call out, "I'm sorry," and there's a thud behind me and Esther as the Redkopf hits the floor. Esther's crying, and I feel bad that she saw that stuff, but I can't do anything about it now except get her out of there. Maybe stabbing Monk or anybody else suddenly doesn't seem like something she really wants to do.

So we're on the fire escape, and when we get to the second floor, I see there's no one left down at the door to The Palm. I shove down the escape ladder, hear the bottom of it scrape against the sidewalk and in a couple seconds we're on the street. I grab Esther by her shoulder, pull her around the corner of Chrystie onto Grand, heading toward Allen and Orchard and the river way past them, because I'm hoping we can turn uptown finally and head up to the dock for Blackwell's. We run a little way and then duck into an alley just as I see a bunch of guys come to the corner and split up, some heading up Chrystie, some down Grand the other way toward The Bowery, and some our way.

They don't see us, though, and we go snaking through some alleys for maybe ten minutes, until I think we've given everyone the slip, but when we're about to come out onto the street, so we can head uptown, I hear some guys calling to each other, so we duck back into the alley and stand in the shadows. And while we're standing there, quiet as we can be, a fat rat skitters up and sniffs at Esther's ankle, so I mash my hand hard over her mouth while I kick the rat a couple feet up in the air. And he lets out a squeal that wakes up some dog that's been dead asleep just outside the alley and sends him charging on in after the rat, which is staggering around and letting out squealy moans, and in a second there's snarling and snapping and squealing and yelping, and anybody who's going to come into the alley to watch the sport is gonna see me with my hand clapped over Esther's mouth and holding her tight up against me.

Well, the guys out on the street stand at the front of the alley when they hear the rat and the dog going at it, but the light's no good, and after a minute, they figure it's just a rat and a dog, and walk on down the street.

Esther and me stand there for a little while more, and the alley's still and quiet now except for the sound of the dog breathing hard and chewing on the rat, and there's a rotten smell. I take my hand off of Esther's mouth, and she leans her head on my shoulder and sniffles and shivers and makes retching noises that she's trying to keep quiet. Then she gets hold of herself a little and asks, "That man that you cut in the neck, do you think you killed him, Morris?"

I whisper back, "Yeah, he ain't ever gonna be with another of Monk's whores."

"Oh, Morris. You're a killer now, for me, and I'm not worth it." And she looks like she doesn't know whether to thank me or be scared of me or just real sad for me.

I say, "Esther, just so you should know the worst, he was the second guy I killed in there tonight. Some guy was trying to strangle me, so I let him have it in his fat belly. I ain't willing to end up like your old man did or like I think my old man is going to. And I won't let anybody turn you into a whore."

And again, she shivers, but she's mad now, "That bastid! If I can't kill him, you kill him! You already did two. One more won't matter, especially if it's him."

And I say, "Yeah, I'll kill him if it comes to that, but mainly we're going to try to get him fried legal up at Sing Sing, so I don't end up there myself. That's if I get away with what I did tonight. But meanwhile let's just get out of here."

So we go out onto the street, which is Canal, just a half-block from the El station, and it's quiet, and for a second I think that me and Esther gave everybody the slip, but I should have known better, because by now Monk must have at least fifty guys fanned out looking for us, and, sure enough, I see three of them a little more than a block away in the shadows under the El tracks, and one of them elbows the others and points toward us. Because of a streetlamp near us, we were standing out too bright, so I give Esther a shove, and the two of us are running.

I could get away myself easy enough, but I won't leave Esther, so I'm ready to try to fight them off with my knife if I have to. But right then I hear the train coming from downtown, close enough that I can see the smoke from its stack and the cinders flying up and sailing down into the dark. So I ask, "Can you sprint in that dress, Esther?" And she says, "We're not gonna let them catch us."

And we get up to the platform just as the train is chugging in.

We climb the three steps into the car and look back at the station staircase we just raced up from the street, and after ten seconds that feels like it's ten minutes, the train is still sitting there and I can see the guys climbing up to the platform hard as they can. But hard as they can go isn't fast right now because it looks like they're not used to running. Another few seconds, and one of them, a heavy guy who looks like he's probably sweating beer, is wheezing, and slowing down, and a guy, who's a couple steps ahead of the wheezer, is no more than a third of the way up, and only one looks like he's got a shot at catching the train.

Well, finally, there's a toot and we start moving, but by now the guy who was ahead of the others has grabbed onto the little iron banister for the steps up into the car, and he's trotting along, holding on, and getting ready to swing himself up. His hat's flown off, and his hair is dripping sweat, and he's red in the face and heavy, but he's only in his twenties and he's got a bulldog look that means trouble.

I tell Esther to go inside the car and I move down to the second step, as the train is starting to chug a little faster now, and the guy looks up now as he's trotting along and hanging onto the railing, and our eyes meet, and he snarls at me and shows his teeth. He's a bulldog, all right, and he howls like a dog, too, when my knife slashes the hand he's hanging on with, but he doesn't want to let go, so I slash him at the back of his wrist this time, and he howls again and lets go, and I watch as he grabs his hand, staggers off balance and goes smashing right into one of the posts that holds up the station roof.

I look back and see him crumpled there while further back the other two guys are running down the platform shaking their fists at me. Then one stops, holds his arm straight out like he's pointing, and I see a flash, and a bullet hits maybe two feet from me and sends some splinters flying. I duck back in, feeling like I did up on the roof just after I'd jumped over the alley. I won't tell Esther they're shooting now because she's scared enough. Anyway, I don't think Monk wants me or her shot dead. The guy who shot must have just been mad that we got away. Monk, I figure, wants us brought back to him so he can have the fun of killing me himself and do to Esther whatever he wants to.

I slip the knife back down my sock, and walk into the car itself and sit down next to Esther. I tell her, "The guy couldn't get on. He slipped and fell down."

Esther says, "Thank God for that, anyway."

Down at the other end of the car are the only other people in it, an old man and old lady sitting next to each other. They look tired, and she's leaning against him. If they saw anything happening out on the station platform, they're not showing it.

Esther asks, "Where are we going?"

"I was going to take you out to a place on Blackwell's Island, where there's a nice lady, a nurse, who could keep you safe till we talk to people who can stop Monk and protect us maybe, but it's too late now to catch the last boat. So I don't know. I could take you to a police station somewhere, but Monk's guys could be watching those already, and besides I don't know yet which cops I can trust. And there's the hospitals, but Monk's guys are probably at those, too. Let me think a minute."

Esther is trying hard not to cry. "You sure my mother's okay?"

"Yeah, she's gonna be all right. We'll get somebody to tell her that you're safe, and that'll make her feel good, and then we'll check on her real soon."

She asks, "Are you hurt, Morris?"

"Nah, not much, just a few scratches." Esther looks over at the old couple sitting there, and she leans to me and whispers, "That's us someday, if we make it that long."

I kiss her on the cheek, and I don't feel real bad yet about killing those two guys or hurting the guy on the platform, even if I probably should.

The conductor comes into our car, just before we pull into Grand Street. When he takes my coins, he says, "You been in a fight, sonny?"

I say, "Yeah, some guy said I stole his gal, and him and his pal jumped me, and I pounded them both pretty good in the nose and they bled all over me, but I'm okay."

He gives me a look like he doesn't believe me but shrugs and moves to the next car. I guess he figures that so long as it didn't happen on his train it's no concern of his, which is all right with me.

A couple people get on at Grand. If anybody notices the blood on my shirt, they don't show it. Not their concern either.

As we go along from Grand to Houston and then towards Ninth Street, I'm looking out the window and I can see into buildings, and in one loft a bunch of people are working at sewing machines, even though it's nighttime, and in the flats, it doesn't seem like most people are doing much but sitting and staring, even if there's somebody with them. And there are guys with their elbows on the windowsill, while they smoke their pipes, just watching us go by while I'm watching them.

By the time we pull into Ninth, I know where I'm going to take Esther. So when the train stops, I tell her here's where we get off.

She asks where we're going, but I don't want to tell her till we get there, so I just say, "I've got a friend who's gonna put you up for the night, maybe for a couple nights, if I figure I can't get you someplace else for a while."

And when we get off, we head back over toward Fifth Avenue and then down to Washington Square, and we pass two real pretty churches, but they're dark and empty now, and then we walk under the lit-up big arch at the entrance to the square, and I look up and read what they've got carved into it. It says, "Let us raise a standard to which the wise and the honest can repair. The event is in the hand of God." And it says George Washington said that. I think to myself, "'the wise and honest,' huh? I guess that leaves me out. And if there's a hand of God, I better watch out that it doesn't swat me one."

But the grass and the trees smell sweet and clean in the nighttime, as we walk through the park, and it's quiet, and you can see the stars, which I guess are still the same ones I was looking at when Davey came down the fire escape back in early June, and I'm thinking it's too bad that Esther and I just can't stay there till morning.

About ten minutes later, we're over at Barrow Street, just around the corner from Bleecker, and we're walking upstairs to where I never thought I'd ever be bringing Esther. It's Miss Friedman's flat. It was a place where I was sure Monk would never figure I'd bring her either, because he knew about how mad Esther was when she heard about me and Miss Friedman. And, sure enough, when Esther stops on the staircase and asks whose place we're going to and I tell her whose it is, she says she's not ever going in there.

I explain to her that Miss Friedman and me made a mistake, but that she's a good person and a good teacher and had gotten roughed up pretty bad by the guys that Monk sent over to the school, and that if Miss Friedman could take her in tonight, Esther should be grateful and that she should remember that she was always Miss Friedman's favorite student.

Of course, as soon as those words went out of my mouth, I knew just what Esther was going to say, and I really couldn't blame her. She says, "Oh, I would have thought that you were her favorite student."

I say, "Like I told you a lot, Esther, I'm sorry, and I figure she is, too. I love you, Esther and nobody else."

She kissed me on the cheek, sighed, and said, "Okay, let's go up and knock on her door."

Just before we knock, I whisper to Esther, "Don't tell her that I killed anybody, Esther, please."

She gives me a look and whispers back, "Don't worry, I won't. You still like her, don't you?"

"Yeah, of course I do. But not in the way I like you. You gotta believe that." She nods like maybe she does. And then she knocks.

Miss Friedman answers the door. She's got her finger in a book, and she looks stronger than last time I was there. When she sees Esther with me, she blushes, figuring that Esther heard about her and me kissing, and she looks like she doesn't know what to do, and then, almost like she's our teacher again, she shows us the book and says, "Have you read *Maggie, a Girl of the Streets*, by Stephen Crane? It's about a girl growing up in tough conditions in an Irish neighborhood not far from where you both live. Things don't turn out... so well," and she shrugs. "You... might want to read it sometime. Well, it's a wonderful surprise seeing you both. Come in."

So we do, and right away Florence and then Miss Friedman see the blood on my shirt and are scared it's mine, so I tell them why we showed up at their place, tell them mostly everything, except about me killing anybody, and say the blood was from one of Monk's guys I had to punch in the nose. And Miss Friedman and Florence tell us we have to stay. I tell them that Esther does, but that I've got stuff to do to get ready to spill the beans about Monk. Miss Friedman says that maybe the best guy to go see right off is this Mr. Schoenwitzer, who runs the *New York Globe*. She tells me that she doesn't know him personal but she knows he was in with Theodore Roosevelt when he was police commissioner and trying to clean things up. So I say that's where me and Esther are gonna go as soon as I get back with the things we need to show the guy.

And then, when I'm leaving, Esther comes over and kisses me, this time on the lips, and says, "Be careful, Morris. I need you safe." And Miss Friedman kisses me on the forehead, and says, "We all want you safe." They're blushing and so am I. I say I'll be back tomorrow afternoon, and I tell Esther not to leave till I get there, and I'll try to have news about her mother.

As I go downstairs, I feel for the envelope my father gave me, which I've been feeling for about every five minutes all night, and it's still tucked inside my shirt, damp with my sweat, but at least not with my blood—not yet, anyway.

XIX

When I leave Miss Friedman's place, it's already after midnight, and my first thought is to get back to Aunt Gabriella and Uncle Giulio's for what's left of the night. But I don't get even a block before I realize that all the streets around their place have probably been crawling with Monk's guys since five minutes after me and Esther ran out of The Palm, and those guys are just hoping I'll try to go home. So, instead of heading back downtown, I go up to the Blackwell's steamer dock on Twenty-Sixth. Nobody'll look for me there, and I can get out to the island first thing in the morning, get the tin box, and go pick up Esther so we can get over to Schoenwitzer and start Monk on the road to the death house, where I hope I don't end up sharing a cell with him after what I did at The Palm.

When I get to the dock, I need a place where I can rest a little, and the *Minnahanock* is right there, so I figure maybe I can go onto it and find a cot they use for the sick people. I climb over a little gate up in front of the gangplank, and when I'm just about to step on the boat, I hear a rough-sounding voice call out, "Where you think you're going?"

I call back, "I'm sorry, sir. I want to go out to my mother's grave, on the first trip in the morning. She died at the TB hospital a few days back, and I couldn't sleep tonight. I miss her too much. I figured if I came out here and just lay down on the boat tonight and waited, I could feel like I was closer to her. But I'll go back over the gate and wait on the dock."

I'm standing in the light of a lantern that's hanging there, and I can see my shadow floating on the dark water below the gangplank. It gives me a chill, even though the night isn't cold. I still can't see the guy except for a little red glow from the cigar or pipe that he's smoking.

The voice, which doesn't sound so rough now, calls out, "That's a sad story, and if it's true, you've got my sympathy, but how do I know that you didn't come out here to steal something?"

I say, "I wouldn't know what you've got on this boat to steal if I wanted to. I don't need a cot or lifesaver, and I ain't a pirate, ready to sail off with the ship, either. I'm a friend of Billy Higgins, who works here. He calls me 'Moe,' which ain't my real name, which is Morris, and I'm a friend of Mary-Margaret Shannahan, who's a nurse out at the hospital where my mother died and who's a friend of Billy's too. You know them?"

I hear footsteps coming toward me now, sort of clomping and uneven, and the red glow from the tobacco is bobbing up and down and side to side. And now I see the guy. He's tall and old, smoking a pipe and leaning hard on a cane, as he comes limping toward me. He reaches out his hand and says, "Welcome aboard, Moe. A friend of Billy and Mary-Margaret is a friend of mine. You can stay the night out here. I wouldn't mind the company."

I take his hand, and he gives mine a good pump, and then yanks me onboard. This was one strong old guy. His hand was big, and callused every inch, and his rolled-up sleeves showed wrists and arms thick as logs. In the dim flickering light from the couple lanterns hanging on deck, I could see his face was long and thin and full of wrinkles and the eyes were set in as deep as I ever saw eyes go in a face.

"Moe," he says, "I'm Carl Habenicht, the night watchman. I'll fix you a cot so's you can get some rest right here on deck."

So five minutes later, I'm laying on a cot, maybe even the cot my mother was laying on when the sanitary board people took her out to the hospital, months back, and this Carl, he's sitting in a chair next to it and smoking his pipe and talking. I'd like to sleep, really, but, like he said, he's glad for the company, and he's being nice to me, so I don't want to hurt his feelings.

For years and years, he used to be a ferryboatman, right here on the East River, he says. But when they finished building the Brooklyn Bridge, they didn't need so many ferryboatmen anymore, and he lost his job. He wasn't mad about it, though. He told me, "I'd had my turn at it, and I was getting long in the tooth, and then I had this bum leg, my souvenir from the war, so when they cut me loose, I shook their hands and told them no hard feelings, because the time comes when one way or another we all have to step off the ferry and let other people get on for their ride, don't you see?"

And I said yeah that I guess I did. And I asked him what he did in the war, and he said that he served down in Virginia.

I say, "I met a man who was down in Virginia during the war, a man named Mr. Norton, who got a scar on his face from a Rebel sword or bayonet or something, and who got to shake hands with Abe Lincoln. You ever meet Mr. Norton?"

And he kind of chuckles, and he says, "No, I never had the pleasure, but you have to remember, Moe, there were a lot of us Yankees down there in Virginia, and we all didn't get to meet each other. And I didn't have the pleasure of shaking hands with or even seeing Mr. Lincoln either, but I'll tell you, Moe, that there were times when I looked into the faces of the men who I was in the cause with, and I knew I was seeing Mr. Lincoln's face. Do you get me?"

"Maybe," I say, "I'm not sure."

"What I mean is that there were times—not all the time, mind you, but times—when we were sticking together and knowing we were working for something good, no matter the odds, and the look we saw in Abe Lincoln's eyes in some of the pictures was in the eyes of the fellows I was serving with. Those were the good times, the best times. You get that, don't you, Moe?"

Yeah, I said, I did.

He went on, "During the war, I did what I did here on the river. I ferried soldiers across the Potomac, and the James, and the Rappahannock, in good weather and rough, high water and low. I saw things I won't forget—whether I care to or not. I suppose it all needs to be remembered. The fellows going across to fight Lee, and the wounded and the sick coming back, lots of them with a leg gone or an arm, some with two limbs left back in Virginia, all with friends left there in the ground, none of that should be forgotten."

He was right, it shouldn't, and I asked, "How did you hurt your leg? If you don't mind talking about it."

"Nope, I don't mind, Moe. It was during a rough day on the Rappahannock. I was bringing back a boatload of the wounded and the sick, and one poor fellow, who had been talking delirious-like about how he could see his wife waving at him from the dock, stood up to wave back and fell over the bulwark right up near the prow. While I was pulling him back, I had my leg swung over the side, and the ferry came in hard and banged into the dock. My leg got smashed pretty good. The docs were able to save it, but it's been a game one ever since."

"So, you were a hero."

"I only did what you would have done yourself, Moe. Am I right?"

I take a few seconds and say, "Yeah, I guess so. Sure."

"There you go," he says. "I think I read my man right."

I'm still sleepy, but I want him to keep talking. He's quiet for a minute, and then says, "Oh, you might find this of interest. Old Walt Whitman rode my ferry a few times back before the war and said some things worth hearing. That name mean anything to you, Walt Whitman?"

I say, "He wrote 'Oh, Captain, My Captain,' right?"

"You got it, Moe." Remember, it tells how Lincoln brought the country through rough waters into a safe harbor and then got killed."

"Yeah, it's real sad."

"Well, Old Walt's been gone now a few years, but according to what he told me when we talked on my ferry, he's really still with us." And Carl took a long puff on his pipe.

"How's that?"

"Well, he told me that life is like a long ferry trip. Being born is like getting on the ferry, and dying is like getting off. And he said that all of us who are making the crossing together, in other words, all of us alive together, Moe, are brothers and sisters. You're you, and I'm me, and Walt was Walt when he was on the ferry, but we're also, he said, all part of the same big eternal soul, or, put it another way, each of us has a little of that big soul in us, which means a little bit of everyone who got off the ferry is alive in us, every one of us. That make sense to you, Moe?" And he took another long puff while he waited for me to answer.

I thought about it for a while. "I don't know. Maybe."

He says, "Fair enough. Keep an open mind about it. There are times when it makes a lot of sense to me, like when I saw a bit of Abe Lincoln in every soldier's face. Walt said nobody really dies, and everyone is still with us and in us. This soul that he was talking about was God, he said, but not the God the preachers all preach about, but a God that's an energy that makes us good, or could, anyway, if we'd let it. He wrote about that in a poem about the Brooklyn Ferry, but he told me about it first, I think, right there on the Brooklyn Ferry itself. Walt was a talker, and so am I, I suppose, leastways tonight. I sit here sometimes and try to work out what he said, and sometimes I think I have it, and sometimes I don't.'"

"It's something to think about, all right."

"Okay," he says. "I've been rattling on, and you came out here to try and get some rest, and it's near three o'clock now. I'll let you sleep. And, come morning, maybe Billy can help you do something about that blood you got on your shirt. I could see right off that you weren't carrying yourself like a guy who was hurt, so I guess it's not yours."

I says, "It ain't," and turn over to go to sleep. I call out "Thanks, Carl" as he goes limping off, leaning on his cane.

I couldn't get to sleep right away, and I laid there for a while, thinking about the stuff that Carl had been telling me. And I was thinking that maybe him and Walt Whitman were right. Maybe the earth is just a big ferryboat, and my mother and Izzie and my uncle Moishe and his Miriam and poor Johnny from the neighborhood, and the two guys I'd killed tonight had all gotten off, just like Abe Lincoln and the killed Civil War soldiers and everybody else who was on the ferry before us had gotten off, and just like my father and maybe me might be getting off pretty soon. And always new passengers were getting on. I kind of liked that idea. I looked out over the river now and saw the stars just like I did from the kitchen window at Aunt Gabriella's, and I could feel the boat rocking gentle under me, so it almost felt like we were going somewhere.

And what Carl said about the ferry made me feel like wherever I was heading in my life I was less alone, because maybe me and Carl and Billy and Mary-Margaret and Esther and Miss Friedman, and Gabriella and Giulio were all part of each other. And if there wasn't any God like the churches and shuls talk about, then it could be there was this big soul that we were all part of that made sure that everything, that even the bad stuff on the ferry turned out good. That was nice and comfortable to think about, while the boat was rocking and while I was laying on a cot that maybe my mother had laid on.

But then I wondered about the two guys I killed. Were they and me part of each other? And what about Monk. Are him and everybody else really part of each other? Me and Monk Eastman? Forever and ever? And I thought maybe a lot of what Carl and Walt Whitman were saying didn't really make so much sense, even if you wanted it to. I couldn't figure it all out, but I was getting sleepy, and then the rocking had me drifting off.

What woke me up was a voice saying "Moe, old pal. It's time to get a move on." And I felt a hand at my shoulder. I opened my eyes and saw Billy smiling down at me. The sun was already coming up over Blackwell's out in the river, and the boat was rocking a little stronger than when I fell asleep, because the tugs and barges were busy by now. The air there by the river was a little cool, but I was warm under a blanket that I didn't have on me when I fell asleep a couple hours before.

Billy says, "Carl gave you that after you fell asleep. He told me about you coming out here after midnight and that I better give you one of the shirts I have stowed in my kit. So here you go, buddy." And he gave me a nice, clean blue workshirt and said I better get washed up, because we'd be pulling out soon. So I go inside of the cabin, where he's got a bowl of water and some soap and a towel, and I wash up, and Billy's watching me when I'm taking my own shirt off, and he says, "You got anything you need to tell me about those bloodstains?"

I just say, "No, nothing to tell, really. The only thing is you shouldn't think I did anything wrong. Nobody good got hurt, and they didn't give me a choice. I swear it, Billy. But I don't want to talk more about it, if you don't mind and if you're not going to be mad at me."

"Okay," he says, "I believe you, Moe. And I ain't ever gonna be mad at you. We're pals to the end. But just always remember you can tell me what you have to, and I won't jump down your throat or rat you out." And he doesn't ask me anything either about the envelope that he sees I've been carrying around inside my bloody shirt or about the key I still got around my neck with the ribbon that's got bloodstains from my mother's lungs on it.

Then he gave me some breakfast and coffee, and while I ate, he gave me some big news. "Moe," he tells me, and he's smiling as broad as I ever seen him smile, and remember, he's always a guy with a smile, "Moe, me and Mary-Margaret are gonna get married."

"Billy, that's great," I say, "Congratulations. You guys will be happy ever after."

"Well, you know we have you to thank for getting us together, old man."

"Aah, you two would have met, anyways. True love is always meant to be, like they say." And right now, I'm thinking that him and Mary-Margaret are part of each other on the ferry and maybe I'm part of both of them too, and it feels good. I can't wait for Esther to meet him and Mary-Margaret.

He says, "The wedding'll be in a couple months, and you're gonna be best man."

"Maybe I'm too young for that," I tell him, and I'm smiling now like he is.

"Naw, "you're the best man we know, so you're it, if you want to be."

"Yeah, sure," I say, and I'm already thinking that maybe he'll be the best man when I marry Esther somewhere later on in the ferry trip we're all maybe making together.

XX

About two hours later, I'm back downtown, heading to Miss Friedman's to get Esther. Out on Blackwell's, I stopped by my mother's grave and told her out loud, just in case she could hear me, that I really couldn't help what I did the night before and I hoped she wasn't mad, and that I would always try to do the right thing from here on, if I could figure out always what it was. Then I went to the statue of St. Jude and took the tin box out from behind it, and everything was just like I left it, and I put in the envelope my father gave me. I hoped he was still okay, but when I looked up in the face of St. Jude, I had this clammy feeling wash up over me that I was probably an orphan by now.

I take a long way round to Miss Friedman's, heading down the west side, where Monk probably doesn't have anyone looking for me. It's turned into a real hot morning, even hotter than usual for this summer. The sky's milky, the sun's only a small yellow hazy spot, and the air feels like you're having to push your way through it, while it's pressing down on you all around.

I'm just a couple blocks from Miss Friedman's, and I realize that I haven't found out anything about Esther's mother, so I buy a paper off of a newsstand, and I don't see any story about a lady on the Lower East Side who got chlorofoamed and then died afterwards, but there is a big story about three bodies they found last night laid out in a row in an alley between the Moskowitz Alte Heym Funeral Parlor and Scheiner's Dairy Restaurant.

None of the bodies had anything on them with their names, but the reporter told what they looked like. One was what he called a "rotund man of about fifty or fifty-five in a cream-colored suit and cream-and-white-checked vest that were drenched with the blood that came from a knife wound to his stomach." The second was a big red-headed guy of twenty-seven or twenty-eight whose throat had been slashed, and the last was "a rather genteel-looking sort of about forty with a gold-and-tan-checked suit and vest and a receding shock of thick curly black hair sprinkled with gray. He had been stabbed in the stomach and slashed across his throat. A note pinned to his lapel with a small knife said, "This rat and the two guys he's laying with was killed by his own son, a young rat who won't live long enough to brag about what he done." The police say they have no leads, though rumor has it that this may be another episode in the long-standing feud between the Hebraic hordes of Chief Rabbi of the Lower East Side Monk Eastman (formerly Edward Ostermann) and the garlic-munching minions of Pope Paul Kelly (née Paolo Vaccarelli). Doubtless, one or the other of these worthies will see to it that the malefactor is apprehended, and justice served well before New York's finest can rouse themselves to, as they say, 'make the pinch.'"

I sat down on a stoop when I started to read all this, and when I finished, I could hardly get my breath, and my legs couldn't have held me steady if I tried to get up.

So they'd got my father, like he figured they would. But I'm thinking maybe they wouldn't have if I hadn't killed the fat guy and the Redkopf. Maybe they would have still been just thinking about it. So maybe the killer's note had it right, that one guy killed all three of them, and I'm the guy. His being dead hit me harder than I figured it would. Things hadn't worked out right for him, and you could say that maybe a lot of it was his own fault, but you could also say that by the time he got mixed up with Monk he'd already been hurt real bad more than once. And he had tried to help me some during the summer, so it hurt now to think of him laying there like that in a crummy alley and not coming home anymore to his Hannah and his little Danny. He was off of the ferry now, and it could be that I was the one who helped push him off, and that kept me sitting there awhile and thinking.

Finally, I got up and walked the last couple blocks to Miss Friedman's, holding the tin box tighter now and trying not to cry. Miss Friedman's place is on a side street that's quiet and shady, and what I'd have liked right then was just to sit down in a nice spot in the shade with Esther and hold hands and talk about how maybe when we're married someday we can live on a street like this. There's a guy sitting on a stoop right across the street from Miss Friedman's building and just leaning back and smoking a cigar. He's got a cute skinny little kid, maybe nine years old, with him. Probably his son, I guess, the two of them just relaxing together.

I have only a few memories of relaxing with my father, back when he was still with my mother and me. There were a couple walks in the park, a trip to Coney Island, when he watched me on the rides, and a couple walks down to the Battery, with us standing and staring at the water without him saying much. I tell myself if I live to have a kid, I'll make sure to spend time with him. The man sees me looking, and I give him a little wave, and he seems surprised, but smiles and waves back. He says something to the kid, and gives him some dough, and the kid goes trotting down the block. I figure he told him to go get himself a treat, something my old man's new little kid isn't ever going to have his father do for him.

When I knock on Miss Friedman's door, nobody answers.

So I knock louder, and still nothing. Then I realize that the door's kind of jammed just short of being shut, like it was at Aunt Gabriella's when I came home from Woodlawn and found them waiting to tell me that my mother was dead. My stomach gets sick, and I'm having trouble getting my breath again, and I shove the door open. And what was there that morning I still see now, again and again, especially at night when I can't sleep and sometimes nights when I do, and I know I'm going to keep seeing it even if I live to be fifty years older than the guy I stabbed and watched die at The Palm.

Laying on her back on the floor in the sitting room, with her hands and legs tied up and a handkerchief stuffed in her mouth was Florence. Her eyes were wide, her throat was cut, and her head was laying in a puddle of her blood that was starting to smell. Laying not far from her, facing down with its pages spread open, was the book she'd probably been reading when they busted in on her. There probably wasn't a thing in it that could have made her ever expect that something like this could happen. Her glasses had been knocked off and were laying a couple feet from her.

Miss Friedman was in her bed. Her arms and legs were stretched out wide and they were tied to the bedposts with ropes they put around her wrists and ankles. And they had done stuff to her that I'll never talk about. And then they'd cut her throat so hard that you could see the head wasn't attached all the way anymore. Her eyeglasses were on the floor all cracked and broken, like somebody had decided that the job wouldn't be finished unless he did that too. The book she was reading about this Maggie girl was laying there on the floor not far from the glasses, and on the wall behind the headboard they'd smeared up in her blood "*shlooche*" and "ML your a rat!" I went running around the place looking for Esther and scared that I'd find her, but she wasn't there. In the kitchen I grabbed hold of the sink and vomited into it.

Then I went and threw covers over Florence and Miss

Friedman. And I had this thought that the ferryboat that everybody was supposed to be on together got rocked hard and a bunch of us got thrown in the river together and were going under. I know I felt like I was drowning as I stood there crying and crying and telling myself that at least two more people were dead on account of me.

Then I hear footsteps behind me, I reach down for my knife as I whirl around, and Esther's standing there, her face gone as gray as the sky outside. Her hands are up to her face, and she's shaking her head, like maybe if she shakes it long enough what she's seeing just wouldn't be there anymore.

"Monk or his guys must have come for us and got them," I whisper. "I just found them."

She just goes on shaking her head and doesn't drop her hands. She looks like she'll scream, so I put my hand on her shoulder and whisper we've got to stay long enough to figure out what to do next. I see now that she's got a lady's clothes on instead of a girl's and that on the floor behind her there's a lady's hat that must have come off of her head when she walked in and saw what was there.

I sit her down next to me on a little sofa, where we can't see Miss Friedman or Florence, and I ask her real gentle, "Where were you?"

She shakes her head and can't talk. I wait a minute, but I don't want to stay here much longer, so I say again, "Where were you?"

She takes a breath and stops shaking her head. "I went back to the neighborhood to find out how my mother was. I know you said I shouldn't go, but I just couldn't sit still here all night. They offered to go with me, said I'd be safer, but I said... I said, no, no, that I didn't want to put them in danger. Oh, God, I should have let them come with me! But I didn't, so they said I should at least let them dress me up in Florence's clothes, which were about my size. A disguise. And I let them."

"Did you find out something about your mother?"

Her lower lip is trembling like crazy, and she stares up at the ceiling. "By the time I got down to the neighborhood, it was late. It was terrible being out alone so late at night. Some men on the street thought I was just some whore and asked how much I cost, and… things like that. When I got to our neighborhood, I slipped into the shop and locked the door. Early in the morning I was going to go and ask some women if they'd heard something about my mother, and if they didn't know anything, I'd go to the hospital, and then, if I had to, the morgue." Again, she can't talk for a minute, and then she says, "But as I was going out, Davey was there."

"That little snaky piece of *dreck*!"

She says, "I begged him not to rat me out. He said he wouldn't ever do that and that he told Monk about what you and I were doing only because he knew we couldn't ever beat Monk and he wanted to protect me by telling him that you were a bad influence on me and that if you were out of the way, then Monk could take care of me again, just like he'd been doing."

"I'll kill that little *shmuck*! 'Cause of him doing us dirt, *this* happened here, and now he's still figuring he can have you when Monk has done everything he wants with you and then tosses you away. I know just how he thinks."

"He told me my mother was taken to Mt. Sinai, that they think she had a stroke, but that I shouldn't go over there, that it wouldn't be safe because they were watching for me, and even dressed up like I was I wouldn't be able to get through. He said I should stay at the shop, and he'd find out what he could about Mama and come back with the news and wouldn't tell anyone where I was. But then he said that if I was willing to lead Monk to you, he'd tell Monk that, and then Monk would forgive me and be nice to me.

"I said that he should go to Monk and tell him I was ready to do that, and if Monk agreed, then I'd rat you out. And as soon as Davey left, I came back here and…" and she put her face down in her hands again and started sobbing.

I say, "Okay, we better get outta here now, because they may come back to watch the place and see if I show up."

But I don't want to leave Miss Friedman and Florence just laying there like that till they start rotting enough so someone notices, and I can't go and get a cop now or even talk to some neighbor, because when the neighbors tell the cops what I look like, the cops could end up framing me for killing them. So I leave the door about halfway open when we go out, figuring somebody will notice it before long and go in and check around and find what's laying there and maybe find some relatives to give Miss Friedman and Florence a decent burial, like I'm not sure my father will get, not for now, anyway.

Well, as we're about to go out the door, I take a look out the window, just in case, and I see that across the street six rough-looking guys are coming along right now with the kid that I saw sitting there, and I realize what I would have before if I'd been thinking a little clearer after I read about my old man, which was that the guy with the paper was Monk's lookout and the skinny little kid with him was his messenger to go and get a bunch of Monk's guys if I was to show there. The little rat actually looks something like what Davey did when we were both kids. Well, these guys stop across from Miss Friedman's and talk for a minute with the lookout, and I see what they're doing. Four of them are going to come up and two guys and the first guy will stay in the street and watch the door and the fire escape.

There's no escape by the roof here because the place has got wide alleys next to it, and in the daytime they'd see us jumping anyway, even if we wanted to try. And we can't go up there to hide, because if they don't find me in the apartment, the roof is where they'll look next.

I say to Esther, "They're coming up in a minute, and we can't get anywhere. But they don't know you're here, 'cause the guy they had watching probably wouldn't think that some lady coming in the building alone would be you in disguise. So hide under the bed, and I'll try to fight them off in the hall, and if they get me, they'll figure they did their job and then you can sneak out later."

And Esther says, "I'm not going to let you get yourself killed now, after all we've been through so far. You're not going to die for *me*. You're not my Galahad or Lancelot. They're only in the books."

"Okay, what are we gonna do, then?"

And she thinks for a couple seconds and says, "You're going to put on one of Miss Friedman's dresses and one of her hats and walk out bent over like an old lady I'm helping."

I tell her, "They'll spot me right off."

She tells me it's the only chance we have, so, a couple minutes later, we're heading downstairs, and I'm wearing a dress and I've got a hat, with flowers and a broad brim, pulled down low, and I'm all hunched over. Esther's got my cap and the tin box in a bag that used to be Florence's. I'm taller than Miss Friedman was but scrunched like I am, the dress comes down over the top of my shoes. Esther's put on another dress and hat that used to be Florence's, just in case anybody was suspicious about her and tailed her from the neighborhood, though we figure nobody did and that Monk's guys outside think I'm by myself.

We step out of the way on the landing at the second floor, as they go tearing up past us. One of them even calls out "'scuse us, ladies." And out on the street, we just walk off, me still bent over and leaning on Esther, while the guys out there are watching the building, and looking up at the fire escape and the roof.

We turn the corner onto Bleecker, go a couple blocks, sit down on a bench in Washington Square, and put our arms around each other, hang on like drowning people, and cry. Too many people went off of the ferry too fast, and I helped push some of them over the side, maybe all of them. Back in June, on the bench down in City Hall Park, my father told me to wise up. I'm thinking now that maybe I'm just too dumb to ever do that.

Finally, I tell Esther we're going to go right now to that newspaper guy at the *Globe*, this Mr. Schoenwitzer, that Miss Friedman told us about. So we go down to Park Row, which people call "Newspaper Row," over near the City Hall. That's where they've got all the big buildings for the top newspapers, the ones that could get the word out on Monk to everyone in the city. The *Globe* building is about twenty stories high and has a dome on top that looks like it could be for a capitol building. And as we're walking down the street toward it, I'd like to duck in somewhere and take off my disguise and walk like myself, but Esther says to wait until we get inside of the building, at least, because Monk might have guys watching all the buildings here.

And he does, strung out all along the street, in front of not only the *Globe* building, but the *Times*, the *Herald*, the *Tribune*, the *World*, and the *Sun*, all of them, and they're giving the once-over to anybody that comes along. So the question is, do we try to go in dressed like we are or is it too dangerous?

We sit down on a bench across the street in the City Hall Park, not far from where me and my father sat, and we see Tick-Tock passing slow and steady along the street, from one newspaper building to the next, and talking to the guys watching in front of each one. Right close to him is Davey, who knows better than the rest what Esther looks like.

And just as I say to her, "Davey's there. We can't take the chance," I see the little rat looking around and then staring our way.

I tell Esther we better go, and we start walking off as fast as we can, me not even pretending to be a bent-over old lady anymore.

I look back and see Davey turn to Tick-Tock and point after us just before we slip into a crowd heading towards the El station half a block off.

XXI

It's still hot and sticky and gray when Esther and me get off
of the steamer at Blackwell's late that afternoon. Billy wasn't
making the run on the one we caught, and I was disappointed,
because I wanted him and Esther to get a chance to meet, but
at least I didn't have to explain why she was there and dressed
like she was older than she was. I had ditched Miss Friedman's
clothes. It made me sad to just leave them laying on top of a
garbage can in an alley. I made sure to fold the dress neat and
put the hat on it careful. Maybe somebody who needed a nice
dress or hat could use them.

I was hoping that we got on the steamer without anybody
seeing us. Davey knew that I'd gone out to Blackwell's a lot
before, and maybe I was only getting jumpy, but I thought I
saw a skinny little guy coming up fast into the shadows of the
building at the dock when we were pulling out. That's also why
I decided not to introduce Esther to Mary-Margaret just yet.
In case anybody was going to follow us out there later that day,
I didn't want her to get mixed up in it. Esther and me would
find a place to hide for the night, see what was happening, and
figure out our next move.

When we got off the steamer onto the island, along with
the sick people they were bringing off of the boat on stretchers,
and got up to the gate to leave the dock, the guy standing there

was new and didn't know me, so when he asks why we're there, I say me and Esther are brother and sister and we're going to visit our mother's grave. He asks me her name and checks his list of the dead people they've got out there and says okay. So we walk off, and I decide I actually want to take Esther to where my mother is, because the two of them would have liked each other. Whether my mother would like me anymore, I really didn't know.

Well, we stand there where they put my mother, and I swallow hard and say to Esther, "It ain't such a bad spot, is it?"

She's choked up, sad about my mother and worried about hers, but nods to let me know it's a good spot.

I say for my mother to maybe hear, "I killed those guys, but I ain't a killer." And then I tell Esther that my father got killed last night.

She just says, "Oh, Morris!" and starts crying, and, of course, there's just so much to cry about.

I tell her, "Look, since there's been all this killing and dying, we've got to make it mean something. We can't give up."

She groans "Oh, I hate Monk so much!"

"I don't think he's on the ferry."

Like I figured, she asks what I mean, so I tell her. I want to give her something good to think about for a change. So I say everything that Carl told me, and that I was trying hard to understand it and to believe that all good people were still part of the crowd on the ferry even if, like my mother and Izzie and Miss Friedman and Florence, they had got taken off early. I was kind of working this stuff out as I was saying it, and I was asking myself whether I was ever on the ferry, or like Monk and Tick-Tock and all the rest of those bums, probably missed the boat from the start.

She's stopped crying before I finish, and then, standing there and looking at my mother's grave, she says, "So you think some little part of your mother's soul is in somehow with all good people, right now?"

I say, "Yes, I think maybe so."

"So your mother's part of me now?"

I say yeah, and that her father is part of me, if I'm on the ferry. And then she smiles a little even with her eyes still full of tears, and she gives me a big hug and a big kiss. And she says my mother's grave has a great view of the city and that she'd love to just lay right down there and take a nap, because she's so tired. But we need to get out of the open in case someone is going to come along looking for us. And I tell her that maybe I got a better idea about where she can get some rest.

So I take her into the church, and I show her St. Jude and tell her that's where my mother had hid the tin box that Esther had in her bag and that this St. Jude was called the saint for lost causes, which meant that if it looked like you didn't have a chance of coming out okay, you prayed to him for help.

Esther says, "I've never been in a church before. Maybe I shouldn't be here, not with that big cross up there, Morris."

"Why? You ain't gonna infect anything or get infected yourself, either. I promise. Look, Esther, none of this in here, or in *shuls* neither, means a thing, I don't think. What's here ain't as real as what's in a store, or a restaurant, or a saloon, or Coney Island."

"No, Morris, don't. Stop talking like that. God will punish you."

"God's only about the soul and the ferryboat, if there's any God at all. He ain't in here."

She says, "I think maybe God can be in both places, but I also think I don't belong here."

Again I ask her why, and she tells me, "Well, maybe it's because I'm a Jew but maybe it's also because I don't belong in any place where people pray to God, not after…"

"Not after what?"

"Well, not after… being so mad at poor Miss Friedman, for instance, and being mean to you, and just not being, well, such a good person."

"You ain't done anything so wrong, Esther. So you were mad at her. Anybody could understand that, and now you're sorry, which means you ain't so bad at all. And maybe you had a good right to be mad at me. And, hell, nobody's good all the time. At least you haven't killed anybody, like I did, or done the kind of terrible stuff that Monk's done. Right?"

She just shakes her head, says, "I'm not good. And I don't even want to talk about Monk."

"That's all right by me. Let's just lay down on the benches and get some sleep. I don't think people come in here much, except on Sundays, so it should be quiet. When we get up later, I'll try to find us some food."

So we laid down on a long bench in one of the middle rows, she's at one end and me at the other, and I'm thinking if there ever was a lost cause, I'm it, and I'm trying not to see Miss Friedman's dead body, and I'm trying not to picture my father laying dead in that alley next to the two bums I killed. Then, after a while, I see Esther's asleep, and then I start to get drowsy. The last thing I see before my eyes close is Jesus, in one of the stain glass windows, smiling down with his hands open wide toward a bunch of little lambs. The stain glass is glowing gold from the sun just then, like it did the morning that I went to church with Aunt Gabriella and Uncle Giulio and talked with Father Basilio.

When I wake up a couple hours later and open my eyes, the stain glass isn't so bright, because the sun's lower, and I know it's just the light, but Jesus looks now like you can't tell whether he's smiling or looking mad and shooing the lambs away.

I look over and see Esther's not there. But then I hear whispering and moaning coming from near the statue of Saint Jude, and I hustle back there and I see Esther on her knees, with her hands together up in front of her face, and she's looking up into the face of the statue and she's praying hard, her voice real low, so all I can make out is "Forgive me," and "Help me," and tears are pouring down her face. If I was a saint, I'd sure do what I could for her, but the face on the statue, it doesn't change any, of course.

After watching her a minute, I say, "Esther, we need to go get something to eat."

She turns and looks at me and says, like she's waking up from something, "Oh, Morris, I had such bad dreams, and I didn't want to bother you, you were sleeping so sound. You looked just like a sweet little boy, lying there on your side, with your head resting on your hands, and your mouth making little puffing sounds when you opened and closed it. Anyway, I couldn't just lie there with what I was thinking. So, finally, I came over here, and I said to myself that if I'm a lost cause anyway, God couldn't punish me worse for praying in a church and maybe it could help."

"You ain't a lost cause, not ever."

"It's not for either one of us to know or say," she tells me. For just a second I think maybe I ought to say a prayer for Miss Friedman and Florence and for my father, and maybe even for the guys I killed, but then I just shrug, and we walk out.

It's almost dark now, hot and sticky, worse than it's been all summer, and I'm coming up with a plan for what me and Esther should do next. I don't want to go back to the city tonight, because if anybody saw us get on the steamer coming out here, they'll be waiting for us when we get off of it coming back. Tomorrow morning, when Billy makes his first run out here, I'll meet him at the dock and ask him if he knows any cops that me and Esther could trust. And if he does, I'll ask him could he get somebody to tell the cops to hurry on down to the Manhattan dock. Then, when they get there, he should tell me and Esther, and we'll come back on the next trip, and maybe when I tell them everything, they could take us to the *Globe* building to meet Mr. Schoenwitzer. But I'm going to make Billy swear on Mary-Margaret that he won't get involved if something happens and there's fighting.

Meanwhile, me and Esther will have supper and then spend the night out here. First, I'm going to take her over to the hospital kitchen and tell them we came out to visit our mother's grave and fix it up a little and could they sell us sandwiches, so we could have something while we're at the grave till the last boat. Then after we eat outside and walk around awhile, then we'll go back to the hospital and tell them we stayed out there too long and missed the last boat back and maybe they could give us a couple cots for the night.

Well, we go to the kitchen, where all the cooks are women that they brought over from the workhouse on the island. You could just look at these ladies and see that things probably haven't ever been easy or fair for them, which is why they ended up where they did.

The kitchen's down in the basement, and it's only got half-windows, up near the ceiling, that go about up to the knees of anybody walking on the ground right outside of them, so you can't really see anything or get a lot of fresh air, even when it's not as hot and still as it is this evening. And ovens and stoves are blazing and big vats of soup and stew are giving off steam that gathers up near the ceiling. Some of the ladies have faces pitted up from the pox, and everybody's faces are red from the heat, and most are hard-looking, like the face maybe of someone who used to be a whore but got too old or too wore out to do it anymore. But when they see how me and Esther are looking and hear about our going to visit our mother's fresh grave, their faces go a little soft and they make us some sandwiches. And when I offer to pay, they don't want to take our money.

So ten minutes later, me and Esther are looking for a nice spot to eat our supper. We see the lighthouse that's up at the north end of the island, which is where they say the currents are the roughest, and we go over near it to sit and look out on the river. If it was daytime, you could probably look up toward the Bronx and see North Brother Island, where Billy was back in '85. On our way, we pass the workhouse, which looks just like the prison behind it. The workhouse is smaller, but it's not small. It looks like a gray stone fortress, like you could imagine King Arthur's knights would attack, but it's a fortress not to keep people out of, of course, but to keep them in.

As we're going by, we hear some lady at her window, singing out loud into the night, and what she's singing is part of a song that I heard before:

> After the ball was over, after the break of morn,
> After the dancers' leaving, after the stars are gone
> Many a heart is aching, if you could read them all.
> Many the hopes that have vanished, after the ball.

Esther and me just stop and listen while we watch the sky get dark and black clouds coming in, with the breeze picking up just a little and lights starting to come on across the water in Manhattan. Then Esther says, "She sounds so sad, like her hopes are all gone, and the stars will never shine again for her. They're gone. Just as sure as Miss Friedman and her friend are gone."

I look up and see that there's no stars showing tonight. I say, "The stars don't ever go away. The clouds block them, but they're always still there."

She says, "Some of them are gone. We're still seeing their light, because it's coming from so far away, but some of those stars went away a long, long time ago."

I tell her I never knew that, but that there were still plenty up there, and she says, "That's beside the point, Morris. You just don't understand. What the song is saying is that once your hopes have vanished, the stars are gone for you, too, even if they're still there in the sky. Understand?"

I did, but I didn't feel like talking about that now. So I just nodded yeah.

And Esther says, "The woman singing in that terrible place

understands that. I can hear her broken heart in her voice." And she starts to cry again.

She doesn't stop crying till we get to the lighthouse, which is maybe fifty foot high. It looks like nobody lives there and that someone comes up every day when it's getting dark and lights the big lantern on top and then leaves it till the next morning.

There's a pretty garden near it, with the flowers giving off a strong sweet smell in the night air. Esther takes a few deep breaths and says, "Those are lilacs, and honeysuckle, too. They have those up in the Bronx, at the Botanical Gardens, where my father took me once. I never forgot how they smell."

When she mentions the Bronx, I think about the night I was up there in the Woodlawn Cemetery, and I remember now that I smelled these same kind of smells, all through the night when I was laying there, feeling dead, after seeing Esther with Monk at the fight.

I put my arm around her and say, "It's pretty right here, ain't it? It's good to be together somewhere pretty. Maybe we deserve it."

"And maybe we don't," she says. And then she leans her head against my shoulder a little and says, "but I like it anyway."

So we eat our sandwiches, which are ham and cheese on rye. Esther never ate ham before, because it's not kosher, and at first she wanted to throw it away and just eat the bread and cheese, but I said to her, "Look, don't be dumb. The ham's already touched the other stuff, which has got some of its taste now, so what are ya gonna do, throw it all away and eat what, the lilacs and honeysuckle? You're hungry and tired, and bad guys are after us. What kind of God is gonna punish you for eating something right now?"

I kiss her on the head, hold the sandwich up to her nose and mouth and say, "It smells good, doesn't it? And you're hungry, so just eat it, okay? You're not gonna make any God angry if you do, but you're definitely going to make *me* angry if you don't, and I'm here and He ain't."

And she takes a bite of it right out of my hand. Then she takes another and another, and she's forgetting that supposably she shouldn't be eating it. And I don't give the sandwich to her to hold, because I like the way it feels to have her lips and teeth and breath close to my fingertips, and she doesn't try to take the sandwich out of my hand, either. She just keeps eating and starts giggling, with her breath warm and moist on my fingers. And as the sandwich gets smaller and smaller in my hand, her lips and tongue are brushing up against my fingertips and her teeth even nip them just the teeniest bit, but it doesn't hurt.

Well, I start giggling myself, and I'm getting swole and hard below, and even though I'm thinking this is wrong after all the terrible stuff that's happened the last couple days, I'm thinking how grown up Esther looks in the clothes she's got on now. And we're both breathing hard, and our faces are close as she takes the last nibbles right from my fingertips. And the honeysuckle and the lilacs are smelling so strong.

When there isn't any sandwich left, I put my arms around her, lean hard against her, and she leans backwards, holding onto me tight, and then we're on the ground, with me laying on top of her, the two of us pressing our bodies together and my tongue in her mouth. And I'm thinking now about how much I love her and how much I dreamed about the two of us being together like this, and that I just don't want what we're doing right now to stop.

I'm scared that in another couple seconds she'll say this is all wrong, but she doesn't. Instead, she's breathing just as hard as I am, kissing me just as hard as I'm kissing her, and rubbing her body up against mine just as hard as I'm rubbing mine against hers as she's laying there underneath me on the soft grass. And when I slide my hand up under her dress and get it inside her bloomers and feel what's up there where her legs come together, she just moans soft. So I just keep rubbing her there, and with my other hand now I'm unbuttoning the front of her dress and then sliding my hand in and feeling her tits, which aren't big like Miss Friedman's but still fit my hand good and feel like some kind of nice small fruit that's just starting to get soft and ripe, and with a cute little rubbery point, almost like a fresh little pencil eraser.

Then without saying anything I unbuttoned the front of my pants, pulled her skirt up to her waist and moved her understuff to the side, and she just spread her legs wider and took me and pushed me into her farther, letting out a big sigh and moan.

Her body was thin, but it had a long, pretty shape. It made me think of a beautiful young girl deer's body, like I saw at the zoo, smooth and graceful. And she moved real quick under me, like a beautiful thing in a forest, or a beautiful young horse that was running across meadows while I was spread out over it and riding. And then after she had gone fast for a while, she shook hard and came to a stop, and just laid there panting and sweating. I thought she was done, but then she says, "Turn over Morris. Let me get on top of you." So I turned over and she rode me while she was sitting up, kind of like I was a race-horse now and she was a jockey pushing me to win the race. And I had to keep going hard, but I knew really that to win I had to get to the finish line fast but not too fast.

I looked up at her while she was riding me and saw her there with the lighthouse behind her and the dark, cloudy sky above that, and up above that there were the stars we still couldn't see on account of the clouds, and the look on her face was like nothing I ever saw on it before. Her mouth was open and her teeth were showing, and her eyelids were almost covering her eyes.

Then we do reach the finish line together, and she lays down on me for a while, both of us breathing hard, and then she rolls off and lays on her back, and I reach out my arm and put it under her head, and the two of us are like that for a few minutes, not saying anything, just smelling the flowers and feeling the breeze that's coming in stronger now from Manhattan across the river.

Then Esther says, "Morris, please don't think I'm a whore."

"Why would I think that?"

"Because I'm not even sixteen yet, and we're not married, and everybody knows what kind of girl does that. And I was so mad at Miss Friedman when I thought that she'd done it with you. I didn't have any right to think what I did about her."

I lean over and I kiss her, and I tell her, "Hey, I did it with you, you know, and I ain't any older than you, and I don't think it was so wrong."

She says, "It's worse for girls, everybody says so."

I tell her, "I ain't everybody." And then I tell her that I love her, and I swear I'll marry her.

"I love you, too, Morris. I really do, but you shouldn't be marrying yourself a whore."

I just laugh, kiss her again, and tell her that after we lay there together like that for just another few minutes we need to go back over to the hospital and ask them to give us a bed for the night.

But just then I hear a low putt-putt-putt sound coming across the water from Manhattan toward where we are near the lighthouse. I get up and go over to the low stone wall they've got around that end of the island to keep the water from coming up over when it gets too high, and I see a boat coming our way. It's not the *Minnahanock*, which makes its run over to the middle of the island, not here to the north end. It's smaller, maybe half the size of a tugboat, but enough, for sure, to carry a few big guys. And I'm wondering who would be coming over like that at night, and I'm hoping it's not who I'm scared it is.

So I duck down behind the wall and peek out over it, but I can't see real good. It's full nighttime now, and even though there's lights flickering on the water, they're not enough to make anything much out except for the boat itself, and it's only got a dim lamp lit. When it's closer I see some guys standing on deck, but I still can't make out for sure who they are. But then they run the boat up into the shallow water just below the wall, tie it to a post, and step out onto the rocks, and I see that one of the guys is lots smaller than the other ones, shorter and skinnier, and I don't know for sure that it's Davey, but I do know that I can't waste any time trying to find out now.

So I stay bent over and run back to Esther and tell her, "Let's get outta here. Somebody's coming, and we better not wait around."

Meanwhile the clouds have thickened up, the wind is blowing hard, and then there's a flash of lightning out over the city that lets me see how scared and sad Esther's face is right then. That look on her face makes me see Miss Friedman and Florence laying there and their faces, and the look on my father's face the last time I saw him alive, and the worry on the faces of Aunt Gabriella and Uncle Giulio, and I got maybe madder about all the stuff that was happening than I'd even been before, and madder, too, about being such a lost cause myself and also maybe getting both her and me killed tonight with another plan that's not going right.

We start to run off then, but we don't go along for more than a minute when the wind roars, the sky opens up on us, and there's a bright flash and a crash of thunder that makes the ground shake. Esther screams, I turn to her, and then, bam, the front of my head is smashed, and I feel myself going down, and then it's all dark.

When I open my eyes again, I'm laying on my back, and my head's hurting bad, and the rain's still coming down, but lighter now, and Esther's wiping my forehead with a wet handkerchief. I start to ask what happened, but she clamps her hand over my mouth and whispers that I've got to be quiet. She says I ran right into a big tree limb and knocked myself cold for a couple minutes, and that she dragged me further under the tree and behind some rocks, where we're hiding, because they're out there, looking for us, for sure.

I whisper that she should have run off and gone to the TB hospital and asked them to protect her, but she whispers back,

"I won't leave you when you're in trouble." And she leans over and kisses me, and I raise my head a little and kiss her back, but I have a hard time not groaning when I pick my head up, and I lay it back down because moving it makes me dizzy.

So we lay there for a few more minutes, and I'm hoping that maybe the guys passed on by us and we could hide out till morning and then get over to the steamer dock. And meanwhile we're soaked through, and the rain's still coming down, and from the rumbling and flashes starting up again over on the Manhattan side, it looks like it'll be coming down lots harder. I see the light up on top of the lighthouse, shining steady there still, and I'm thinking that plenty of people would say that it's like God shining bright for them and showing the way when everything's dark and rough. But I'm also thinking that I'm not one of them.

Then I hear some rustling around not far away and I can't tell for sure that it's not the wind, but maybe there's some voices, too. I nudge Esther, and the two us lay there as still as we can, trying not even to make noise breathing.

And then I hear some wheezing and then a ticking sound, real close, from a watch that's lots louder than most, and I know it's got to be Tick-Tock, with his buttoned-up black coat, his black cap, his long pale face, and eyes that never see anything that changes the dead expression on his puss. And I remember Davey telling me way back, that if Tick-Tock Tannenbaum is looking for you and you hear the ticking, it's just about the last thing you'll ever hear. I reach down, take the knife out of my sock, and unwrap the cloth I've got around it.

The ticking and wheezing get closer and closer, and I've got my hand tight on the knife handle and, dizzy or not from my head, I'm going to spring up and stab the bastid right in the neck, where his goddamn black coat's not reaching, but then the ticking starts moving away. And I'm hoping that maybe him and the guys with him will head off somewhere else, but then I hear a voice that I know real well saying, "They gotta be somewheres around here, Tick-Tock. I seen them running off when we was getting to the wall, and then they suddenly was gone. They must of just dropped down somewheres. I got real good eyes, which is why you brung me along in the first place, right? It was me that spied them getting on the boat to get out here, and I ain't gonna let you and Monk down."

"Shut up, punk," Tick-Tock says in his flat voice, like he's just telling you a fact. "For all I know, they ain't even here, and you don't know *bupkes*."

Davey says, "I know they ain't far. I just know it."

I can't make out their faces, but I can see there are two other guys there, and one of them sounds mad and says to Davey, "Shut up, punk."

Tick-Tock says to the other guy, still in his calm voice, "I already told him," and then, just as some lightning is making everything bright for a second, just as sudden as that, he flicks out his arm, fast and hard, and smacks Davey across the mouth with the back of his hand.

It's dark for a couple seconds, and then there's another flash and I see Davey laying there and rubbing his jaw and sniveling. The thunder is louder.

Then, when it's quiet for a couple seconds, I hear Tick-Tock say, "Abie, light up the flash lantern and you and Droop-Eye just walk around a little and see if they're hiding around here. Meanwhile I'm gonna take a piss." So he opens up his coat, and is unbuttoning his pants, while the others walk off with the lantern, and just then a bug flies up into my nose. I hold off and don't make a noise, but because I'm so surprised by it, my hand shoots up and swipes at my nose, and this makes Esther jump a little and let out an 'oh!' It's soft but not soft enough so that Tick-Tock doesn't hear it, and without taking time to button up his fly, he comes toward where me and Esther are, and he's reaching into his coat pocket for something.

Well, I've got something for him. And when he gets to a couple yards from us, I spring up and stab him in the left side of his neck, and for a second, he stands there, like he doesn't know what happened. I'm not going to give him any chance to figure it out, and I stab him again and again right there in the same spot on him. He's gurgling, but not loud. Then he takes a short step or two, like a baby that's just learning to walk and his arms go out, like maybe there's a mother or father he's trying to get to. But he doesn't get to anyone. He goes down, pushes himself up a little, and then flips over on his back and lays there bleeding and still breathing some, his fly spread open.

There's a flash of lightning, and Esther sees his face, and lets out a little scream. The rain is coming down harder now. I reach to see what he was going for in his pockets, and I come out with a blackjack, a pistol and a razor. I open the razor and cut his throat, just to be on the safe side. The rain is washing the blood into the ground as soon as it's coming out of him. I also reach into his vest and take his watch and chain and put it in my own pocket.

Esther stares at me. I look around and see the lantern coming our way now, and I tell her to get out of there, to head back to the hospital and tell them her and me got separated in the storm, and I probably got out of the rain somewhere else on the island, and she should ask could she stay there till morning, when she figured I'd show up. She nodded, and I told her to make sure not to lose the bag with the tin box in it, and she nodded again and ran off.

I turn back and I see that the lantern's right up close now, and then I see the light from it shine right on Tick-Tock's feet. There's a break in the wind and thunder, and you could hear the watch that I took off of him, and a voice says, "Tick-Tock? It's Abie. You okay?" He comes closer and sees what the lantern shows him when it shines all over Tick-Tock. "Oh shit!" he says.

It's the last thing Abie does say. I smack him on the back of his head with Tick-Tock's blackjack, and then when he's laying there, I open the razor and cut Abie's throat.

I close the razor, put it and the blackjack in my pocket, and grab the pistol. I pick up the lantern, and in a minute Droop-Eye Leibowitz comes over, the same guy who was having so much fun on the bridge the night Izzie went off of it. Well, Droop-Eye sees the bodies laying there and me just standing and looking at him, with the lantern in one hand and the gun in the other, and he turns and takes off running toward the boat. I start after him, fire once and miss. And then I figure I don't need to kill the bastid, not if he's going off and leaving me and Esther be. I read that Billy the Kid had killed nineteen guys by the time he got killed when he was twenty. Maybe it made him feel good, I don't know. And now I'm standing there out on Blackwell's, just almost sixteen years old, and I already got me four, but it doesn't make me feel good, or bad either. I just know I'm not out to set a record.

The storm is blowing strong again now, as I'm coming after Droop-Eye, making sure that he's leaving. And he is, just racing toward the lighthouse and the boat tied up at the wall there. He falls a couple times, scrambles to his feet and keeps going, looking back again and again to see me coming after him steady, with the lantern and the gun. Then I see Davey come running up to him. He's pointing back at me, like Droop-Eye really needs to get me, but Droop-Eye smacks him just like Tick-Tock did before, and Davey falls down, then jumps up and starts running after Droop-Eye toward the boat.

I keep coming after them, the lantern glowing just as steady in all that wind and rain as the light up in the tower up above us. The lightning flashes come and go, but me and the light I'm holding keep coming.

Davey is scared, so scared he keeps slipping and stumbling as he tries to catch up to Droop-Eye. His neck is so thin, I figured Tick-Tock's razor could go right about through it with just a flick of my wrist, but I tell myself I won't rush after him. If he gets away on the boat, fine, it's not over yet, and if he doesn't, well, we'd just see, because I haven't figured that out.

Well, when Droop-Eye gets to the wall and crawls over it, he can see that the boat's getting tossed all around by the river, which is higher and faster than I ever saw it and swirling like crazy too. It's gotten so high that more and more it's sloshing up over the wall. There's a guy on board, the captain or pilot or something, and Droop-Eye's yelling at him to start up the motor real fast, which he does. And Droop-Eye yanks on the rope and pulls the boat over so it's close enough for him to jump onto it. Then, when he's on it, and Davey's up on the wall and ready to jump onboard, too, Droop-Eye gets the rope off of the post the boat was tied to. I can see he's not waiting for Davey, because he knows I'm coming and that I don't mind killing.

Davey jumps for the boat, just as a wave comes up and smacks him head-on, and he doesn't make it. Right away, I've got one leg over the wall, and I'm looking down at him. On a usual night, he'd be standing on some rocks and sand, but this is no usual night. Tonight, once you're off the wall on his side, you're in the river, and it's high and fast and swirling. And he isn't much of a swimmer. He's yelling for help, but the boat is heading off and it's not going to turn around.

A swell rushes up, and he rides it with his arm out towards me, and without thinking about it, I lay down on the wall and grab his arm, and the two of us are hanging onto each other, him in the river and me on the wall, with the river splashing up over me. He's screaming, higher than the wind, "Don't let me go, Moish. I'm sorry. Please, please, *please!*" Stuff like that. I'm on my stomach, with one leg still on the ground side of the wall and the other dangling into the water, which is pushing and pulling all around at it. And the rain is still pouring down, and the thunder's still banging, and the lightning's still flashing, and every time it does I can see Davey's face absolutely clear, just like times we were sitting across a table from each other at Aunt Gabriella's, having some pasta together, or at Davey's, having some gefilte fish that his mother made out of what his father brought home from where he worked. His face right now doesn't look any older to me than it did when we were ten.

And now he's yelling, "I can't hang on much more, Moish! Moish! I don't wanna die!" The river is splashing up over his face and choking him while he's screaming and crying.

I'm crying some too, remembering Davey the way he used to be and thinking how much I hate him now.

Then there's the biggest clap of thunder and the brightest flash all night, and a swell pushes Davey up, and the two of us look right into each other's eyes. And he's *so* scared, just a frightened little guy who's maybe real sorry now that he did me dirt. And then there's another hard swell and Davey's shooting down the river, his arm still out towards me. I hear a high-pitch scream, and when there's another flash of the lightning, I see his hand reaching up out of the water, and then, when there's a flash right after, you can't see the hand or Davey Blumenthal anymore.

The lantern, which was laying on the ground while I had Davey's hand, has gone out now, but I make it over to the lighthouse and try the door, which is locked, so I huddle up against the lighthouse, cry some, and close my eyes, while the storm passes by.

XXII

I slept some, finally, and when I opened my eyes, the sky's getting a little gray over on the Queens side of the river, and it's not long before the sun's going to come up. I was wet and stiff and chilly, but I figured moving around would take care of some of that, and I sure had to get moving because I had a lot of stuff to do, and Tick-Tock's watch was telling me that I didn't need to be wasting any time getting started.

First off, I went over to where Tick-Tock and Abie were laying. They hadn't moved an inch, neither of them. I had this feeling that maybe I ought to say something for them, some kind of prayer, but right off I say to myself that I don't owe neither of them a thing. They were off the ferry and that was that.

It was tough dragging them to the wall, and tougher still getting them over it, so I could drop them into the river. One good thing was that the river was still up from the storm and from it also being high tide right then, so there was no chance they'd be just laying there on the rocks for somebody to find them. And they went floating off, one after the other until they both went under.

It was strange hearing Tick-Tock's watch going the whole time that I dragged him and watched the river take him away. Just after he went under, I gave it a good winding. Tick-Tock and Abie's faces didn't have any expressions, except maybe a little surprised. I wondered if my own face looked different from just a couple days before. I washed it with river water just in case there was any blood on it. And you could hardly notice the few flecks that were on my shirt and pants.

Then I sat down and rested for a bit and noticed again the smell of the honeysuckle and the lilacs. But the watch was ticking, and after a couple minutes I touched the key on my mother's ribbon and started moving.

The sun was getting above the houses and trees over in Queens when I got to the TB hospital. Esther was there in the lobby of the rothunder waiting for me. She said she told the nurses just what I told her to and that they'd been real nice to her, but that she hadn't slept all night, worrying about me. When she asked me what happened after she left, I shrugged and said that Monk's guys walked by close, looking for us and Tick-Tock, but then they just went back to the boat and headed off.

"Are you telling me everything? You mean they just gave up?"

"It was so wet and dark and stormy. Oh yeah, in fact, I heard one of them say 'I don't need this kind of *tsuris*.'" And I shrugged again and said, "It worked out okay."

"Yeah, it worked out just swell," she says, like she doesn't mean it. "I can hear that awful watch of his. Can't you please just throw it in the river, which is where you probably threw him?"

"I think I'll keep it for a while because it can keep reminding me that I've got to be careful. And remember, none of this is our fault, at least not yours, anyway, and I'm gonna do what I can today to start making things better."

"You mean *we* are, Mr. Big Shot," she tells me.

"No, I mean *me*. You're going to stay here, where they won't be looking for you. Monk's guys will be watching for the two of us now. It'll be easier for me to give them the slip by myself."

Well, she keeps arguing, and then I see Mary-Margaret come into the place, and I tell her that Esther is my best friend, and we've got some bad guys after us and that she needs to stay here and be safe while I go to the newspapers and the cops. I don't tell her much more, except that these guys killed Esther's father and we want to get them for it. I don't name names, because, like I said, I don't want Mary-Margaret involved, though right away she wants to be, of course. She even says we should stay there and either she'll go and tell the cops what we've got to tell or that her, and maybe Billy, too, can at least go and get them and bring them out to the island.

I think about Miss Friedman and Florence, and I don't want Billy floating dead in the river that he always crossed in the little steamer he loves and I don't want Mary-Margaret laying somewhere with her dead eyes staring out in opposite directions. So I tell her nothing doing, and that how she could really help is just to take care of Esther till things settle down. She doesn't look so sure, but she finally says okay, but only for a day or two, and meanwhile she'll be worried sick.

I say not to worry, that I can take care of myself fine.

Then she helps me finally convince Esther that she shouldn't go with me. Esther, I can tell, likes Mary-Margaret right off, even though, like me that first day I met her, she has trouble knowing how to look at Mary-Margaret when she talks to her, because of those eyes.

So a little later, with some breakfast in me and with Esther safe for a while, I headed for the dock. I've got the tin box with me in a little beat-up brown briefcase that Mary-Margaret said some doctor out there had tossed away. And when she wasn't looking, I stuck the gun and the knife and the blackjack in it, too. I kept the razor in my pocket.

And I decided not to wait to see if Billy could round up some decent cops. I couldn't take the chance that there might be a rotten apple in the bunch. No, I was gonna go straight to Schoenwitzer myself and get him to write the story up so big that the mayor and police commissioner and even Tammany couldn't do anything but finally go after Monk, and if they took down Paul, too, well, I didn't owe him anything, did I?

Billy's working the steamer that day, like I hope. I don't tell him more than that my girl Esther is out at the hospital with Mary-Margaret and that there are some guys looking for me and her but that I'm going to get to people who can help us if he can just get me off back at Twenty-Sixth Street without me being recognized. He wants to do more than that, but all I let him do is give me another clean workshirt to change into.

Well, Billy gets me off of the boat in a way that not only is sure to keep me from being recognized but is also going to keep anybody from even coming near me. He gets me off under a sheet on a stretcher that him and another guy carry down the gangplank. The captain doesn't mind because Billy told him it was part of a friendly joke they were playing on somebody.

And it works. I don't know if anybody's there looking for me or not, but everybody who's there stays away because Billy's saying stuff like, "Watch out, folks. Steer clear. This poor fellow died on the way out this morning, and they're gonna have to do an autopsy over at Bellevue 'cause he could have something contagious real bad." Of course, by the time Billy has gotten me someplace where there's no one looking and he can take the sheet off, I'm wondering whether I could be laying under a sheet again before the day was over and not because I was pretending.

Billy hugs me and tells me to be careful. Then I go over to Lexington Avenue and start looking for a uniform store, which is what I need for the plan I've got now. Before I get there, though, I see a newsstand, and I see that one of the front-page stories is about two dead ladies that got found in an apartment down on Barrow Street. It's about Miss Friedman, of course, so I buy a couple papers and sit down on a stoop and read what they say about what happened. One says the bodies were mutilated and that one of the women was "obviously assaulted in a manner that can only be described as fiendish. The details are too horrifying for the printed page to bear." The top detective said that none of the neighbors saw or heard anything unusual. He also told the reporters, "Boys, what we've got here is work that's as nasty as anything I've seen in a long time. I'd guess it was perpetrated by a depraved madman. There are a number of strange sorts among the Bohemian types who make their homes in this Greenwich Village neighborhood, and I for one would not be surprised if one of them is the monster we're looking for."

The *Globe*, Mr. Schoenwitzer's paper, had drawings of the apartment and 'X's where the bodies were laying in it. It had a drawing of Miss Friedman that they must have copied from a photograph that they got over at the apartment. It showed her wearing her glasses and smiling. The story said that she was a teacher and also that she was "a tireless fighter for the downtrodden in society, a valiant woman lost to a vicious criminal." I was sweating now, I wanted so bad to get to Schoenwitzer and tell him who the boss vicious criminal was.

I fold up the papers, leave them there on the stoop, and head down the avenue till I find a store that sells messenger uniforms. And I buy one and wear it out of there. I have the store clerk fold the clothes I wore in into a nice tied-up package. Then I go into an alley to stick the package into my briefcase, which I didn't want to open up in front of anybody.

While I'm doing it, I remember the thick yellow packet that my father's writing says not to open unless he's dead, and which I had forgot all about. So, I get it out of the tin box and open it, and there's a note from him, like I figured, and it says, "Don't be a *shlemiel*, be smart with this. I was not so good to you, so I want you should have what's here. I was hoping to live longer so I could get this back from your mother and give it to you when you're old enough to know what to do with it, but I suppose I haven't made it that long." And in the packet there's more greenbacks than I ever saw in my life, and I don't mean small bills, either. He must have swindled it all from Monk and was afraid to have it anywhere close around. Now it was mine. I took a little of it out and put it in my pocket. I had to sit down on a garbage can and calm myself a little before I left.

Then I went along till I found a bicycle shop, and I asked the guy there could I rent one. He says, "What security do you have?"

I ask, "How much does a bicycle cost that a messenger uses?"

"Forty dollars would be about it for a kid your size. Sorry, lad."

I pull out two of the greenbacks. "Okay, here's the price of it. Keep this if I don't bring it back, and if I do, charge me what's fair for the rent. But you've got to write me a signed note that you got the cost of the bicycle from me." I'm really not going to be a *shlemiel* with my dough, you see.

The guy writes me the note, and in a few minutes I'm riding down toward Park Row, with my briefcase in the basket on the front of the bicycle. I only rode a bicycle once before, when I was about nine or ten, and my old man took me to the park and let me rent one for an hour and I got to where I was okay on it. And after a couple wobbles getting started now, I was doing all right, though I skidded some, running over horseshit or getting caught in trolley tracks for a second, and I got yelled at by some wagon drivers for getting in their way.

When I pull up at the *Globe* building, I see that some guys are out there still watching for me, but I know that three of them ain't Tick-Tock, Abie, or Davey. I've got my hat pulled down low so they can't see my face so good, and I just act like I'm just a messenger minding his own business. I get off the bicycle, all matter of fact, lock it to a post with a lock and chain the guy at the store told me I've got to have, and trot on inside the building.

The lobby is a great big hall, and in the center of it is a globe, a couple stories high and turning real slow. Shining on it is a lamp that's supposed to be the sun, so you could see where it's daytime on the earth and where it's night. New York is out of the shadow of last night now, but as it heads slow around over the rest of the day, the shadow is still there, waiting around the bend.

A bald guy with thick glasses at a desk asks me who I'm looking for, and when I say that I have a message for Mr. Schoenwitzer, he tells me he'll give it to one of Mr. Schoenwitzer's secretaries. I says that I was told to take this direct to Mr. Schoenwitzer himself and wait for a message to take straight back from him personal. He says that he can't allow that, so I say could he ask someone, because it's real urgent. I figure "urgent," which is a word I never used before, sounds more serious than just "important." He asks me who's it from, and I tell him, "I'm not at liberty to say," a line I read once in a story about a spy working for a countess who's in danger.

Well, when he hears that, he takes off his glasses, rubs his eyes, like he's thinking deep about it, you know, showing me he's somebody important, with another big decision to make in a job that's so full of big decisions it just wears him out, even early in the morning. Then he puts his glasses back on and says, "All right then, I'll call upstairs and see what they say." There's a bunch of speaking tubes hanging on the wall next to his desk, and he pulls out one that says, "Twentieth Floor," and he blows a little whistle into it and then puts the tube up to his ear. And nothing happens. He blows in again, sticks the tube up to his ear again, and still nothing.

"Mr. Schoenwitzer's secretary must be away from his desk," he says. "Wait here, and I'll find someone to take the elevator up and see if Mr. Schoenwitzer wants to receive you personally." And he goes down one of the halls that branches off from the lobby.

But I'm not waiting for him to come back. Instead, I grab a pencil and an envelope laying on his desk for notes to send upstairs, and I scribble quick on the envelope, "I can't wait. Here's the message. Maybe it ain't so urgent after all." And I grab a piece of paper and fold it up inside, lick the envelope shut, and put it and the pencil back on his desk. Then I run for the staircase.

Twenty flights up, I stop and get my breath. Then I open the door there a crack and peek out just when a kid a couple years older than me is talking to two men. One of them is about thirty in a crisp gray suit, with his hair slicked smooth and parted straight down the middle, and the other is an older guy with a pointy beard. He's wearing pinchnose glasses pressed right up to his eyes and his dark suit is rumpled. He looks like he might be a rich guy who wants to do some reform stuff. The kid is telling him, "Mr. Devlin sent me up, Mr. Schoenwitzer, because he couldn't reach Mr. Miller through the tube. Mr. Devlin wanted me to ask if you want to see a messenger boy who says he has an urgent message that he needs to hand you personally."

Well, before Mr. Schoenwitzer can answer him, I lean more on the door than I mean to, it squeals some, and they all turn to me, and I say, "I'm the guy he's talking about, sir. I couldn't take the chance you were gonna say no, because I do have to show you what I've got, right in person."

Mr. Schoenwitzer looks at me for a couple seconds and asks, "Who sent you?"

I say, "I came on my own, and it's important. But I need to tell you private."

He studies me some more, and I say, "Please, sir."

"All right, young man," he says. "I'll give you a moment, which is all I've got just now." And he thanks the kid and says to go tell Devlin it's okay, but that Devlin should be more careful about watching the stairs from now on. And he asks the other guy, who is Mr. Miller, his private secretary, to go into Schoenwitzer's own office and wait there for just a second. I guess he doesn't want to spend the time to take me into it.

As soon as me and Schoenwitzer are alone in the secretary's office, I talk real fast and tell him, "Miss Rachel Friedman, who you've got the story about in the paper today, the teacher lady that got murdered in Greenwich Village, she told me a few days back that you were somebody that I could trust. It was Monk Eastman had his guys kill her, and he killed that Judge Goldman, too, a few years back. I've got all sorts of stuff on Monk, stuff that will send him to the death-house. And I've got some stuff on Paul Kelly, too, but he didn't have anything to do with those two killings."

Schoenwitzer takes off his pinchnose specs, gives them a quick wipe, puts them on again and says, "I will be pleased to hear personally what you have to say, if you'll be good enough to just wait here and make yourself comfortable for a little while, perhaps a half-hour to an hour, at most, as I have some gentlemen coming to see me in just a moment, and I'm afraid they're always quite punctual. Mr. Miller will see to your comfort." Schoenwitzer had an accent that was like my father's a little bit, but not near as thick.

I told him I'd wait, and when Mr. Miller came back in and asked if I wanted coffee or something, I told him that I didn't need anything, that I'd be fine just resting a little.

And two minutes later, four guys walk in, two of them preachers, and one of the preachers is Reverend Fanshawe, still wearing the same toothy grin he was wearing the night that he made Miss Friedman cry so bad. I figured the bastid had seen the papers and knew what had happened to her, but that grin of his said to me that he didn't care any more than if he'd read that a bunch of Chinamen drowned over in China. "Too bad" he'd say, tell himself something like "it must be part of God's plan," and then turn the page.

I heard Tick-Tock's watch and thought of what I wouldn't mind doing to that Fanshawe, but because I'm not really a killer, I just watch him grin and chat. I know Fanshawe won't recognize who I am, even if he notices for a second, which he probably doesn't, the messenger kid sitting there in the secretary's office, with his hat a little low over his eyes.

So Fanshawe and the others go into Schoenwitzer's office, and the door shuts behind them. Mr. Miller sits down at his desk, smiles over at me, and says, "Mr. Schoenwitzer doesn't ever see people without an appointment, so he obviously took what you said quite seriously."

I said, "Well, it's serious stuff," and I get up and look out the window.

"It's a remarkable view from up here," Miller says.

I say, "Yeah, it is." Schoenwitzer's office up there on the twentieth floor is in the dome part of the building way up on top, and the whole floor up there is a circle. Tall windows go all around it. The secretary's office takes up maybe a quarter of the circle. One of its windows looks right down on the City Hall park, where me and my father sat when he told me Monk wanted to see me, and how I needed to wise up. Whether the me up here on the twentieth floor was wiser or dumber, better or worse, than the me that was back then I couldn't say yet.

Two windows over the other way, you could see the river and the bridge. I stared at them for a while, until Mr. Miller said, "If you don't mind being by yourself for a few moments I have to go down to the chief accountant's office for a while."

I said that, yeah, I'd be fine.

As soon the elevator door closed behind him, I was over at Schoenwitzer's door with my ear pressed up to it. I just figured I might hear something important.

What I heard first was Schoenwitzer's voice saying, "So, then, we're agreed, are we not, that if you gentlemen of the cloth and you secular reformers would be willing to help the campaign of Mr. Schuyler, who is a close personal friend of mine and a fine progressive fellow, I think the *Globe* can see its way clear to support these charity initiatives of yours and to give you a significant markdown on our advertising rates for some of the fine firms in which you've invested a portion of your organizational funds."

Then I heard some voices saying that they did find that real agreeable, and, after a couple seconds, I heard Schoenwitzer's voice again. "By the way, you may have noticed a young fellow in a messenger's uniform sitting in Mr. Miller's office. He made a special effort to see me, as he claims to have some information of interest. He said, for example, that he knows who's behind the murder of these teachers that is one of our lead stories today. This Miss Friedman seems to have been involved in the progressive cause. Did any of you happen to know her?"

I hear Fanshawe say, "I knew her slightly. What does this fellow know about her murder?"

Schoenwitzer answers, "He tells me that he has information that it was Monk Eastman's cutthroats who did the poor woman in, and he tells me, as well, that he can prove that Eastman was behind the death of Judge Goldman."

A voice I don't know says, "Do you really think he knows anything?"

Schoenwitzer says, "I'd like to find out. He may be merely trying to bilk me, of course, because I'm sure the young scoundrel wants a tidy sum for his so-called information. But if he does have anything, it will make a story that will double our circulation for as long as we can milk it. Hearst and Pulitzer will be sick with envy. And our editorials can trumpet that Monk and Paul Kelly and their kind have to go if we ever want a clean city."

So I hear this, and Tick-Tock's watch is keeping time to everything they're saying.

Next I hear Fanshawe say, "Well, we might wish to leave Kelly out of it. He's still contributing a good deal to the cause, whatever his motives may be."

Then somebody says, "If the boy really has something, do you think it will put Eastman behind bars?"

Schoenwitzer says, "I think not. He's paid off too many people. And even anonymous jurors would be justifiably terrified that he'd manage to get their names. And do you think any of his hooligans would ever testify that he ordered these murders? But, gentlemen, why should we want such a one in jail, anyway? For me he is good copy. Monk Eastman stories sell papers. And over time, his behavior will bring more and more people to see that the present situation fosters such corruption. A man like Monk Eastman is unwittingly more effective on our behalf than five hundred political speeches and eventually will bring the masses here in the city to the progressive cause. If we did not have a Monk Eastman, we would have to invent him. He and his mischief are means to a glorious end at last."

Fanshawe says, "Please God, that it's so." And a couple voices chime in with their amens to that, and Schoenwitzer says, "Well, now gentleman, if you'll excuse me, I'll tend to this young purveyor of a tale, and if there's enough there to spin into a five-day sensation, I'll give him his turncoat's blood money and wait eagerly to hear the healthy ring of coin piling into the *Globe*'s gaping coffers." And then him and the others laugh.

I hear chairs moving, and then I'm going fast, out of the secretary's office, and down the stairs, carrying my briefcase with everything I got on Monk, even Judge Goldman's ring still on the bone from his finger. I'm thinking, "So nothing's gonna come of this! And there ain't anyone I could go to who could make something happen. Well, I know what I gotta do now."

Five minutes later, I'm back on the bicycle, pedaling away from the *Globe* building, and I'm heading uptown, and I don't stop till I get to a neighborhood where swells live, the kind of place where Mr. Norton's house is. And I find a bank and take care of what I've got to there.

And then I'm pedaling hard and fast again, this time back downtown, and I make sure that I've got my razor, my knife, my gun and my blackjack, and even while I'm dodging trolleys and wagons, and loud curses, I'm still hearing the ticking, and it's almost like it's louder as I'm getting closer to where I'm going.

When I get off my bicycle at The Palm, around lunch-time, Monk's at his usual table, with an oyster in one paw, an oyster knife in the other. Sadie's on his right and some whore I haven't seen before on the left. A bunch of his guys are around, and they see me, just as soon as I step inside, and so does Monk.

He grins, waves to me with his knife, and yells, "Look what da cat drug in! It's me old buddy Moishele. Long time no see. I been missing youse and dat little tart Esther, who ain't got so much meat on her, but still feels good to your mitts, no? And not bad in da hay, neit'er, is she?"

I just stand there staring him straight in the face.

He says, "You look like you went and got yourself some honest woik. You got a message for me? Tell me what ya got. Is it from Esther or dat *zaftig* Friedman bitch? Make me happy, Moishele, since you interrupted my lunch here." The guys are all chuckling, and, meanwhile, even with the grin still on his ugly mug, Monk is slipping on his brass knucks and fingering his club, and little Sadie is looking kind of worried for me. Guys are getting up from their tables and from the bar and circling around where me and Monk are, some of them blocking the door and the stairs.

None of it is stuff I didn't expect. And I say to Monk, "Funny, you should ask if I've got something for you, because it just so happens I do. Tick-Tock said to say, 'Hi and good-bye,' because he ain't gonna be around anymore. He told me to let you listen to this to remember him by. I guess he doesn't need to know the time anymore." And I pull out the watch, and swing it slow back and forth on its chain. Monk isn't grinning now, and everybody is as quiet as the sawdust and spit and oyster shells laying there on the floor. All you can hear is the ticking. And then I say, "Abie and that little rat Davey Blumenthal say to tell you they went off with Tick-Tock and ain't gonna be around anymore, either. But I didn't hear any of the three of them say, 'Having a good time, wish you was here.'"

Guys are whispering. It sounds like this is all news to them and they're shocked. It's just what I figured. If Droop-Eye and the boat didn't go down last night, he hasn't worked up the nerve yet to come back and tell Monk to his face what happened out there on Blackwell's.

Monk is so mad now he isn't even trying to show me he ain't. He grabs his club, and he starts to get up. I've got my briefcase up at my waist now, and I could pull the gun before he gets to me and shoot him a couple times before his guys kill me, and so me and Monk could go off of the ferry together, if either of us was ever really on it.

That's not what I want, though, so I just say quick, trying to sound as calm as you please, "Hold on, Mr. Eastman, I've got another message for you. This one's coming from me, and it's this: You want to beat me into *kishke* and kill me. I know that, and I understand. No kidding, I really do. But killing me ain't a smart thing for you. And here's why. You see you were right not to trust my old man. He had just got printed up somewhere five copies of lots of stuff he knew about you, like what businesses you've got your paws in, how much dough you have and where you keep it, who you're paying off and how much, that kind of stuff. He also wrote up everything he knew about killings you did or told people to do. By the way, he also had Judge Goldman's ring and even the poor guy's finger bone. That's what was in that tin box he gave my mother to hide and that I was going to use on you, and was dumb enough to tell Davey about, so that he ratted me out to you. Anyway, my old man got these five copies stamped legal, and he was going to keep them like insurance against you bumping him off, but your guys got him before he could tell you what he would do to protect himself."

Monk's sitting back down now and listening hard. He wants so bad to kill me. And I'm worried that, like my father said Monk could do, he'll get so mad that he'll kill me even if killing me was gonna make things tougher for him.

I go on anyway, and I still have Tick-Tock's watch swinging in my hand, and it's the only sound in the place, except for me talking. "But my old man did get all the stuff to me, Monk, and also a little bit of money, and I did the kind of thing that he was going to try to do. I went to a big lawyer that ain't from around down here, some guy who ain't in politics or with the cops, some swank and honest guy, and I paid him most of the dough that my old man gave me, because this kind of lawyer doesn't come cheap. And I said for him to keep one of the copies of what my old man printed up and the tin box with the ring and the piece of Goldman in it, and I said if I didn't come around about every two weeks and let him know I was okay, then he should take what he had to the cops uptown and the papers and anybody he knew was honest who could do something about it.

"And then I took the other four copies and I gave them to four other people, people you will never know the names of, and I told them the same stuff. Now, don't worry, Monk, I've got it all in sealed-up envelopes, with my name scrawled across where it's sealed, and they ain't going to open anything, unless I don't show up. That's a promise."

Monk's fingering the notches on his club and running his hand over the brass knucks he got on, but he's listening. I say, "Your boys kept me from getting to the newspapers down at Park Row yesterday, so I had to figure out something else to do, and now you know what it is.

"Monk, you might still beat the rap if you were to kill me, but, then again, you might not. And even if you did, Tammany might not want you around anymore, anyway, because they'd figure you just make too much noise. And do you really want to take that chance, Monk? I mean, am I really worth it? And is Esther? What I'm saying is, you let me out of here in one healthy piece, and you call off your guys and you just leave me and Esther alone, and what's it gonna hurt you? We ain't going to ever bother you again, because there ain't any point. You're a smart businessman, right? And, besides, you already hurt us both plenty."

And then I looked at him real cold. "You're getting off

easy. It could be worse, you know. I could be the messenger boy of Death." And I reach into the briefcase and pull my gun and aim it at him, my arm out straight, and hardly trembling at all, even though my heart's banging like it's going to drown out the ticking watch. And meanwhile these crazy words come into my head, "Moishe the Kid's last stand." But I know that I'm not Billy the Kid and I don't want to die in some last-stand shootout, even though it'd almost be worth it to put holes in Monk's belly and head.

I was bluffing, of course, about the five printed copies and all that stuff. I didn't give anything to anybody. I didn't know anybody I could trust who could do anything. So I got a safe deposit box up at the bank, just before, and put everything in, including all that dough. But I wasn't bluffing about shooting this bastid if I had to.

After a few seconds, it turns out that Monk doesn't want to make me have to shoot him.

He leans back, smiles that nasty smile of his that I've seen way too often this summer, nods, and says, "Dis kid must piss fire. You sure Asher's really your old man?"

"I'm sure. You ain't saying anything against my mother by that, are you?"

He laughs now. "He pisses fire and craps cannonballs, dis *gantse meshugener*, don't he, boys?" And, nervous-like, they all laugh with him. "Okay, okay, Moishele, you t'ink you're a *gantse k'nacker* now, don't you? Well, you ain't, and don't you forget it, or I won't be so patient wit' you next time like I am today. You wanna shoot me after all, go ahead. You don't, just get the hell outta here and tell yourself it's your lucky day, 'cause it is, *momzer*. And don't never let me catch you in here no more."

I don't budge, and I still have the gun on him. I say, "Okay, I think we've got us a deal, then. It's all square between us, and me and Esther ain't gonna have to see your ugly puss anymore or worry about any of these mugs coming after us?"

All he can let himself do in front of everybody is just give me the slightest nod he could make, but he does it, and says, "Beat it, *putzkopf,* while you still got two legs to run out on! Go back to your skinny *shlooche* that I wouldn't waste two spits on." And Sadie, she gives me just this cute little smile and tiny wink that Monk, of course, doesn't see.

I nod back at Monk just the way he did to me, and I lower the gun, put it back in my briefcase, and then I turn my back on him and walk towards the door, like I ain't rushing. I'm scared plenty, but I have to do this with no gun on him so I'll know right now that Monk's decided, just like Droop-Eye did last night on Blackwell's, that he doesn't need the *tsuris* that going against me could bring him. I'm also thinking that if him or his guys kill me this second, I'm going to die real, real bitter that I didn't shoot him just now when I had the chance.

My steps and the ticking of the watch are all you can hear, and Monk's guys move away from me. When I'm almost at the door, one says, "Get lost, you bastid punk! And another one says, "Monk's bein' too generous wit' ya, get outta here, we can't stand lookin' at ya!"

And then I'm out on the street, the sun's shining, and I'm pedaling through the crowds and the wagons and trolleys for my next stop. When I get there, maybe half an hour later, and walk in, Paul, who's sitting at a table with a tiny cup in front of him, tells the two guys with him to go to another table, nods to me with no expression on his face, and motions for me to sit down beside him.

He asks me if I want a cup of what he's drinking. I say, yeah, sure. It turns out to be the bitterest, strongest coffee I ever had. He sees my face screw up when I swallow, and he says, "You'll want to drink that slow, Massimo. Sip it. It's bitter, right? Put some sugar in it. You have to develop a taste for it, like you have to do for most things."

I say, yeah, I suppose so.

"Now I don't say that I've developed a taste for everything

that's bitter for me, but I learn to deal with it as well as I can. And, Massimo, could you guess what's bitter to me right now?"

I answer, "Yeah, the kid sitting down with you at this table right here."

He smiles a little and takes a small sip. I look at the small Vesuvius painting on the restaurant wall, *sterminator Vesevo.* "You're not dumb, Massimo." He takes another tiny, tiny sip. "Monk still out to kill you? That why you have that outfit on, a disguise, maybe?"

"Yeah, it was a disguise, but I don't need a disguise for Monk anymore."

"That's a surprise. You did kill a customer and the big redhead at Monk's place the other night and then another of his guys on the train platform, didn't you?"

"Yeah, I didn't have a choice, but I didn't know the guy on the platform died. I figured he might, though." Then I take a real tiny sip this time. "I killed three more of his guys last night."

He smiles a little more. "Do tell. That watch I hear ticking so loud, would that possibly be a trophy you took off the menacing Tick-Tock Tannenbaum?"

"Yeah, I guess it would."

"I see. You've been a busy messenger boy, and you've done me some favors, it seems. So why isn't Monk panting to chew you up and wash you down with a growler of suds?"

I tell him what just happened at The Palm.

"So you're off the hook with my pal Monk. Any reason why you should be off the hook with me, though, even if you did me some little favors? It's not like you had it in mind to be a pal to me by doing them, right? And, like you just said, you left me with some bitterness, the kind that I haven't acquired a taste for. You know, like, for instance, by your getting my men gunned down because you were playing me and Monk off against each other like a couple of saps." And he takes another tiny sip. He's still smiling a little, and I figure he could have that same smile on his face while he saw me bleeding out my life in the alley behind his place.

I tell him the reason to let me off the hook is like the one Monk has, that I have something big on him. I recite some names and stuff off my father's list to prove I'm not bluffing, and I tell him I gave sealed-up copies to some people, but it won't be used so long as nothing bad happens to me.

For almost a whole minute he stares at me, like he might want to kill me right there, and then he says, "Well, your old man was a smart weasel while he lasted, and you are, too, ain't you, you big sneaky bastard? A little bit crude, 'untutored,' as the polite people uptown would say, but far from stupid." He studies me some and says, "Well, maybe from the first you just did what you had to do. You hadn't been put in any easy position. I don't know if I would have had you killed if you didn't have this over me. Probably not. But now, no, certainly not. You win, Massimo. You've got moxie, kid. So you won't need any disguises now, at least not the visible kind, if you know what I mean. Your old man ever talk to you about the sort of disguise that has nothing to do with what you wear"?

"Yeah, he did, Paul."

He nods. "No, he wasn't dumb. He would have done all right for a while longer, if he hadn't brought you into things."

"Monk didn't give him a choice."

"No, Monk didn't. You want some more of my espresso, Massimo? You have to drink it slowly and sweeten it some. Then you'll learn to like it."

I say, yeah, that'll be fine.

Then he says, "You have to do something else, too."

"What's that?"

"Don't get run over by a trolley or a train, because I don't want your pals to take what you have on me to anybody. It would be more than a little embarrassing, so to speak."

"I'll take care of myself."

"I know you will. Now tell me one more thing. What are you planning to do with yourself from here on out?"

"I ain't given the future much thought."

"Okay, some advice from me." And he laughs a little. "Here I thought I might be having my men kill you, which, let's face facts, you might deserve, but now I'm giving you advice. So here it is. You've got brains, you've got, like I said, plenty of moxie, and you're a big, good-looking kid. But you speak like a dumb thug. Stay in school for a while, learn how to speak better, read some good books and read the papers. You can become somebody."

"Like what?"

"Who knows, kid? Whatever you want. Hell, be a lawyer. You could end up either putting people like me and Monk away or helping us beat the rap. It's up to you. Now, scram. And don't let me see you again till you've taken my advice and you're ready to show me how it turned out."

I say okay and thanks and walk out of Vaccarelli's, and I get on my bicycle again and head off on my way. A picture pops into my mind from the night I first met Paul, when me and Miss Friedman took the trolley up to Mr. Norton's. It's the advertisement for learning how to become a lawyer.

XXIII

So, it all started, like I said, that night in early June just a few years back, when Davey came down the fire escape to get me, and, I guess you could say it all ended that afternoon when I sat with Paul in Vaccarelli's and he gave me his advice and told me to get lost. Well, I know it all ain't, or I should say, *isn't* really over and probably never will be. But all the dangerous stuff with Monk and Paul is, anyway, and that's okay with me. I don't want to ever kill anyone else, and I'm following Paul's advice and working on my grammar, you see. But I decided I would tell my story of that summer just about how I would have told it back then.

I don't feel guilty about the killing I had to do. I see Davey's parents on the street, and they look older and even more tired than they did before. They don't know what happened to him. His body has never washed up. I miss him sometimes and wish things hadn't gone bad with him, because he was a good pal before he changed and hurt me and Esther.

I feel kind of bad about Esther, too. Things didn't work out so well for her, either. Her mother died from the stroke that she had on the floor of the shop, and Esther took it hard, of course. In the same summer she lost both her mother and her father, and she had nobody else. And what we decided, Mary-Margaret and Esther and I, was that Esther was going to stay out on Blackwell's and go to the nursing school there. She'll make a good nurse. You know, it's like she started early with her little sister who was sick and died. We decided that Mary-Margaret would look after her, which she's still doing, and that I'd come out and visit all the time, which I did at first.

But none of us knew that Esther was pregnant. And when she discovered she was, she got scared, told Mary-Margaret, and said she wanted her to help set up an abortion. Mary-Margaret said, "Massimo's the father, right?" And Esther, crying hard, nodded her head that, yes, I was, and so Mary-Margaret said that the right thing would be for Esther to talk to me about it.

She told me Esther was really frightened about becoming a mom so young and that I should be nice and gentle talking to her, which, of course, I was going to be. And, obviously, it was scary for me, too, the thought of becoming a father so young, but I was also proud and happy, thinking of Esther and me having a kid together. I took her out near the lighthouse again, where the smell of honeysuckle and lilacs was still so strong, and told her that she shouldn't be frightened, that we should get married, have the baby, and then more babies as the years went by, but she cried and cried and said she didn't want this baby, that we could have others when we were more ready.

Something about how hard she was crying, how terrible the thought of having this kid was to her, made me remember suddenly how she'd been praying to that statue of San Giuda Taddeo and how worthless she said she was that day, and I recalled Monk's taunts at my last meeting with him, and I said, "You're upset because it could be Monk's kid, right?" She just cried harder, which was all the answer I needed.

Well, after that I couldn't love her anymore. I couldn't hate her, of course, but I couldn't love her. From then on, every time I saw her, I would imagine her in bed with Monk, and I couldn't stand that. That's why I don't see her much now, and why I gave up my dream of marrying her. Like I say, I feel kind of bad about that, but what else could I do, really? And I always will do the best I can for her.

Mary-Margaret is married to Billy now—I went to the wedding, of course, and I think she's a little disappointed that I changed about Esther, even after I told her that the baby was somebody else's, a guy that Esther wanted nothing to do with. Well, a woman is going to feel that way, I suppose. It's only natural. I give her some money each month to get stuff for Esther and her little girl, and Mary-Margaret, who kept Esther from getting the abortion, says that she's helping Esther learn to love the baby. I've never seen the kid.

I gave Mary-Margaret and Billy a good wad of money when they got married. They didn't want to take it, but I said it was from a big inheritance I got from my father, so they did end up taking half of what I offered, anyway, which they put down on a little house they wanted to buy in Queens, not far from Blackwell's. They're there now, and they invite me to dinner pretty often, but they don't invite me anymore when Esther visits, because, after the first time, I told them that I didn't want that. I think they both understood but weren't happy about it.

Aunt Gabriella and Uncle Giulio are doing okay. When I finally came home, they were so glad to see me alive and in one piece that they weren't even really all that angry that I had never told them what was going on. What I said was that Monk had been furious at my father and was out to get me because of that, but that everything was okay, and I'd be safe from now on. When I told them I had inherited money from my old man, and I wanted to give some to them, they told me they didn't want a cent of it, that I could do whatever I wanted with it, but that they wouldn't want their hands to touch it or anything that I would buy them with it. I couldn't argue them around on that. But they're happy to have me safe and staying with them for at least the next couple of years.

And as for me, I think I'm doing all right. Uncle Giulio wants me to learn to carve headstones, but that's not for me. Besides, I've seen too much death, as it is. I've got plenty of money, and I go to school to work on sounding and thinking less like what Paul would call a thug. I think I'm going to become a lawyer, as Paul suggested. I haven't decided what I'll do when I'm a lawyer, but I'll figure it out and be somebody.

I feel awful about Miss Friedman still, and I miss her a lot. I give money to buy milk and clothes for poor kids, and I always tell them it's in honor of Miss Rachel Friedman and Miss Florence Cohen. And I'm always going to do that. But I'm not going to give a cent to any socialist crowd, or to any political party, for that matter. Not ever.

Sometimes I feel a little lonely, but I see Sadie once in a while. She was always smart, and she always saved the money she got from Monk, and after he got tired of her and she bought her way out from working for him, she and a couple of cousins of hers got together and opened up a little dress shop that's starting to do okay. I give her some money sometimes to help them out with it and I get a small cut of the profits, and she and I have some good times together. We're comfortable because we know that all we want from each other is a bit of a good time.

I also see Hannah and Danny a lot, and if my old man had some money put away for them, like he did for me, Hannah says she doesn't know anything about it, and I pretty much believe her, so I make sure they have whatever they need. I take them places, like Coney Island or the Polo Grounds, where we sat in the best seats for the baseball game, which neither of them understood, but I explained it to them. And they like the Central Park, which I took them to a couple of times. The kid sailed a boat in the pond, and they both liked the zoo, and they thought the Belvedere Castle was beautiful. Hannah and I go to bed together sometimes, and, even though she's shy, she's as much fun in her way as Sadie, though neither one feels as good as Esther did.

And I've been following Paul's advice and reading the papers. I read them carefully. Now that Spain surrendered to us, and we've got Cuba and the Philippines, America's going to be booming for a long time, I think. And my old man said to use his money wisely, so I'm going to get a smart businessman to find me some good investments for some of the dough, not a lot of it, though, and only big companies, because I know there are ups and downs. I've learned that much.

When I see Monk or his guys out on the street, they act like I don't exist anymore, which suits me just fine.

A couple of times, lately, I go out to the middle of the Brooklyn Bridge at night and look down the river, toward the bay and the ocean past that. And I always remember feeling when Izzie dropped into the river that I was the first person in my family to die in this country, feeling that from then on I'd never do what I was supposed to, not really. Maybe that night I fell off the ferry. I don't know. Anyway, that's the sort of thing I can't help thinking about sometimes when I'm out on the bridge. And I don't like to think it. Still, I keep going out there. But every time I do, I also turn around finally and come back into the city.

About the Author

Allen Stein was born in the Bronx and is Professor Emeritus of English at North Carolina State University. His stories and poems have appeared in numerous journals, among them *The Hudson Review, Poet Lore, Prairie Schooner, Valparaiso Review* and *Salmagundi*. He is also the author of two poetry collections, *Your Funeral Is Very Important to Us* and *Unsettled Subjects: New Poems on Classic American Literature.*

www.ingramcontent.com/pod-product-compliance
Lightning Source LLC
Chambersburg PA
CBHW011515240626
47154CB00010B/3033